TRUTH AND HONOR

LIGHT *in the* EMPIRE

TRUTH AND HONOR

CAROL ASHBY

CERRILLO PRESS

Cover and interior design by Roseanna White Designs
Cover images from Shutterstock.com

ISBN: 978-1-946139-33-7 (paperback)
       978-1-946139-34-4 (ebook)
       978-1-946139-35-1 (hardcover)

Cerrillo Press
Edgewood, NM

But even if you should suffer for righteousness' sake,
you will be blessed. Have no fear of them, nor be troubled,
but in your hearts honor Christ the Lord as holy,
always being prepared to make a defense to anyone
who asks you for a reason for the hope that is in you;
yet do it with gentleness and respect.
1 Peter 3:14-15 (ESV)

Jesus said, "Truly, I say to you, there is no one who has left house
or brothers or sisters or mother or father or children or lands,
for my sake and for the gospel,
who will not receive a hundredfold now in this time,
houses and brothers and sisters and mothers and children and lands,
with persecutions, and in the age to come eternal life.
Mark 10:29-30 (ESV)

And we know that for those who love God
all things work together for good,
for those who are called according to his purpose.
Romans 8:28 (ESV)

To my children, Paul and Lydia,
for their love, support, and encouragement
and my new granddaughter, Payton,
for the joy she brings to our lives.
And especially to my husband, Jim,
whose love and encouragement
make every burden lighter.

And most of all, to Jesus.

Soli Deo gloria.

A Note from the Author

Skepticism and resistance. For many, that's their initial reaction to anything related to Jesus. For some, it's social conditioning from a childhood where no one at home or school or in the media ever said anything positive about God. For others, it stems from seeing how suffering touches everyone, whether they believe in Jesus or not.

When God's answer to prayer is no and suffering or death comes to someone we love, it's natural to ask why.

For those who believe, who know the reality of the Holy Spirit in our lives, we may not like how something ends, but we trust there's more going on than we can see. Somehow, God is working all things together for good for those who love Him.

The more I see of life, the more I can look back and glimpse the greater good that came from what only seemed bad at the time.

But for those who don't know God, who haven't recognized Jesus as Savior or felt the Holy Spirit in their lives, there's an unanswerable question hanging over them. How could a good God, a God with the power to do anything He wants, let bad things happen to the people who claim He loves them?

Truth and Honor explores that question in one man's life. Glabrio never met his grandfather, but he knows he was executed by the emperor for the crime of treason after he became a Christian. His father ordered him not to ask about what his grandfather believed because that could get him killed, too. But when the best people he knows share his dead grandfather's faith and consider it worth dying for, what's a person who values truth and honor above all else supposed to do?

Sometimes we're presented with opportunities to share what we believe and why we believe it. The surge of excitement when an unbelieving friend seems ready to listen for the first time is indescribable. But it can be frightening, too. What if our friend is turned off by what we say? It's so easy to back off, to wait for a more opportune time. We might lose our friend if we don't, but what will our friend lose if we never say anything?

i

As Jesus promised the Holy Spirit would give the right words to speak before hostile governors, He'll guide what we say to our friend when we ask and then listen. It's good to remember that "Rome wasn't built in a day." Great things can be accomplished through many small acts of friendship, through the living example of how God is important in our own lives, and when the time is right, through sharing the hope we have in Jesus in the words the Holy Spirit will guide us to use.

May we have many opportunities to be the friend who's there to answer those first hard questions about whether God is real and whether Jesus really did what Christians claim is true. May we know the joy of seeing our friend discover the truth and be set free.

Characters

Family Relationships and Social Standing: What Roman Names Tell Us

The rules for naming a Roman citizen were well defined, leaving little room for creativity but revealing a lot about the person and their relations.

The Roman *familia* is the Roman family unit consisting of the *paterfamilias*, his married and unmarried children regardless of age, his son's children, and his slaves. Wives and freed slaves (freedmen) are sometimes considered part of the familia. When a paterfamilias died, his oldest son became the new paterfamilias of his father's familia. His daughters and other sons became *sui iuris,* a person who is not under the power of another person. Each of the sons became a paterfamilias over their own children and any slaves they acquired.

Romans took names and what they said about family connections very seriously. The three-part name (like Gaius Acilius Glabrio) meant you were a Roman citizen of the clan Acilius and family Glabrio. Using a three-part name if you weren't a citizen was actually a crime. Which name of the three you called someone depended on the closeness of your relationship. There were only twenty male first names in common use, and one-in-five Romans was named Gaius. Only close friends and immediate family called you by your first name. Others used your last name, both your second and third names when being formal, and sometimes your first and third names.

When a male slave was freed by a citizen so he became a citizen, too, he took the first and second names of his former owner with his slave name added as his third name. Women were named the feminine form of their father's clan and family names. Married women kept their maiden names because they officially stayed part of their father's familia, not their husband's.

The Glabrio Familia
Gaius Acilius Glabrio (21): tribune who replaced Titianus commanding the XI Urban Cohort

Manius Acilius Glabrio, consul in 124, and proconsul of Africa in 139/140, father of Gaius

M'. Acilius Glabrio: consul in AD 91. Exiled by Domitian and executed in AD 95 for treason for becoming a Christian, grandfather of Gaius

Marcus Acilius Glabrio: consul suffectus in 33 BC and governor of Africa in 25 BC

THE PUBLILIUS FAMILIA

Publilia Martina (19): a Christian, moved from Cigisa estate to Carthago when parents died of fever; lived 8 years with her grandfather, G. Publilius Martinus

G. Publilius Martinus (deceased): Martina's grandfather, duumvir and decurion of the council of Carthago

Juliana (deceased): Martina's step-grandmother, Gaius Martinus's 2nd wife, died 6 months before start of story, a Christian

Volero Publilius Martinus (39): Martina's uncle, decurion of the council of Carthago

Artoria Prisca (35): Volero's wife

Priscilla (17) and Sufina (15): Volero's daughters

Platana (25): Martina's lady's maid since Martina was 12, a Christian

Clavus, Colina, Lepus (11), Myrtis (13), and Petale: the slaves in Martina's town house

Ceraulo, Scalptor, Speculo, and Cherida: slaves at Martina's glass shop

Figulus: steward of Martina's pottery shop in Utica

Atriensis: chief steward of the Cigisa estate and Utica shop since Martina was a girl

TITIANUS AND LENAEUS FAMILIAS

Titus Flavius Titianus (31): ex-tribune of XI Urban Cohort

Pompeia (26): wife of Titianus

Kaeso Lenaeus (20): brother of Pompeia, business partner of Titus

Sabina (23): Kaeso's wife

Melis (17): business manager for Kaeso and Titus

THE URBAN COHORT IN CARTHAGO

Acceptus: centurion responsible for road patrols

Dubitatus: centurion responsible for the Forum (where government buildings are) and the agora (large central marketplace)

Longinus: centurion responsible for the public entertainments (circus, amphitheater, theater, and the area around them)

Verus: centurion responsible for the harbors, the quays, and the warehouses and merchants around them

Placidus: optio in the harbor station (Verus is his centurion)

OTHER IMPORTANT COHORT MEN

Sartorus (25): optio from the warehouse district of Rome; accompanied Glabrio to Carthago as his aide

Nepos: Tribune of the XIII Urban Cohort who was replaced by Glabrio

Saturninus: M. Lollius Paullinus Valerius Saturninus (59): Glabrio's commander, Urban Prefect of Rome AD 124-134, also consul of Rome in 125

Hortus: Saturninus's optio serving as his aide at headquarters in Rome

THE MESSALA FAMILIA

L. Vipstanus Messala: friend of Tribune Nepos; son of a councilman of Carthago

Ahenus and Ferreus: metalsmiths in the metal shop at the Messala estate

OTHER PEOPLE IN CARTHAGO

Paternus: one of two duumvirs who were the co-mayors of the city

Viator: councilman who owns a glass shop

Lupulus and Lucretius: members of the city council

HISTORICAL PEOPLE

Truth and Honor is set in the early summer of AD 128, the year that Emperor Hadrian toured several provinces along the coast of Africa, including Africa Proconsularis and its capital city, Carthago. The following were real people who lived during the Roman era.

M. Lollius Paullinus Valerius Saturninus (59): Urban Prefect 124-134, also consul in 125; (commander of fictional Gaius Glabrio),

M'. Acilius Glabrio: consul ordinarius in 124 (Jan.-April); (father of fictional Gaius Glabrio)

M' Acilius Glabrio: consul ordinarius in 91 (Jan.–April); exiled in 91; executed in 95 by Domitian for being Christian; (grandfather of fictional Gaius Glabrio)

M. Acilius Glabrio: consul suffectus in 33 BC, governor of Africa 25 BC)

L. Stertinius Noricus: governor of Africa 127/128, consul suffectus in 113

L. Publilius Celsus, consul suffectus in 102, and consul ordinarius in 115; executed for plot to assassinate Hadrian in 118 (distant relative of the fictional Volero Publilius Martinus and his niece Martina)

Locations

Ad Gallinacium (6): military station on the road to Utica.

Bagrada River (A): Silting has moved the river's path and the shoreline away from Utica since AD 128. Dashed line is my estimate of the ancient shoreline. Now the Medjerda River.

Carthago (1): capital of Africa Proconsularis; rebuilt by Augustus where Phoenician Carthage had been destroyed in 146 BC in 3rd Punic War; 4th largest city in the Empire, population over 300,000. Near present-day Tunis, Tunisia.

Cigisa (2): town with garrison on the Bagrada River, close to Martina's estate. Now Sidi Thabet, Tunisia.

Hadrumentum (11): port city south of Carthago. Now Sousse, Tunisia.

Inuca (4): town on road going southwest from Carthago. Now Gourbis, Tunisia.

Leptis Magna (9): major port city in Africa Proconsularis province. Near present-day Khoms, Libya, 81 miles east of Tripoli (130 km).

Mare Nostrum: "our sea," what the Romans called the Mediterranean Sea.

Ostia and Portus (8): port towns at the mouth of the Tiber, main ports for Rome.

Pupput (10): port town south of Carthago. Now Hammamet.

Puteoli (12): port city in Italia south of Rome, third major port serving Rome. Now Pozzuoli, Italy.

Roma (7): capital of the Roman Empire, population approximately 1 million in AD 128.

Utica (5): port city on Bagrada River and capital of province of Africa before Carthago was built by Augustus. Utica is only ruins. No longer on the coast where it once was a major port, but further inland because deforestation and agriculture upriver led to massive erosion so the Medjerda River silted over its original mouth. The dashed line is my approximation for the ancient coastline. About 30 km from present-day Tunis.

Uthina (3): Small city established by Augustus for retired legionaries (a *colonia*) from the XIII Gemina Legion with a garrison of the III Augusta Legion stationed there in AD 128. Near present-day Oudna, Tunisia.

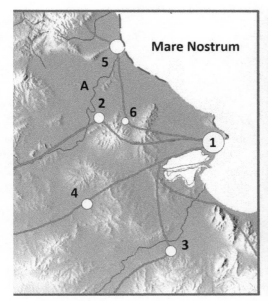

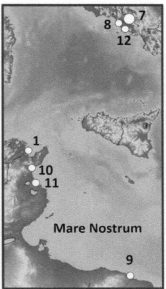

Chapter 1

THE NEW MAN IN CHARGE

Urban Cohort headquarters in the Praetorian Fortress.
Rome, Day 1, AD 128

With a snap, Tribune Gaius Acilius Glabrio shut the last of the wax tablets and added the report to the finished pile. In the warehouse district, a small fire, quickly extinguished, might have been arson. The nighttime robbery of a jeweler's shop in Trajan's Market had ended in the murder of the owner and the disappearance of his goldsmith and the slave girl who tended the shop. The goldsmith was Glabrio's first suspect, but was the girl an innocent victim, an accomplice, or the real murderer?

He closed his eyes and rubbed his forehead. Hunting lawbreakers and bringing them to justice had become his passion since he took over as tribune of the XI Urban Cohort several months ago. He'd been trained by the best as Urban Prefect Saturninus made him shadow then-tribune Titus Titianus on his last investigation before he retired.

But the lessons about honor and truth he'd learned as he spied on Titianus for his commander made him an uncompromising copy of the tribune Saturninus despised. The prefect was a close friend of Glabrio's father, but even if the affection Saturninus showed Father was real, it did not extend to him.

He'd irritated his commander with his failure to discover and betray what Emperor Hadrian's Praetorian Prefect had ordered Titianus to conceal. Since Glabrio took over the XI Cohort, he'd angered his commander each time he refused to discuss details of a case until he had enough evidence to arrest and convict the guilty. He'd infuriated the prefect when he refused to ignore some wrongdoing by a client of one of Saturninus's personal friends.

Glabrio rubbed his jaw. No one died in the fire, so the robbery and murder would get his full attention this morning. With his fingers laced atop his head, he leaned back in his chair and contemplated the spider that had spun

1

its web where wall met ceiling. The tiny hunter was the picture of patience as it waited to kill and eat.

Had the goldsmith watched and waited for the right moment to kill his master, take the gold, and run? Or was someone else guilty of murder, and the goldsmith ran because he feared he'd be blamed and executed for not stopping it? Had the girl run for the same reason?

The scraping of Plancus's chair legs on tile drew his eyes to the door.

"Prefect." The thud of his *optio's* fist hitting his chest triggered an eyeroll, but Glabrio stopped it before Saturninus stepped through his doorway.

Glabrio stood and struck his chest. "Prefect. What may I do for you?"

"I dined with your father last night." Saturninus lowered himself into the guest chair and motioned for Glabrio to sit. "We discussed you."

Glabrio sat and rested clasped hands on his desk. Did Saturninus want a response or respectful silence? Either could trigger his commander's frown, but a smug smile appeared instead.

Saturninus picked up Glabrio's stylus and rolled it between his fingers. "While you served here in Rome, we both thought you would form some good friendships of your own with your father's colleagues and supporters. But with your disregard for friendship, family obligations, and the privilege of rank that you learned from that equestrian you replaced—you've made that less likely than we thought."

"Getting to the truth and delivering justice matter." Glabrio's words triggered the tick at the corner of Saturninus's mouth that declared his commander's disagreement.

With a flick of his hand, Saturninus swept Glabrio's words aside. "You've squandered this first opportunity, but I proposed another to your father. He sees the benefit you're certain to gain from it."

"Father does have exceptional skill at seeing a political advantage." Glabrio's smile was more subdued than what his commander probably wanted. But it was unwise to act too pleased when he didn't know what was coming. "As you do as well."

Father considered Saturninus a good friend, but Titianus had told Glabrio more than once that what passed for friendship often wasn't. The friend of your father wasn't always your friend. He might even be your enemy, but he usually wouldn't strike while he still wanted your father's friendship.

The warmth of Saturninus's smile as he received the compliment didn't reach his eyes. "We do, and I can make certain you take proper advantage of this opportunity. The tribune of the XIII Urban Cohort in Carthago is moving up to be a *quaestor*. I'm transferring you to take his place."

"Carthago." He barely stopped his jaw dropping before Saturninus saw. Father had said a year in Rome should be enough before he transferred to a post with a fighting legion on the frontier. But being in charge of the men who policed the fourth largest city in the Empire—he never expected that.

Glabrio cleared his throat. "Being the new man in charge there should prove highly advantageous, as you say. When will I be going?"

"Now." A slow grin crept across Saturninus's face, reminding Glabrio of a cat with a dead mouse between its paws. "Tribune Nepos will be sailing for Rome in two weeks. You need to go before then so there's no break in the command there."

"I have a few matters to tie up, but I can be ready to sail in six or seven days. Then Nepos will have enough time to tell me about the cases I'll need to continue working." Saturninus's eye roll drew Glabrio's broad smile, but the prefect would probably think gratitude inspired it. "I look forward to the challenge. Thank you."

Saturninus stood, and Glabrio followed his lead. His fist stuck his chest as his commander left the room. Then he sank into his chair.

Within a week, he'd be on a ship to the capital of Africa Proconsularis and a highly visible posting. The grin had barely formed before it faded; then the corners of his mouth drooped. Politically, it was highly desirable, but it came at a cost. For however long he would command the XIII Cohort, he'd be leaving the true friends he'd made through Titianus. Would he find even one friend he could trust where Saturninus was sending him?

Carthago, capital of Africa Proconsularis, morning of Day 1

Martina closed Grandfather's eyes before taking his still-warm hand in both of hers.

"Find my uncle and tell him Grandfather's gone."

She swept aside the first tear before Platana, her lady's maid, passed her a dry handkerchief and slipped out of the room.

He'd told her to go to bed, to get some rest since she'd been at his side for hours. He'd promised not to die while she slept. It was the only time he'd given her his word and failed to keep it.

She shook out the handkerchief and wiped each cheek in turn.

His death came too soon. Not only because he was the last of the family who'd truly loved her, but because she couldn't be sure she'd see him again.

When her parents died of the fever eight years ago, Grandfather had sent the carriage and bodyguards to bring her from the estate near Cigisa to the town house in Carthago. Stone-faced, he'd met the only child of his favorite son like the Stoic he was. She'd lowered her gaze to his feet as he crossed his arms and stared at her. But it was only grief that had made Grandfather so cold that day.

His second wife, Juliana, had stepped forward to wrap a broken-hearted girl of eleven in her arms. She'd held Martina from the first whimper through the racking sobs to the final shivering sigh. Then she'd loved Martina more than even Mother had, and she'd told Martina how God loved her, too.

When Juliana died six months ago, Martina had no doubt of their future reunion with Jesus in heaven. Her grandmother's last words as she left this world to be with their Lord still echoed in Martina's mind. Convince the man they both loved so dearly to embrace the truth before it was too late.

He wasn't interested. Whenever Martina tried to tell him what Jesus had done for every living soul, Grandfather smiled indulgently and told her what he'd told Juliana. She could believe what she wished, but don't let anyone outside their *familia* learn of her faith.

But this week, as Grandfather's vigor drained away, he'd listened. He'd asked questions. But what had he decided?

At the sound of footsteps, she squared her shoulders. Uncle Volero had been jealous of Grandfather's greater affection for her father. Envy of his brother became resentment toward her when Grandfather favored her over Volero's children.

And now he was her guardian.

Her uncle only glanced at her before his gaze locked onto Grandfather. His jaw clenched, silencing any sounds of grief before they could escape. She'd seen the same with Grandfather when Juliana died. Grandfather raised his sons as Stoics, and such men kept their tears stanched and their cries of anguish stifled when someone they loved died.

But even a man who could hold in his tears couldn't hide the haunted look of a new orphan when the father he loved was gone.

If only she could comfort him with words about the promise of eternal life with the Lord, like God had given Juliana. But she couldn't. She didn't know herself what Grandfather had decided about Jesus.

But even if she did, Uncle Volero would only mock what she said and then get angry at her for saying it. If anyone discovered the Martinus family had been infiltrated by Christians, that would undermine his influence in the council. Even his wife and children didn't know her secret.

"You should have called me in time for the final kiss to receive his soul as he died and then to close his eyes." He glared at her. "I'm his son. That was mine to do."

"He died in the night." With her handkerchief, she caught the escaping tear. "He made me leave and go rest for a while. When he promised me he wouldn't die before morning, I believed him." She tightened her lips to stop the quiver. "I closed his eyes without thinking, or I would have let you do it."

Uncle's sigh was deep. "What's done is done."

As he stood across the bed from Martina, Uncle took Grandfather's hand from her, removed the signet ring, and slipped it onto his own finger. He placed first one, then the other hand on his father's chest. "I always thought it a waste of time when my tutor made me memorize so much of what Seneca wrote. But Father had memorized it when he was young, so he insisted." He placed his hand atop Grandfather's. "'It is not that we have a short space of time, but that we waste much of it.' Father quoted that so often. He used to say we'd be given enough time to accomplish the greatest things if we only invested the time we had wisely."

He rubbed his mouth. "But it doesn't feel like enough right now."

Martina bit her lip as she wiped away a new teardrop. It hadn't been enough. Not because Grandfather hadn't accomplished many things because he had. He'd been *duumvir* of the city, served for years on the city council, enlarged the family estates, added the glassworks to his business holdings, and made her uncle an important man in the city as well.

But he'd died before he told her what he decided about Jesus. A fresh tear trickled down her cheek, and she swept it away. How could she bear the uncertainty? She could tell herself he must have chosen to believe. How could he not? But that didn't mean he had.

"Father was duumvir, and many will come to pay respects. So, the funeral rites will be public and here in Carthago." The corners of his mouth turned down when his gaze shifted from Grandfather to her. "They will also be completely Roman rites." His eyebrows dipped. "You will do nothing that would make someone suspect Father was hiding Christians in his household."

Did Uncle think she was that reckless? She couldn't count how many times Grandfather had stressed that point.

"I will also make offerings for my step-mother as part of the rites for Father. I don't want anything from you that would suggest to anyone that she wasn't a pious Roman matron. Father buried Juliana with Roman rites, even though it was only our family and a few close friends out at the estate. He would want that reputation preserved."

Martina clenched her jaw. The hypocrisy of Grandfather pretending Juliana wasn't a Christian and cremating her in the Roman way with all the rites and offerings, as if she believed in the pagan gods she'd rejected—it hadn't surprised Martina, but it heaped grief upon grief as she was forced to pretend Juliana would have wanted what they did.

"I'm not stupid, Uncle. I know that could be dangerous to me and embarrassing to you."

"You were stupid enough to let Juliana convince you to think a crucified rebel died for you both and then came back to life as a god. You still believe that ridiculous story."

"It's not ridiculous, and Grandfather was considering it when he died."

Volero inhaled sharply, and his frown became a scowl. "Don't ever repeat what you just said. Father remained a Stoic and a good Roman."

Anger had swept the grief from her uncle's face. To choose to antagonize him now, when her authority as *domina* over the household had died with Grandfather—that would be stupid. But being faithful was more important than being smart.

"I don't know what he decided, but you don't need to worry. I won't say what I don't know for certain, and I don't plan to tell anyone who comes that I'm a Christian, either." She squared her shoulders. "But don't ask me to say or do anything as part of those rites that would look like I'm worshipping the gods of Rome. I won't betray my God that way. Besides, your daughters can do whatever people will expect, and they won't mind at all."

"If it wouldn't look strange and spawn gossip, I'd pack you off to one of my estates before the funeral." His eyes narrowed. "I'll let nothing tarnish Father's reputation among the elite of the city."

She raised her chin. Her grandfather had the right tell her what to do, but not her uncle. "Grandfather may have made you my guardian under Roman law, but you are not my *paterfamilias*. I'm *sui iuris* now, and you can't order me to go anywhere."

After drawing a deep breath, she blew it out slowly. Uncle had no official power over her, but he could make her life difficult. Roman law said he had to approve her major financial decisions as long as he was her guardian.

She softened her tone. "I know you only have my best interest at heart, Uncle. Let's not argue when grief might make us say what we don't really mean."

Her sad smile formed, then faded. "If I leave Carthago, I'll go to my own estate near Cigisa. It became mine when Mother died, and it's been well managed by her family's steward these past eight years. But for whatever Grandfather might have bequeathed to me, I'll welcome your guidance. Grandfather always said you were wise in the ways of business. You made him proud."

Uncle Volero had been bristling like an angry guard dog, but her last words relaxed his scowl into a slight frown. "I'll decide how to handle that after Father is properly buried as the important man he was. You can wait for me to deal with his will until we finish the nine days of mourning."

"Of course, Uncle."

"But what you propose for the funeral...we can do that. My girls are eager to move to town from the estate, and my wife will want to take on all the hostess duties you've been doing for Father. They'll gladly do what the Roman rites require." He squeezed the back of his neck. "I've sent word to the undertaker, and he'll be here shortly to prepare everything for Father to lie in state. If you would oversee that, at least…"

A sigh drained his lungs, and for a moment, the proud, capable man who helped run the city looked more like a lost child.

"You don't need to worry about that. I helped with Juliana, and you can leave it all to me." Preparing Juliana's body for a pagan funeral had driven a dagger into her already-wounded heart, but Grandfather had needed her help. Uncle Volero needed it now.

His frown relaxed into the slight downturn of heartfelt grief. "My son can't return from Alexandria in time, but I've already sent the message for Artoria and my girls to come from the estate." He rubbed the bridge of his nose. "You can stay here as long as you wish, but we'll continue keeping your religion secret from the three of them."

"Thank you, Uncle. I agree that's wise." She'd stay for a while, but this house that had been a home while Juliana and Grandfather lived was only a building now. How long she would stay…only time would tell.

Uncle Volero drew the sheet over Grandfather's face and flicked his hand to send her out of the room ahead of him. As she passed through the doorway, she looked over her shoulder. Grandfather's body would have a Roman funeral, but his soul…

God, please let him have decided to believe. Let him and Juliana be together once more, joyful in Your presence until someday I join them, too.

Chapter 2

Almost the Last Time

The Martinus town house, Carthago, midmorning of Day 1

Martina wrapped her arms around herself as she stood watching the undertaker lay Grandfather on the mosaic floor in his bedchamber. She turned her eyes away as the man began the washing and anointing with perfumed oils that would prepare the empty shell to be draped one final time in a toga for viewing.

With feet toward the door and a wreath encircling the brow, his body would lie in state for a few days on the two mattresses atop the ornately carved funeral couch. The platform it would stand on was even now being assembled in the twenty-foot-wide *vestibulum* where Grandfather used to hold the salutation for his clients and friends.

A flaming torch would stand at each corner, and two head-high vases would be at the far end of the platform, garlands of fruit and flowers hanging between them.

Grandfather always planned ahead. He'd sent his steward to order everything two weeks ago so it would be premade and ready to assemble when the time came. If only that planning had been unnecessary...

Martina wiped her cheeks with the slate-gray handkerchief that matched her tunic and the *palla* wrapped around her. Juliana had worn both when Martina's father died. Martina had worn them a few months ago after Juliana's death. When Platana had folded them and placed them at the bottom of her tunic trunk, Martina hadn't expected to wear them again for years. Why couldn't God have let that be true?

Wearing nothing but grays and blacks had been a painful reminder that Juliana had left this world behind. But with Grandfather's eternal fate a question not to be answered before her own passing, everything hurt more this time.

A quick glance, and she looked away again. The undertaker hadn't quite finished his work.

No longer Grandfather, it was only a body that lay on the floor, but it meant a lot to Uncle Volero that the family mourned him properly.

Roman noblemen were expected to control their grief, to press on and fulfill their duties even when loved ones died. So, Uncle had donned the charcoal-gray toga and tunic Grandfather had worn for Juliana, masked his grief as a good Stoic should, and gone to the council meeting to serve Carthago and Rome, just as Grandfather would have expected.

When he returned, the important men who'd been Grandfather's colleagues and friends would also come to pay their respects.

She would have everything ready. The paid female mourners, their hair down and disheveled, would be beating their chests. The flute player and singer would be filling the vestibulum with quiet dirges. Uncle would be grateful for all she'd done to prepare his father for their visitors. His eyes would show it, even if he never spoke the words.

When his wife, Artoria, came from the estate, she would take over as domina, and Martina could retire to grieve in private. That couldn't come a moment too soon.

She closed her eyes and tipped her face heavenward. *God, please give me strength and wisdom to make it through these days of mourning without betraying my faith in You. You know my heart and mind belong to You, but I must endure everything Uncle will do to honor the Roman gods like he thinks Grandfather would have wanted. Please let Uncle be wrong about that because Grandfather is with You now.*

The Glabrio town house, Rome, evening of Day 1

When Glabrio rode into the stableyard of his father's town house, he was late for dinner. He'd planned to be early, but he hadn't expected the urgent summons from the centurion who'd been inspecting the jeweler's shop. What should have been a quick visit turned into a painstaking examination because all was not as it should have been.

A crowbar blow to the head had killed the owner. The bloody weapon still lay by the strongbox, where the metal hasp had been pried free with the lock still attached.

But wouldn't the goldsmith merely have taken the key on the chain around the owner's neck and unlocked it? Much faster, much quieter. But the long brass chain still hung around the dead man's neck with the key hidden under his tunic, halfway between throat and stomach.

Of course, the gold that had been in the strongbox in the windowless storeroom was gone. Any thief should have taken all the precious metals and any jewels in the steel box, which was bolted to the floor on the inside so no one could carry it away without unlocking it to unscrew the bolts first.

The gold and silver were missing, but several small boxes remained. Some held garnets, carnelians, and amethysts, shaped into cabochons and carved with images, ready to be made into rings. Others held emeralds, sapphires, and rubies. Several more held pearls, sorted by size.

When his centurion found the fortune in jewels that shouldn't still be there, he'd sent for Glabrio.

Had the goldsmith been afraid that trying to sell them would get him caught? Or had the thief not known he left a treasure behind?

That triggered Glabrio's search of the entire shop himself. Every drawer, every cabinet, the underside of every shelf and piece of furniture in the sales room, store room, and the room where the goldsmith slept—nothing had gone unexamined, and he found more things that shouldn't have been there if the goldsmith committed the murder.

In a hidden compartment in the cabinet in the goldsmith's bedchamber, he'd found an exquisite filigree necklace set with pearls and emeralds and some matching earrings. Whether the goldsmith had stolen those and hidden them from the owner or whether the murdered man put them there so someone with access to the strongbox wouldn't see them—either way, the goldsmith should have taken them as well as the gold.

He dismounted, and Father's stable slave led his stallion to its usual stall as he bounded up the portico steps and into the peristyle. Father wasn't in the *triclinium*, even though the salad course had already been set on the table between the three couches.

A deep breath ended in a sigh as Glabrio headed for the library. In less than a week, he would be on a ship headed for Carthago. Would his late arrival spoil one of their final meals together before he sailed?

But when he entered the library, Father set down his scroll and raised a hand in greeting. "I thought you might be delayed. Marcus Saturninus told me what he planned for you last night. When I saw Marcus at the baths today, he said you were planning to leave before week's end."

A wry smile lifted one corner of his mouth as Father returned the scroll to its cubicle. "He seemed to think you'd simply leave things to the next tribune, but I expected you'd be tying off as many loose ends as you could."

Father waved his hand toward the door. "I told the stableman to let the kitchen know when you arrived. Let's go eat."

Glabrio stepped into the atrium and waited for his father. These meals together, just the two of them—he'd miss these as much as he'd miss dining with Titianus's family.

"Saturninus told me this morning he's transferring me to Carthago. I'll be taking over the XIII Cohort, but..."

He removed his helmet and placed it under his arm. "How long should I plan to stay there? We'd only planned on me serving a year in Rome, so it's almost time to ask for a posting with a frontier legion."

They'd reached the triclinium, and Glabrio set his helmet on the right couch. Father reclined on the host's couch to the left while Glabrio released the clasps on the side of his bronze cuirass. Before taking the center couch of honor, he set his cuirass and skirt of leather straps beside the helmet.

Father raised his gold-lined silver goblet for the wine slave to fill. "Marcus surprised me when he suggested it, but he's right that it's an unusual opportunity to give you a position of some power where you'll be noticed."

He took a sip and set it on the table. "Hadrian will be touring Mauretania, Numidia, and Africa Proconsularis this summer. If he passes through Carthago, he'll see what a fine job you do policing the fourth largest city in the empire. Marcus will have told him you're there, as will I if I get the chance before Hadrian leaves Rome."

Father dipped a hard-boiled egg in the pine-nut sauce before taking a bite. "One of our ancestors governed that province less than twenty years after Augustus rebuilt Carthago as a Roman colony. Most of the colonists were the poor of Rome, but some are now wealthy enough to be equestrian. A few are even senators, so the elite of the city should be worth adding to your acquaintances."

"I can see the possible advantage, but the timing..." Glabrio selected a purple carrot slice. "He's known for some time that the tribune of the XIII was moving up. Saturninus wants me in Carthago before Nepos sails for Rome in two weeks. I'll be leaving in less than one. I wonder if my commander is using this to get me out of Rome before I gather enough evidence against one of his good friend's clients." He dipped the carrot in the sauce.

A wry smile accompanied Father's shrug. "You might be right, but it's better for everyone if you go. Besides, your commander can send you anywhere he wants whenever he wants, and this is an excellent opportunity."

"I can see that, and I've told him I appreciate it. Besides, I might make some powerful enemies, Saturninus among them, if I stayed."

"Enemy? That's too strong a word. He hasn't been pleased that you do some things exactly like Titianus did, but I think he has your best interest in mind with this transfer. He is, after all, my friend."

Glabrio forced a smile. "Hunting those who break Roman law—perhaps that makes me naturally suspicious of everyone, even when I don't need to be."

He bit off the end and dipped the remaining carrot in the sauce again.

The friend of your father is not always your friend, and what seems like friendship might not be. Those were two pieces of wisdom that Titianus had shared, and Glabrio had seen both in action. But Father's friendship with Saturninus was of such long standing it probably was real, and Saturninus's dislike for him hadn't changed that.

"I thought I'd sleep here until I leave." Glabrio selected an egg. "It's only a four-day voyage to Carthago. Perhaps you can visit."

"I will." The love and pride of a father for his son warmed Father's eyes and broadened his smile.

"Good." With that one word, Glabrio spoke all the love and respect the best of fathers deserved. Then the conversation turned into their usual comfortable give-and-take between friends.

Father had confirmed the wisdom of the transfer, but in the morning, Glabrio would stop by Titianus's house on his way to the fortress.

Before his friend and mentor started teaching his noble students tomorrow, Glabrio would share his news and ask for practical advice on how to oversee a city where he knew no one. Titus had spent ten years as an outsider to the elite circles of Rome, and no one could have policed the city better. How to do that himself—that was advice that only Titus could give.

Chapter 3

THE NEW ORDER

The Martinus town house, Carthago, evening of Day 1

Martina leaned her elbows on the dressing table and buried her face in her hands. When Uncle returned from the council meeting, a *duumvir*, both *aediles*, and what felt like half the councilmen came with him to pay respects to Grandfather. Many had dined with Grandfather since Juliana died, and those who'd seen her as domina of his household spoke condolences to her.

How could it be that words meant to console hurt so much? Every mention of Grandfather being at peace and enjoying a reunion with his ancestors in the Elysian Fields tore at her heart.

There were no Elysian Fields. The only hope for eternal life, for eternal peace and joy, came from believing in Jesus, who'd died to pay for his sins. Had Grandfather understood and decided to believe in time?

Platana came behind her and massaged her shoulders. "What can I do to help?"

A deep breath turned into a deeper sigh. "What you're already doing. Pray." Martina rubbed her forehead. "It's been harder than I expected, but something worse is coming."

"Your aunt?"

Martina closed her eyes and nodded.

A knock on the doorframe forced them open. She turned in the chair to find Lepus, whom she'd moved from his usual post at the front door to the back to watch for the carriage from the estate.

"The carriage and a wagon are here, Mistress."

"I'll be right down. You can go back to the vestibulum door." As the boy left, she placed her palms on the tabletop and pushed herself up from the chair.

This morning, she'd moved her things to this room off the small courtyard balcony. Since coming as an orphaned child eight years earlier, she'd slept in the bedchamber next to Juliana's, one off the peristyle where the murmur of water from the fountains had seemed like musical accompaniment to the loving words spoken there.

But both of the people who'd filled that house with their love for her were gone, and Artoria would want that room for one of her daughters. It was better to move herself than be told to do it by the new domina.

She paused by the barred window. It let a refreshing breeze pass through while giving a lovely view of the harbor. One corner of her mouth lifted. With the discord that was about to descend on the main floor, this would seem a haven of tranquility.

"I wish their coming had taken longer. Artoria has never liked me. She hated how Grandfather preferred me to her girls."

Platana adjusted the folds of Martina's gray palla. "If her daughters weren't so...so much like her, perhaps your grandfather would have liked them better."

"Having the three of them here..." Martina didn't even try to stop the sigh. "The last time I saw Priscilla, she taunted me about my parents being lucky they were dead so they didn't have to be around me. Juliana told her to stop when she overheard, but Priscilla used that sneer she's perfected. She said Juliana wasn't her grandmother, and she had no right to be giving orders to the daughter of the next paterfamilias."

With arms crossed, Platana glared at those words. "Those two want your place even more than their mother does. You're *sui iuris* and wealthy, pretty, smart, and kind. They're only the daughters of a rich man with a son who'll get most of it. Any man worth marrying will consider you a better match, and they resent that."

The mother-lion loyalty Platana always showed her triggered Martina's smile. "I'm not any prettier than they are, and they can be pleasant enough when they try. With them living here in Carthago now, Uncle will be able to find them suitable husbands soon enough."

She fingered the silver necklace with a cameo of a resting lamb that Juliana had given her right after she declared her commitment to the Good Shepherd. "Grandfather used to complain that me being a Christian forced him to tell anyone who asked that he wasn't seeking a marriage for me. He made up an excuse that Father had informally committed me to someone, and he was waiting to see if that deal went through."

As if committing to spend a lifetime with someone was a business contract between the fathers. In a way it was, but to hear it talked about that way...

"I'm glad he did. I have enough that I don't have to marry, and I'd only want a man who already shares my faith. It broke Juliana's heart that Grandfather wouldn't even listen to what was most important to her." She shrugged. "But I'll probably never find one. I don't even know where to look."

From the cabinet, Platana took a clean handkerchief and traded it for the damp one Martina was clutching. "Maybe you won't have to look. Maybe God will bring one right to you." She offered a subdued smile with her shrug.

"Hmph." Martina shook her head. "He could, but maybe He has other plans for me." With steepled fingers, she rubbed the side of her nose. "But right now, I need to welcome my aunt and turn over this household to a woman who hates me. I'm glad you were Juliana's and never Grandfather's. She gave you to me, so Artoria can't treat you like she does her own people. But stay out of her way until I make sure she knows that."

With shoulders squared, Martina headed down the stairs to face the woman Grandfather had called a Gorgon with a pretty face. Martina barely knew her because he didn't want "that woman" in his house after she'd snubbed Juliana.

Martina placed one hand on her stomach as she headed toward the commotion in the peristyle. Maybe her aunt wasn't as bad as Grandfather said. Juliana never spoke ill of her, but she never spoke ill of anyone.

As she stepped out of her courtyard into the larger room, Priscilla's arm shot out, finger pointing. "There she is."

Artoria made a stately turn and tilted her head to look down her nose. "I'd expected you to greet your new domina at the door, Martina."

Martina swallowed the response those words deserved and summoned a welcoming smile instead. "Welcome. Uncle Volero isn't here at the moment, so let me get you settled in your new home."

Artoria scanned the wall of bedchambers. "Of course, I'll be using Juliana's old room, so you'll need to find another."

With a sweep of her hand, Martina directed Artoria's gaze toward the second-largest bedchamber next to Grandfather's. "Actually, I never moved out of the room I used as a child when Juliana died. I've already had the domina's room freshly cleaned in preparation for your arrival." Her arm dropped, but her social smile stayed in place. "I assumed you'd want your girls near you, so I also had my old bedchamber and one next to it prepared."

She tipped her head back to match Artoria's angle.

"Uncle told me to take any room I wanted, so I've already moved to one on the balcony off the smaller courtyard."

"You forgot to comb your hair before you came down." Sufina wrinkled her nose. "And that gray makes you look ugly."

"Your mother didn't explain mourning customs yet?" Martina raised her eyebrows. "Or if you've forgotten what she said, I'm sure she'll tell you again." She turned back to Artoria. "I sent one of the older housemaids to buy some dark tunics for you and my cousins and matching stolas for you. She also got the dark tunics for the house slaves. You'll each find the mourning clothes in your rooms."

Sufina stepped into her room and came out with the slate-gray tunic held against her. "This is hideous, Mother. Grandfather didn't like us enough to have us live in town with him, so why should we make a big display of mourning him? Wearing this, wailing, leaving my hair down and messy like Martina—do we really have to do that? We didn't do any of it when his wife died."

"Stop complaining." Artoria's glare shifted from Martina to her younger daughter. "Your grandfather was a very important man in the city, and the funeral rites will be worthy of such a man. You want to impress those who attend with your willing participation in everything your father has planned to honor his memory." A smug smile appeared. "Besides, the leading men in this city with sons who could become your husbands will be watching. This is your chance to show what fine daughters-in-law you'd be."

"It's ugly, but we don't have to wear them for long." Priscilla glanced at her mother. "The whole thing will be like a play where people only pretend to grieve. Everyone knows that."

"Your father isn't acting." Martina crossed her arms. "He is mourning his father, not just in public but in truth."

Her cousins looked at each other and rolled their eyes.

"As I am." The words from Artoria's mouth were contradicted by her smile and shrug, and they drew another eyeroll from her daughters. "We'll all do what's appropriate to honor your grandfather as the great man he was, and you'll do it without complaint."

Pricilla's mouth opened, but it closed without uttering a sound when her mother scowled.

"And I'll make sure all the slaves understand what I expect of them." Artoria turned another glare on Martina. "You do know I became domina here the moment my Volero became paterfamilias. I'll expect no interference from you in how I direct this household."

"It's between Uncle Volero and you to decide what's proper." Martina straightened to her full height, which made her taller than the tyrant who'd soon be making life miserable for the familia. "I'll expect you to remember my maid Platana has belonged to me since Juliana died, so she's not part of your household. She'll obey only my commands, not you or your daughters."

Martina managed a gracious smile, but it wasn't easy. "I'm going to my room for a while before dinner is served. I've already dealt with the undertaker to get everything in place for Grandfather to lie in state, but I know how much you need to do overseeing a house where death has come." She directed another smile at her cousins. "And with two daughters to help with keeping watch over his body and calling out his name, I'm sure you don't need me."

Artoria stared at the funeral couch where Grandfather's body lay, and she blanched. "How long is that going to be there?"

"Uncle didn't say, but I'd expect at least three days, maybe more. The burial will be public with the whole city invited, but I'm sure you'll manage everything well."

Her aunt shuddered.

"I'll leave you now." Martina turned and walked away.

Was Artoria afraid of dealing with Grandfather's corpse? Afraid of facing death itself?

Thank You, God, that Juliana told me the truth about You so I'm not mired in fearful superstitions like my aunt. Please let Grandfather have broken free from them before he died. Let him be at peace now with You.

She entered her new room and closed the door. The warm breeze caressed her, and the warbles and trills of an unseen bird came through the window.

"I should have moved up here earlier." She squeezed the back of her neck. "It's been a long day. I think I'll take a nap until dinner."

She held her arms out, and Platana unwrapped her palla.

"I told Artoria and her daughters that you're mine and they are not to be giving you orders."

"I wish you could protect the others from her, too."

"So do I."

Martina moved to the window for one more look before sleeping. A large grain ship had just been pulled out of the harbor. Its sail unfurled, and as the wind filled it, it headed out to sea on its way to Rome.

She should have moved to this room sooner. With the view of the harbor out the window, it was easier to remember that the future was filled with possibilities, that she wasn't trapped in this household if she didn't want to be.

With neither Juliana nor Grandfather there, being down on the main floor didn't feel like home anymore. But where should her next home be?

Chapter 4

Unexpected Opportunities

The Titianus town house, Rome, morning of Day 2

When Glabrio rode into Titianus's stableyard, the stableman was brushing his friend's gray stallion just outside its stall. Glabrio slipped from his horse and raised a hand in response to the man's wave. He slapped his own stallion's rump, and it ambled toward a manger of fresh hay.

Then he headed into the private part of the town house unannounced. Titus had told him it was wrong for a good friend to do otherwise.

As he passed the kitchen, the corners of his mouth drooped. The easy familiarity, as if Titus and Kaeso were his brothers and their wives were his sisters—nothing like that awaited him in Carthago. He hadn't known it was possible before Titianus. Would he ever have it again?

Voices came through the opened panels of the tablinum wall that faced the garden. When he stepped inside, Titus and his brother-in-law Kaeso were bent over the desk, their gaze fixed on a pile of coins their business agent Melis was sorting.

Titus straightened "Good morning. To what do we owe this pleasure?"

"I've been transferred to command the XIII Cohort in Carthago." He set his bronze helmet with its red horsehair crest on the guest chair. "I'm looking forward to the greater responsibility, but it will seem strange not to have Plancus sorting what needs my attention when I enter my office." He shrugged. "I'll miss Gellius in Subura, too, and my centurions and optios at the other stations."

He looked at the three men standing before him. He'd miss them as well, but that wasn't something he could say aloud.

"Carthago." A smile accompanied Titus's nod. "That could be an excellent move to advance your career. You'll be in charge of a city Rome depends on for grain. Even Alexandria contributes less."

18

"Father said Hadrian will probably pass through Carthago this summer, so it's a chance to gain his notice. Father was highly pleased by that prospect, so I think you're right."

"There's already a problem there for you to fix." Melis tossed a coin in the air before catching and handing it to Glabrio.

Glabrio stared at the shiny silver denarius. It was one of the newer ones minted by Hadrian commemorating his tour of the provinces.

Melis's chuckle made Glabrio's brow furrow.

"What am I not seeing?"

Melis took it and turned it to show the edge. "See this?"

A thin line looked less shiny. Glabrio put his thumbnail in it and twisted. A shiny flake popped off, revealing the dull gray beneath.

Glabrio's eyebrows rose. Silver had been plated onto base metal and stamped to look like one of Hadrian's new coins.

Melis placed another coin on his palm, this one a golden *aureus*, and showed it to Glabrio. "I was just telling Titus and Kaeso about their captain getting change for his purchases of raw glass slabs partly in counterfeit coins. He bought from the shops of several foundries, getting change from each. He didn't notice when someone gave him the coins, so he doesn't know which cheated him."

Glabrio's smile grew until it was a crooked grin. "I hadn't expected something so significant to investigate."

His grin triggered Titus's frown. "Significant often means dangerous. Counterfeiting is a capital crime. The opportunity for huge profits is enough to tempt powerful people to be behind it, and that ramps up the danger to those who hunt the criminals. The mildest punishment for the elite is deportation to an island. For others who were born free, it's the beasts, the mines, or crucifixion. For a freedman or slave, it's however the governor decides to execute them. You know from my experience that a powerful man has men who will try to kill you to stop you finding out who he is."

Glabrio sobered. "But I can't turn a blind eye to it."

"I'm not telling you to, but you'll need to be especially vigilant in a city where you don't know who can be trusted."

"So, what do you suggest?"

"Can you take any of your men with you?"

"I don't know. I haven't discussed it with Saturninus."

"Ask to take a squad of men you know you can trust. Also take one of your optios as your aide, someone who can be your second set of eyes and ears."

Glabrio rubbed behind his ear. "I have twelve good men to choose among. Which do you recommend?"

"I want to check into something before I say. Stop by this evening, and I can tell you."

After tossing the coin in the air, Glabrio gave it back to the young man who missed nothing, just like Titus, his former master.

Melis dropped it back on the pile. "I'll prepare a list of the glass shops we deal with in Carthago. I can't be completely certain they're honest, but I haven't seen anything to make me think they aren't. They might have been victims themselves."

"That will be give me a good starting place."

Melis swept the coins off the desk into a leather bag. "I'll also bring Titus more counterfeit coins to give you. They were mostly denarii, but there were a few where gold had been plated to make a fake *aureus,* like the one I just showed you. I'll show him what betrays them as counterfeits so he can teach you before you leave."

Glabrio donned his helmet. "I'll swing by on my way to dine with Father tonight. After you decide whom I should take, I'll talk with Saturninus."

Titus stood. "I'll take care of that now. Melis, can you start my geometry class today?"

Melis's quick nod and smile were his answer.

Titianus rested his hand on Glabrio's shoulder. "I'll walk you to the stable. I'll need my horse, too."

The Martinus town house, Carthago, morning of Day 2

When Martina came down from her room and entered the peristyle, the doors to Artoria's bedchamber and those of her daughters were still closed.

That was what she'd hoped for. Eating alone in silence was much better than listening to the complaints of the daughters and the scolds of the mother.

But she'd scarcely entered the triclinium when Uncle Volero came through the doorway. After a curt nod, he reclined on the host's couch to the left of the table. Honored guests used the center couch, so she chose the one to the right. Artoria would insist her daughters take the center where Martina had always been with Juliana and Grandfather. But as Artoria had replaced her as domina, Volero's daughters had displaced her from honored granddaughter of the household to merely tolerated relative.

"Good morning, Uncle."

"That remains to be seen." The frown he already wore when he walked into the room deepened.

Lepus and Myrtis, who were children of one of the undercooks, entered with plates of bread, cheese, and dates. Martina waited for her uncle to take his share, then selected some for herself.

The silence was broken only by the sound of them chewing and the distant gurgles of the peristyle fountains.

Finally, Uncle Volero tipped his head back to drain the last drops of wine from his goblet. "It's time to discuss my father's will." He glanced at his wife's still-closed door half-way down the right side of the pool and this side of his own chamber. "Go to the tablinum. I'll be right with you."

She rose and followed him. At the end of the pool that ran the length of the peristyle, she, turned left to the tablinum as he turned right.

Martina's stomach clenched as he approached Artoria's door. Whatever Grandfather had given her, her aunt would think it was too much. But Uncle walked past without knocking and entered his own room.

Inside the tablinum, the desk where Grandfather sat every day stood before her. Stacks of tablets and papyrus scrolls awaiting his attention should be piled on the left side, but there were none this morning.

Past the desk, a set of shelves divided into cubicles spanned half the wall. Many held documents related to the estates. Others contained the accounts of Grandfather's other businesses. But the cubicle on the upper right held some scrolls of Seneca's writings. Grandfather often took one down and read for a while when he took a short break from his work.

His favorites were still in that cubicle—except one. The one he read most, the one with the lion-head knobs on the end of the scrolls—it was missing.

Juliana had surprised Grandfather with that one when they were first married, before she became a Christian, and the ruby eyes in the silver lions were treasures themselves. Was Uncle Volero already selling what Grandfather had loved?

One missing scroll was no reason for tears, but Martina still wiped the corner of her eye. If he'd only told her what he planned, she would have offered to buy it. A gift of love to the one who loved it should remain with someone who knew how much it meant.

Her uncle's footsteps grew louder, then stopped. The soft thud of a door closing and the click of a bolt sliding home made her turn.

From the scroll cradled on his arm, four ruby eyes greeted her. Uncle returned the scroll to its usual place of honor.

Martina wiped her other eye as a sad smile grew. He'd been reading it in his chamber. Grandfather would have been pleased.

"That was Grandfather's favorite scroll."

"I know. When I was a youth, he'd read the start of a saying, then expect me to finish it." He stroked one lion's mane. "He did the same with my son." He placed it atop the other scrolls and turned it until the lions looked straight at her. "Someday I hope to do the same with my grandsons."

He settled into the desk chair and motioned for her to take the one opposite. "What my father gave you is none of my wife's business, but she'll think it is. So, I'll give you a quick summary now and tell you more later."

He leaned back in his chair. "You've inherited Father's glass business. He owned it for only a few months, so it's still being run by the men he bought with it. From its performance since then, it appears likely to bring in good income for you without any significant attention on my part."

"What does that include?"

"The foundry where bulk glass slabs are made. It's outside the city, but there's also a glass-blowing shop here in Carthago. It fronts a small town house not far from the harbor that includes four other small shops. They're all rented right now. The glass shop comes with a shop steward who also blows glass, two other men who are glass blowers and sculptors, and a woman who does whatever is needed. That's where the raw glass slabs we ship to Rome and other ports are sold as well."

"There's a town house?" Martina touched the lamb cameo. Property in Carthago presented possibilities and choices she hadn't anticipated.

"The town house is usually rented, but the tenant just moved out. I expect I'll have another one arranged within the month, and that will also add to your steady income."

"I've never run a business." She bit her lip.

"And you won't have to run this one. The shop steward knows what he's doing, and the man over the foundry has been doing it for many years."

"But it's wise for me to learn. I want to know what's involved for when I have to replace one of them. No one lives forever. Not in this world, anyway."

The corners of Uncle's mouth turned down. "No, they don't. Some die too soon." A deep sigh followed.

She offered a sad smile, and he returned a sadder one.

Not in this world, but this world wasn't all there was. Juliana and she would live forever, but would Grandfather?

Uncle cleared his throat. "So, you are welcome to remain here, but it's imperative we keep your faith secret from Artoria and the girls." He raised an eyebrow at her. "Not just for Grandfather's reputation, but for your own safety." One corner of his mouth curved. "Perhaps you'll be a good influence on my daughters. The contrast between you and their mother...it's one they need to see."

He pointed toward the small door that opened into her courtyard. "Leave that way. My wife might be up now."

"Thank you, Uncle."

His hand flicked toward the door, but his nod and slight smile whispered the "you're welcome" his lips wouldn't speak.

Chapter 5

THE RIGHT MAN FOR THE JOB

Guard station in the warehouse district, Rome, morning of Day 2

Titianus dismounted and tied his reins to a ring on the guard station wall. He paused by the door as a squad of men he used to command passed by him, heading out on patrol. Several nodded in respect, and he returned each nod. When the last man passed, he entered.

Optio Gaius Flavius Sartorus sat at his desk, writing on a wax tablet. When he raised his head, first his eyebrows rose, then he stood.

"Tribune." His fist struck his chest, then a wry smile curved his mouth. "Old habits return easily. It's good to see you, Flavius Titianus."

"And to see you, Sartorus." Titianus pointed toward Glabrio's office. "I need to talk with you privately."

Sartorus followed him into Glabrio's office, and Titianus closed and bolted the door. He pointed at the guest chair as he settled into his old seat behind the desk.

"Tribune Glabrio will be commanding the XIII Urban Cohort, which polices Carthago and the surrounding area." He leaned back in the chair. It felt as if he'd never left. "I told him I would recommend someone to go with him as his personal aide."

"His personal aide." His old optio rubbed the back of his hand. "I would think he'd want Plancus."

"That might seem an obvious choice, but I plan to recommend you." It took Titianus some effort to keep his mouth straight when Sartorus's eyes saucered. "It might lead to your promotion, although it might not. But I would like you to go along to make certain he stays safe and succeeds there."

Sartorus's head drew back "Why me?"

"Your background as a tradesman and what you've learned about merchants, both good and bad, while serving seven years in this district. On the

23

last voyage to Carthago, my ship's captain received counterfeit coins, and Glabrio is eager to hunt the counterfeiters there."

He'd picked up a stylus and was rolling it between his fingers. When he felt the nick in the wooden handle, he stared at it. It was the same one he'd left there.

"He's going where he knows no one, and he was raised to understand how senators think, not merchants or common thieves. Without someone who can advise him about whom he can trust and protect him from those he can't, that could prove fatal. He'll need someone who'll watch his back."

Sartorus's fingers moved from rubbing his hand to massaging his wrist. "Tribune Glabrio is a man of honor, like you, and I'd be proud to serve him in that role. But I don't know why he'd pick me when he could have someone like Plancus or Gellius. They've worked closely with him since he first came. I've done nothing special to draw his attention."

"He'll take my recommendation, and I've chosen you for one more reason." Titianus leaned in and rested his forearms on the desktop. "I think you know Someone who can help with any problem if you ask."

"I don't know anyone in Carthago."

"That's not what I meant, and my next question—however you answer, it will go no further than the two of us."

◆

"Ask me anything, Tribune." Sartorus's mouth twitched. Old habits of address die hard.

All emotion vanished from Titianus's face. The icy gray eyes Sartorus had seen make bold men squirm focused on him, and silence filled the room.

Sartorus's breath froze. The one question he dreaded answering—was it about to be asked? He could only answer with the truth. But where would that lead?

Titianus leaned forward and with his fingertip, traced a curve that made half a fish on the desktop.

Sartorus's eyebrows shot up. Titianus tapped twice on the curve he'd drawn. Sartorus watched his former commander's face and drew the second curve to complete the fish.

The straight mouth relaxed into a warm smile, and Sartorus returned it with a nod.

"You, too?" The tribune had always acted with honor and taken risks for justice, but he was the last man Sartorus would have guessed would be a Christian.

"Yes."

"How did you know I am?"

"When I used to attend camp worship with all of you, I saw some eager to take part and others only going through the motions because it was required. But you seemed uncomfortable at times. I didn't understand it then, but I do now."

Titianus leaned on his elbows and steepled his fingers. "Glabrio is my friend, and several of us will be praying for him. While you're serving him, I'd like you to do the same."

"It will be my pleasure. If Tribune Glabrio asks me to go with him, I'll say yes." Sartorus rubbed his jaw. "Is he one of us?"

"Domitian executed his grandfather for treason for becoming one, but Glabrio's father chose a safer path. My young friend has taken the safe path, too." One corner of Titianus's mouth lifted. "But I don't think that can last. When a man values truth enough, resistance is futile. I'm proof of that."

"Faith comes at a cost, but it's been worth it." Sartorus massaged his right hand again. "When would we be leaving?"

"Within five days."

Titianus stood, and Sartorus rose as well. "I'll be ready, Tribune, and I thank you for the opportunity."

"You deserve it." Titianus opened the office door. "And he deserves you."

As Titianus headed out the station door, Sartorus returned to his own desk. He still had to finish the daily reports that would be going to Glabrio.

But it took some effort to keep from grinning.

God, I never expected to be singled out like this. Please let it be the start of something good.

The Titianus town house, Rome, late afternoon of Day 2

When Glabrio walked into Titus's library at the end of a hectic day, he found his friend in his favorite wicker chair, codex in hand.

"What are you reading?" Glabrio settled into the matching chair.

"My new copy of Phlegon's *Chronicles.* He's describing the darkness at midday from the sixth hour to the ninth during Tiberius's reign. That was just before Jesus died, when all our sins were placed upon Him. Phlegon wrote it was only an eclipse of the sun by the moon. But that's impossible. Jesus was the ultimate Passover sacrifice to pay for our sins. The Jewish Passover is at full moon, and the moon cannot both block the sun and be full at the same time." Titus closed the codex. "But I think you didn't come to hear about full moons, strange darkness, and what Jesus's death did."

"No. I came for a name." Glabrio's smile turned wry. "If I could choose based on whom I'd like to keep working with, I'd pick Plancus or Gellius. But Plancus is too valuable for keeping the XI Cohort working as it should when there's a new tribune who's as ignorant as I was. Gellius is unmatched at ferreting out information in the archives. I've had him work cases for the other tribunes because they have no one as good as he is."

Glabrio blew out a long, slow breath. "I asked the other tribunes, and each recommended a man I hadn't heard of before."

Titus chuckled. "They won't want to part with their best men, so I wouldn't expect any to name the best choice."

"Like Saturninus recommends Victorinus to someone he doesn't want to be too successful."

"Exactly. But if I were you, I'd take Sartorus from the warehouse district."

Glabrio's head drew back. "Why him? His centurion has never particularly commended him."

Titus set the codex on the small table beside him. "He hasn't needed what Sartorus can give you. Carthago is both the capital and the main merchant port for its province. Your father has been training you for success among Rome's governing elite, but you're not wise in the ways of tradesmen and merchants, equestrian or otherwise."

Arms crossed, he stretched out his legs. "Sartorus comes from a tradesman family, and he'll see things you'd miss. You could use a man who's been something other than a soldier, and policing the warehouse district has broadened his knowledge even more."

Titus pulled his legs back and leaned forward. "But more than that, you need a man who can advise you about whom you can trust, one who'll protect you from those you can't. I trust him to watch your back."

He leaned back in his chair again and rested his hands on the arms. "Tell him I recommended him and then ask if he'd like the assignment."

"I'll do that. Then I can speak with Saturninus about taking him and a squad, as you suggest."

"Good. Melis gave me a thorough lesson in identifying the counterfeits. I'll show you now."

They had just finished studying the last bad coin when a tap on the doorframe drew their gazes. Titus's wife Pompeia stood in the doorway, and that triggered a smile and a curl of his fingers to invite her in.

"Theo said Glabrio's horse was in the stableyard." She strolled to Titus's side, and he wrapped an arm around her. His hand rested on her bulging belly, and she patted it. "Are you joining us for dinner?" She glanced down at the baby growing inside her. "Sabina's almost as big as me now, so it will be chairs at a table for a while, but there's always room to add you."

"Normally, I'd say yes, but Father already sent a message that he'd like me to join him for as many dinners as I can since I'm leaving in five days."

"I understand. I hope you'll write often to let us know how you're doing.

We'll all be praying for your safety and success while you're there." She wiped a tear from the corner of her eye as her smile turned shaky.

"Thank you. I'll do that." Glabrio stood. "Father's waiting, so I'd better go."

He clenched his jaw. Leave-taking was too hard when it meant saying farewell to true friends.

Titus rose, and the two men gripped forearms. "May God be with you, my friend. Stay in touch."

"I will." He squared his shoulders and strode from the room.

When he reached the stableyard, he looked back. Titus and Pompeia stood watching, and Pompeia's smile accompanied her final wave. He raised his hand and mounted.

As the stallion carried him into the street, his mouth curved down.

They would pray for him, but prayers to their god didn't stop Domitian from killing his grandfather. If they didn't protect a man who worshiped the Christian god, it was unlikely they would protect a man like him who didn't.

Chapter 6

Good Enough

Guard station in Tiber warehouse district, Rome, morning of Day 3

Glabrio usually ended his day in the warehouse district, but today he would start there. Before he rode out to the Praetorian Fortress to make his request to Saturninus, he needed to talk with the optio Titianus recommended above all others.

He tied his stallion to one of the wall rings and strode past a saluting soldier.

Sartorus was at his desk, writing on a wax tablet that was undoubtedly meant for him to read later. He stood, and his fist hit his chest.

"Tribune. What can I do for you this morning?" He picked up the tablet and offered it. "I haven't finished yet, but I can finish with another tablet if you want this now."

Glabrio took the tablet and waved it toward his office. "I want to speak with you privately."

He strode into his office and set his helmet on the side table before taking his chair. Sartorus entered behind him.

"Close the door and sit."

Glabrio leaned back and crossed his arms. This was the first private talk he'd had with Sartorus, and his optio sat at attention on the front of the guest chair.

One corner of Glabrio's mouth lifted. "This is not a reprimand. Quite the contrary, but it's not to be discussed among my men here until after I speak with Prefect Saturninus. I'm being transferred to command the XIII Cohort in Carthago, and today I will be asking to take an optio to be my assistant, much as Plancus is here in Rome. Titianus recommended you."

Sartorus's back remained straight, but the tightness at the corners of his eyes and mouth relaxed. "I'm honored by Tribune Titianus's recommendation.

It was always my pleasure to serve under him, and it's been my pleasure to serve under you as well. I would be pleased to go with you."

"Has Titianus already spoken with you about this?"

"Yes, Tribune. Yesterday morning. He wanted me to have a chance to think about it before you asked." A subdued smile warmed the optio's features. "Even though a soldier will go where he's told. I don't expect to be asked if I want to."

"For an assignment like this, I prefer asking to ordering. In a city where I know no one, I need a man who wants to be there to help me, a man I can trust."

"I can be that man, Tribune."

"Good. I'll be speaking with the prefect when I leave here to request your transfer to be my aide when I take command of the XIII."

"When would we be leaving and for how long?"

"In four days, we'll take a ship out of Portus. Plancus will be making arrangements for both of us and will let you know the details. How long—I don't know. I expect not more than a year."

Glabrio rubbed his jaw. "There's something you must do today or tomorrow to prepare for the first major crime I plan to investigate there."

Sartorus's back had been relaxing, but it straightened again. "What, Tribune?"

"I'll begin looking for counterfeiters as soon as I assume command of the Thirteenth. I want you to check with Titianus or his business manager Melis to learn how to identify counterfeit coins."

"I know Melis. He's usually at Titianus's warehouse in the morning, but he's elsewhere in the afternoon. With your permission, I'll go see him now if there's nothing more."

"That's all for now." Glabrio opened the tablet Sartorus had given him and laid it on the desk. "You're dismissed."

Sartorus stood, and after saluting, he left the office and disappeared into the street.

With a satisfied smile, Glabrio took a blank tablet from his desk drawer and began the prioritized list of the cases at this station that his replacement would need to pursue.

The Martinus town house, Carthago, morning of Day 3

"It's not fair, Mother. I'm sick and tired of sitting there with Grandfather's body, calling out his name whether there's someone paying their respects or not." Sufina wrinkled her nose. "It's starting to smell in there, even with the perfumes."

She balled up her napkin and threw it on the table. "Why can't Martina do it? He treated her like a daughter. She should act like one."

Martina drew a deep breath, but before she could respond yet again to her cousin's complaints, Artoria slapped the dining couch.

"That's enough. I don't want to hear even one more complaint out of you. Your father said you and Priscilla were to do it, and if you know what's good for you, you'll do it as if you cared for your grandfather."

Artoria scrunched her eyes and rubbed her forehead. "I have enough problems without you causing more. I've never overseen a funeral before. I still have to figure out how to do the burial banquet at the grave after the cremation."

When her eyes opened, worry filled them. "What with the procession, sacrifices, cremation, and putting what remains in the family mausoleum... how am I going to get everything organized to be ready at exactly the right time? I have no idea who must receive a personal invitation and who might simply show up."

Martina moved her napkin to her lips. It would look like she was wiping off some of the sauce she'd just dipped an egg into, but it was really to hide a smile.

A smile she was a little ashamed of. It wasn't fair to expect Artoria, after so many years living in the country where Grandfather had sent her, to know who and what mattered among Carthago's social elite.

It was time to lighten her aunt's burden. "At least the governor is down in Leptis Magna holding court sessions, so many of the important imperial officials are there with him. Uncle can probably name the ones who are still in the city. As for the others, the duumvirs and aediles, members of the council, some of the heads of the government offices in the Forum, many of the wealthier businessmen who worked or traded with Grandfather...I can help with those lists. You'll also need plenty of extra food to share with the poor who need the food most."

With a snort, Artoria shifted her glare from Sufina to Martina. "We don't need to be spending your uncle's money on the riffraff of the city."

"Well..." Martina drew out the word. "You might save a little money now, but the city will remember Volero as a miser who disgraced the memory of his father."

Artoria's eyes saucered. "We can't have that! We'll provide more than ample amounts of food for the poor. Enough that they'll speak of my Volero with gratitude for many months."

That was the one good thing would come of this funeral. Martina kept her smile subdued so Artoria wouldn't change her mind.

Her aunt squeezed the back of her neck. "But that's the easy part. How many of the people who matter will be there? How can I find out who those are going to be?"

It was tempting to let her aunt stew over the questions, but Martina already knew the answers. It would be unkind not to share them.

"Grandfather arranged everything with the undertaker before he died. Maybe he told the man some of what we'll need to know. But even if he didn't, the undertaker can tell me what kind of food people usually serve and how much. He'll know when you should send word for the servers to bring it. He'll even know who usually comes to the funerals of other councilmen."

Martina swung her legs off the dining couch. "I'll go this morning and get all the details he can give us."

The aura of panic that surrounded Artoria faded. "Yes, go do that. Priscilla and Sufina will continue the vigil." She turned a glare on her daughters. "Without any more complaining."

With a nod toward her aunt, Martina left the triclinium, and as she walked up the balcony stairs to tell Platana they were going out, a genuine smile leaked out.

An hour or two without the animosity of the aunt or the contempt of the cousins awaited her.

There had been no peace in the household since they came. Martina was bone-tired of it, and each time she made herself hold her tongue, it became harder.

Two hours of tranquility wasn't much, but for restoring some of her patience, it might be enough.

When the door to the undertaker's shop closed behind her, Martina's shoulders drooped. She'd taken Platana with her and Clavus, both as her escort, because an elite woman didn't walk the streets of Carthago without a male slave along, and as a scribe to write down anything the undertaker said that would need repeating to Artoria.

If she were to forget something important, she'd never hear the end of Artoria's verbal assaults over it. Since the satchel hanging from Clavus's shoulder held four wax tablets of notes and names, that was now unlikely.

But it was time to return to that house of strife, and the thought made her wish she had somewhere, anywhere else to go.

They were passing a glass-blowing shop when she paused midstride. "There's another matter I think bears checking out."

"What, Mistress?" Platana stopped beside her.

"Grandfather left me his glass business, and the shop here in Carthago has a town house attached." She pinched her lower lip. "It has no renters at the moment, so it's a good time to inspect my property and meet my people who work there."

She turned to her escort. "Do you know where that might be? Grandfather only owned it a few months, and I don't know if it has its old name or whether he renamed it."

"He kept the old name, Mistress, so people who'd traded there before or had heard of its fine reputation could still find it. It's called the Palace of Glass."

He shifted the satchel strap. "It's closer to the harbor than the master's town house. I can show you."

"Lead the way." Martina pursed her lips to stop the smile that would have been most unsuitable for a woman in mourning clothes. She was no actor, but at least she could keep from looking too pleased should they meet anyone who knew her or Uncle.

After only a few blocks, her party stood before the glass shop. Next to it was the entrance to the town house, and past that were four more small shops.

"Before we see the glass shop, I think I'd like to inspect the town house."

She pointed at the door, and Clavus knocked.

No answer, so he pushed, then pulled on the door handle. It didn't budge.

"No one's here, Mistress, but sometimes the largest shop has a door into the town house."

"We'll ask after I meet my new people."

He opened the glass-shop door, and she led them all inside.

Three men and a woman sat around a small table in the back with half a loaf of bread and some sliced cheese between them. The oldest, a man who looked about Uncle Volero's age, stood and came to the counter.

"May I help you?" The words were spoken without enthusiasm.

"I'm Publilia Martina." She cleared her throat. "Your new mistress."

His eyes widened. He scanned the three of them, each dressed in dark gray, and swallowed. "I beg pardon, Mistress. We heard of Master Martinus's death when Cherida went to market, but no one came to tell us about it or who owned us now." He placed a hand on his own tan tunic. "We didn't have any mourning clothes, and I was afraid to spend the money. Our last owner would have been angry if I had. I didn't know what Master Martinus would have wanted."

"My grandfather would not have been angry, and he would have considered it unnecessary for anyone not living in his town house." She gave him a sad smile. "As do I. It's the respect for the living man and the regret that he's died that matters more than what one wears."

Both eyes and body of the shop steward relaxed at her words. "He bought this shop only a few months ago, so I only saw him a few times." He cleared his throat. "But I hear those who knew him do regret his passing. I'm sorry for your loss."

Martina wiped the corner of her eye. It was not time for tears. "Death comes to us all, although this one came too soon." She squared her shoulders. "But since I was nearby, I wanted see the glass shop and meet you all." Palm up, her hand swept toward the table.

"I'm your shop steward, Ceraulo, and that's Scalptor, Speculo, and Cherida." He pointed at the two men, then at himself. "We blow and sculpt glass. Cherida takes care of us. As steward, I handle raw glass sales. Many come here to get our glass slabs for glassblowers around the empire." His chin rose as pride filled his eyes. "They also buy the glassware and sculptures we make in this shop."

"I look forward to seeing more of what you do. Unfortunately, I must return home to help with funeral preparations today. But before I do, I would like to see inside the town house. I understand there's often an entrance from the main shop."

"There is, and Master Martinus gave me a key when the renter moved out." Ceraulo pulled a chain with three keys from inside his tunic. "In case someone wanted to see it. I was supposed to stay with them while they looked because it has furniture he owned."

"Since I own it all now, you needn't waste your time escorting me." She held out her hand. He removed the key from the chain and gave it to her.

Her fingers wrapped around it. "I'll return it for you to keep for me when we're through, but I'm not interested in renting it...at least not at the moment. I might have another use for it."

She handed the key to Clavus, who unlocked the door and held it open for her.

"As you wish, Mistress." As she walked into what might become her new home, Ceraulo returned to the table to finish his meal.

As Martina strolled through the town house, her smile grew. It was in very good shape and had enough furniture she wouldn't need to add more.

"Clavus."

"Yes, Mistress?"

"You are not to say anything to anyone at Uncle's town house about our visit here."

His eyebrows rose, then a slow smile appeared. "Yes, Mistress. We went to see the undertaker, and if Domina Artoria asks what we did, that's what I'll tell her."

"How long do you think it would take to get this ready to live in?"

"It hasn't been empty long. It's a little dusty, but if you don't mind being here while it's cleaned, you could move in right away."

Martina drew her finger along the tile at the edge of the pool. A tiny pile of dust remained when she withdrew her finger. "Not as bad as we used to see at the estate after a wind storm. I wouldn't mind at all."

Her gaze swept the modest-sized room and lingered on the small pool and garden. It wasn't as large as the villa near Cigisa nor as elegant as Grandfather's town house, but it was good enough.

Praetorian fortress, Rome, midmorning of Day 3

When Glabrio entered Saturninus's office, the prefect looked up from writing on a wax tablet and greeted him with a frown. "Make it quick. I'm expected at the Forum, and I'm already late."

Glabrio removed his helmet and held it against his side. "I would like to take a troop of eight men and an optio with me from Rome."

"Why would you need eight men from here? You'll have a full cohort there."

"I don't know any of those men. It's important to have some men I know I can trust. An officer's enemies are sometimes wearing Roman armor."

"Hmph." Saturninus set his stylus down. "That sounds like something Titianus would say. There's never been any unrest in the troops there in the whole time I've been Urban Prefect, nor was there for the man before me." He snapped the tablet shut. "Request denied."

Disappointment surged, but Glabrio wasn't ready to give up. "I would like to at least take an optio with me who's familiar with the way I command."

Saturninus crossed his arms. "You can't take Plancus. Your successor will need him to help with the transition."

"I wasn't planning to ask for Plancus. I want Sartorus from the warehouse district."

"Sartorus?" Saturninus's brow furrowed. "I never heard of him. Why that one?"

"Carthago is a commercial city at its core. The men who govern that city are businessmen, not senators whose families have governed for generations. Like you, I have no personal understanding of how merchants and tradesmen think. But the grandson of a freedman who's worked in the family businesses before enlisting does, and that should prove useful."

Saturninus leaned forward to rest his crossed arms on the desk. "You're parroting what Titianus said when he met your uncle Aviolo."

"A statement that's true bears repeating. His centurion says Sartorus is trustworthy, hard-working, and smart. That got him made optio quickly. He has a healthy ambition for further promotion, so I expect he'll be diligent in all I ask of him. He was born and raised here in Rome, but he's willing to spend a year with me in Carthago to gain skill and knowledge that will advance his career."

Saturninus rubbed his jaw. "I promised your father that this would be an exceptional opportunity. If you don't think you can perform well without this man, then you can take him."

"The right tools for doing a job well need the right men to wield them. I believe Sartorus is the right man to help me with that. Thank you for providing him."

"If you don't need anything else, you're dismissed." Saturninus opened another tablet and proceeded to ignore him.

"Prefect." Glabrio's fist struck his chest. He executed a parade turn and left the office.

As he strode toward the stable to reclaim his horse and go tell Sartorus, his smile grew.

It wasn't everything he wanted, but it was better than nothing. If Sartorus was a good as Titianus said, it was probably good enough.

Chapter 7

The Funeral

The Martinus town house, Carthago, Day 4

It had been three days since Grandfather died, and the smell of death hung heavy around Martina. But strangely, it didn't make her gag like it did visitors. Perhaps, a person becomes deadened to its presence when it's there long enough. Juliana had said sin was like that. If you tell yourself often enough it's not real or it's not a problem, you grow comfortable with the stench. It had broken Juliana's heart when the man she loved wouldn't let her tell him what the only way to be free of the stench was.

As Martina stood by the wall, waiting for the funeral procession to start, she adjusted the charcoal gray palla that she'd pulled up to cover her hair. Grandfather had let her tell him how Jesus could cleanse anyone from sin. Had he gone past listening to believing?

Uncle Volero exchanged words she couldn't hear with the undertaker. Then the man tapped the gong that was used to summon guests to the dining couches. "I summon you all to follow Gaius Publilius Martinus to his final resting place among his illustrious ancestors."

He walked toward the vestibulum door, turned, and clapped his hands.

The four torches were removed from the corners of the bier and held by men in black. Eight muscular men, two on each pole, raised the bier bearing the couch and body to their shoulders. Then Uncle Volero walked to the head of the bier and placed his shoulder under the pole, replacing the first man.

Martina stood behind Priscilla and Sufina as befitted the niece of the new paterfamilias, waiting to join the procession as the bier moved past.

But Uncle turned toward her. "Martina." He summoned her with a curve of his fingers.

All eyes followed her as she walked to his side. "You're all that remains of your father, so you'll walk by the man behind me. He bears this load in my brother's stead."

36

Artoria's eyes narrowed, and if she'd been closer, Martina might have heard her aunt's teeth grind.

"Yes, Uncle." It was a great honor, but why did he have to bestow it? He'd promised she wouldn't have to do anything that would seem like denying God.

Then she drew a deep breath and relaxed. When they got to the pyre at the family mausoleum, she'd be able to step away and become only a spectator who knew it was all a farce.

Six other men who'd been close friends of Grandfather took the other positions from the slaves who'd raised it shoulder high.

It was time.

The undertaker pulled open the double doors of the vestibulum to signal the start of the procession. The first two torch bearers marched out the door, followed by four pipers, two horn blowers, and a trumpeter. Two paid women with disheveled hair followed them, alternating between raising their hands and beating their breasts. The final two torch bearers walked just ahead of the bier.

As the bier passed from the darkened room into the sunlit street, Artoria and her daughters fell in behind.

Martina glanced down at the comfortable old sandals she'd chosen for today. It would be a long walk. Sufina had insisted on wearing her new pair set with silvery-black hematite beads. She'd pointed out how they matched the black tunic that made her look almost as ugly as Martina, so there was no good reason not to wear them. After fussing to get to wear them so at least something she wore would be pretty, she deserved the blisters they would almost certainly rub raw.

That was a mean thought, Lord. Help me to do better.

Dozens of black-clad councilmen and others of importance in the city waited there, and they joined the procession as it passed.

The long walk to where Grandfather's body would be burned and entombed had begun.

With each measured step, Martina braced herself for the pagan rites that lay ahead. The Roman gods weren't real, and the rites were only a play being performed with no divine audience. The only thing that mattered was what Grandfather decided before he died.

God, is Grandfather with You now?

A cemetery by the road outside Carthago city limits

Martina found it painful listening to Uncle Volero deliver the eulogy from the podium by the family mausoleum. Not because he wasn't a good orator because he was. It hurt to watch him mask his true feelings, like a good Stoic, when inside he was suffering like an orphaned child.

She knew those feelings too well. For the fourth time in her life, someone she loved had left her behind in this world. Only Juliana was she certain to see again.

When Uncle finished, he placed the coin in Grandfather's mouth that was meant to pay Charon to ferry him across the River Styx and opened his father's eyes. Then he scooped up a handful of dirt and tossed it on the body to make it a proper burial in the eyes of the Roman gods.

All who were gathered called out Grandfather's name one last time.

Then Uncle took one of the torches and joined the men lighting the kindling beneath the bier. First smoke, then flames spread through the wood upon which bier, couch, and corpse stood.

The musicians who led the procession played as the flames grew, singing praises to the Roman gods and urging them to remember the many good deeds Grandfather had done and the great things he'd accomplished.

Martina closed her eyes and prayed instead to the only true God, asking Him to open the eyes of the lost ones surrounding her before it was too late.

The flames leapt and danced and did their work, devouring both wood and flesh. When the dying embers gave off their last light and nothing was left where Grandfather's body had lain but bone fragments and ashes, Uncle doused what remained with wine. First it sizzled and steamed, but soon everything was cool enough to handle. He gathered the burnt bones and ashes into a marble box carved with his father's image and name. In silence, he carried it into the mausoleum his great-grandfather had built. When he came out, the trumpeter blew three quick blasts.

The rumble of wagons on the stone-surfaced road announced the arrival of the funerary feast. A small army of slaves set up tables, then loaded them with platters of food and pitchers of wine. Ground cloths were spread so the mourners could sit or recline as they gathered into smaller groups to eat and talk.

Artoria strolled among the mourners, accepting condolences for her loss and compliments for her feast. As she moved from one group to the next, her eyes met Martina's.

And for the first time since her aunt had come from the estate, she gave Martina a genuine smile.

Chapter 8

NOT TO BE TOLERATED

On the ship bound for Carthago, Day 7

Plancus had bought passage on a fast ship headed to Carthago. Glabrio's ever-efficient optio had reserved him a room in the cabin. Sartorus would be sleeping on deck, but his aide had stowed his helmet and trunk in Glabrio's room before taking a place alone at the rail.

As soon as the rowboats towed them out of the harbor, what had been gentle motion turned into a deck that rocked side-to-side and up-and-down as the ship rode the waves.

They'd spent last night with Titus's man in Portus, and he'd fed them both a hearty breakfast.

Big mistake. As the ship rose and fell, Glabrio's stomach turned unsteady. He'd expected to read in his room, but...

He reached the rail before losing everything, and he managed to keep from launching that breakfast into the sea. Outside the cabin wasn't as bad as inside...but it wasn't good.

Sartorus appeared beside him. "You look like the morning after, Tribune. Stomach problem?"

Glabrio nodded. "Our chef had something for guests who drank too much. I never needed it, but I should have brought some."

"It probably wouldn't have helped, but I have something that should."

Sartorus disappeared into the cabin and returned with a thick, branching root.

"Suck on this."

"What is it?"

"Ginger root. It helps when you're seasick."

Glabrio sniffed it before he put it to his mouth and licked it. "I thought you were born and raised in Rome. When did you go to sea?"

"I haven't."

39

"So how did you know to bring this?" Glabrio put one tip in his mouth and began sucking.

Sartorus shrugged. "If a man keeps his ears open, he learns all sorts of useful things. There are enough people in the warehouse district who go to sea often, and they laugh at the ones who get sick because they didn't take ginger. Licorice root is supposed to help, too. I have a piece of that as well."

"I'll see if this does it first. How long do I suck?"

"No one ever said. But I think if you keep your eyes on the horizon, that's supposed to help, too."

Glabrio nodded and fixed his gaze on the distant line between sea and sky. Sartorus leaned on the rail a few feet from him, wearing that slight smile that his mouth seemed to relax into.

After several minutes, Sartorus moved away to join a group of men who were in animated conversation. But once there, he listened in silence.

The ginger was doing its work, and Glabrio was able to move back from the rail and rest his back against the cabin wall to watch the man he'd brought as his aide.

When someone addressed him, Sartorus answered, usually with a smile and always with only a few words. He was the embodiment of one of Titus's favorite sayings. God gave us two ears and one mouth, so a man should listen before he talks and listen again afterward.

A commotion toward the bow of the ship drew Glabrio's gaze from his optio. A pretty young woman was surrounded by three men. Two small boys clung to her, while she tried to reach a baby one of the men was holding over his head. Pleading in a language he didn't understand, she reached as high as she could but still couldn't touch the now-crying baby. The man feigned a toss toward the rail as another man touched her where a stranger shouldn't.

Before Glabrio could move away from the wall, Sartorus walked up behind and lifted the baby from the man's grasp. With the baby cradled on his left arm and its head resting in his hand, he dropped his right hand to his dagger and partly drew it as he stepped back.

"You've picked a bad way to amuse yourselves. Babies aren't toys, and women aren't playthings. Why don't you go throw some dice"—his voice chilled as he tipped his head toward the bow—"as far away from her as this ship allows."

The baby's cries had silenced. The three men took a couple of steps back, then paused.

Sartorus tipped his head toward Glabrio, who was halfway to reaching them. "That's the tribune over the XIII Urban Cohort that polices Carthago. He does not tolerate the mistreatment of women. If you show any sign of that being your intent, you will be arrested the moment we reach port."

Three pairs of eyes turned toward Glabrio, then back onto the man with a baby held against his chest with one arm while his other hand still gripped the dagger. The infant quieted and began playing with the leather strips hanging from Sartorus shoulder.

"If you're wise, you'll stay at least ten feet away from her until we land, and you'll leave her and any other woman who doesn't want your attentions alone when we reach Carthago."

Glabrio had reached Sartorus's side. "Will you be causing further problems?" His own glare sliced into the troublemakers.

Vigorous shakes of three heads accompanied a "no, Tribune."

"Wise choice. Now go over there where he told you."

As the three men moved away, the woman came with outstretched arms. Sartorus transferred the baby from his arm to hers and received a glowing smile. Glabrio didn't need to speak her language to know she showered him with thank-yous before gathering her boys and returning to her belongings.

Glabrio looked at the man beside him. "You calmed that baby quickly."

Sartorus chuckled. "I'm from a large family. I've been keeping my little sisters and cousins quiet and content since I was scarcely larger than a baby myself."

"I was surprised when Titianus said you were the best man to bring with me. It looks like he was right."

"It's a great honor that he would recommend me. I'd do anything Titianus asked of me. I owe him for my promotion to optio, and I owe him for this opportunity." The usual slight smile broadened. "But he's a man I'd want to serve even if I didn't owe him anything."

Glabrio nodded before walking back to his place against the cabin. So, loyalty to Tribune Titianus was the reason Sartorus was so willing to leave everything and become his aide.

Titus always said it wasn't who a man knew that gave a man value, but what that man was himself.

But if Sartorus hadn't known Titus, Glabrio would never have suspected the value of the man who'd be watching his back.

The Martinus town house, Carthago, morning of Day 7

Martina laid her head back against the wicker chair and smiled. Uncle Volero had left early, so she'd sent Platana to the kitchen for some cheese, rolls, and fruit. A simple cold breakfast with her best friend was infinitely better than the usual array of delicious dishes served with bickering between the cousins and snide remarks from her aunt.

When Platana returned to their upstairs room after taking the breakfast dishes to the kitchen, she closed the door and leaned against it. Her eyes were spitting fire.

Martina closed her codex. "What's wrong?"

"That cousin of yours."

"Which one and what did she do?"

"Priscilla." Platana drew a deep breath. As she released it slowly, the fire cooled to a smolder. "When I went into the kitchen, I found Myrtis wrapped in Colina's arms, sobbing. When she moved back so I could see her face, she had an eye swollen shut and a half-inch lump right here." She touched her temple.

Martina set the codex on the end table and leaned forward. "What did Priscilla do?"

"She's been meaner than a hyena to Myrtis since your aunt made the girl her personal maid. This morning, she wanted her hair combed and perfumed, even though she has to leave it hanging down her back for another day. It was badly matted, and Myrtis was trying to work the knots and tangles out. She'd almost finished when Priscilla turned her head suddenly to say something to Sufina. That made Myrtis pull her hair."

Platana put her fists on her hips. "That she-beast picked up a hair brush and hit the girl on the side of her head several times. A little farther to the right and she could have taken Myrtis's eye out."

Martina clenched her jaw. "Artoria said she wanted no interference in how she treats the people here, but this is not to be tolerated." She closed her eyes and rubbed her temple. "So, I must find a way to get Artoria to think it's her idea to tell her daughter not to hurt the girl or anyone else again."

She stood. "With God's help, I can do this."

By the closed door, she turned back to Platana. "Stay here until I return, and pray for me."

"Always, Mistress."

Martina headed downstairs, first to the kitchen for a bowl of fruit as an excuse for seeing Myrtis's injury, then to wherever her aunt was.

She found Artoria in her bedchamber reading once more the tablets Clavus had written at the undertakers.

"May I speak with you, Aunt?"

God, please guide me in this. Please show me what to do and say.

Peace descended upon her. Skirmish or battle, she was ready for the confrontation.

With tightened lips, Artoria shifted her gaze from the tablet to Martina, and her mouth turned down. "What do you want?"

"I know that you are domina here, but it's been a number of years since you last lived in Carthago. Most of the important people Uncle Volero deals with don't know you. It's as if you've come to town as a stranger, and they are watching you."

She selected a raisin from the bowl and popped it into her mouth.

"Fairness and self-control are highly valued by the councilmen who were Grandfather's friends. Uncle Volero is welcome in their midst because he's like his father in that. Your husband's colleagues would not want to have a daughter-in-law who flew off the handle at the slightest provocation."

She pushed the dates aside to get another raisin from beneath. "One of the duumvirs already spoke with Grandfather about looking for a wife for his grandson soon."

Of course, she was the object of his interest, but her aunt didn't need to know that.

"He's a man whose wife treats her slaves well and is proud of how peaceful her house is. Her daughter-in-law also runs a peaceful household. A city familia isn't like your farm slaves, where you can treat them like animals without someone criticizing you."

Artoria's eyes threw daggers as she crossed her arms. "How I treat my husband's property is not your affair."

Martina set the bowl on the chair by the door and mirrored the crossed arms. But she added a subdued smile, even though her aunt deserved a scowl. "No, but Uncle cares about his reputation, especially the opinion of his Stoic colleagues. If they come and see slaves with cuts and bruises when they never saw those here before, they might not say anything, but they'll wonder why."

She shrugged. "Women have the reputation of being terrible gossips, but I heard enough when Grandfather entertained to think these men might be even worse." She rubbed the underside of her chin. "Especially about a man they'd like to keep from rising any higher above them than he already has."

Artoria's hands fisted as she moved them to her hips. "You're all sweetness and modesty on the outside, but you're a schemer underneath."

One corner of Martina's mouth lifted as she uncrossed her arms. "A person doesn't have to be a snake to know when one is going to strike and what to do to avoid getting bit." As she turned away, she looked back over her shoulder. "I know you have a lot to do getting ready for the end-of-mourning banquet. I'll leave you to it now."

She picked up the bowl and headed for the balcony stairs. Her aunt's snort followed her, but no angry words joined them.

Thank You, God, for giving me the right words so she'd listen. Let what she heard guide her actions, whether she wants them to or not.

Artoria was furious over being challenged, but she'd rein in her daughters. Too much might be lost if she didn't, and no woman who was so eager to rise in Carthaginian society would risk that.

Chapter 9

THE OPINIONS OF OTHERS

The Martinus town house, Carthago, Day 10

W hy you don't keep the carriage in town where it's convenient is beyond understanding, husband. You keep a horse stabled nearby for you."

Martina moved back against the wall. Wearing black was considered very poor manners for the end-of-mourning banquet on the ninth day after Grandfather's death, so she'd chosen a beige tunic and brown palla for the occasion. But would it let her fade into the background enough that her aunt wouldn't vent her frustration over anything irritating on her?

"You should have told me before this morning that you wanted to be carried instead of walking to the mausoleum like we did before." Uncle had donned his Stoic face that he wore so often when Artoria or his daughters started fussing. "I sent a messenger to the estate to fetch it as soon as you decided you had to have it."

"You should have known without me telling you." Artoria's lips tightened. "Any man smart enough to help run the city like you do should have realized that."

"I planned on walking, and I'm leaving now so I won't be late for the final public celebration of my father's life. You're welcome to join me, or you can wait for the carriage. It will get here in time for you to not miss the banquet's end."

"What will people say when your wife and daughters aren't there?"

"I doubt they'll say anything to me. What they think and say to others... that will reflect only on you, wife, not on me."

He took two steps toward the door, then turned. "Martina, you need to come with me in your father's place." He glanced at her sandals. "At least you were sensible enough to dress for walking." His lips tightened. "Unlike the rest of the women in this house."

Artoria's eyes flamed, and the fiery gaze moved instantly from her husband to Martina.

Stay or go? Martina drew a deep breath. Either way, she'd have to listen to Artoria fussing about this for several days. But maybe she could lessen the pain of this final goodbye for Uncle. Only someone who'd known grief already could share that burden.

She pulled the palla over her hair and stepped away from the wall. "I'm coming."

Between Rome and Carthago, Day 10

It was the last full day at sea, and Glabrio was glad of it.

The ginger root had mostly solved his nausea, but mostly was not the same as completely. He could keep down the bread and cheese and dried fruit the ship's cook served at every meal, but his stomach wasn't cut out for the mariner's life.

The wealthier passengers who slept in private rooms were served under the canopy behind the cabin where they slept. That had been eye-opening for a man from the elite circles in Rome, where he was a welcome addition to any gathering.

Most were merchants returning to Africa from Italia, if not from Rome itself. He'd had to introduce himself first before they told him their names. One with a Roman nose but curlier hair than any Roman Glabrio knew wore an enormous emerald and two small rubies set in more gold than Glabrio's signet. If that ring was any indication, at least one of his dining companions had more than the 100,000 denarii required to qualify as an equestrian.

When ring-man and two others launched into an argument over what kind of wheat would give the higher yield if the rains were lighter than usual, Glabrio remained silent. The day before, he'd tried to join a discussion of how many years before some fruit tree he'd never heard of would bear heavy enough crops to repay the cost of planting the orchard. After a cool appraisal of him, the men switched the conversation from Latin to whatever language they spoke at home.

Was that because he was young and uninformed or because he wore a uniform representing Roman power?

Titianus would have kept his face emotionless and joked about it later because what other men thought of him didn't matter. So many times Glabrio's mentor and friend had said a man's worth didn't depend on any man's opinion of him. Only his god's opinion mattered.

Glabrio tried to control his face even though he didn't always succeed. But some men's opinions did matter because they could alter a man's future. There were limits to how freely he could discount those. But what a god thought, if they ever did, didn't matter at all.

He left the canopy and strolled to the front of the cabin. There he leaned his back against the wall and scanned the lower-class people who slept on deck. Each time he'd done that, he'd found Sartorus as part of a circle of men. It wasn't the same men each time, and he always looked like he was welcome among them, even though he seldom spoke.

Why was that? His optio was in uniform, too, so they must know he was a military man on official business.

As if he felt Glabrio's gaze, Sartorus turned. Then he came over.

"Is there something you want, Tribune? Is the ginger keeping your stomach steady, or should I get the licorice root?"

"Steady enough, for the most part. Good enough for only one day more. This time tomorrow, we should be in Carthago. It will be good to have solid ground under my feet again."

Glabrio pointed toward the group of men Sartorus had left. "I've seen you talking with a lot of the passengers. Did you learn anything useful?"

Sartorus's smile looked like he was laughing at a secret joke. "Not really. But people like to talk about themselves, and when they find someone who's willing to listen, conversation flows. A question or two to start it off, and who knows what you might learn."

"Your last tribune wasn't one to start a casual conversation."

"No, but I think our lives before the Urban Cohort were very different."

"I know some of Titianus's history, but nothing of yours. He said you were involved in some kind of trade before enlisting. Why did you leave it?"

"My grandfather decided a fullery was a good addition to the family businesses. I was seventeen when I was sent there to help run it. But it wasn't my idea of a good future, so I asked a cousin on my mother's side who'd served as an optio in Dacia to write me a letter of recommendation. It got me into the Urban Cohort." He flashed a toothy smile. "I prefer the smells of a military camp to that from vats of urine. I wasn't the one stomping on the togas and tunics in it, but it made me want a different way to make a living."

Glabrio had never been inside a fullery, but even from what he'd smelled walking by, he agreed with Sartorus's career change.

"Fortuna smiled the day you made that choice."

Sartorus shrugged. His back settled against the cabin wall next to Glabrio, and silence descended between them. Not the silence born of conflict, but a companionable silence between two men who'd said all they had to say.

Chapter 10

THE NEW COMMAND

Carthago, Day 11

When the buildings atop the hill called the Brysa appeared, Glabrio walked to the bow for a better view. An important temple and the homes of the Carthaginian elite had been there before Rome won the final war with Carthage. The old Punic city had been torched and razed when Scipio Africanus defeated its last defenders. It had been rebuilt in the Roman style when Julius Caesar and Augustus restored it as a Roman colony.

Many hours of reading Polybius's eye-witness history of Scipio's victory still fired his enthusiasm for seeing the circular harbor that had housed the war fleet that made Carthage so formidable. Even better, he'd be landing in the rectangular inner harbor used by the merchant fleet that made her so rich.

But their ship didn't head for the narrow entrance to the inner harbors. It stopped offshore from a quay along the narrow strip of land separating the famous harbors from the open sea. Two rowboats towed it backward and maneuvered it into place with its stern near the quay and slightly below it. A long ramp was lowered to connect ship and shore, and the deck passengers gathered up their belongings and climbed the ramp. One corner of his mouth lifted as he watched the three men Sartorus had challenged stay as far from the young mother as possible.

Dockhands began descending into the hold and carrying crates and amphorae out.

"I'll get help for the trunks." Sartorus appeared beside him, helmet already on his head. Before Glabrio could reply, his aide strode up the ramp and exchanged words with the overseer, and when he returned, he had two men following him. "If you'll show them what's ours, Tribune, I'll watch it up there"—he pointed at the quay—"until we have it all. Then I'll find someone to take it to your lodgings while you guard it."

Glabrio scanned the quay. "Plancus sent notice of what ship we'd be arriving on. I expected someone to meet us."

Sartorus looked up and down the quay as well. "Apparently, they didn't get the message. But the harbormaster's office will know where the Urban Cohort is headquartered, and I can get us directions there."

Glabrio led the men to the room and pointed to the first of his three trunks. It held civilian clothes: purple striped tunics, toga, and personal items. The second held his dress uniform, extra armor and weapons, and footwear, while the third was his library and the folding gameboard made for *tabula* on one side and *latrunculi* on the other. He wore his usual bronze cuirass that proclaimed him an officer even without the red-crested helmet.

One chest was all Sartorus brought. His optio was a citizen, but that chest was too small to include a toga.

Glabrio rubbed his lip to conceal too large a smile. A soldier of the Cohort wouldn't need more than his military tunics to declare his citizenship to anyone who would care. Wearing a toga was a nuisance at times. He preferred just the uniform himself.

After he followed the final trunk up the gangplank, Sartorus left him to exchange words once more with the overseer of the dock slaves, then he strode into the warehouse where the ship's cargo was being stored.

It wasn't long before he returned with a small wagon pulled by two men, who loaded their trunks and gripped the twin handles, ready to follow.

As they headed up the quay toward an opening between buildings, the failure of anyone to meet their ship gnawed at Glabrio. Perhaps it was too much to expect the departing Tribune Nepos to come himself to extend the courtesy of greeting his replacement, but he should at least have sent one of his centurions. Or even an optio with a handful of men, but to send no one?

The passageway led to the inner harbor. Two rows of ships lay before them, each drawn into the wharf stern first, dock hands treading up and down ramps like two lines of ants.

Sartorus entered the closest warehouse for only a moment. When he emerged, he pointed left toward the end where the commercial harbor ran into the curved walls separating it from the circular one. "If we go through there, it will take us to the guard station at the gate from the harbor into the rest of the city."

"Lead on." As Sartorus strode toward the passage, Glabrio fell in beside him. The clatter of wagon wheels followed them around the half-circle and through the gate.

Across the street from the gate hung a sign, "Cohort Urbana." A soldier in cohort armor stood by the door. After telling the wagon pullers to wait there with his trunks, Glabrio led Sartorus past the saluting guard and into the station.

An optio sat at the desk just inside. As Glabrio marched toward him, his eyes widened, and he leapt to his feet, knocking his chair over. His fist hit his chest. "Tribune."

"I expected someone to meet my ship." The downturn of Glabrio's mouth brought worry to the man's eyes.

"No one told me you were coming today, Tribune."

Glabrio raised one eyebrow. "What's your name, soldier?"

"Gaius Alfenus Placidus." The optio blanched.

"Placidus, where is your centurion?"

"I don't know, Tribune. Maybe at headquarters." Placidus swallowed hard.

"Hmm. Where are the cohort headquarters and my tribune quarters?"

"Just a few blocks and near the Forum. They're in the same building." He turned toward the barracks door and yelled. "Ambustus."

A man with black curly hair like the wealthy merchant who'd encouraged the others not to speak to him came out and saluted.

"Escort Tribune—" The optio bit his lip. "Pardon me, Tribune, but I don't know your name."

"Your new tribune is Gaius Acilius Glabrio." Sartorus answered before Glabrio could.

The optio nodded once. "Escort Tribune Glabrio to headquarters."

Ambustus squared his shoulders and saluted again. "Follow me, Tribune."

Then he led them through the door and back into the swirling crowds of people buying, selling, and doing who knew what in this merchant quarter between the harbor and the Forum.

When they finally reached the cohort headquarters, the outside looked like a smaller version of the headquarters in the Praetorian Fortress. Inside was another matter. Six offices large enough to hold a desk, two chairs, and not much more lined one side of the inner courtyard. The other side had two larger rooms with closed doors. Straight ahead and flanked by two smaller rooms, the door to his office stood open.

But in the antechamber to his office, where an optio should have been organizing daily reports, there was no one. Glabrio glanced at Sartorus. It was good he'd brought his own man who knew what should be done.

Five of the six centurion offices were also empty. In the sixth, a centurion sat eating his lunch.

Ambustus tapped on the doorframe. "Centurion, the new tribune is here."

The centurion stood and saluted. "Tribune. Tacitius Dubitatus, commander of the century policing the agora and Forum districts, at your service."

He opened his mouth, paused, then closed it. After clearing his throat, he continued. "We weren't told who was coming or when you'd get here."

Glabrio's eyebrows plunged. "Where is Tribune Nepos?"

"He left for Rome eight, maybe nine days ago."

It was hard not to look shocked, but Glabrio tried. Saturninus had said Nepos would brief him on the activities of the XIII Cohort before heading to Rome. Either Nepos left early without telling Saturninus, or his commander sent him knowing he'd be assuming command without knowing what investigations were ongoing or important to begin.

"Then the tribune quarters are vacant now." He turned to Ambustus. "Show Optio Sartorus where those are. He'll be quartered there as well. After they deliver my trunks, send the dockhands back to the quay and bring Sartorus back here."

"Yes, Tribune." Ambustus struck his chest. "It's just down there." He pointed toward a passageway next to Glabrio's new office and vanished into it.

Sartorus raised his eyebrows, and Glabrio answered with a nod before the only man in Carthago that he knew he could trust disappeared from view.

"Since Nepos chose to leave early, did he leave a written summary of investigations I would need to take over?"

"No, Tribune."

"Then I'd like to see the reports from your district for the last week."

"Reports?" The furrows on the centurion's brow almost made Glabrio's eyes roll.

Glabrio donned the cool expression Titianus always used with the men who reported to him. "I want all my centurions in their offices here first thing tomorrow morning. I'll explain what I expect in the reports that you'll start preparing daily."

"Yes, Tribune." An affirmative answer, but with the down-curve of his mouth and resentment in his eyes, would Dubitatus provide what he would be demanding?

"I'll be in my quarters for a while."

Dubitatus saluted and headed back to his office.

As Glabrio entered the passageway Sartorus had taken, he finally released a sigh.

This was not an auspicious beginning to his new command, but an Acilius Glabrio would never let another man's irresponsibility or anyone's failure to perform his duties stop him from doing as good a job as anyone before him.

He let his mouth relax into a wry smile. Not just as good, but better.

Glabrio rested an elbow on the desk in his quarters and rubbed his forehead. Sartorus sat across from him, waiting in silence for Glabrio to speak. What he'd like to say wasn't something his aide should hear. Losing his temper in the presence of subordinates was something Titianus never did, and Glabrio tried to do the same. But if anything had ever called for a string of curses that would make a brothel slave blush, it was what he was finding in Carthago.

Nepos had been in command there for three years. But when Sartorus searched the records room off the courtyard that should have held Nepos's reports on significant events during his time as tribune, he found a few tablets from the first three months and then nothing.

Had Nepos sent reports to Saturninus about what was going on in Carthago? At the very least, copies of those should have been among the records. Had they never been there, or had someone disposed of them?

Surely Saturninus would have expected reports, even if he didn't read them carefully. Did he know this command was in such disarray when he ordered Glabrio to take it?

Glabrio closed his eyes, and a deep breath was followed by a deeper sigh.

Had Nepos not bothered to do his job at all? Had he left everything to the centurions, like Victorinus did? The experienced men should have known reports were required. Had Nepos told them not to bother with them?

At least some of the questions could be answered by his centurions, but that would have to wait until morning. Until then...

"I'm hungry." Glabrio stood. "We might as well start familiarizing ourselves with the city by finding a good place to eat."

"There are usually good ones near a harbor. Captains eat at the best of them. Placidus will be able to direct us to one." Sartorus rose as well. "We can look for the glass shops Melis listed on the way."

Glabrio lifted his helmet from the desk, then put it back. He used the helmet to project authority without doing anything. All he wanted right now was a hearty meal with no risk of losing it into the sea.

"You can leave yours here, too."

His optio's usual slight smile broadened, and Sartorus set his helmet beside Glabrio's.

With Sartorus at his side, Glabrio headed for the harbor.

Tomorrow, when the centurions came to headquarters first thing as he'd ordered Dubitatus to arrange, he would find out how the cohort had been doing its job while Nepos was in charge.

Then, whatever it took to fix the problems, he'd order the changes to get it done.

Chapter 11

MEETING THE MEN IN CHARGE

Urban Cohort head/quarters, early morning of Day 12

After a quick cold breakfast of bread and cheese, Glabrio sat in his headquarters office, drumming on a blank wax tablet with a stylus, both eager and nervous about the first meeting with the centurions of the XIII Cohort. Sartorus had taken over the antechamber desk, and he'd be escorting the men into the office as soon as the last one arrived.

Sartorus had offered to find extra guest chairs and try to fit them into the room, but Glabrio preferred to have the men stand. He was in charge now, and keeping them standing was a subtle way to make that point. He'd be asking for changes in how they kept their commander informed, and it was natural for men who'd served longer than he had to resent that.

It didn't help that he was only twenty-one, and his subordinates were both older and many years more experienced than he was. Although his helmet now sat on the end of his desk, his bronze cuirass, skirt of leather strips, and leather armguards carried the necessary message. What a man wore declared the power he had, making words unnecessary.

A tap on the doorframe drew his gaze.

"Your centurions are here, Tribune."

"Bring them in."

Four men entered, each in armor that included their helmets. What he would have said if they hadn't shown that respect...it was good he didn't have to find out.

"I understand from Optio Placidus that you received no notice that I would be arriving, so I'll introduce myself. I'm Gaius Acilius Glabrio. I've been commanding the XI Urban Cohort in Rome for some time now, and I welcomed this transfer to command the XIII here in Carthago. I look forward to working with you all to serve this city and Rome better than anyone has before."

With open wax tablet and stylus in hand, Sartorus stood at the wall where he could watch the facial expressions of all four. Glabrio kept himself from glancing toward his aide, lest his centurions realize they were being analyzed by someone of lower rank.

"Let's begin with each of you telling me your name and which district your control."

As the men answered in turn, Sartorus wrote on the wax tablet. Dubitatus, Longinus, Acceptus, and Verus—four men, not six like in Rome, but Carthago was only a third as large as the imperial city. Fewer made sense, but Saturninus hadn't mentioned it.

"You will find I am much more involved than Nepos was with the day-to-day work of those reporting to me. I appreciate a job well done and dedication to truth and justice."

No one rolled their eyes, but none nodded in agreement.

"In Rome, I visited the guard stations in each district regularly and knew what problems were facing my men there. I'll be doing the same here."

The two older men, Longinus and Acceptus, relaxed slightly. Dubitatus and Verus remained at attention.

Glabrio cleared his throat. "Each day, I'll expect a written report of the problems you deal with, drawing my attention to those you believe are especially important. Which brings me to my first question."

He pointed toward the door. "In the records room here, I find only a few reports from Tribune Nepos's first three months in Carthago. After that, nothing."

He crossed his arms. "Have the daily reports been kept in your stations instead of here in headquarters?"

Acceptus glanced at the other men, then spoke first. "Mine are, but not daily reports. Not every day has something of note happen when my men go on patrol. Squads are stationed in many smaller garrisons spread along the roads that are important for commerce. It helps keep robbery and kidnapping in check. I visit them on a regular basis and record what the squad leaders tell me."

He fingered the strap beneath his chin where the helmet cheek guards let him. "Those reports I keep at the first guard station south of the city. I use that as my main office. Tribune Nepos had no interest in copies being sent here. Since you want them, copies will be made and brought to you as soon as I return from each inspection."

Verus tipped his head back. "I've been centurion in the XIII for ten years. Some tribunes wanted regular written reports. Others did not. Tribune Nepos said he found no particular use for them, so it was not a priority."

Dubitatus and Longinus nodded their agreement.

"It is a priority with me. What I receive from you will be the basis for the regular reports I will be sending the Urban Prefect, to whom we all report. This tribune"—he tapped his chest—"considers good record keeping to be an essential part of the job. What Acceptus is doing is fine for his situation. For those of you policing the city, one of your men will deliver the daily report to me, drawing my attention to anything you feel is especially important."

Glabrio stood. "I will be touring each of your districts with you to familiarize myself with what you consider important there. I'll do that on a regular basis."

Acceptus smiled, and Longinus nodded once. But Dubitatus and Verus started to tighten their lips before erasing emotion from all but their eyes.

"Any questions?"

Four heads shook.

"Then you can go back to your districts."

The centurions filed out. Dubitatus went into his office, and the rest left the building.

Glabrio closed the door and turned to Sartorus. "Your thoughts?" He kept his voice low.

"Acceptus was keeping records on his own. He's glad you want them. Longinus is comfortable with doing it. Dubitatus and Verus–I think there's some resentment of a young tribune from Rome telling them how to do their jobs. But you are the commander of the XIII Cohort, and every military man knows the commander has the right to say how things should be done. I expect all of them to provide what you ask."

"What they think of me now doesn't matter much. I'm sure that will improve with time."

He picked up his helmet. "It's time to start meeting the men who govern the city. The council is in session this morning, so we're going to join them."

He settled the helmet on his head but didn't fasten the strap. "They're the ones who can tell me what's wrong in the city and which problems I might help solve. Hadrian will be touring the province this summer, and I want to have something accomplished that's worthy of showing him."

With Sartorus beside him, he strode toward the Forum and his first meeting with the elite men who governed a major city. It would be a relief to once more deal with the kind of men he'd been raised to understand.

The Martinus town house, early morning of Day 12

Martina had made a habit of dining early with Uncle Volero while her cousins slept in. Simple food eaten in companionable silence was better than the best work of Grandfather's chef seasoned with bickering and criticism. When Artoria joined her husband, a helping or two of criticism was usually served, but at least she didn't have to put up with the cousins.

This morning, Artoria entered the triclinium and reclined on the honored guest couch. "Husband, I'd like to have a dinner tonight and invite the duumvir who spoke to your father about needing a wife for his grandson. I want to get that conversation started between you and him before he looks elsewhere."

Volero returned the roll he was about to bite to his plate. "It hasn't even been two weeks since Father died."

Artoria picked up a slice of cheese. "And mourning ends after nine days. Aren't Stoic men like you and your father supposed to resume the duties of life right away? Arranging a good marriage for your daughters is one of your duties, husband. Priscilla would make a better wife for the duumvir's grandson than any other maiden in Carthago."

Volero glanced at Martina. "He was Father's good friend. He and I are only friendly acquaintances. I can't throw my daughter at him and make the suggestion."

"No, but you can invite him here to start turning what you have into a true friendship. And he'll see how lovely and well-mannered she is. Later we can have his son and grandson join us for an intimate dinner. His grandson will see Priscilla's beauty and grace are irresistible."

"As I saw with you." His mouth twitched.

"Yes." Her smile turned seductive. "You excited every young woman's imagination then. Handsome men father children pleasing to the eye, and ours are all exceptional."

"The girls are pretty, but no prettier than Martina."

Artoria shot Martina a disgusted glance. "Your niece is...reasonably pretty, but she's nothing compared to Priscilla. And Sufina will be just like her sister in a couple of years." She refilled his goblet and passed it to him. "So, can we have a dinner this week?"

"We can have it tonight, if you can manage that. Just don't make it too extravagant for so soon after Father's passing."

"Then only invite the duumvir and some of the councilmen you think important. It can be simpler if their wives won't be here judging me as hostess." She leaned close and drew a finger down his cheek. "It's the food you men notice, anyway." The seductive smile reappeared. "And the pretty women like our girls."

Volero swung his feet off the dining couch. "I'll invite twenty or so, men only and those with unmarried sons or grandsons for the girls to impress."

Artoria rose as well and placed both hands on his chest.

"You're such a good father. Send me word as soon as you can on how many will be coming."

When she reached up to stroke his cheek again, he caught her hand and kissed her palm. "I'd better leave now so I'll have time to speak with several of my colleagues before the meeting begins."

She stood on tiptoes to plant a kiss on his cheek.

The gentle voice and fond eyes vanished the instant he left the room.

"You." Artoria stabbed the air with the finger she pointed at Martina. "You will not be joining us on the dining couches tonight. I won't have you trying to lure the men away from Priscilla."

Martina rose from the couch and raised her eyebrows. "No, you won't have me trying to lure anyone tonight. I have no intention of trying to entertain Grandfather's friends so soon after his death. As for their sons and grandsons, my cousins are welcome to any they can get. But you might warn them that men don't like women who complain all the time. They might want to work on that before the marriage."

With a condescending smile, she turned and headed for her balcony chamber.

Artoria had done her a favor. Grandfather had kept interested suitors away with an imaginary agreement between her father and a friend near Cigisa. Uncle would do the same. But it was easier to never attract a young man's interest than to try to douse it once it had begun.

Carthago Council chamber, morning of Day 12

As Glabrio approached the council chamber with Sartorus behind him, the two soldiers on guard saluted. But first their heads had drawn back in surprise at seeing him.

They slipped into the back of the chamber and stood against the wall. The only person likely to notice them there was the sixty-something man speaking from the rostrum.

Glabrio scanned the room. It was filled with men ranging from their late thirties to well past seventy. The rostrum at the front, the chairs and benches in rows curving around that focal point—it felt very much like the Senate chamber in Rome. But there were no wide purple stripes on the tunics, and fewer than half the men had narrow ones. All wore togas, but there were only a handful with purple edging to show who were magistrates at the moment.

He leaned back against the wall, crossed his arms, and watched what he expected to see in any council chamber in the empire. Men rising to speak on the topic at hand, some being listened to carefully and some not. All in Latin, but with an accent he'd not heard in Rome.

He made special note of the ones whose words were considered worthy of full attention. They were the men he wanted to get to know first. Some he might want to know well.

Sartorus stood silently beside him, watching with the fascination Glabrio would expect of a man who'd never seen a council in session before.

It was already time for lunch when the man on the rostrum raised his right hand. "That concludes this session. We will resume next week at the usual time."

As the men rose and milled around, the speaker came over, accompanied by a councilman whom most had listened to carefully, even though he was only about forty.

"Welcome to our city. I'm Lucius Aemelius Paternus, duumvir of Carthago, and this is Volero Publilius Martinus."

Glabrio placed his hand on his chest. "Gaius Acilius Glabrio. I'm very pleased to meet you." He gave Martinus his social smile. "Publilius. Are you perhaps cousin to Publilius Celsus?"

"The consul executed on behalf of our illustrious emperor by his Praetorian prefect?" Martinus chuckled. "Very distant cousins and not among those our emperor would consider allied in any way with my infamous relative. My own family's loyalty is always to Rome and whomever the gods have chosen to make her emperor at the moment."

"The transgressions of our ancestors shouldn't determine the kind of men we are or what others think we are." Glabrio rested his hand on the hilt of his sword. "A wise man told me that a man's worth doesn't depend on his relatives, his friends, or his wealth. It's his own honor."

"I agree." Volero adjusted the drape of his toga on his left arm. "The Acilii Glabriones have a long history here in Africa. Your relative, I assume, was governor here shortly after Augustus made Carthago the provincial capital. My own family has been in Africa that long."

Volero glanced at Paternus beside him. "I'm having Duumvir Paternus and several other members of the council to dinner this evening. If you're not otherwise engaged, I'd be pleased to have you join us."

"I'd be delighted. I want to get to know the city leaders, like yourselves, who can tell me what problems might need my attention. The tribune I've replaced was supposed to have sailed a few days after I arrived, but he left eight days before he was supposed to, and he didn't leave anything in writing to give me that understanding."

Volero's brow furrowed. "Nepos left early? He always seemed to enjoy his time of service here." His mouth twitched as he said service. "Very fond of the chariot races and always a jovial addition to any dinner."

"You entertained him often?"

"No. Until two weeks ago, I lived at the Martinus estate that's an easy ride from the city. I've only moved into the Carthago town house since my father died. He was duumvir once and a member of the council for years. My father preferred more serious guests than your predecessor." He fingered the toga again. "I enjoy the same, but a light-hearted gathering can also give pleasure. My acquaintance with Nepos is from the dinners given by younger, livelier council members and their sons."

"Nepos's early departure has made the transition less smooth, but I'm sure you and your fellow councilmen can tell me what I ought to know."

"When it's known that you'll listen, I'm certain we will." Martinus arched an eyebrow, and his smile turned wry. "I'll send someone to your headquarters with instructions on how to find my house and the time the dinner will be starting. My wife hadn't finalized that when I left this morning."

"Getting to know people over fine food and good wine is always a pleasure. I thank you for the invitation, especially as we've only just met."

Silent laughter lit Martinus's eyes. "There are many who'll be eager to gain your acquaintance. Nothing could make my wife happier than the new tribune coming to her dinner before anyone else could invite you."

Paternus pointed at three men by the rostrum. "Come, and I'll introduce you to my fellow duumvir and our two aediles. The four of us bear the most responsibility for the governing of our fair city."

Martinus rested his hand on Paternus's arm. "Until later." A nod toward Glabrio, and Martinus headed for the council-chamber door.

As he followed Paternus toward the top leaders of the city, Glabrio's satisfied smile grew. Despite Nepos's disregard for preparing him to do this job well, his own time of service as commander of the XIII Cohort was getting off to a decent start.

Chapter 12

FIRST DINNER IN CARTHAGO

The Martinus town house, evening of Day 12

Whatever dangers lurked in Carthago after dark—they should be less than in Rome, but Glabrio still took two soldiers as bodyguards to Volero Martinus's town house for his first dinner with the men who governed the city.

As he passed through the town house's front door, his men stepped to the wall on each side of the doorway, turned to face the street, and stood at parade rest. Since he didn't know what else they'd be expected to do, he left them there.

He'd expected a narrow hallway leading into an atrium as the main public room. Instead, he found himself in a large L-shaped room, twenty foot wide where it led directly into a peristyle garden with the part of the L along the outer wall being almost as wide.

In his toga and a short tunic with its narrow purple stripes, he would have been inconspicuous at a gathering in Rome. Here, most wore togas, but only a handful had the narrow stripes of equestrians. None bore the wide stripes of senators.

He masked his surprise. These were the councilmen of Carthago, the fourth largest city in the empire. It was unlikely even one of them didn't have the fortune of 100,000 *denarii* required to be equestrian. So, had most of these men not been put forward to Rome for admittance into that order? Or, like Titianus, did they sometimes not don the striped tunics they were entitled to wear?

Martinus was talking with the duumvir and an older man Glabrio had seen at the council meeting, but he left them and headed toward Glabrio.

"Welcome, Tribune." He swept his hand across the room. "Many are looking forward to meeting you tonight." His host's gaze paused on three women at the end of a reflecting pool before returning to Glabrio. "I'm sure you'll find some of them worth knowing."

Two young women still dressed as maidens stood by a woman about Volero's age. The younger nudged her sister and giggled as he looked at her. The older one looked down, then straight at him, then down again. He'd seen both reactions before, and one corner of his mouth lifted. He wasn't a vain man, but being handsome, rich, and from one of Rome's top political families naturally inspired the admiration of women and the interest of men with marriageable daughters.

Two middle-aged men entered from the street, wearing broad smiles. "Two soldiers guarding your door, Martinus? Are you expecting someone to attack us tonight?"

"They aren't mine. They belong to our city's new tribune." He held his hand out, palm up, toward Glabrio. "Tribune Acilius Glabrio of the XIII Urban Cohort, these are Drusinius Lupulus and Flavius Lucretius. We serve together on the council."

Lupulus chuckled. "Two soldiers in full armor as bodyguards—whoever told you that you'd need those is probably laughing that you believed him. Your predecessor Nepos always said he could protect himself, but he never had to prove it."

Glabrio donned a social smile. "My predecessor as tribune of the XI Cohort in Rome almost died in one assassination attempt while going home from a dinner and would have died from a second if he'd been alone. That taught me to be careful."

The eyes that were laughing at him opened wider in surprise. Lucretius nudged Lupulus. "Perhaps Nepos will become more careful when he discovers there's yet another reason why it's better to live here instead of Rome."

Martinus crossed his arms. "So, what did he do that made so many enemies?"

Glabrio raised his chin. "He enforced Roman law, as I have since taking over his command. As Nepos should have been doing here."

Silence was followed by some uncomfortable clearing of throats.

"Well, I expect you'll have plenty of opportunities to dine with my fellow councilmen, and your guards will be as welcome at their homes as they are here." Martinus's redirection drew relieved smiles from Lupulus and Lucretius. "I think you'll find Carthago a more congenial city than the capital of the empire."

Glabrio smiled at each man. "If all men here are like yourselves, I'm sure I will."

The woman who'd been at the far end of the peristyle pool was moving toward Glabrio, her gaze locked on him like a falcon on a rabbit. Behind her trailed the two girls, faces alight with anticipation of meeting him.

The woman walked up behind Martinus and touched his arm. "Who's our young guest, husband?"

Lupulus and Lucretius tipped their heads to Glabrio and moved away.

Since following them wasn't an option, Glabrio turned his best social smile on what must be Martinus's wife. He placed one hand on his chest. "Gaius Acilius Glabrio, tribune of the XIII Urban Cohort."

"Glabrio has replaced Haterius Nepos policing the city." Palm up, his hand swept the three women. "My wife, Artoria Prisca, and my daughters, Priscilla and Sufina."

"Volero told me we'd be the first in Carthago to entertain you. I'm delighted to have that honor. I'm sure you'll find much to enjoy here. I've just moved back to the city myself."

Glabrio acknowledged mother and daughters with a tip of his head. "As this is my first time in Carthago, I appreciate being included this evening even though Martinus and I only met today."

"I would have been appalled had my Volero not invited the newest tribune Rome has sent to take care of our city. It's not often someone from a family that's so important moves here."

The temptation to shift his gaze from the wife to the husband to see her Volero's response to his wife's fawning was almost irresistible, but Glabrio kept his gaze on Artoria and his I-care-what-you-think face in place.

A tilt of her head and a smile she meant to be charming joined self-assured eyes. "I've never been to Rome myself, but my older sister is married to a senator there. Her beauty enthralled him when he served here as quaestor, and nothing would do except marrying her before he returned to Rome. He said he'd never find a woman who was her equal among his acquaintance in Italia."

Glabrio wanted to roll his eyes, but instead he donned the smile that he'd discovered would charm most women. "I see beauty runs in your family." He turned the smile on her daughters before turning toward Artoria again. "And it passes from one generation to the next."

Sufina blushed and giggled, and Priscilla tilted her head and batted her eyes at him.

Volero took one step back. "I invited Glabrio so he could meet some of Carthago's leading citizens. I want to complete some introductions before dinner is served. He can talk with us later at a private dinner."

"That will be delightful." Artoria beamed at her husband, then at Glabrio. "We'll do what we can to keep you from being lonely here."

"I'll look forward to that." Glabrio had taken two steps backward before finishing the sentence.

Volero led him from the women toward a man who looked younger than thirty. "Nepos found a friend in Messala shortly after he arrived. Perhaps you will, too. His father is now on the council. Messala will be someday."

They reached Volero's target, whose smile was friendly while his eyes remained cool.

"Tribune Acilius Glabrio, this is Vipstanus Messala. His family provides vast quantities of wheat and oil to the people of Rome."

The duumvir raised his arm and summoned Volero with a curl of his fingers.

"Excuse me, Glabrio. I'm needed, but I leave you in good hands." Volero crossed the room to join Paternus.

"Welcome to Carthago. Nepos enjoyed his time of service here. It's a fine city with many entertainments, and he partook of most of them."

"I'm here to command the XIII Cohort, but I look forward to enjoying what the city has to offer."

A serving girl paused to offer some wine in gold-lined silver goblets.

Messala took two and handed one to Glabrio. "The circus here is almost as large as the one in Rome. It's an irresistible destination for those who like to gamble, as Nepos did. We spent many a pleasant afternoon together. The sweet taste of victory becomes sweeter still when you placed your wager on the winner. There's no better way to spend a day than some betting between friends."

Glabrio took a sip. "Many in Rome would agree with you, but it's a fool who wagers more than a few day's wages, even with friends. I enjoy watching fine horses racing to beat the wind, but I seldom bet on a race."

Messala's smile cooled. "Perhaps I'll see you there sometime, but right now"—he tipped his head toward two men about his age at the far end of the pool—"I need to ask Rusticus about something. May Fortuna smile on you during your time in Carthago."

Chapter 13

An Independent Woman

Glabrio's gaze followed Messala's progress toward the two men, but that changed when the man who liked taking money from Nepos passed a young woman who was conversing with a man old enough to be her grandfather. With straight lips and serious eyes, she asked him a question too softly for Glabrio to hear. A look of sympathy washed across the man's face before he patted her upper arm and began to speak.

What followed looked like her asking short questions and him giving longer answers, and they looked like they were discussing something important that interested both. It looked nothing like a flirtatious young woman and an older man flattered by the attention chatting about pointless social topics.

She wasn't dressed in black mourning attire, but wavy dark brown hair still cascaded down her back, although it had been combed. Wearing the black of mourning after the end-of-mourning dinner was considered bad manners, but she'd chosen beige for her tunic, dark brown for her palla, and a single silver bracelet, even as Volero's daughters were clothed in bright colors and expensive jewels.

Whoever she was, she was still grieving. Volero had mentioned his recent move to the town house since his father died. Was she the father's young wife, Volero's sister or niece, or some more distant relative who'd lived here with his father?

With a smile that was real, not social, Glabrio strolled over. As he moved into place beside them, the older man shifted to include him in the conversation.

"Martinus said our new tribune would be joining us tonight. Welcome to Carthago." He placed an age-spotted hand on his chest. "Marcus Calventius Viator." He extended his hand toward the woman. "And this is Publilia Martina."

The words were spoken politely yet without enthusiasm. But for an elderly councilman, Glabrio would be only one more of a long line of young tribunes who'd passed through Carthago on their way to more prestigious positions serving Rome.

"Gaius Acilius Glabrio."

"Glabrio. Any relation to the recent consul?"

"He's my father."

Viator's raised eyebrow was followed by a wry smile. "We usually get the sons of less illustrious men posted here. I supposed you'll be leaving soon for something more important, as Nepos did, but you can expect many dinner invitations before you do."

"I consider this command as important as any future one, and I look forward to getting to know many people here. I plan to be remembered long after I leave as one who cared about Roman law and justice and served Carthago well."

Duumvir Paternus left a cluster of older men and approached. "Viator, we need your opinion over here." Paternus looked first at Publilia Martina, then at Glabrio. "I apologize for this interruption, Glabrio, but a young man like yourself should find more pleasure with a pretty young woman than an old councilman, anyway."

"No apology needed when duty calls."

As the two men walked away, one said something too softly for Glabrio to catch the words. The other one chuckled.

"Your duumvir is a man of great wisdom." Glabrio turned his back on the rest of the room before crossing his arms. "Should I call you Publilia or Martina?"

She mirrored his crossed arms. "Most of Grandfather's colleagues call me Martina."

Silence followed her answer—not the usual response he received. It was more like what Titianus did to people than like the talkative women he was used to in Rome. It was a point of pride that he could get anyone to talk to him, even the shyest women. But with such confident eyes meeting his gaze, shyness wasn't the problem.

He liked challenges, and this woman offered one certain to entertain him tonight.

"You and Viator seemed engrossed when I joined you. What were you discussing that was so interesting to both of you?"

"How to run a business."

He waited for more, but she said nothing.

"What business?"

No teasing glint lit her eyes. She wasn't being cryptic to catch his interest, but she'd snared it anyway.

Her eyebrows dipped, then relaxed. "I own a glassworks now, and Viator has many years of experience running one. I was asking his advice on how to run mine well."

"A glassworks?" Melis's captain had received the counterfeit coins when he was buying raw glass slabs. He had the list of sellers to start his investigation. If her shop was the one that passed off bad coins—that could explain her aloofness toward him.

He tightened his lips to hide he was laughing at himself. Titus had warned him that this job could make a man too suspicious.

"Yes. This city is famous for the raw glass we ship all over the empire for local glass shops to use."

"I have a friend who buys Carthaginian glass. It is lovely. But doesn't your guardian take care of business matters?"

"Volero Martinus is my uncle, and he's my guardian now. But Uncle has more important things to do than oversee what I own. When I need his help, I'll ask, and he'll give it."

"So, do all the young women of Carthago choose such independence from their guardians?" He offered the teasing smile that made most young women fluttery. "Or are you unique among them?"

"I can't say what all women do." Her lips tightened, but not in anger. She was laughing at him and trying not to show it. That was not a reaction he'd seen before, but at least she was warming up to him. "Nor can you. Perhaps my independent nature comes from growing up on an estate far from the city. When what we do isn't fodder for gossip, we can be what we truly are, not what others say we ought to be."

The last hint of amusement faded from her eyes. "I value truth more than what others think of me."

"As do I."

"Hmm." Her lips tightened again.

He raised one eyebrow. She didn't believe him. Calm eyes, a cool smile—not even the slightest hint of a flutter in her response to him. Her cousins' eagerness made them boring. She was anything but.

"Where is your family's estate where you felt so free?"

"My estate. It's not far from Cigisa on the Bagrada River."

"Is it a large one?"

She raised one eyebrow. Was she mimicking him? "Large enough. Why do you ask?"

His head drew back. Why had he asked? He didn't usually interrogate young women he'd just met. But most didn't pique his interest like she had.

"It's my first time in this province, and there's much I don't know. I thought you could enlighten me."

Her eyes narrowed, then relaxed. "I see. It's smaller than some of the estates around Carthago, larger than others." She looked past him, and the trace of a smile that vanished as quickly as it appeared seemed sad. "But it's not size that makes an estate special."

A serving girl appeared beside them and offered a platter of sliced fruit and cheese. Martina smiled at her as she shook her head. He took some cheese.

"What does?"

She met his gaze as her mouth opened, then closed.

He was about to ask again when she spoke. "Coming from the imperial city, I don't think you'd understand."

"You might be surprised."

Her lips twitched. What did she find amusing about those words?

"I have been before." The slightest shrug accompanied a sad smile. "Perhaps it's the people and the memories that make it special. You'd find it quite ordinary, I think."

Her estate might be ordinary. Publilia Martina herself—definitely not.

"So, like all the estates here, you grow wheat and olive oil to feed the people of Rome?"

"There are clay deposits as well. The pottery my people make is well known."

His lips twitched. "Well known?"

"In Utica and Carthago, anyway. I doubt a man like yourself would know of it."

"What I know might surprise you. I commanded the men who policed the warehouses on the Tiber and Trajan's Forum in Rome. I've had to learn much about the goods that come into the Tiber ports since I took over that post."

"A crescent moon marks our red slip pottery. We make stamped designs for ordinary use, but we're best known for our appliques." A slow smile grew as she held out her hands and wiggled her fingers. "These are good for more than displaying expensive rings. I enjoyed making appliques as a child."

His brow furrowed. "You worked in the pottery shop?"

"I wouldn't say 'worked.' Mother and Father encouraged my artistic efforts. That they could be used to make money...that was never the goal, but I liked how others got to buy and enjoy them. If I move back there, I'll try my hand at it again."

"Are you planning to go soon?" He tipped his head toward Volero's daughters. "Surely your cousins would miss you."

Her lips curved into the first full smile he'd seen. "I think not." Then the enchanting smile faded as quickly as it had appeared. "With Grandfather's death, I'm sui iuris and no longer domina of this house. Doing nothing is boring. Getting more involved in the pottery and glass trades—that seems a worthwhile use of my time."

She shrugged. "I'll probably stay in Carthago for a while. Now that I own Grandfather's glassworks as well as the estate, there's much to learn."

"That should prove...interesting. I've seen how having an intimate knowledge of traders and craftsmen is an advantage for policing Rome."

"Really?" One of her perfectly matched eyebrows rose again. "Uncle said the Acilii Glabriones have been senators helping rule Rome and her provinces for generations. I wouldn't have expected you to be a merchant."

He chuckled. "I'm not, but the man I replaced in Rome imported wine and other goods for repackaging for resale. That gave him insight into how the criminal thinks. Most of the lawbreakers he hunted were not from the noble orders. I expect the same here."

Odd. Her eyes had veiled, and a slight frown appeared.

She hugged herself as he said "lawbreakers" and rubbed her arm at the word "hunted." "Carthago's elite are merchants, not senators. Being a merchant doesn't mean you think like a criminal."

His careless choice of words had lit a fire in those cool eyes. He reached for his neck but stopped himself before rubbing it. "I never said that it did."

"People hear more than the words that are spoken." She stroked the hollow of her throat. "Carthago doesn't appreciate the arrogance of Rome. Offense can be quickly taken, even when it isn't meant." She lowered her hand and laced her fingers at her waist.

"My apologies. I didn't mean to offend you."

"You didn't. I'm hard to offend." Her gaze swept the room. "But many here are not."

Volero's daughters had moved from their mother's side and now stood across the pool from him. If eyes could throw daggers, Martina would be bleeding. No wonder his suggestion that the cousins would miss her drew that smile. It would have triggered a hearty laugh had she been a man.

One whispered to the other, and they started over. Why had he let them catch him watching them? They'd interpreted his glance as an invitation rather than an appraisal.

The sisters flanked Martina, and Priscilla placed her hand on Martina's upper arm. "Martina is so serious all the time, so we thought we'd come and give you something more enjoyable to talk about before dinner."

The fake smile the older cousin directed at Martina received a genuine one in return.

"It's most fortunate you came over, cousins. The tribune is very interested in the estates here. Since you've just moved into town from your father's estate, surely you can answer his questions better than I can."

Martina patted her cousin's hand before stepping away from her. "So, I believe I'll leave him in your care." She stepped back. "Farewell, Acilius Glabrio."

The sisters moved closer to each other, leaving no room for her should she want to return.

No doubt she wouldn't. Wearing a palla without a stola declared her unmarried. She was not much older than the cousins, yet she was an independent woman, willing to correct him, not a man-hunting girl. But why had Martina been so pleased that she could withdraw from their conversation? That was one more intriguing thing about her.

He'd only known one other woman who'd found his irresistible charm so easy to resist, but that was because she was already in love with another man. Now both were his good friends, and he knew her lack of interest had nothing to do with him and everything to do with how exceptional the other man was.

Young elite women, even some of the married ones, always wanted his attention. As an Acilius Glabrio, he was a matrimonial prize of the highest order in the eyes of their fathers, and his good looks and ability to make anyone he spoke with feel as if he were interested in their thoughts could set female hearts fluttering.

Why was Publilia Martina immune to his considerable charm? Perhaps being domina of her grandfather's house had made her old beyond her years, but even mature women enjoyed conversing with him.

His eyebrows began to dip, but he forced them to relax before the girls asked what triggered his frown. Was there a more sinister reason Martina didn't want to talk to the tribune in charge of policing the city? One corner of his mouth rose. Suspecting a woman of criminal intent simply because she didn't want to talk to him went past reasonable wariness to paranoia. The other side of his mouth lifted to complete the smile. Or maybe injured vanity was the real reason.

He glanced past the chattering sisters to see Martina exchanging a quiet word with another older man before stepping into the smaller, unlit courtyard and disappearing from view.

He rubbed behind his ear as he focused his eyes and his smile on Volero's daughters again. But his host's independent-minded niece remained the focus of his thoughts.

Her grandfather had been duumvir, and her uncle was a city leader worth getting to know better. Especially if that meant more opportunities to talk with the enigma that was Volero's niece.

His smile broadened, and the giggle from the younger daughter showed she thought she had caused that.

Volero signaled his steward, who tapped a gong, drawing all eyes toward him. "Dinner is served."

His host summoned Glabrio with a curl of his fingers. As Glabrio expected, he would recline on one of the three couches nearest his host.

As he moved away from Volero's girls, he glanced once more at the dim courtyard where Martina had vanished.

Carthago doesn't like the arrogance of Rome, and many will be quick to take offense, even when none was meant. In their first week together, Titianus had shared many such insights that had helped him succeed.

He would remember her warning and thank her for it when next they met.

Chapter 14

Time for Some Changes

Martina climbed the stairs to the balcony of the dark courtyard. Many bronze lampstands, each holding several clay lamps, lit the peristyle where Uncle's guests were gathered, but the balcony leading to her bedchamber door was in deep shadow.

She paused for a last look into the peristyle before walking the final steps to her private haven where Platana waited. The tribune was still talking with her cousins. The focused gaze he'd used on her was fixed on Priscilla. The crooked smile that accompanied his first questions was directed at her cousins now, and Sufina was vying with her sister for his attention. He gave both equal shares.

Handsome face and muscular physique, family wealth, political power—he knew he had them all. She'd never met a man from the noble families of Rome before, but he was everything she'd imagined a Roman officer would be, including the extreme confidence bordering on arrogance.

Why he'd come over to talk with her was a mystery.

Her lips twitched. It was silly to think he had. He'd come to speak with Viator and been stuck with her when Paternus took his old friend away.

The tribune glanced her way, and she froze. She should be hidden in the shadows, but she didn't want him to think she was watching him. The man responsible for enforcing Roman law in the city was a person she should avoid. Anyone whose personal goal was to hunt lawbreakers wasn't safe for someone who followed Jesus to allow too close.

It was good Artoria had decided Martina had no place on the dining couches tonight. What if he'd decided to recline beside her?

A gong sounded, and the guests headed toward the triclinium. When the tribune turned away from her, it was safe to move again.

She slipped into her room and closed the door. As she leaned back against it, she blew out a long, slow breath.

"I'm glad that's over. Uncle said I should be there because many would ask about me if I wasn't. Artoria didn't want anyone seeing me and thinking I was still domina of this household."

Platana rose from the wicker chair. "Or for anyone to compare her spoiled childish daughters to a gracious grown woman like you."

Martina held out her arms so her lady's maid could unwrap the palla and fold the long rectangular fabric.

"She needn't worry about that. I don't want to marry any of the men she wants for her girls. None that I know follows Jesus like we do. I watched Juliana try for years to get Grandfather to let her tell him about our Lord." Martina fingered the silver filigree bracelet Juliana had given her just before she died. "Her last words were a plea for me to get him to listen and then believe."

She clenched her jaw to stop the quaver. "I wish I knew what he decided." She wiped a tear from the corner of her eye. "With Grandfather gone and Artoria and her girls so disagreeable, this isn't home anymore."

With her eyes closed, she massaged her neck. "Tomorrow Priscilla and Sufina will be worse than usual because that tribune showed too much interest in me."

She sat on the bed and flopped onto her back. "Maybe it's time to move out."

Platana took Martina's sleeping tunic from the chest. "To the Cigisa estate?"

Martina rose, and Platana began removing the clips that held her daytime tunic in place at the shoulders. "Not yet. I was talking with Viator about how he runs his glassworks, and there's still so much I need to learn. I do own that small town house next to the glass-blowing shop that Grandfather left me. It's not rented right now, so we could move there."

With the last clip removed, the tube of fabric dropped to the ground, and Martina stepped out of it.

"It takes many people to run a house properly." Platana dropped the sleeping tunic over Martina's head. "Where will you get them?

"I supposed I could bring some from the estate." Martina squeezed her eyes shut and rubbed her temples. "Or I could buy some here." Her eyes opened. "Which is better?"

"Maybe get some here. Your people at the estate won't want to be parted from family and friends there."

Martina sat at the dressing table, and Platana began brushing her hair. "I know nothing about how to buy slaves. Maybe Uncle would sell me some we already know." She looked over her shoulder at Platana. "There are probably many here who'd love a different mistress than my aunt."

Platana choked back a laugh. "The whole household would want to go with us."

With her elbows on the dressing table, Martina rested her forehead on her palms. "I'd love to get Christians so we wouldn't have to hide our faith, but I don't know where to find any. We do need people we can trust to keep our secret even if they don't believe as we do."

Her maid kept brushing. "We can probably trust some who served Mistress Juliana and knew of her faith. Those who truly grieved for her would be good choices. Many have known you since you were a girl of eleven. Loyalty to your grandmother and to you should prevent a betrayal."

Martina ran her fingers through her hair before staring at her face in the mirror. "I'll speak with Uncle about that tomorrow. I think he'll say yes. It can't be enjoyable for him to watch Artoria picking at me all the time or to listen to his girls' nasty comments."

She returned to the bed and lay down. With her arm draped across her eyes, she sighed. "I don't enjoy it either, but I know putting up with it instead of saying something cruel back pleases God." Another sigh drained her lungs. "But I'm ready for some peace."

The Martinus town house, morning of Day 13

Martina rose early, hoping to catch her uncle alone in his *tablinum* before anyone came to see him. Many of the men who used to come to Grandfather came to Uncle now.

She tapped on the small door that opened into the courtyard beneath her balcony. The last thing she wanted was for Artoria to see her at the double doors opening on the peristyle. That woman wouldn't be able to resist coming to join them, and this conversation needed to stay private.

"Enter." The voice sounded tired.

Last night was the first dinner in the house with the duumvir and so many of the council since Grandfather died, and Artoria had outdone herself to make it memorable. Martina had awakened more than once to hear lyres, flutes, and singers. All tastefully done with only the best performers, but late was still late, no matter how elegant the entertainment.

She opened the door only enough to slip in and closed it softly behind her.

Uncle sat at his desk with stacks of tablets on both sides of him. He closed the one lying open before him and moved it to the side. Then he leaned back in his chair and crossed his arms. "What is it?"

She walked to the desk and clasped her hands. "I appreciate you letting me stay with you for a while, but I think it's time for me to go."

His mouth curved down. "Where would you go?"

"Since Grandfather gave me the building with the glass shop and the small town house, I thought I'd move there for a while. I'll still be close, but I won't be in anyone's way."

His frown had deepened. "There's no one there to look after you."

"Platana will go with me, of course, but I will need a few slaves. Not many since I won't be entertaining anyone." She donned a hopeful smile. "I was wondering if you'd sell me a few from this household. Ones I know we can trust."

"Trust?" His eyes narrowed.

"Yes. Trust to look after things well...and to keep my secret."

He leaned forward to rest his elbows on the desktop and rubbed both sides of his nose. "Why now?"

"I feel that my presence here is...no longer needed. Artoria has the household well in hand, and your daughters can help if she needs it."

He snorted. "What you mean is my wife hates having you here. She knows the slaves wish you were still domina, and young men can't help preferring a woman like you to our daughters. She didn't like how the new tribune so obviously enjoyed talking with you."

"She—"

"Don't bother making excuses for her. I saw how it is for you last night. I can't blame you for wanting a change." He sighed. "As your guardian, I approve of you moving into the house you already own. I can still watch over matters for you while you live in the city. Artoria plans to invite Glabrio to family dinner often, and if he's as sharp as I think he is, there's a risk he'll realize why you're different if he sees too much of you. You'll be safer if you move out."

"Thank you, uncle."

The easy part was accomplished. Now for the harder request.

"About the slaves..."

"Which do you want?"

She held up one finger. "I'd like Clavus. He's good with his hands for fixing things, and he can read and write. I know how to handle the household accounts myself, so I can train him to be a good steward. He and the underchef Colina have a son and daughter, Lepus and Myrtis."

As she spoke each name, she raised another finger. "They're old enough to help take care of the house. I'd like those four plus Petale. Juliana found she could do anything that she asked her to do."

She raised her thumb from her palm and spread the fingers out in front of her uncle. "So that makes five. I think that's all I'll need for the moment." She lowered her hand. "When Juliana died, their grief was real. They're all loyal to this family, so if they learn what I am, I'm sure they'll keep our secret."

"The day Father died, you told me he'd said I was wise in the ways of business, that I made him proud." One corner of Volero's mouth lifted. "If he could see you now, I think he would say the same about you. Those five will go with you."

Her shoulders relaxed. Who would have thought this would be so easy?

"After I get settled, I hope you'll visit often, maybe even come for dinner."

"As your guardian, I'm responsible for checking on you, so you can expect I'll do that." He massaged his neck. "That town house was usually rented, so I've never seen inside it. But it's a decent neighborhood. I have visited the attached glass shop with Father."

His gaze shifted to the closed double doors before returning to her. "I had them make a small statue of an antelope in Artoria's favorite colors for her last birthday."

"What a lovely gift. She must have appreciated that."

"As much as she appreciates anything I do." He shrugged. "She's wanted to move back into Carthago every day since Father sent us out to the first estate your great-grandfather acquired."

He picked up the ivory-handled stylus with bronze tips that had been Grandfather's favorite. "She's thoroughly delighted that I'm paterfamilias now. She's wanted that for a long time." He rolled the stylus between his fingers. "I gave this to Father when I was Sufina's age." A deep sigh escaped. "I wish he was still here to use it."

"I do, too." Martina wiped the tear from her eye before it could trickle down her cheek. She didn't want her own grief to make it harder for Uncle.

She bit her lip. How sad it was that he didn't have a wife like Juliana. Or one like her mother who, even though she wasn't a Christian, was kind-hearted, generous, and a loving wife and mother. Artoria looked on her marriage to Uncle as a path to social position and the source of the daughters she did love. As much as any self-centered person could love, anyway.

"She's made my daughters just like her." He opened a new tablet, and the stylus hovered over the pristine wax surface. "I wish they were like you."

He cleared his throat. "Tell my steward to prepare the bills of sale for the ones you want at the lowest reasonable price, and tell him I said to pay the sales tax on that amount. If my wife asks, you bought them from me, but I'm giving them to you. I consider their price to be part of your inheritance."

"Thank you, Uncle."

He flicked his hand toward the door and focused on the tablet.

As Martina slipped out of the room, she glanced back. Uncle Volero was more like Grandfather than she'd ever realized.

Chapter 15

SETTLING IN

Urban Cohort headquarters, morning of Day 13

Glabrio drew a blank tablet from his desk drawer and picked up the brass stylus. As he rolled it between thumb and middle finger, he contemplated the untouched wax.

What should he say in his first report to Saturninus? If he wrote what he truly wanted, he'd ask his commander if he knew Nepos hadn't been doing any more than the good-for-nothing Victorinus back in Rome. Did he know Nepos had already left even before Glabrio sailed from Portus?

But he couldn't write that without it seeming to accuse Saturninus of sending him to a posting where failure was almost certain.

So, he'd only report the facts and not ask a single question. He pressed the stylus into the wax and began.

> G. Acilius Glabrio, tribune of the XIII Cohort, to M. Lollius Paullinus Valerius Saturninus, urban prefect, greetings. If you are well, then I am glad. I write to report my arrival and the state of affairs in the XIII Cohort as I have found them.
>
> Although we expected my early arrival to allow four days for Haterius Nepos to brief me about the activities and ongoing investigations of the Cohort, I have learned that he left for Rome eight or nine days before my arrival. His centurions did not know I was coming, and he left no written reports on what he considered important for me to continue.
>
> To make up for the lack of direction from Nepos, I planned to use his earlier reports. I expected to find useful information in the Cohort archives, but I found reports for the first three months of his command and nothing thereafter.

His centurions tell me he didn't use their reports so he didn't require them. Consequently, most did not prepare them.

I want to commend Centurion Flavius Acceptus, who oversees the troops protecting the provincial roads. On his own initiative, he has been keeping records of important events. He will continue as he has been doing and will provide me with copies for the cohort archives.

I have told the other three centurions that they are to provide daily reports in the future, as you have the cohorts do that police Rome. When they understand what I consider priorities, I expect they will perform as well as the men who were my centurions of the XI.

I have begun meeting with the important men of the city to learn what they see as the problems with which I can help.

Since counterfeit coins have been given to traders from Rome at glass slab venders, I have begun looking into the glass trade to find a trail to the men responsible.

I look forward to serving the people of Carthago as the Cohort better fulfills its duty to protect the city and the interests of the empire.

I hope all will continue to be well with you. May the gods guard your safety.

He set aside the stylus. "Sartorus."

"Yes, Tribune?" The optio appeared in the doorway.

"Seal this, and find out how reports are sent to Rome. I assume some ships must carry correspondence between here and Portus."

"Placidus at the harbor station should know."

Glabrio stood and took his helmet from the side table. "Now is a good time for us to inspect part of the city between here and the harbor. Do you have the list of glass sellers from Melis?"

Sartorus glanced at Dubitatus's office; the centurion wasn't there. "It's on the shelf with your codices and scrolls. I didn't have a key to the desk drawers or the strongbox in your quarters, and I thought it wise to put it where unauthorized eyes wouldn't see it." One corner of his mouth lifted. "Titianus used to say hiding something in plain sight could be almost as good as a locked drawer."

Glabrio chuckled. "We both learned well from the same teacher. I want to look at it again, and then we'll go."

He led Sartorus out of his office and down the passageway to his quarters.

Titianus had chosen wisely. Sartorus was the right man for this job.

Martina's town house, Carthago, Day 13

Martina wiped the dust from the cubicles that would soon hold the codices and scrolls that had once been Juliana's. Uncle had given her more than she expected from Grandfather's collection as well. When she asked if he was certain Artoria and her cousins wouldn't want them, his answer was a snort and a roll of his eyes.

She'd chosen to unpack her library herself. Her new home's tablinum was smaller than the intimate three-couch triclinium where family dined in Grandfather's house. Uncle's tablinum reflected the dignity of generations of councilmen and a few duumvirs. Grandfather's portrait bust had joined the other ancestral busts and masks on the wall behind the desk.

Hers felt almost cozy. With a strongbox for her money and private documents, a small desk with a single guest chair, and a padded wicker chair with matching footstool that was perfect for curling up with something to read, it was all she'd need.

Clavus carried a new chest into the room and set it at her feet. "Master Volero just had this delivered. It's the records from the glassworks and the shop that he had at his office."

She selected the top leather binder of papyrus sheets and scanned the first page. "I'm sure this makes perfect sense to Uncle, but it might take me a while to understand it all." One corner of her mouth lifted. "For *us* to understand it. Since you're going to be my steward in Carthago, I want you to become familiar with the businesses here. The glassworks, the glass shop next door—I want to understand what's done at both, what's important for success."

Clavus squared his shoulders. "I'll do my best to serve you, Mistress."

Petale knocked on the doorframe. "Mistress, the glassblower is at the shop door. He asked to speak with you."

"We're coming."

With Clavus beside her, Martina approached her shop steward. He stood just inside the door to the glass shop, but he was looking intently at everything in his field of view.

"Ceraulo. Did you want to speak with me?"

"Yes, Mistress. I see you have very few here in your household. He's the only man." He tipped his head toward Clavus.

"This is Clavus, steward for this household and my assistant for business matters."

The men exchanged polite nods, but it felt like Ceraulo was taking her man's measure.

"So, what did you want to tell me?"

"Sometimes it takes more than one man to get something done. I wanted you to know one of us could usually come over if you need a second man to help with anything."

"I'll keep that in mind if that becomes a problem. Thank you for letting me know."

Ceraulo tipped his head back and inhaled deeply. "That sure smells good."

"Colina is an excellent cook. What she prepares tastes even better than it smells."

He drew another deep breath.

"I believe she made only enough for the familia today, but she can prepare some extra stew next time for you to enjoy along with what Cherida cooks."

"That sounds good, Mistress." He closed his eyes for one more deep breath. "If you need us, just let us know."

"I will."

He went back into the shop, closing the door behind him.

Martina bolted the door. "Until I get to know them, I want to control when they can come in. I don't want them to overhear something that they shouldn't, and I don't know if the men can be trusted around women."

"That's wise. I'll do everything I can to look out for you, but as Ceraulo said, I'm only one man." Clavus squeezed the back of his neck. "I want to thank you for choosing me to serve you here. For rescuing my whole family from Mistress Artoria. For saving Myrtis from Mistress Priscilla."

"No thanks are needed. I would have rescued everyone in Grandfather's familia if I could, but that wasn't possible."

"Mistress Juliana was always kind, but that's the way with Christians. You're just like your grandmother."

Martina rubbed one arm. Would Clavus already knowing she was a Christian be a good thing or bad?

"How long have you known about our faith?"

"Many years. Neither Mistress Juliana nor you made the morning offerings at the household shrine. Always Master Gaius did it, and when he was out of town, his steward did. The master's first wife often performed the household rites. She acted like they did something important."

"Does the rest of your family know?"

"Colina does, and Petale. My children, probably not. They were born after Master Volero's mother died. They never saw the difference."

"Please be careful not to tell anyone without asking me first."

"I won't tell. Only a fool would want to trade a Christian mistress for one who might be like Master Volero's wife."

His words drew Martina's nod and knowing smile. Only a fool would want to marry a woman like her cousins if they knew what the girls were really like. But both women and men conceal their faults before their marriage, and a woman's beauty could ignite a man's desire while dousing his good sense.

But it wasn't only men who could be fooled. The new tribune was everything her cousins thought they wanted—handsome, masculine, rich. He'd encouraged their flirting, but what seemed like interest—she'd be willing to bet it was only a game to him.

No doubt he knew how he affected young women, and he found it entertaining. The son of a consul of Rome would have his eye on a political marriage, not a girl from the provinces with nothing but beauty to offer.

His conversation with her was only a game as well. But she hadn't played it like he wanted, and she'd come away the winner.

Her smile faded. The last thing she wanted was a rematch. Leaving Uncle's household should protect her from that.

She returned to the tablinum and opened the final chest of scrolls. No more criticism from Artoria, no more irritations from her cousins, and no more attention from the too-confident tribune. She closed her eyes, and a satisfied sigh escaped.

Thank You, God, for giving me this place for my new home. Let it always be a household filled with Your peace.

Chapter 16

SETTING EXPECTATIONS

Near the Carthago harbor district, Day 13

As Glabrio and Sartorus strolled along the streets between the Forum headquarters and the harbor, they watched for the glass shops on Melis's list. They'd almost reached the agora before spotting the first. It occupied part of a building that also housed several small shops and a town house.

"Palace of Glass." Glabrio raised an eyebrow. "An impressive name for such a small shop."

Sartorus craned his neck to look down the alley beside the building. "It's larger than it looks from the front. It goes more than halfway to the next street. I'd expect the bulk glass foundries to be outside the city, so they wouldn't need much space to display samples of what they sell. The shops that only sell bulk glass slabs could be much smaller than this. One this size should have glassblowers, like Titianus's shop in Rome, who make glassware for export and special designs for custom orders."

"Make a note of the location and size of each shop as we find it." Glabrio rubbed his chin. "I think I'll have you visit them out of uniform. You can find out what they sell and get an impression of the kind of men who work there before we pay an official visit to ask about the counterfeit coins."

Sartorus's usual slight smile broadened. "I've never worked as a spy before. Titianus used to use Melis as his eyes and ears where a young slave could blend in like a piece of furniture." The smile turned into a grin. "I can do that easily among tradesmen."

They crossed the agora with its permanent shops surrounding the open plaza. Temporary stalls and tables were arranged in rows in the plaza itself, offering an endless variety of goods to the crowds shopping there. A few more blocks, and they reached the guard station for the harbor district where they'd first met Placidus.

When they entered, Placidus rose and struck his chest. "Tribune. How may I help you?"

"I'm here for Centurion Verus to give me a tour of his district."

Placidus opened his mouth but paused before speaking. "Centurion Verus isn't here right now."

"Where is he?"

Placidus blinked too fast. "Patroling his district, Tribune."

"When will he return?" Glabrio crossed his arms.

"I don't know, Tribune."

"Then you will escort me and point out the typical problems you deal with down here until we find Verus to take over."

"Yes, Tribune." Placidus stood and cleared his throat. "Ambustus!" His bellow brought the soldier who'd taken them to the Forum headquarters through the barracks doorway. "Take my post until I return."

Ambustus came to Placidus's desk by the station door and sat.

As the nervous optio led them toward the entrance to the circular harbor, Glabrio raised an eyebrow at Sartorus. With tightened lips, his aide nodded once.

His visit had made Verus's optio too nervous. Men who were doing their jobs well were unfazed by the visit of their superior officer. Something was not as it should be in the harbor district. How long would it be before he knew what it was? How long would it take to fix it?

Duumvir Paternus's town house, evening of Day 13

With great satisfaction, Glabrio selected another fruit-topped pastry from the platter and listened to Paternus and Viator discussing the quality of last year's wines and speculating on what this year would produce.

A day that had started with a report to his commander of the dismal state that Nepos had left the XIII Cohort in was ending with promising new relationships that could help him turn that around.

He'd returned to headquarters midafternoon after a several-hour tour of the harbors, quays, and adjacent warehouses. Several hours spent with an optio instead of the man in charge of the port district. After three years with do-nothing Nepos, how long would it take Verus to recognize there was a tribune in charge again?

When he walked into headquarters, a pleasant surprise awaited him—a boy with an invitation to dine at the dummvir's house that evening. Deciding what to do about Verus could wait.

He probably didn't need an armed escort in Carthago, but he brought one to Paternus's house anyway. The two soldiers who accompanied him to Volero Martinus's dinner had been discussed by so many that it would raise eyebrows if he didn't bring them now.

When he saw the size of the party and the dignity of the men gathered there, he'd expected to be assigned to the third set of couches farthest from Paternus. When he was summoned to share the couch across from his host and next to Volero Martinus, it was hard to keep his smile from becoming a grin.

The wine slave reached for his half-empty goblet to refill it, and Glabrio waved him away. The man who stayed sober never said things he'd regret later. He also learned things others might not want him to know.

He took a sip of the excellent vintage. Tonight had gone well. He owed a large part of that to Martina's comment that Carthaginian elite were merchants, not senators. The duumvirs, the aediles, and all of the councilmen he'd met were businessmen as well as landowners. So, he asked each what businesses they were involved in and whether there were any particular problems he should be addressing for them.

Each time he asked, polite social words were replaced by a genuine conversation. In one evening, he'd shown many of the men who mattered that he wasn't just one more arrogant Roman who'd come for his own benefit with no desire to serve Carthago well.

"Tribune." Volero Martinus's voice ended his reflections. "We have some unfinished business."

Glabrio shifted on the couch for a better view of Martinus. "We do?"

What that might be was beyond him.

"We do, indeed. I want to invite you to dinner at my house tomorrow. With as many as you've met these last two days, you may have forgotten, but I haven't." One corner of Martinus's mouth rose. "I haven't been allowed to."

Glabrio's raised eyebrows asked the question and triggered Martinus's chuckle.

"My wife promised you a private dinner with my family. She's been reminding me several times a day that it wouldn't be hospitable if I fail to extend the invitation as soon as possible. She's afraid you might think she didn't mean it."

A family dinner at Martinus's house. That should include his intriguing niece. How would she respond when he thanked her for her sage advice? Would it be surprise or silent laughter that would enliven those observant brown eyes?

But the daughters would be there, too, and a mother too eager to snare a wealthy husband for one of them.

"I'd enjoy that. Few things give more pleasure than a small dinner gathering. What I miss most since leaving Rome are the private dinners with my father and with the family of my predecessor as tribune of the XI."

"Did you leave a wife and children in Rome as well?" Volero watched him over the rim of his goblet as he took a drink.

Glabrio lifted his goblet to wet his lips but didn't drink any. Time to make his intentions clear before frustrated expectations became resentment. "Father almost arranged an excellent political marriage last year, but the woman, although admirable in many ways, wasn't well suited to the highly public role she would have to play. A Glabrio wife must be able to shine in the top social circles of Rome. It will be challenging, but Father will find me the right woman."

Volero's chuckle was unexpected. "I commend you on your tactful way of declaring you expect to remain unattached to any woman of Carthago. Artoria might want to repeat what happened with her sister, but I'd rather have my girls marry a local man with large estates and other thriving businesses than a man destined to serve all over the Empire. My father enjoyed helping his grandson grow into a fine man. I want to do the same."

"It's good when men understand each other's goals and priorities." Glabrio raised his goblet in a silent toast to Volero. "A relaxing dinner with new friends is always welcome. I like to listen to those who know things I've not yet learned, and good conversation over good food satisfies both stomach and mind."

"Then we'll expect you tomorrow evening." Volero returned the toast. "I can promise the food will be excellent. The conversation...I'll leave it to you to decide whether that satisfies as well."

The crooked smile that most women loved...it escaped before he could stop it. He'd be willing to bet any conversation with Volero's independent-minded niece would more than satisfy.

Chapter 17

Not Like in Rome

Morning of Day 14

With Sartorus beside him, Glabrio headed back to his office after another breakfast in the barrack's dining hall. Titianus had eaten with the regular soldiers for years. How on earth had he endured that?

Glabrio had taken an underchef from his father's house to prepare his private meals in the Praetorian Fortress. But his tribune quarters in Rome were like a small town house with atrium, peristyle, and standard kitchen. In Carthago, he had a three-couch triclinium barely big enough for the couches, a small tablinum that doubled as his library, and a handful of small rooms no bigger than a horse's stall, all overlooking a tiny peristyle garden with a pool no larger than the smallest tub in his father's private bath. But no kitchen.

"That porridge—it couldn't be more tasteless if the cook tried. Is there anything that could be done to add some flavor?"

"I had porridge every day for breakfast as a child, but my mother added a little rosemary or thyme to it. I always thought it tasted good."

Glabrio fingered his lip. "Are those too expensive if you're feeding eighty men?"

"We had eight in my family, plus a dozen or so slaves. We all ate the same porridge. Those chest-high bushes with the little blue flowers we've been seeing—those are rosemary. It should be cheap to buy here."

"Have the cook look into trying some. If I'm going to eat with the men, they need to eat something decent."

"You'll soon be their favorite tribune of all time for making that change." Sartorus pushed open the headquarters door. "You're already in my top two."

"You've only had two."

A shrug and laughing eyes were his optio's reply.

As they walked by the tribune offices, Dubitatus raised a hand in greeting.

"Tribune." Verus pushed back from his normally vacant desk and approached, wax tablet in hand. "My report for today. My optio tells me he gave you a tour yesterday. I regret that our paths failed to cross while we were both inspecting the harbor district."

He held the tablet out to Glabrio, and Sartorus took it.

"Placidus probably showed you some of the important places in the district, but he might not have provided an adequate explanation of why each is important. I would like to take you on a second tour to provide you with that information."

"We can do it now."

Verus struck his chest, then strode back to his desk to get his helmet. Glabrio tapped his head, and Sartorus fetched theirs as well.

The way from the Forum to the harbor led past the agora, which was Dubitatus's responsibility.

As they walked along a street lined with shops, Glabrio scanned each one. Were the counterfeiters working within the city? They needed a way to melt metal and a way to stamp the hot metal with the patterns found on real coins. So, any shop that needed a metalsmith for their wares might be a possibility.

But they also needed someone who could make the mold for stamping the pattern. An engraver could copy the new designs being issued by Hadrian to commemorate the different provinces he was visiting. Metalsmiths, jewelers… these would be his starting focus.

But melting metal for coins might not need a regular forge. Even a place like a bakery had ovens that might be used. How many bakers were there in a city the size of Carthago?

"When do we pass from Dubitatus's district into yours?"

"We've been in mine for the last two blocks. The quays along the seashore, both inner harbors, and the warehouses serving them are mine. Also, the shops in the warehouse district. Over there"—Verus pointed to the right as they stepped into a broad street filled with carts and wagons—"is the harbor station with the barracks just past it. You've already seen it, but we can stop there later, if you wish. The inner harbors are through that archway."

"I'd hoped to land in the inner harbor, but our ship from Rome docked against the seaside quay."

"Most ships do." Verus led them along the half-circle around the old military harbor. "It's easier to maneuver into position for unloading, especially for the bigger ships. If a ship needs repairs, they might choose the inner harbor. No waves." He pointed to eight soldiers in full armor flanking a door where the circle necked down to form the entrance to the old commercial harbor. "That's one of the fee stations where the captains pay their wharfage fees. There are others along the quay. The harbormaster's main office is on the island." He pointed to the circle of land in the center of the military harbor.

He turned a wry smile on Glabrio. "Nothing happens in a harbor that doesn't cost someone money. Docking space, rowboats, crews that load and unload, customs and freight fees on the cargo. The captains pay for anchorage off the quay. There's even a lighthouse fee to pay for the oil that keeps it lit."

Glabrio's brow furrowed. "Is there a fee for the security our patrols provide?"

"Not directly, but whatever an emperor provides always comes from someone else's purse."

Sartorus cleared his throat, and Glabrio raised his chin. "Emperor Hadrian is coming to Carthago in late summer when he visits this province. He inspects the troops wherever he goes. Our cohort will have an opportunity to display our respect and loyalty then. I'm sure we both want him to consider it one of Rome's finest."

Verus's jaw twitched. "Of course, Tribune."

An uncomfortable silence followed as they walked by the soldiers, who each struck their chest and stood at full attention as they passed.

As they entered the commercial harbor, Verus pointed at the two-story building running the length of the wharves. "Warehouses for temporary storage of cargo moving on and off the ships. More permanent warehouses are on the other side. Similar buildings line the quayside."

"Where are the wheat and olive oil for Rome warehoused?"

"Follow me."

Verus turned into a narrow passage that led to the seaside. As he walked ahead of them, Glabrio raised his eyebrows at Sartorus. He got a shrug and that subdued smile that was his optio's standard response. He'd ask what they really meant later when they were alone.

As they strolled along the quay, Verus described the range of activities before them, from the ships lying at anchor awaiting a turn at the wharf to the rowboats maneuvering the back end of a ship against the quay to the rows of slave carrying cargo on and off each ship.

The level of detail was far beyond what he needed, but when he glanced at Sartorus, he'd usually see a quick tip of the head to confirm it was a good explanation.

But Glabrio's own interest lay not with the details of cargo handling but with how a counterfeiter might fit into the scene.

"If a captain needed metal work done, where would he go?"

Verus's mouth opened, then closed. Unreadable eyes stared at Glabrio.

Then the centurion cleared his throat. "There are metalsmiths at several of the marine supply shops. They're mostly a block or two back from the cargo handling areas. Common fittings in bronze and iron are often in stock. Custom work is easy to hire when needed."

"I'd like a list of all the shops in your district with metalsmiths."

Verus's eyes narrowed and then relaxed so quickly Glabrio almost missed it. "I can have Placidus prepare and deliver that list for you."

"Good. Besides your district, where might I expect to find metalsmiths?"

Verus's mouth straightened. "Dubitatus should have some. More than captains need custom metal work in the city. Longinus…maybe he knows of some, but not as likely as Dubitatus. Acceptus…there might be some outside the city, but many estates have their own metal shops, so I don't know how you'd find those."

"I see. If I wanted some metal engraved…I'd like a list of shops where I might get that done."

"Dubitatus is more likely to have jewelers in his district, but I'll ask Placidus to prepare the list of any in mine."

"Good."

Verus pointed toward a huge ship floating at anchor. "That's one of the larger ships that make up the grain fleet, and…"

With his I-care-what-your-saying expression, Glabrio listened to Verus describe the one-hundred-eighty-foot-long, forty-five-foot-wide ship that carried over a thousand tons of grain to Portus. By the time Verus finished, he was more than ready for the tour to end.

Verus looked over Glabrio's shoulder to Sartorus, then back. "What would you like to see next, Tribune?"

"I don't want to keep you too long from your regular duties. I would like that list of metalsmiths and engravers as soon as you can prepare it. But I would like to tour the areas away from the docks with you soon. For now, you may go."

Verus's satisfied smile mirrored Glabrio's own. "Whenever you want that, let me know, Tribune. If you follow that street,"—he pointed toward a narrow street lined with shops—"you'll reach the agora."

Verus's fist struck his chest before he executed a parade turn and strode back along the quay.

With Sartorus beside him, Glabrio headed up the street. "One thing is clear. Verus knows his district and is overseeing the harbors and the warehouses as well as my centurion did in Rome."

"It's clear he knows his district." Sartorus drew in a breath and blew it out through pursed lips. "But whether he's overseeing like your centurion in Rome…I'm not so sure."

Glabrio's head drew back. "What makes you say that?"

"Well, maybe it's only a difference between a seaport and where river boats dock. Maybe what the Cohort garrison does in Portus is like what Verus's men are doing here. I don't know what they do differently than what my old centurion does."

"What did you see that seems wrong?"

"Verus has eighty or so men under his command. I would expect most of them to be out on patrol. I didn't see as many as I expected out walking the wharves."

"Maybe some are out in parts of the district that aren't right by the harbor. Verus didn't show us the whole district, just the parts near the harbors and quays. And maybe part of them are in battle training, like my men did weekly at the Praetorian Fortress."

Sartorus rubbed his jaw. "That could explain part of it, but your centurions always conducted that training for their own men, and Verus was with us."

"Maybe the centurions share training responsibilities for all the districts."

"Perhaps. Do you want me to find out?"

"No, but let the centurions know I'd like a description of their training program in their next report."

Sartorus's mouth twitched, then he released a wry smile. "If I were a betting man, I'd bet Acceptus has the best one."

Glabrio returned the smile. "I am a betting man, and I wouldn't bet against you on that. I would bet that anything Acceptus does will be done well."

As they continued in silence, Glabrio glanced at the man walking beside him. He'd willingly bet that no matter what he asked of Sartorus, his optio would try his hardest to do it well.

Chapter 18

DISAPPOINTMENT

Volero's town house, evening of Day 14

As Glabrio approached the entrance to Volero's town house, he looked forward to an entertaining conclusion to a satisfying day. Sartorus had chosen two different men from Dubitatus's century as escorts for this evening. His astute optio pointed out that standing for hours outside a door while his commander enjoyed a sumptuous dinner inside would not inspire his own loyalty, even if he already liked and respected the man. It was wise to choose different men each time and spread the miserable assignment around.

Two raps on the door, and a youth opened it. "Welcome, Tribune. Master Volero wanted me to tell you your escort is welcome to join his slaves for dinner and then relax inside rather than stand outside the door."

Glabrio glanced over his shoulder at his men. Two smiles announced their approval of Volero's offer. "Enjoy Martinus's hospitality. It's good to know your faithful service is appreciated by him as well as by me."

"Follow me." The youth led Glabrio into the peristyle garden and his men on toward the back of the house.

Volero sat in a wicker chair beside his wife, and his daughters stood in front of the fountain, framed by an array of flowering plants and dressed in tunics whose colors complimented their floral background.

His crooked smile leaked out. Artoria made masterful use of color and staging to focus a man's attention on her pretty daughters. But it wasn't physical beauty that snared his interest. It was a sharp mind, the courage to graciously correct him, and a sense of humor that made him wonder what she'd find amusing next.

It was her niece...who was missing from the room.

Perhaps she was joining them later. If not...

Volero rose and strode toward him. "Welcome. Canis will have told the kitchen that you've joined us and dinner can be served." Palm up, his hand swept toward the family dining room. It held only three couches. To the left, the host's couch. In the center, the couch for honored guests, and to the right, the couch for the remainder of the company.

The salad course was already on the table between the three tables. Two plates each for the right and left couches. Only one in front of the center couch.

Disappointment flooded through him. The one person he'd been looking forward to seeing all day wasn't going to be there. Volero's niece was unusual, and he liked that. Her grief was real but not flaunted to impress others. She found her cousins' attempts to take his attention from her amusing rather than irritating. She'd been willing to tell him something he needed to hear even when she thought he wouldn't like it.

Her quiet confidence, her gracious treatment of the hostile cousins, and her seeming indifference to his family's wealth and political importance—all reminded him of Titianus's wife Pompeia, and he'd found as much genuine pleasure in Pompeia's company as he had with the men in her household who were his friends.

But disappointment was never an excuse to be rude, and a good guest made do with whatever company the host provided. He reclined and waited for Volero to take the first bite.

"We're delighted you were able to join us so soon for a family dinner." Artoria picked up a carrot stick and dipped it into a white sauce. The crunch of Volero's first bite of carrot should have started everyone eating, but Artoria merely dipped her carrot again. "Our son is still in Alexandria. He will be for another month or so, but it's our great pleasure to have you join the rest of our family. We've missed the company of a young man here."

"I look forward to meeting your son upon his return." He swirled his carrot stick in the white sauce. "It's my pleasure to dine tonight with most of your family, but your niece is missing."

Artoria's beaming smile froze. "She stayed here and served as domina for Volero's father after his wife died, but now that the funeral and mourning period are over, she's moved elsewhere."

Artoria kept her voice matter-of-fact, but there was an undertone of irritation that he'd pointed out Martina's absence.

"It was her choice." Fake sweetness had replaced irritation. "Once a woman has been domina, it's hard to step back and be merely a member of the household."

"Where did she choose to go?" He gave Artoria his social smile. "I'd like to talk with her more about her glass business."

Artoria's brow furrowed before she caught herself. "Her glass business?"

Glabrio glanced at Volero and caught him wiping his mouth to hide a broad smile. But silent laughter enlivened his host's eyes.

"Father left her the glass foundry, the glass shop, and the building near the agora that houses it. It includes a small town house and several small shops as well. Martina decided to move there for now rather than return to her estate near Cigisa. As her guardian, I heartily approve of her staying in Carthago where it will be easy for me to look after her interests, as needed."

"Before I leave tonight, I'd like directions to the glass shop."

"I'll draw you a map." Volero dabbed at his lips again. "It's well situated for those wanting to buy raw glass slabs for export or artistic works made of glass."

Artoria found her smile again. "Volero's father was a brilliant man of business and served Carthago as duumvir and councilman for many years." She rested her hand on Volero's arm. "My Volero is carrying on the family tradition of service to the city and to Rome."

Glabrio lifted his goblet. "To the men of the Publilii Martini and their invaluable service to both city and empire."

Volero's broad smile bordered on a grin as he raised his goblet in response. "And to the brilliant career we expect for the latest tribune of the Acilii Glabriones."

Artoria and her daughters drank the toast, but her satisfied eyes told Glabrio she had no idea why the men grinned.

It was late when Glabrio strolled back to his quarters. He would have left earlier, but Artoria had done her best to delay his departure. She'd also extended an invitation to come whenever he didn't have another dinner to attend.

If this were Rome, he'd have feigned appreciation but politely declined. But when Volero was so swift to urge him to accept her invitation, he'd said he would. Being forced to spend too much time alone with his wife and daughters couldn't be pleasant, and he could spare Volero from that fate.

Besides, the food was excellent. Volero had promised good food, and he'd delivered. Glabrio had no personal chef like he'd kept at his quarters in Rome, so he'd joined Sartorus eating in the barracks with Dubitatus's men. While it was good for the men who were now his to see him there, what was served by the garrison cooks was merely edible, not something to look forward to.

Satisfying conversation...his host had only partly delivered. Volero had described the rebuilding of Roman Carthago on the site of the destroyed Punic city and his own family's role in it. For a lover of history like himself, that had been more than satisfying.

But Artoria had appeared bored with her husband's stories when Glabrio looked at her. And the daughters watched him continuously, or so it seemed.

Each time he glanced their way, Sufina blushed and Priscilla smiled alluringly and sometimes batted her eyes.

Priscilla asked too many questions about what it was like to live in Rome. Many he'd been unable to answer. He didn't shop for fine fabrics, embroidered sandals, or fancy women's jewelry. But his ignorance didn't dampen her urge to ask him more pointless questions.

He sighed. Martina reclining near him would have made the conversation as satisfying as the food.

But tucked into his tunic was a map to her new home. Tomorrow he'd start his investigation of the glass suppliers and the counterfeit coins that one of them gave Melis. The first place he'd visit was hers.

She'd been too happy to end their conversation at Volero's dinner. He had the perfect justification for visiting her now and the power to make her talk with him.

He'd take Sartorus there tomorrow. While his trustworthy tradesman examined the glass shop records, he could question its owner. And what would begin as official questions should easily shift into friendly conversation.

His crooked smile started small and grew. Trading words with Martina felt like a game, and no one loved a good game more than he did.

Chapter 19

A Visit from the Tribune

Martina's town house, morning of Day 15

With Sartorus carrying a satchel of wax tablets beside him, Glabrio knocked on the door of Martina's town house.

The door remained closed. He knocked again...and still he waited.

The third time, he pounded.

"Did we miss something on the map?" Sartorus shifted the satchel on his shoulder. He reached in and pulled out the papyrus sheet Volero had given Glabrio the night before.

Together, they examined it.

"I don't think so."

The muffled sound of a bolt being drawn back was followed by a boy of about eleven pulling one of the two doors open. His gaze swept their uniforms, and his eyes saucered.

Glabrio stepped past him into the wide vestibulum, and Sartorus entered behind him. "Tell Publilia Martina that Tribune Glabrio is here to speak with her."

The boy closed and bolted the door. "Yes, Tribune."

He scurried into the peristyle.

At the far end under the portico, Glabrio could see two women at looms. One had brown hair in a braid pinned at the back of her head. The wavy, dark brown hair of the other hung almost to her waist. Even in the drab beige tunic she'd worn when he first saw her, the sight of her triggered a smile.

The boy reached her and spoke too softly for him to catch the words. But she spun to face him, and shock, not pleasure, was her first reaction.

He turned off the smile.

She placed her shuttle on the small shelf at the top of the loom and walked toward him.

"Tribune. To what do I owe this visit?" Her smile was cool, and her eyes matched it.

He'd come for official business as well as pleasure. It had taken a question that she thought odd for her to warm up to him before. There would be time for that after he took care of business.

Since her glassworks gave him a believable reason to visit, he could make as many opportunities to talk with her as he wanted. Once she decided she wanted to talk with him as well, he wouldn't need a reason to come.

"I told you before that a friend of mine buys Carthaginian glass. The last time his ship was in Carthago getting glass slabs, his captain received counterfeit coins as change from one of the glass sellers. I want to find the source."

She crossed her arms. "But why did you come here?"

"Some of the glass was purchased from your glassworks. Your uncle provided the address." One corner of his mouth lifted. "Since I don't think you're a counterfeiter, if the coins came from your shop, then I assume your shop steward was paid in counterfeit coins for something he sold."

"So, how do you think I can help you? I've only just inherited the business, and Grandfather only owned it for a few months before that."

"I want to see your record of sales, how much and to whom for the past few months."

Her brow furrowed, and that tight-lipped smile that suggested she was laughing at him appeared. "Will a nobleman like yourself understand what you're seeing or will my steward have to interpret it for you?"

"He can continue with his usual work. It's true I'm not a merchant, but if a wise man doesn't know something himself, he finds an assistant who does. I brought one of my optios from Rome. He comes from a family of tradesmen and worked in the family businesses before enlisting in the Urban Cohort."

"Very well. I'll take you to the steward of my glass shop."

She led them to a door that was bolted and had a bar across it. After she lifted the bar from its rack, she slid the bolt back. When she swung the door open, they stepped through into the workshop where two men were blowing glass and a third sat at a desk with a stack of papyrus.

"Ceraulo, I'd like you to show these men any records of sales they want to see."

Her shop steward frowned as he stood and came forward. "As you wish, Mistress." The frown turned into a stiff smile. "The records are in the sales room. Follow me."

Sartorus pulled out a wax tablet and went into the next room.

As Glabrio followed his optio, he looked over his shoulder and gave her a warm smile. "Thank you for your willingness to help."

"It's my pleasure." With a fleeting smile that declared those words more social convention than truth, she disappeared into her house.

A stack of tablets sat on the counter. Her steward opened one, and his finger moved across from column to column as he spoke softly to Sartorus.

A quick tip of his optio's head and a smile sent the steward back to the workshop.

Glabrio leaned on the counter beside the wax tablet Sartorus was writing on.

"So, what am I looking at?"

Sartorus pointed at each column in order across one sales tablet. "Date, amount paid, quantity, what kind of glass, and the one who bought it." His finger rested by one entry. "Here's Titianus's purchase. We only need to look at entries older than his."

"What will this tell us?"

"By itself, not much. But if we inspect the coins each shop has on hand and find more than one with counterfeits that look like they're from the same source, we can narrow down the suspects to those who traded at all those shops. If there's only one, we'll have the one who used the bad coins."

"But what if only one shop has bad coins?"

"We'll still have a list of possible people, but we might need to check them all to find the right one."

Glabrio glanced at the door to the workshop. "So, I need to tell Martina we'll be inspecting the coins in her shop's strongbox or wherever else they might have been stored when they were paid out to Titianus's captain."

Sartorus nodded, and they returned to the workroom. Sartorus asked Ceraulo to show him their coins, and Glabrio strode to the door through which they'd entered.

It swung open silently. At least she hadn't locked him out.

She'd returned to her loom, and he stood a moment, watching her weaving the shuttle back and forth. She used a comb to control the loops at the end and to tap the yarn from the latest pass up against the earlier rows to become the fabric.

She worked faster than the woman beside her, and the edge was perfectly even. But precision and efficiency from Volero's niece were what he expected.

He stepped lightly to let the gurgle of water in the fountain mask the soft clicks of hobnails on the tile floor. He waited to speak until he was right behind her. "I see those fingers can work with wool as well as clay."

She jumped at his voice, but by the time she turned to face him, any sign of surprise was gone.

"Have you finished already?"

"No. I need to examine the coins in your shop's strongbox to see if any are counterfeit. If they are, Sartorus will need to make copies of some of your records."

"Ceraulo oversees the shop without my help, but you can tell him I said to let you do whatever you think necessary."

"Sartorus already started the inspection." He gave her his irresistible smile. "I thought I'd find it more interesting to interrogate you than to look at coins with my optio. But if the coins come from here, you're probably a victim, not a criminal."

Her lips curved into an ironic smile. "I'm flattered that you don't think I'm committing a capital crime like counterfeiting, but if I refused to help you, you'd be forced to suspect me, even though I'm innocent."

He donned the emotionless face he'd learned from Titianus. "Perhaps you are committing a capital crime, but I don't know what it is."

The color drained from her face. An odd response from an innocent person.

He let his expression relax into his woman-pleasing half-smile. "You aren't committing a capital crime, are you?"

As she fingered the filigree bracelet she'd worn when they met, an enigmatic smile played on her lips. "You could hardly expect me to tell you if I was." Her light chuckle almost erased the wariness from her eyes. "But you can rest easy, Tribune. I'm not involved in anything that's a threat to the Empire or to the peace and good order of the city you're responsible for." Her smile broadened, and to the casual observer, her eyes would seem to match.

But he was no casual observer.

"I think I can take your word that you're no counterfeiter, but I may need to get to know you better before I abandon all suspicion."

"If you want to waste your time that way..." She shrugged. "But you'd get a more enthusiastic response to your interest from my cousins."

He rolled his eyes, and the laugh that evoked was as genuine as any he'd ever heard.

The clicks of hobnails on the tiles behind him announced Sartorus's untimely arrival. The laughter that had danced in her eyes quenched as her gaze locked onto his optio.

"Did you find any counterfeits?" Glabrio asked the question as he turned to face the man behind him.

"Yes, but only a handful. Three denarii and eleven aurei. I think the coins were struck with the same dies." Sartorus opened his fist to show some of the coins.

Glabrio took an aureus and turned back to Martina. "I'll be taking these as evidence. You couldn't spend them, anyway, now that you know what they are."

She'd turned pale again. "I didn't expect you to find any."

"There are few enough that it's clear you took them as payment for something. So, I won't be accusing you of any crime today." He gave her his crooked smile. "But I still need to get to know you better."

The smile he expected didn't appear.

Her lips straightened instead. "Was that a large part of what Ceraulo had in the strongbox?"

He tossed the aureus to Sartorus, who pulled a small bag from the satchel and dropped the coins into it. "Was it?"

"No, Tribune."

Martina bit her lip. "Did you show Ceraulo what marked them as counterfeit? I'd like him to know so we don't take any more of them. Giving away glass for what isn't real money—I can't afford to do that."

Sartorus shook his head. "I did not."

Glabrio stroked his jaw with his thumb. Volero Martinus was a wealthy man, but was Martina living off limited funds?

He opened his purse and took out good coins equal to what she was losing.

"To make up for your loss...this time." He held out the coins, but she placed her hands on her stomach instead of taking them.

"That's your own money, Tribune. It wouldn't be right to take it. We can stand the small loss."

"Are you sure?"

"Yes, but I appreciate your generosity, even if I don't take advantage of it." Her eyes and smile both confirmed the truth of those words.

"We'll be back to train your steward so it shouldn't happen again."

"Please show all of my people who might be serving customers."

"Sartorus will train them all, and I'll train you."

The smile he received was too small and fleeting to suggest she wanted such attention from him. But that should change as she saw more of him.

And he'd make certain she did.

"You can repay me later with more advice on how to keep Roman arrogance from offending in Carthago. Your comment at Volero's dinner has proven most helpful. I could use your guidance about how things work and how people think here." He let his crooked smile appear. "I don't want to give offense unless I really mean to."

Her brow furrowed, as if she didn't remember what she'd said. "I doubt I have any other advice you'd find useful."

"I want it anyway." He cleared his throat. "We have other shops to visit today, but we'll be back."

"Then I won't keep you from your duty. Lepus will let you out. Goodbye, Tribune." With a social smile and a nod, she turned back to her loom.

Glabrio erased all emotion from his face again, but it took some effort this time. He'd never been brushed off like that by a woman before. But somehow, it felt more like a challenge than a rebuff. There was something about her that intrigued him enough that he'd keep trying to breach her defenses.

As he led Sartorus back through the peristyle, the boy scurried ahead and opened the door. When they stepped into the intense African sun, a bolt slid into place the moment the door closed behind them.

He stopped his eyebrows before they dipped enough for Sartorus to see. Why did she keep that door bolted midmorning with no one ready to open it? Was she trying to hide something she didn't want others to see? He pursed his lips to stop a wry smile. She'd barred and bolted the door to her glass shop as well. He hadn't seen anyone else in the town house but the woman at the second loom and the boy. Were they all she had there to protect her?

"Where next?"

Sartorus consulted the copy of Melis's list he'd put in the satchel. "Two shops one block off the docks of the inner harbor."

Glabrio nodded, then strode toward their next destination.

He often asked Sartorus for his thoughts after an encounter. But this time he wouldn't. Sartorus was too good at seeing through what people said to what they were thinking. He didn't want to hear what his optio thought of his exchange with Martina. He was fairly certain his aide wouldn't want to tell him, either.

◆

Martina listened for the sound of the bolt sliding home before she turned around.

"I thought I was through with talking to him when I moved out of Grandfather's house. Why did he come to my door instead of the glass shop? Surely Uncle wouldn't have told him where I moved. He said himself it was safer if Glabrio didn't spend time near me. He sees the danger if a tribune finds out I'm a Christian."

"But if the tribune asked about the glass shop, how could your uncle refuse to tell him? Wouldn't that make him suspicious?" Platana set her shuttle on the shelf atop her loom.

"Maybe he already is. You heard him asking if I'd committed a crime he didn't know about." Martina rubbed her forehead as she stared at the front door.

"But his eyes and that smile said he was just teasing." Platana moved behind her and massaged her shoulders beside her neck. "He's only a man, and any man with eyes and ears would want to spend more time with you."

Martina glanced over her shoulder at her closest friend. "I moved here partly to avoid seeing him, and now he's threatening to come often for more advice."

"What did you tell him that impressed him so much?" Platana continued the massage.

"Only that Carthago didn't appreciate the arrogance of Rome, and he'd be offending people even if he didn't mean to."

Platana chuckled. "And he liked you calling him arrogant and offensive so much that he wants more of the same?"

"When you put it that way, it seems even stranger that he'd want more of my critical comments. How I treated him today should have told him I have no desire to spend more time with him than I absolutely must."

"What I heard made that clear, but maybe he's a man who likes a challenge." Platana kept kneading Martina's still-stiff muscles.

"That feels good." Martina closed her eyes, but an unwelcome image of the tribune's teasing smile made her open them again. "That crooked smile of his and those eyes that seem like he's listening to every word made my cousins all fluttery trying to impress him. I was so glad when they interrupted us and I could politely get away from him."

The continuing massage had drained most of the tension from her body. "Artoria would like him to marry Priscilla, but Uncle said men like him from the powerful families in Rome always make political marriages. They don't care if their wives are beautiful, smart, or even agreeable. It's the political alliance and the dowry that they look for. Or rather, that their fathers look for. Acting so interested in my cousins and me—I think it's just a game for him."

She looked over her shoulder at Platana. "So, when he comes next time, I'll simply have to show him that I'm too boring to play that game with."

"I'm not sure you can be that boring, even when you try."

"I'm sure I can when it's this important." Martina looked over her shoulder and grinned at Platana. "I'll giggle like Sufina and flutter my eyelashes at him like Priscilla. He'll lose interest in no time." Her demonstration drew a chuckle from both of them.

Platana ended the massage, and both returned to their looms. Martina moved the bar to separate the warp threads and wove the shuttle between them.

God, is he going to lose interest before he suspects I follow You?

With many sweeps of the comb, she pushed the yarn up against the growing fabric.

He's not impressed with my cousins, but surely You could have him meet some councilman's daughter who can make him forget about me.

A push on the bar made the front and back sets of warp threads change places, and she wove the shuttle back the other way.

Maybe Uncle could introduce them—she fought the grin—*without letting Artoria know, of course. I wouldn't want her to make his life miserable just to spare me from Glabrio's attentions.*

After slipping the last tooth of the comb through the yarn where it turned at the side, she held it to control the selvedge loop while she pulled the yarn tight.

Smooth on the edge and tightly woven, she always made the fabric exactly what she wanted. Why weren't people so easy to deal with?

She could try to discourage his interest, but she couldn't control what the tribune thought of her...or anyone else, for that matter.

You always know what's best for me, God. Help me to trust You to provide it

Chapter 20

ROAD TRIP

Urban Cohort headquarters, early morning of Day 16

Glabrio placed his hands atop his head, leaned back in his chair, and arched his back. For their breakfast, Sartorus had gone to get some fresh-from-the-oven rolls from the bakery up the street that Dubitatus said was superb.

For five days, Glabrio had been in charge of the XIII Cohort. Nepos's early departure, his neglect of his duty for almost three years—not a promising beginning, but he'd already turned that around.

His centurions in Carthago would now be doing what his men in Rome had. He was already accepted among the men who ruled the city, and the most important ones knew he intended to do what he could to address any problems they brought to him.

He'd found the first link between a glass seller and the counterfeit coins.

A smile started slowly and grew. That first link gave him an excuse to visit Volero Martinus's intriguing niece for more conversations. The smile faded. Twice she'd spoken with him because she had to. Each time, she'd been eager to end their conversation.

Did she really think he was arrogant and offensive? He rubbed his jaw. Probably. She was honest in a way he'd seldom seen with elite women. She'd learn he was neither as he spent more time with her.

But why did she tense up yesterday when he joked about her breaking a Roman law he didn't yet know?

A knock on the door frame interrupted his musing. One of his centurions stood in the doorway in full armor, including helmet.

"Acceptus." Glabrio pointed at the guest chair. "Sit."

His conscientious centurion settled into the chair and tucked his helmet under his arm. "You said you wanted to tour our districts with us. My district includes many of the roads within a hundred miles of Carthago. So, since I'm leaving today to ride a route that includes several major roads, I thought you might want to join me on the first day's ride."

"You were right." Glabrio's smile made Acceptus relax. "But I'll need to get horses first. A quality one for me, a decent one for my optio."

"There's a horse trader near the harbor who can provide both. Next to him is the saddlemaker where I buy for my own horse."

Glabrio stood. "Let's go."

When Glabrio returned to the station, Sartorus sat at the antechamber desk, stylus hovering over a wax tablet.

"We'll be going on an inspection with Acceptus today. He's with the horses outside."

Sartorus closed the tablet. "Horses?"

"He took me to the horse market. My new gray stallion was sired by one of the champion chariot stallions, and the mare was from Hispania. He's larger than most and has enough spirit I'll enjoy the ride. I also got you a bay gelding that's fit for distance travel. There were no military saddles, so I bought Scythian. They'll be more comfortable, anyway."

He slapped the desktop. "Let's go. Acceptus wants to reach Uthina before evening, and we're starting later than he normally does."

Sartorus stood and placed his helmet on his head.

Glabrio stepped into his office for his own helmet. When he returned, Sartorus had the satchel slung from one shoulder and a sword hanging by his opposite hip.

They mounted, and Acceptus led them west toward the amphitheater and circus.

With his centurion beside him and his optio behind, Glabrio nudged his horse into a fast walk. The XIII Cohort was stationed in Carthago to make sure nothing kept African grain from reaching the city's wharves. It was time for his first view of the grainfields and olive orchards that fed the people of Rome.

As they rode past the circus, he slowed. "It's larger than I expected, maybe three-quarters the length of the Circus Maximus. And those awnings over the seats and even the stalls..."

"Our African sun would make it too hot for afternoon races without them." Acceptus's mouth twitched. "Tribune Nepos liked this part of Carthago best. He said it was a good place to meet with the leaders of the city." He cleared his throat. "He met with them often."

Glabrio's stallion tossed his head and pulled at the bit. That triggered Glabrio's smile. A horse that got impatient at a slow walk was what he liked best.

He leaned forward and patted its neck. "I like spirited horses, and watching champion teams race gets my heart pounding like the hooves on the sand. But a man's life needs a purpose beyond entertainment. Watching the races is fine as long as you don't do it too much, and only a fool bets more than he can afford to lose on the races he does watch."

Acceptus's tight-lipped smile and quick nod proclaimed his agreement... and his approval. This centurion who'd done what was proper even when his commander didn't want it was a man whose good opinion was worth having.

Glabrio returned the nod before focusing on the road ahead of them. Acceptus nudged his horse into a trot, and Glabrio's mount kept pace as the road turned and headed southwest.

They'd gone a quarter mile when Glabrio glanced over his shoulder. Sartorus, the man who seemed comfortable no matter what he was doing, was grim-faced and bouncing on his horse's back.

He dropped back beside his optio and slowed to a walk. "Have you ever ridden before?"

"No, and it's not something I could learn listening to others talk about it." His wry smile accompanied a shrug. "Titianus taught Melis so he wouldn't slow them down when he took his spy out of town." He lowered his voice. "Looks like you'll have to do the same with yours."

"It's not hard. Move with your horse. Don't squeeze your knees so tight, don't lean forward, and let your body float as he goes up and down. Relax into the motion, and you won't bounce."

Sartorus drew a deep breath and blew it out between pursed lips. "You make it sound easy."

"It is, once you figure out how to do it. Watch me."

As the two horses switched from walk to trot and back several times, Glabrio watched Sartorus. "Straighten, relax, float." As his optio settled into the rhythm of the trot, Glabrio increased the speed.

"Ready for a few hours of this now?"

"Probably, but I won't be asking to transfer to the cavalry."

"I wouldn't approve the request, even if you made it."

Acceptus was some distance ahead, twisted in his saddle and watching them. Glabrio flexed his calves, and the stallion shifted into a fast trot.

The hoofbeats behind him kept up, and they rejoined Acceptus.

They'd gone by another mile of wheat fields before they rode past the large villa of the man who owned them. No wonder Africa could send twice as much grain as Egypt to feed Rome.

He rubbed under his chin where the cheek guards weren't in the way. Martina owned an estate that grew grain. She said it was larger than some, smaller than others, but what did that mean? It probably had a villa, but she'd chosen to live in the small town house off the agora with almost no furniture and very few slaves. Why?

"Does this road go to Cigisa?"

Acceptus's head drew back, and he slowed to a walk where talking was easier. Then he turned curious eyes on Glabrio. "Cigisa?"

"Yes." Glabrio put on his emotionless face. If he seemed too eager, Acceptus would be wondering why he asked that question. His centurion didn't need to know how much Martina intrigued him, that seeing her estate, even from a distance, might give him something to discuss that would spark some interest in talking with him.

"No. It's on the road to Bulla Regia, halfway between Carthago and Thuburbo Minus. I have a guard station there. That road goes west out of the city and reaches the Bagrada River near Cigisa. From there, it follows the river valley southwest."

Acceptus waved his hand at the road ahead of them. "This road splits into three, with one going to Inuca, another to Uthina, and the third to the coast at Pupput. I'm taking you to Uthina. Augustus made it a *colonia* for the XIII Gemina, and a garrison of the III Augusta is there. It's where we'll spend the night. When you head back to Carthago, I'll ride southwest from there to Lucana, Thignica, and Agbia, then north to return on the road that passes through Inuca. I should be back in Carthago in eleven or twelve days."

Glabrio's stallion tossed his head again and shook his mane. Acceptus nudged his horse, and they resumed a distance-swallowing trot.

Countless fields of grain and plantings of olive trees flanked the road as they traveled endless miles.

When Uthina appeared in the distance, Glabrio knew two things for certain. Acceptus was the right man for this district, and it would be a long time before he accepted an invitation to join the tireless rider on another inspection.

When he saw the small fortress ahead, the prospect of getting out of the saddle was almost as appealing as that of trading the constantly moving ship for solid ground.

But Acceptus rode by without slowing. Glabrio glanced over his shoulder. Sartorus was close behind them, shoulders sagging. But when he felt Glabrio's gaze, his back straightened and a slight smile accompanied one quick nod.

Acceptus slowed to a walk as they entered the town. "The guard station is just off the agora."

When he finally reined in, the soldier guarding the station door stuck his head in and called out two names.

The centurion swung his leg over his horse's neck and slid off. Glabrio also dismounted and handed his reins to the first soldier who appeared. The second took Acceptus's horse.

A grunt came from behind before Sartorus led his mount up beside them. Glabrio had seen soldiers less weary after a twenty-mile forced march with full gear.

Acceptus chuckled. "Looks like the ride aged you twenty years."

Sartorus's answer was a wry smile and a shrug.

The centurion held out his hand for Sartorus's reins. "Go in and tell my optio to get quarters ready for you and our tribune."

Sartorus's fist hit his chest. With short, careful steps, he disappeared through the door.

When Sartorus was out of earshot, Acceptus handed the reins to the man holding his horse. "Stable them. I'll need mine early. Have the others rubbed down and ready an hour after mine."

A fist hit each chest, and the horses were led away.

Acceptus turned to Glabrio. "You have a good one as your aide. I kept us at a trot half the time. For a first day riding, only the toughest could take it like he has." He tipped his head toward the street leading from the garrison to the agora. "There's a good private bath a couple of blocks down there. You should take him for a hot soak and get him a good massage while you're there. If he ever wants more action than he'll get serving a tribune, I'll gladly take him as one of mine."

One corner of the centurion's mouth lifted. "If you're not used to riding this distance, you might need a massage yourself." The wry smile turned into a chuckle. "You'll probably want one even if you are. When you return, I'll take you both to a better place to eat than in the garrison."

Glabrio followed Acceptus into his office and left his helmet on the side table there. The centurion took a wax tablet out of the desk drawer and picked up a stylus, so Glabrio walked outside to watch the people on the street.

As he waited for Sartorus to come back from the barracks, he leaned against the wall. With only a few hours' observation, Acceptus had seen his optio's worth and wanted his service. When it was time to return to Rome, he could offer Sartorus that choice. A wry smile escaped. He'd be a fool to offer the choice before then. Until the day he left, he wanted Sartorus's dedication and skill for himself.

Chapter 21

PROBLEMS WITH TRIBUNES

Martina's town house, Day 17

Martina was working at her loom when she heard Lepus behind her. "Welcome, Master."

By the time she placed the shuttle on the shelf and turned, Uncle Volero had walked through the vestibulum and was halfway down the peristyle.

"Uncle. It's good to see you."

"The council adjourned early today, so I decided to check on you before I join some friends at the baths." His gaze swept everything that was in view, and his mouth turned down. "I haven't been inside this place before, but I thought it was furnished."

"It is. Furnished enough, anyway. I don't have clients or colleagues coming to visit me during a salutation, so I don't need anything in the vestibulum. I'm not entertaining friends, so I only need those two wicker chairs here in the peristyle." She offered him a smile. "It's very pleasant to read what you gave me from Grandfather's library with the fountain gurgling nearby."

His frown had relaxed back to straight lips. "But when you do have visitors, what will they think?"

"Before you came today, the only visitor I've had was Carthago's new tribune, and I certainly don't want him sitting in something comfortable so he'll stay longer than he has to. I stayed well away from the chairs while we talked so he wouldn't sit without my invitation." She shrugged. "I can't imagine him discussing my Spartan living conditions with anyone."

"I figured it wouldn't take him long to come see you." One corner of Uncle's mouth lifted. "Artoria was quite unhappy with me after he joined us for a family dinner the day after you left." A full smile appeared. "He asked where you were when he noticed there was no place set for you. She was quick to tell him you couldn't stand not being domina so you moved out."

106

He settled into one of the two wicker chairs near the fountain and pointed at the other for her to sit.

Martina relaxed against the back cushion and rested her hands on the blue cloths she was using to avoid getting splinters from the chair's arms. "I'm glad I wasn't there. He's a big part of why I wanted to leave your house so quickly. I don't want to encourage him. Carthago's tribune being too friendly with me might let him discover my faith."

She fingered the fringe on the arm-cloth. "I didn't tell him the name of my glass shop, but he came here first and asked for me by name. I don't know why he assumed I was living next door."

"I gave him a map."

"You did what?" Her eyebrows rose, then plunged. "Why on earth would you do that?"

"He asked me for directions to where you were living. He said he wanted to talk with you about your glass business. I couldn't refuse him when he made it sound like something official." He leaned back in the chair. "After he left, Artoria fussed at me over that. She doesn't want you to distract him from Priscilla."

He lifted the cloth that covered the arm of his chair and picked at a loose wicker strand. "These are worn out. I'll have two new ones delivered. You can move these to the vestibulum for any visitors you don't want to stay long."

He laid the cover back over the rough spot. "Artoria was still mad the next morning, and her saying Glabrio was too interested in you put Priscilla in a foul mood. I ordered her to stop behaving like a spoiled brat. I can't in good conscience encourage any friend to take on a daughter-in-law who can't control herself."

"Priscilla is welcome to him." Martina bit her lip. "I tried to discourage him when he came to look for counterfeit coins in the glass shop. He still said he'd be back the next day to teach me to identify the fakes. But that was two days ago. I'm hoping he's forgotten."

Uncle snorted. "That's unlikely. I think Glabrio is a man who loves a challenge, and you trying to avoid him will make him even more eager to get to know you. Perhaps I should invite him to another family dinner where you join us."

"What would Artoria think of that?"

"She'd hate it, but it's my house, not hers, and you are my niece and ward. The alternative would be for you to invite Glabrio and me to dinner here."

Martina couldn't help but laugh. "I can't do that. He'd think I was succumbing to his manifold charms. You've seen how he is with your daughters."

"I have. It's all he can do not to roll his eyes when Artoria starts flattering him. I don't know how he manages to be so polite to my girls. The only time he got visibly irritated with them was when Sufina said something too critical of you."

She rubbed the back of her neck. "I really haven't done anything to earn his good opinion or to encourage his interest. He's not the kind of man I'd ever want to marry."

"He has no intention of marrying a woman here. We discussed it the night after Artoria's banquet when I dined with Paternus. He's expecting a political marriage to a woman his father chooses. I think he simply finds conversing with you entertaining."

"So, if he shows up here again, I'll try to bore him or offend him so he'll find someone else to entertain him. Getting a woman to like him is a game with him. I saw him playing it with Sufina and Priscilla that first night. No intelligent man could be as interested in what they say as he appeared. My lack of interest bruised his ego, that's all."

"I don't think so. Your modesty is the only reason you think that. He's not looking for a wife, but you intrigue him. For any intelligent man, you're an interesting companion. And if there's one thing I can be certain of with Gaius Acilius Glabrio, it's that he's an intelligent man."

He leaned over and patted her hand where it lay on the chair's arm. "I do intend to have him dine with me again. I gave him a standing invitation. He actually listens to what's said, even if he's faking it with my girls. He's well read and thinks before he speaks. I enjoy his company, and living in a city where he knows almost no one must be lonely. But I won't make you spend any more time with him than you want."

"I think that's best for all of us."

He stood. "Some of the council will already be at the baths." As he walked toward the front door, she strolled beside him. "I'll arrange for two new chairs to be delivered."

Lepus opened the door.

"Thank you, Uncle. I'll look forward to using them." She smiled up at him. "And thank you for dropping in. I hope you'll do it often."

"I intend to. Maybe I'll pick out a chair I like myself and send three." He returned her smile. "Even if you don't need me to take care you, Father would want us to be friends."

He passed through the doorway, and Lepus closed and bolted it.

Martina's smile grew as she headed back to her loom. Grandfather would have been pleased with their growing friendship.

And so was she.

The Baths of Trajan, Rome, late afternoon of Day 17

Saturninus climbed the steps out of the hot-water pool and took a towel from the stack on the nearby table. He toweled first his chest and then his hair.

Hortus, his optio from the Urban Cohort headquarters, entered the room, and Saturninus waved. When Hortus's gaze fell on Saturninus, he strode toward his commander, wax tablet in hand.

That evening, Saturninus was dining with one of his oldest friends. Manius Glabrio was father to the exasperating tribune he'd just transferred to Carthago. It was an excellent opportunity for young Glabrio, but it also meant the young man's zeal for enforcing the letter of the law for both the rabble and the men of the noble orders would no longer cause political and personal inconvenience.

He'd left orders for Hortus to bring anything that came from the latest tribune over Carthago to the baths so he could share news about his son with Manius.

Hortus held out the tablet. "From Portus by courier, Prefect."

Saturninus flipped the seal box lid open. The wax seal was already broken, but that was to be expected. Hortus always prepared the reports for his inspection. But this time, his normally unflappable optio seemed nervous.

As Saturninus scanned the report, his mouth shifted from slight smile to frown and then to scowl.

Nepos was gone when Glabrio reached his new post. He left Carthago eight days before Glabrio's arrival.

He wasn't the most conscientious of his tribunes, but Nepos had always sent his reports on time, even if they were sparse on details. Nepos knew his replacement was coming, and Saturninus had told him he would need to brief Glabrio before he returned to Rome. Nepos had replied that he would do that before catching a ship home.

So, why would Nepos leave more than a week before Glabrio arrived?

As Saturninus rubbed his lower lip, Nepos's father entered the *caldarium* and strolled toward the hot pool. The perfect man to answer that question removed his sandals and stepped into the water.

"Get me a tablet and stylus."

"Yes, Prefect." Hortus strode toward the exit, and Saturninus strolled toward his friend.

"Salve, Lucius." Nepos turned at Saturninus's greeting. "I trust your son is enjoying being back in Rome."

"Marcus." Nepos greeted him with a smile. "I haven't seen him yet. His ship was supposed to dock in Portus yesterday afternoon. I expected him last night, but he'd written that a friend had planned a farewell dinner the night before his departure."

"A friend of your family?"

"He didn't say who. He might have missed his ship, or perhaps he ran into some friends on the way up from Portus and was invited to celebrate his return. Or maybe it took him longer to get his replacement briefed than the half-day he expected." Nepos's smile broadened. "We all enjoyed our friends' company most when we were his age, but I expect him by this evening."

"We did." Saturninus tried to make the smile that was forced appear natural. "I transferred Acilius Glabrio to replace him. He's notorious for his concern about even the smallest details. If something caught Glabrio's attention, he'd ask enough questions to more than fill a day." He tossed the towel across his shoulder. "I'm expected for dinner, so I'll see you later."

Nepos stepped into the hot water and sat on the underwater bench that left the waterline just below his neck. "I'll let my son know you asked about him. He'll probably stop by your headquarters soon."

"I'll look forward to that." The words were easily spoken, but speaking with the missing tribune soon was not what Saturninus expected. Gone for eight days when Glabrio arrived might mean gone forever.

Hortus approached, tablet and stylus in hand.

Saturninus took it. "This message must go by courier tonight to be on the first ship to Carthago tomorrow."

Hortus gave one quick nod. "Yes, Prefect."

Saturninus sat on a bench against the wall, and Hortus positioned himself to keep others away.

He drummed on the tablet's wooden frame with the stylus. He might be putting the son of one friend in danger to find out what happened to the missing son of another.

Nepos had wanted a safe posting for his son. Carthago was a city as civilized as Rome. No Jewish zealots who would kill a Roman officer when given the slightest chance. No barbarian tribesmen eager to cross the Rhine or the Danube for prestige from killing a Roman officer. Being Tribune of the XIII Cohort should have posed no danger to Nepos's son.

Would he have to tell his friend that his only son died in the service of Rome before his political career had even begun?

With a slight shake of his head, he set that thought aside. It was too soon to assume the worst. If Nepos was alive and still in Africa, Glabrio was the man to find him. If Nepos was already dead, Glabrio would get his body home for a proper Roman burial.

Since Titianus was almost killed twice in the year before Glabrio took command of the XI Cohort from him, the young man was fully aware of how dangerous hunting a murderer could be. Caution was born from experience and inclination, and a naturally suspicious man like his close friend's son should be safe enough.

Saturninus rubbed his mouth. It was too late now, but maybe he should have let Glabrio take those eight men he was certain he could trust.

With a sigh, Saturninus pressed the stylus into the wax and began the letter he didn't want to write.

> M. Lollius Paullinus Valerius Saturninus, urban prefect, to G. Acilius Glabrio, tribune of the XIII Cohort, greetings. If you are well, then I am glad. I received your report on the state of affairs in the XIII Cohort upon your arrival, and these are your new orders based on what it contained.

Chapter 22

FAKE AND REAL

Martina's town house, morning of Day 18

Glabrio had allowed enough time for an elite woman to get up and eat breakfast before he led Sartorus to Martina's town house again. If she hadn't still been wearing her hair down three days ago because of her grandfather's death, he would have doubled the time he allowed. Curling and pinning and arranging hair on what looked like scaffolds…that could triple the time to get what some women he knew in Rome would consider presentable.

"You'll be training anyone who might handle coins in the shop. I'll take care of Publilia Martina."

"Yes, Tribune." Sartorus started to walk past the town house door to the entrance to the shop.

"We'll enter like we did before." Glabrio raised his fist and rapped on the plain, weathered planks of the door that opened into her vestibulum.

Rapped, and then waited. But this time he wasn't surprised when the door didn't open right away. He counted to twenty and knocked again. He was about to knock a third time when the door swung open to reveal the boy she called Lepus.

His eyes widened. Lepus meant rabbit, and from all Glabrio had seen, the name fit.

Glabrio stepped in before her rabbit could keep him out. Not that the boy would try. A tribune of Rome could enter any house, any time, but he'd show her more courtesy than that.

"Go tell your mistress Tribune Glabrio is here to teach her to recognize fake coins."

The boy scurried down the peristyle and into a passage at the back of the house.

Glabrio strode to the archway between the vestibulum and peristyle and stopped. He had the right to enter the private part of the house without her invitation, but she'd probably see it as the arrogance of Rome.

Lepus reappeared and came to stand before him. "Mistress Martina said she'd be here shortly."

A nod sent the boy back to close and bolt the door before disappearing into the passage again.

Glabrio crossed his arms and watched where Lepus had disappeared. Only the gurgle of the single fountain broke the silence. It was long past "shortly" by now, and she hadn't appeared. Was she deliberately making him wait, even though she'd be ready for other visitors?

Sartorus shifted beside him. Glabrio glanced at him and found him staring at the passageway with the emotionless expression he'd seen so often on Titianus. When Glabrio turned a fixed gaze on his optio, Sartorus's gaze shifted from doorway to him, and his optio's mouth relaxed into the usual slight smile before he shrugged.

When Martina finally came through the passage, he couldn't help but smile. The wait had been worth it. Her hair hung down to her waist, shiny, wavy, and swinging as she turned to say something to the maid coming behind her. Whatever she said, her maid nodded and went back the way they'd come.

Martina was still in mourning, or maybe he'd interrupted her dressing so she hadn't had time for a fancy style like her aunt and cousins wore. Whatever the reason, it looked good on her...very good.

She stopped three feet from him. "Tribune. Lepus said you wanted me."

"We've come to train your people so they can recognize counterfeits, as I promised."

She offered a social smile. "I see. You and your man can always go directly to the shop. You don't need my permission each time to do that."

One corner of his mouth lifted into a half-smile. "I'm still trying to figure out what crime you might be committing, and I can't do that talking to your shop foreman."

Her eyes widened, as they had before when he teased her. Why was that if she really wasn't doing anything wrong?

When Glabrio held out a hand toward his optio, Sartorus took a sack from his satchel and placed it in Glabrio's palm. Then Glabrio pointed toward the door into the glass shop, and Sartorus left without either saying a word.

He bounced the sack of coins just enough to make it jingle. "Is there a table where I can spread these out?"

She glanced at two wicker chairs and a small table with a tabula board between them.

He felt a smile start before he could stop it. He'd be willing to bet she was good at the game, and he'd challenge her to play after they finished with the coins. He'd go easy on her until he gauged her level of skill.

Or maybe not. Pompeia played well enough to beat Titus often, and Titus often beat him. Would Martina accuse him of Roman arrogance for assuming he was a better player before the first game?

"There's a desk in the tablinum."

He stopped his eyebrows as they started to dip. Once more she'd steered him away from something warm and personal to something cool and businesslike.

He took off his helmet and put it under his arm. "Lead the way."

In the tablinum, she walked through a narrow space between the desk and the wall to reach her chair. Palm up, she directed him to the guest chair. "Please sit."

The room was smaller than the family triclinium at Volero's house. The desk was half the size of the one in his office, which he considered barely large enough when he set his helmet on one end. The guest chair had no arms or cushion, and there was no side table.

A wicker chair sat in the back corner. On it, a scroll nestled against some pillows that had seen the passage of many years. To reach that chair to set down his helmet, he'd have to squeeze past her or step over the strongbox that filled most of the space between the desk and the other wall.

So, he put his helmet on the floor by his feet.

With the grace of a dancer, she lowered herself into her chair, rested her elbows on the desktop, and laced her fingers. "I trust this won't take long."

"That depends on how quickly you learn." He tried a smile and got her straight lips in return. "We'll practice until I think you're proficient."

"Then it won't take long." She leaned back and crossed her arms.

After shaking the counterfeit coins onto the desktop, he spread them out. Then he took some real coins from his purse and stacked them beside the counterfeits. "I'm going to teach you to identify the bad ones first. Then I'll mix real and fake together, and you can sort them."

Her arms remained crossed. "Real and fake." She drew a deep breath and released a sigh.

"Yes. Like the smiles you give me."

Her eyebrows plunged. "I do not give you fake smiles, Tribune. I haven't given you a fake anything, nor do I intend to."

"So, as I watch your smiles run warm and cold, am I seeing what you're really thinking?"

Her lady-like snort raised his eyebrows. "No one can see what another person is thinking. With someone you know well, it's sometimes possible to understand how they feel. It's much harder with strangers, like we are."

"For deep understanding, that's probably true. But I don't have to know you well to guess some of your feelings. I'll get better at it as we get to know each other."

Her eyes veiled. "Perhaps you won't like what you learn."

"That doesn't worry me...unless you really are breaking Roman law."

Her lips tightened, but this time it wasn't to hide her laughter.

He leaned toward her. "I understand that look. I didn't mean to offend."

Her mouth relaxed, but there was still something wrong about her eyes. "You didn't. I told you before that offending me isn't easy." She picked up a coin. "So, what tells me this one is bad?"

First with five of the aurei from her shop, then with three of the denarii Melis had found, he explained the tell-tale signs that cheap metal lay underneath a gold or silver surface.

"I believe I'm ready for your test now." She swept his stack of real coins into the pile of counterfeits, mixed them up, and proceeded to sort them perfectly the first try.

When she finished, she raised one eyebrow. "It appears I've mastered the lesson."

He swept the counterfeits off the desk and into their sack.

After seeing the shabbiness of the furniture in her office, it was tempting to leave the real coins. But there was no way he could "forget" to pick them up without her noticing. She'd already told him she didn't want his money to replace the fakes he'd taken. Was that from pride or because she didn't really need them?

He scooped up the real coins and dropped them back in his purse.

"For someone to learn so quickly...that seems odd, you know. A counterfeiter could do it..."

Her chuckle was the response he'd hoped for. "You seem determined to find some crime I'm guilty of. I can assure you, if there is one, you won't discover what it is."

"I have discovered that you're a woman of many talents, one of them being an uncanny ability to say something I find useful."

"Indeed? That hasn't been my intention. Most of what I say has little value. You'd be wiser to ignore me and seek advice from someone like Uncle Volero. Any advice you get from him should be sound. What I might tell you...well, I've only just begun to be on my own, so it's not from much experience. You'd be wise to seek advice elsewhere."

His smile turned wry. She'd been domina over the household of a rich man who helped run the city. Lack of experience wasn't her problem.

"You're too modest. I've already taken your advice to keep my Roman arrogance concealed, and I've found it most helpful for making me less offensive."

Her head drew back. "That's not what I said…not in those words, anyway."

"Close enough. That and your comment about Carthago's elite being businessmen, not senators, has helped me convince many of the councilmen that I truly want to help solve their problems."

"Hmm."

"So, I'll be expecting more words of wisdom from you during my next visit."

Her eyebrows lowered, "Next visit? Haven't you already shown me all I need to know about these?" She patted the sack of fakes. "I know I've already told you all you need to learn from me."

"About identifying a counterfeit coin…maybe I have. But I still have things to learn from you after I visit the other shops. I told you that yours was the first. If we find bad coins at the others, I'll need to compare your list of customers with theirs."

"But that's something my shop foreman can do. You won't need my help."

"Who knows what I'll need?" He picked up the coin sack and bounced it in his palm. "A city of this size has problems other than counterfeit coins."

She straightened in her chair and tipped her head to look down her nose at him. "Of course, I'll do what I can to help you solve your counterfeiter problem. Like Grandfather always said, it's a citizen's duty to help an officer of Rome when he needs it." Her eyes veiled as she gave him a social smile. "But Uncle tells me you're an intelligent man. I expect you'll do fine without my help."

The click of hobnails on tile came closer, and Sartorus appeared in the tablinum doorway.

"I see your man has finished with my shop people, and it's clear you've finished with me." She stood. "I'm sure you have important duties awaiting you, so don't let me keep you any longer."

She was brushing him off again, and it vexed him more each time. He'd done nothing to deserve it.

He stood and scooped up his helmet. She crossed her arms as he placed it on his head.

If all she wanted was cool formality, that was what he'd give her.

"Thank you for your help, Publilia Martina. It will be noted in my records."

"You are most welcome." Her smile stiffened, and palm up, a wave of her hand invited him to leave.

He made a parade turn and strode from the room. As he led Sartorus toward the front door, his jaw clenched.

Frustrating woman! Just when it seemed they were starting a friendly conversation, something made her draw back.

Maybe Volero could explain it next time they spoke. But if her uncle was trying to find her a husband now, would he discuss what her problem was where others might overhear? Glabrio had heard enough at Father's banquets with the leaders of Rome to know how eagerly gossip was used to undercut political rivals.

At her age, why wasn't she already married? Had her grandfather felt he couldn't part with her? Had he chosen to make his own life easy by having her run his house when he should have found her a husband to give her one of her own? Was there some problem that kept him from arranging a marriage?

Glabrio opened the front door before Sartorus could reach for the handle and pulled it shut behind them. She could bolt it herself. She obviously liked keeping people out.

Or maybe it was only him she wanted at arm's length.

The scorching sun beat down on them from a cloudless African sky as he led Sartorus at a brisk pace back to headquarters. Armor that was comfortable enough in Rome was too hot here.

He rubbed under his chin where the helmet's cheek guards didn't get in the way. His fingers came away damp with sweat. Perhaps he'd start going bareheaded when he walked around the city. At least until the provincial governor returned. His body armor already declared him the tribune in charge.

He took off the helmet and wiped more sweat from his forehead. If he went to the baths for a swim to cool off, Volero might be there. His eyes rolled at the thought of another evening of the flattering mother and the flirting daughters, but if her uncle was dining at home tonight, he'd ask to join him.

If he was going to overcome Martina's dislike, he needed to know what caused it. Was the problem with him or something about her? He had a standing invitation to dine at Volero's house. It was time to use it.

◆

Martina followed the tribune to the office door, but not so quickly he'd see her. This visit had not started well. Why did he keep trying to get her to talk with him, teasing her in a way that would actually be gratifying if she wanted his attention?

She shook her head. She didn't, of course, even if Artoria was convinced she did. Handsome, rich, and powerful didn't matter in her eyes any more than they did in the eyes of God.

But his last words and the way he left gave some hope that he finally got that message. He called her by her full name, not just Martina as if she were a friend. His "it will be noted in my records" was as cool and businesslike as she could ever have wanted. But the set of his jaw betrayed the anger underlying those words.

There really was no reason for him to seek her out again. Anything he needed related to the fake coins he could get from Ceraulo.

She rubbed the back of her neck as Lepus scurried through the peristyle to bolt the door behind the tribune and his assistant. Thank goodness that optio had come when he did. It gave a good reason to end their conversation. At least it felt that way to her.

But there was that flash in his eyes when she said she considered his business with her finished. The lift of his chin as he placed the helmet on his head. And the way he turned, like she'd seen soldiers do after saluting an officer.

Platana appeared beside her. "How did it go?"

"I finally made him angry." Martina fingered the hollow of her neck.

"Did you offend him enough to drive him away for good?"

"I don't know." She wrapped her hand around the lamb cameo. "I hope so. The way he keeps asking if I'm breaking Roman law...he says it like he's only teasing, but what if he discovers I really am?"

Chapter 23

A New Plan of Attack

Baths of Trajan, afternoon of Day 18

At the baths, Glabrio slipped his bronze cuirass and sandals into one sack and the padded vest, skirt of leather strips, forearm guards, and tunic into another. He tied the sacks together and draped them over the shoulder of the youth who would follow him around until he got dressed again.

The helmet he handed to Sartorus. "Take this back to headquarters. I'm looking for Volero Martinus, but I won't need you for the rest of the day. Bathe, relax, do whatever you want. I'll see you tomorrow morning."

"Thank you, Tribune." Sartorus tucked the helmet under his arm and left.

Glabrio strolled through the tepidarium with its warm pool, the caldarium with its steamy atmosphere and hot tubs, and the frigidarium with its cold tubs without finding Volero. But when he returned to the tepidarium for a massage, Volero stood near the wall where his valet was applying scented oils and scraping them off with a *strigil.*

Martina's uncle raised a hand upon seeing him, and Glabrio strolled over to join him.

"It's good to see you, my young friend. I didn't expect to find you frequenting the baths so early in the day."

"After a few hours in armor under your African sun, I came for a swim."

"I was heading there myself." Volero swept his hand toward the door leading outside to the pool in the center of the garden where men also exercised.

They strolled through the arched exit, and Glabrio cleared his throat. He'd never asked a man if he could eat at his house before, but Volero had made the offer himself the other night.

"I was wondering…if you're dining at home soon, would you be wanting some company?"

Volero's broad smile answered before he spoke the first words. "Come this evening. I have no other commitment. If you'd like, we can play tabula or latrunculi before or after dinner. Or both."

"I'd like that."

"Good. It should be more entertaining than my daughter interrogating you about the shops in Rome."

"She was merely curious. It's a common thing with women. But I'm sorry if it bored you to have such…" What could he say without offending?

"Stimulating conversation?" Volero chuckled. "It's common when a man has two daughters of marriageable age and a wife eager to get them married. It was amusing to watch you try to hide how bored you were."

"But your family's history in this province…that was anything but boring." Glabrio couldn't have planned a better opening for satisfying his own curiosity. "Your niece…she's of marriageable age as well, almost past that age if she were living in Rome. Why is that? She should appeal to any father looking for an intelligent wife for his son, and any man with even one eye could see she's a beauty."

Volero's smile stiffened, then relaxed. "I was already living at one of the family estates off the road to Uthina when my brother died and she came to live with Father. Before Father's health failed, I didn't really get to know her. She's about the same age as my oldest girl, so she was too young to draw my attention when I visited Father."

Valero paused, as if he'd said all he meant to. But what he'd said had no bearing on the question. Odd, because his question had been clear enough.

"But your father didn't arrange a marriage for her." Stating the obvious should bring Volero back to the question.

"My brother moved to his wife's estate when they married. Her family has owned it since before the land became a Roman province, and she didn't like city living. Their Roman ancestry dates back to a centurion who fought with Legion III under Scipio Aemilianus. After Carthage was destroyed, he became part of the garrison of the new province with the governor in Utica and never left Africa."

"The estate near Cigisa. She mentioned it was a special place."

Volero massaged his neck. "I've never been there. It's on the Bagrada river. Very convenient for shipping wheat and olive oil down to Utica and then along the coast to Carthago."

"Is it a large estate?"

"Smaller than any of mine, but it's fairly large. It has excellent clay deposits for most pottery, and its ornamental red slip wares are prized, at least in this province."

"Martina said she made appliques for that part of the business as a child.

But that doesn't explain why she isn't married." He'd raised the question three times now. Why did Volero keep sidestepping it?

Her uncle's mouth opened, then closed, as if he was weighing his next words. "My brother had an informal agreement with a friend. Father decided to honor it. I don't know the details. Martina is sui iuris now, so what she chooses to do about it…that's not my responsibility. Her Cigisa steward runs that estate without oversight. I'll help with her glassworks, as needed. Beyond that, she likes to make her own decisions." Volero led them down the steps into the swimming pool. "As you might have noticed, Father raised her to have opinions of her own."

"Like many Roman women, given half a chance."

Volero's wry smile mirrored his own.

At last, his question had been answered. Glabrio rubbed his jaw. How to ask the next question without making it seem Volero was derelict in his duties as a guardian? "I've been inside her town house. It wasn't quite what I expected."

Volero chuckled. "You mean the furniture? That's what was left behind by the last renters. She claims it's all she needs, but I ordered three new chairs for the peristyle. The ones she was using had lumpy cushions and splinters on the arms. I told her she could move the old ones to the vestibulum for the visitors she doesn't want to stay too long. I haven't seen what's in the rest of the house yet."

Volero ducked under the water and then stood, pushing back his wet hair from his forehead. "She's a gracious woman. She won't turn down my gifts. She'll appreciate any thing I do, no matter how small, even if she protests that I'm helping too much."

"Hmm." She'd had no qualms about rejecting his help. But maybe she only accepted it from family.

Volero tipped his head toward the changing room. "I'd better skip the swim and let Artoria know we have company coming. I told her already you weren't looking for a Carthaginian wife, but she'll want the girls to dress for you anyway. But we'll retreat to the gameboard in the library as soon as we eat."

He signaled his valet, who was standing near the entrance to the tepidarium. "Grandfather encouraged Martina to read so he'd have someone to discuss what he read himself. She loved that room so he put a chair in the corner especially for her. I often found them both reading, but I never find my daughters there."

Volero climbed out of the pool. "When will you be coming?"

"I'm going to swim a few lengths of the pool and attend to something at headquarters first."

"Later, then." Volero and his valet left.

Glabrio pushed off from the pool wall. He was a powerful swimmer, and each stroke washed away tension. He'd always found the pool a good place to think. Something about the rhythm of the strokes cleared his head.

Maybe he just needed to find the right gift, and she'd take it from him. She loved her grandfather's library. A new scroll or codex from Titus always made Pompeia happy. But what did Martina read? Greek as well as Latin? Philosophy, history, natural history? Would a duumvir of Carthago have the poetry of Ovidius or Lucanus? He'd have Virgilius's Aeneid at the very least. Even men who didn't like poetry had the Aeneid in their libraries in Rome. It was Rome's founding tale, but Carthage was in it as well.

After Volero told him why she kept him at arm's length, he'd ask what gift for her library could help him change that.

Volero's town house, evening of Day 18

When Glabrio arrived at Volero's town house, a boy took him through the peristyle and into the side courtyard. Before entering the library where Volero sat reading, Glabrio scanned the balcony above to see where Martina's room had been. No trace of her remained that could tell him.

Volero rolled up the scroll and pointed its silver lion-head knobs at the desk before placing it in a cubicle. On the desktop sat a tabula board made of marble inlaid with two opposing rows of black onyx triangles

Glabrio picked up a game piece of polished jade. "Your board reminds me of the one Father has." Smooth and cool, the stone felt good in his hand. "I brought a wooden board that folds. It has tabula on one side and latrunculi on the other. With bone rondels and kings that were antler tips, it's light and small enough to fit in a compartment inside the trunk with my scrolls and codices."

A jade vine encircled the onyx playing area, and he traced a tendril. "The trunk and board were a parting gift from a friend whose father had given them to him to take to his first legion posting."

Volero joined him at the desk. "So, your board has traveled more of the Empire than I ever hope to."

"No. His father's health began failing before he could join a frontier legion. So, he stayed to care for his father until he died and spent ten years over the XI Urban Cohort. This is the board's first trip away from Rome."

Volero's finger traced a jade leaf with an inlaid stem of gold. "This board was my father's and my grandfather's before that. Someday it will be my son's."

A corner of Glabrio's mouth lifted. "It's the history that makes something precious, not what it's made from."

"Indeed." Volero's smile drooped. "Father and I spent many hours at this board." He cleared his throat and forced a smile. "It will be a while before the dinner is ready. We can start a game now and resume it whenever the dinner conversation grows…tiresome."

"I leave the decision about when to resume playing to you." Glabrio lifted the strap holding his sword over his head, wrapped it around the brass-and-wood scabbard, and laid it by the board.

"You brought no guards with you tonight." Volero fingered the brass inlay on the scabbard. "And no helmet. Have you decided the hazards of Carthago don't require the precautions you took in Rome?"

Glabrio rested his hands on the back of the guest chair. "I suspect even this is more than what's required. My friend who was tribune in Rome before me almost never took a guard. He often said, 'If a tribune in full armor can't walk safely through Rome at night, no one can.'"

"Was that before or after someone tried to kill him?"

"Both. But it had changed from something he believed to a family joke by the time I heard it." Glabrio fingered the handle of the dagger he still wore. "He'd found it true in Rome for his first eight years. Then the client of a powerful man hired an assassin to keep him from tying a senator to two murders. I haven't been here long enough to make that kind of enemy."

"Nepos found it safe, so I'm sure it is." Volero gripped the hilt and pulled the gladius from its scabbard. When he felt the blade's edge, his brow furrowed. "It's sharp enough to kill. I expected a duller edge…more for show than anything."

"In Rome, my men trained like legionaries at the Praetorian Fortress. I brought my optio from there, and he likes to keep weapons battle-ready."

Volero sheathed the sword. "May the gods guard your safety so you don't ever need that."

Glabrio shrugged. "Serving Rome well isn't always risk free."

He scanned the shelves that lined one wall of the room. "You said Martina loved this library. I can see why. She must miss having one."

"She doesn't have as many scrolls, but she has some. Whatever her father had was left at the estate, but she inherited what her grandmother owned here. I sent some of her favorites from this collection with her. Father liked her to read Seneca aloud to him. He was a committed Stoic, as I am." Volero touched the scroll with red-eyed lion-headed knobs. "I gave her the one she was reading to him the day before he died."

"Would she like others?"

Volero stared at him, then one eyebrow rose. "Why do you ask?"

"I brought a few of my own favorites from Rome, but not enough. I'll be adding to my library here. Martina is helping me with a counterfeiting problem, and I'd like to show my appreciation with a scroll she'd enjoy."

Volero's mouth twitched as he masked a smile. "I can find out, if you'd like. She might or might not enjoy your way of showing appreciation."

"I'd like that."

They sat and faced each other across the board. Glabrio picked up a handful of game pieces. His were disks of rust-colored jasper, polished to a soft shine. Volero used the jade. They had each made several plays when the girl appeared at the door.

"Dinner is ready, Master."

Volero placed his next piece and returned the others in his hand to a small stack beside the board. "We'll finish this after dinner, and I hope you'll come often for more of the same."

"With pleasure."

As Glabrio followed his host to the family triclinium, he was content with what he'd learned today. Her uncle didn't seem to know that she'd been reluctant to talk with him, and maybe it was better not to tell him. Perhaps the right scroll would change that, anyway.

Good games, good food, good conversation...this evening at Volero's was providing everything he wanted, including a new plan of attack for getting Publilia Martina to see him as more than an arrogant Roman destined to remain a stranger.

Chapter 24

STRATEGIC MOVES

The entertainment district, Day 19

With Centurion Longinus leading the way, Glabrio headed southwest from the cohort headquarters by the Forum. Today was his tour of the entertainment venues that Longinus's men watched over when thousands gathered for races or gladiatorial games.

As they approached the stone walls of the circus, Longinus pointed back the way they'd come. "There's a theater north of the Byrsa, but we won't visit today unless you especially want to. It holds about five thousand people. I station men there and in the neighboring streets when plays or musical performances are scheduled. That's mostly to make certain there aren't too many robberies as people are going home afterward."

"That won't be necessary." Glabrio turned back to face the two stories of arches that made the outer wall of the circus. "I'll be attending a performance there soon, and I'll see what your men do then."

"You probably won't see them do much. There's never a problem with the ones who attend." Longinus cleared his throat. "It's mostly the upper classes there. It's not like with the circus, where people are so caught up in whether their teams are winning. Fights break out between fans of opposing factions, especially the Greens and Blues. Both factions train charioteers here to get them ready for the circus in Rome."

Several trumpet blasts sounded, and most who'd been talking in the plaza around the circus headed toward the entrances. A squad of soldiers stood by each doorway.

"Sometimes fights start inside the circus. Sometimes they're outside between races." Longinus pointed at a squad, then swept his finger along the length of the building where two dozen more were stationed. "The circus will seat about forty-five thousand, so most of my troops are in and around it on race days."

He pointed at the amphitheater a few blocks away that towered over the adjacent buildings. "We'll visit there next. It can seat about thirty thousand. There were games before the governor left on his tour of the main cities along the coast. There won't be more until after he returns. But there are races at the circus three or four times a week."

"Do you know the doorkeeper for the stalls and staging area behind the gates?"

Longinus's head drew back. "No. If I may ask, is there a reason I should?"

"The Praetorian Guard does what your men do here, but the areas around the Circus Maximus and Flavian Amphitheater were part of my cohort's responsibility in Rome. The tribune before me found it valuable to talk with the doorkeeper at the circus to learn about potential problems. I did as well. Sometimes a slave sees and hears things you want to know because men don't watch their tongues around those they see as little more than furniture or livestock."

Messala, the son of a councilman who liked to gamble with Nepos, approached with his hand raised in greeting. Glabrio lifted his in reply.

"Anyone, slave or free, who thinks you value what he tells you is often eager to help when you need it."

Lowered eyebrows accompanied Longinus's frown before he nodded. "I see your point." A crooked smile appeared. "There might be others worth knowing as well."

"Tribune Glabrio." Messala stopped when he reached them. "It's a pleasure to see you again. I was just thinking about how much I miss having Nepos join me here." He sighed. "But...while a departed friend can never be fully replaced, it does leave room for adding a new one."

Missing a friend? Glabrio's mouth twitched. Messala's eyes didn't match what his mouth was saying. Messala was missing Nepos's willingness to bet more than he should on teams that didn't win.

Messala's gaze swept Longinus before returning to Glabrio. "My friends and I attend the races often. Perhaps you'd like to join us?"

"Perhaps." Glabrio glanced at Longinus in time to see his centurion's fleeting frown. "I hear Tribune Nepos joined you regularly."

"He did. He's a man who appreciates fine horses and the men who love winning more than staying alive." Again, the eyes didn't match the friendly smile. "Perhaps you're one of the same?"

"For most people, staying alive is considered winning. If a man's going to die, it should be for a reason greater than thrilling the crowds."

Messala's chuckle sounded forced. "But wealth and fame come to those who win enough while Fortuna smiles. That's true of the charioteers and of the men who bet on them to win. Great risks bring the greatest rewards. Will you join me today? Or perhaps next week?"

"Not today, but perhaps in the future." Glabrio felt his centurion tense beside him. But Longinus needn't worry that he had another commander who spent more time on his own pleasure than on his duties. "As I don't know yet what I'll need to be doing next week, I must answer your invitation with no more than a perhaps."

Messala's smile stiffened as the fake friendliness faded from his eyes.

"Duty comes before pleasure, and as tribune, I plan to set an example for my men. If I do come, it won't be for the full day. But perhaps we'll run into each other. Longinus tells me as many as forty-five thousand attend, so I can't guarantee I'll find you in that size of crowd."

The two men Messala had joined at Volero's banquet had stopped by an entrance. Messala raised a hand in response to their wave.

"I see your friends are waiting. May Fortuna favor you if you choose to bet."

"She usually does." With a cocky grin, Messala strode toward his friends.

Glabrio turned to Longinus. "What next?"

Longinus pointed toward the amphitheater. "There are no games right now, so I can get you a private tour of the areas where the gladiators and animals wait for their fights. The holding cells for criminals are there, too."

"Excellent. I never toured the underground chambers of the Flavian Amphitheater in Rome."

As the centurion over public entertainments led him toward the amphitheater, Glabrio glanced over his shoulder. A race had started, and the high-pitched screams of the women blended with the bellows of the men to drown out the words Longinus was speaking.

But that didn't matter. Longinus would gladly repeat them if they might be important. Glabrio had now seen what Sartorus had predicted after his first meeting with his centurions. Longinus knew his district, and he was content to have a tribune who wanted to know what was going on, who wanted to do his duty. He hadn't liked that Nepos didn't.

Verus, Acceptus, Longinus—three of his four centurions were men he could count on to do their jobs well. Dubitatus—he was adequate, anyway.

Perhaps Father was right that Saturninus had given him an exceptional opportunity for a young tribune to show what he could do. For whatever reason that was, he would make the most of it.

Martina's town house, morning of Day 20

Knock and wait. It was what Glabrio expected when he came to Martina's town house. He'd sent Sartorus ahead to find the shops they were looking for. A tribune in armor would only get in the way of his optio observing the shopworkers without changing what they'd normally do.

His knuckles hadn't hit the third time before the door swung open. Lepus jumped like a startled rabbit as Glabrio stepped across the threshold.

"Tell your mistress Tribune Glabrio is here."

"I can't, Tribune." Fast blinks accompanied the boy's nervous smile. "Mistress Martina isn't back yet."

"When will she return?"

"She has returned." The feminine voice behind him triggered a smile. The rabbit had opened the door right away because he was waiting for her.

Glabrio turned to find Martina with her maid and a man he hadn't seen before. So, she had at least three serving in her household, but there couldn't be many more.

"Martina, I'm glad I found you at home. I was in the area, so I thought I'd update you on the counterfeit situation."

Her eyes narrowed. "In the area."

"My optio is checking into something for me, and I thought it best if he did it alone. Having a tribune along…" He tapped his cuirass. "People notice this, and I didn't want my presence to change what people would normally do."

"I see."

The man with her had gone on through the peristyle and into a passageway that probably went to the kitchen. Her maid still stood behind her.

Martina looked over her shoulder. "The tribune doesn't want his presence to change what people do, so you can go work on what we discussed."

"Yes, mistress." With a tip of her head toward first Martina, then Glabrio, her maid followed the man.

Palm up, Martina swept her hand toward two wicker chairs by the wall in the vestibulum. They were the shabby ones he'd seen in the peristyle, the ones Volero had told her to offer to visitors she didn't want to stay too long.

But an invitation to sit, no matter how worn out the chair, was still an invitation to sit. He settled into the larger of the two and stretched out his arms along the back and arms of the chair.

"I should get one of these. It's more comfortable than the chair I have in my quarters."

He mirrored her palm-up gesture toward the other chair.

She remained standing. Then she moved a step closer, triggering his smile. He was a tall man, and she was a short woman. Somewhere she'd learned how to counter that disadvantage by standing close to a sitting man. Artoria didn't use the trick with Volero, not that it would work on him anyway. Martina would soon learn it didn't work on him, either.

"You said you were going to update me on the counterfeits." She clasped her hands at her waist.

"I've found more that were used for something other than glass. One of the councilmen told me his steward had some, but he wasn't sure which of his enterprises had received them. His steward narrowed it down to three, so Sartorus is checking for shops selling the same kind of merchandise on the streets around your workshop."

He fingered the fringe on the blue cloth draped on the chair arm. "I have to wait somewhere for him to return, and I don't want to draw attention to myself by standing in the street outside your house. That could get your neighbors wondering why an officer of Rome was leaning against the wall by your door. People are intrigued by anything odd, and the smallest thing can be fodder for the local gossips. But if I appear to be visiting a beautiful young woman…"

He let his best crooked smile leak out. "That's the kind of gossip that wouldn't endanger my investigation."

Her mouth twitched, but was that almost a smile that she kept from escaping or irritation that she concealed just in time?

"I'd rather have my neighbors wondering what you were doing outside my house than what you were doing inside."

His laugh escaped before he could stop it. Depending on the meaning of that twitch, what would she think of him laughing?

"Your uncle would approve of that answer if he was trying to arrange a marriage for you. But he told me your father arranged something unofficial many years ago. A dowry contract could make it hard to change, but an unofficial agreement is just that…unofficial. The slightest thing could change it. Perhaps your caution is warranted."

Her eyebrows lowered, and what the twitch meant became clear. "I don't know why Uncle told you about that, and I hardly think that's something we should be discussing."

"He told me because I asked."

Her brow furrowed. "Hmm." Her delicate hand slipped beneath the thick, wavy hair cascading down her back to massage the back of her neck. "I can't imagine why."

Footsteps in the peristyle grew closer, and her man came with them.

"Mistress Martina, Colina has a question about the next step you were showing her, and there's something in the household accounts you'll want to look at."

"Thank you, Clavus. I'll be right there."

As her man headed back toward the kitchen area, Glabrio had to admire her strategic planning. He'd be willing to bet he'd just seen what Martina had told her maid to work on before sending her to the kitchen.

"Please, go take care of that. The sound of your fountain is relaxing, and this chair is comfortable enough, so I don't mind waiting alone for however long it takes you to attend to what your steward needs. I'll be looking forward to talking with you when you return."

She lifted her chin and looked down her nose. "I don't know what else we could discuss that you'd find interesting."

Some women used that move while flirting, but it was always followed by a seductive smile and inviting eyes. He could safely wager she didn't play that game.

But if she really didn't know what would interest him, he had two good options.

"I just dined with your uncle, and we played tabula in his library. He mentioned it was one of your favorite rooms. Two people can always discuss what they like to read."

"I suppose they can." She fingered the silver filigree bracelet that she'd worn each time he saw her.

He tipped his head toward the peristyle. "And I noticed you have a tabula board set up by the pool. That's always a good way to spend time together. Volero and I found that we're well matched when I dined with him two days ago. We're planning to play often."

Her gaze locked onto the tabula board and the cluster of three new chairs near the fountain. Then she sat in the shabby chair near him.

It was hard not to chuckle. She'd made another strategic move to keep him from rising and going to the gameboard without her express invitation.

But when it came to strategy, a woman of Carthago was no match for a tribune of Rome.

"I assume you have that board out so you and your uncle can play. Perhaps you'd enjoy me as an opponent as well."

She steepled her fingers and rubbed both sides of her nose. "Perhaps."

If that meant what it did when he rubbed his own nose...

Three thuds from a fist hitting the door pulled her gaze away from him.

With no sign of her rabbit nearby, Glabrio rose and let Sartorus in.

The quiet gasp behind him as he bolted the door brought a wry smile. She hadn't expected his optio in civilian clothes.

"Sartorus is my spy today. A man out of uniform will learn many things a man in uniform cannot. So, I really did need a place to wait where I was out of sight. The report of a tribune patrolling the area could stop a criminal from doing what he usually does, even when he thinks no soldiers are watching."

He stood. "But if anyone saw me today, I would appear to be visiting a beautiful young woman. That's the kind of gossip that can't hurt our investigation." His mouth curved into the woman-pleasing smile that had no effect on this woman. "And it has made the wait much more pleasant. So, I thank you for once more helping an officer of Rome."

She gave him a subdued social smile. "I'm only fulfilling the duty of any good citizen." Her smile broadened, but her eyes didn't warm. "But since I'm not looking for a husband and you certainly don't want me for a wife, your visits might seem less suspicious if you visited my glass shop instead. Ceraulo would let you sit in the sales room or workroom while you waited. You might enjoy watching the glassblowers, and leaving with something you spent money on would appear less suspicious than spending time with me."

Glabrio felt Sartorus stiffen beside him. He didn't need to see his optio's face to suspect what his aide was thinking.

"But neither could match the pleasure of talking with you. I learn something valuable each time."

"I don't know what that could be." She crossed her arms.

"Maybe I'll tell you next time."

She opened her mouth, then closed it before speaking. He'd pay a day's wages to know what she almost said.

"Thank you for your hospitality. If you ever come to the cohort headquarters when I'm there, I'll be pleased to return it."

"It's been a pleasure." Her lips formed the expected words, but her eyes contradicted them. Still, there was some truth in them. It had been a pleasure for him.

He led Sartorus out the door and turned toward the Forum. When they'd walked three blocks, he turned to his aide. "Did you find what you were looking for?"

"Maybe. At least in part."

As they continued walking, Glabrio listened to Sartorus's description of the three shops he'd found that might be of interest. But his thoughts kept drifting to Martina's "perhaps" when he suggested they play a board game. Might she enjoy it as much as he knew he would? Next time he came, he'd find out.

Chapter 25

NICE ENOUGH

This time, Martina didn't wait for Lepus to come bolt the door. With some satisfaction, she slid the bolt across and turned the handle down so no one could work it back from the outside. That should keep the tribune out if he returned.

A sigh escaped. Of course, she'd have to let him in again if he did. He really hadn't done anything that could justify refusing him. It was silly to think he'd try to enter uninvited.

Uncle liked him. If she didn't have to hide her faith from him, she might find talking with him pleasant herself. After the way she dismissed him the last time, who would have thought he'd forgive the insult and act like he'd forgotten it happened?

Why had he asked Uncle if she was betrothed? They both knew it had no bearing on him.

She massaged her neck, as she had when he'd confessed his unwarranted curiosity about that. If Clavus hadn't walked up, would he have explained why it interested him?

She covered her mouth with steepled fingers and shook her head. How much clearer could she make it that his visits were not welcome, that he should talk with her shop steward, not her, if he needed them to help?

He'd be back. Next time, would she be able to keep him from sitting at the gameboard and insisting they play?

Uncle thought she should be boringly pleasant to make him go away. Would playing a game where she deliberately lost speed that up? Could she lose a game convincingly, or would he know she was deliberately making stupid moves?

A throat cleared behind her, and she turned to find Clavus.

"When you didn't come, I thought I should check on you."

"He was going to wait until I came back, so I decided to stay and keep trying to get rid of him."

"Do you want me to find a reason to stay in the peristyle whenever he's here, just in case?"

Clavus's concern drew her warmest smile. "No. He wouldn't try to do anything you could protect me from, but I appreciate your willingness." She squeezed her neck and arched her back to relieve the tension the tribune caused. "Uncle thinks he's a good man, and I have no reason to question that. He's just too…curious about me, and I don't want to encourage him."

She followed a deep breath with a deeper sigh. Was now the time to let her steward know her secret? A still, small voice inside her said yes.

"It wouldn't be safe for him to learn I'm a Christian."

"About that, if you don't mind my asking…" He looked into her eyes, then down at his feet, then back at her face.

"You can ask me a question any time, Clavus." A dangerous offer to make, but there was no taking it back.

"It's not just my question, Mistress. Colina and Petale have been asking, too." He clasped his hands and looked down again.

"What have you all been asking?" Martina laced her fingers at her waist and tipped her head to show her interest. She wasn't Artoria. He didn't have to fear her if she didn't like what he said.

"Mistress Juliana…she treated all of us like people, not just something she owned like your grandfather's first wife had. We thought it might be because she was a Christian, but it never felt safe to ask."

Clavus glanced over his shoulder when Platana walked up behind him. "Your grandfather always led the daily rites for the household gods. He did it like they were important, like they actually did something. So does Master Volero. Mistress Artoria acts like they matter, and only a fool would risk making her angry with a question she didn't like."

He rubbed his jaw. "But you never led them, even when your grandfather was out of town." He lowered his gaze to the floor, then raised it to her face. "Or when he was dying. You're just like Mistress Juliana in how you treat everyone, so we thought you might be a Christian, too."

He cleared his throat. "So, now that the risk of what Master Volero and Mistress Artoria might do is gone, we want to learn about the god you believe in."

Martina's heart skipped a beat. Like Juliana, she'd longed for years to live where she never had to hide her faith.

Thank You, God, for bringing to me this freedom to share what I know of You. Please let them listen with all their hearts and decide to believe.

"You're right. Juliana was a Christian, and she taught me about what Jesus did and why she believed in Him. I saw the truth in everything she said, and I became a Christian, too." She looked past him to see Platana nodding. "And so is Platana."

Clavus turned toward Platana, eyebrows raised. Her nod and smile turned him back to Martina.

"I'm delighted to know that you want to hear about our faith in Jesus. We'd both love to tell you. This evening, after everything is done for the day, we'll meet around the table where you all eat. Platana and I will start explaining everything."

The widest grin she'd ever seen lit Clavus's face. "I'll go tell the others, Mistress."

He tipped his head to Platana as they passed, and she joined Martina in the vestibulum.

"It looks like God is answering your prayers about finding Christians for this household."

Martina grinned at her Christian sister and best friend. "It's a start. Each person must choose whether to believe, but I think they will."

Platana took an end of Martina's palla, and Martina turned to unwrap herself from the long rectangular shawl.

"So, how did your conversation with the tribune go? He seemed very glad to see you."

"He was more satisfied with it than I was." Her gaze settled on the door through which he'd gone. "He didn't tell me anything I needed to know, so it was only an excuse to bother me."

Platana folded the palla. "Bother or impress? It's obvious he likes you."

Remembering the tribune's teasing smile triggered Martina's frown. "It's probably impress, but not because he likes me. I think that's a game he plays with all young women. I've become a challenge, and he's determined to win."

"What if you let him think he has?"

"Maybe he'd go away, but I wouldn't give false hope to a man who was actually interested in me. I can't in good conscience encourage one who really isn't."

Platana tucked the folded shawl under her arm. "Maybe you can be just nice enough to let him think you find his company pleasant so he doesn't feel you're a challenge anymore?"

"I suppose I can try that. What I'm doing certainly isn't working. But if any of my people decide to believe as we do, then there's a risk to everyone if he figures out my faith. In a Roman tribune's eyes, that would put us all on the wrong side of Roman law."

With eyes closed and steepled fingers, she rubbed both sides of her nose.

It wouldn't only be in the tribune's eyes. In truth, they would be, and she knew what that could mean.

With the gurgle of the fountain beside her, Martina sat in her new chair, reading, when Lepus trotted past her to answer the knock on the front door.

Her uncle entered and strolled into the peristyle. He settled into the chair beside her that he'd selected for himself.

"It's good to see you, Uncle." She patted her chair's arm. "This chair...it's delightful to sit in it. The height and curve of the arms, the thickness of the cushions...it's like they made it especially for me."

"I described you to them, and they gave me what was most often chosen by women your size." He leaned his head back against the cushion of his high-backed chair. "This is comfortable, too. Perhaps I should get another one just like it for my library."

He stretched out his legs. "What are you reading?"

"Viator lent me some writings about glass." She set the scroll aside. "I just finished the section in Plinius's Natural History. Did you know glass was discovered by accident when some merchants built a fire on a beach near Ptolemais in Syria? There weren't any rocks there, so they used some lumps of the nitre they were carrying as cargo to support their kettles. Where the nitre sat on the sand, it made little streams of molten glass."

Lepus stood before them, holding a tray with two goblets and a flagon of diluted wine.

"Hmm." Volero tapped one goblet, and Lepus half-filled both. "Good things sometimes come by accident."

"He wrote that you can blow it into shapes, turn it in a lathe, or engrave it like silver. My men do all of that next door."

She rested her hand on two more scrolls that lay on the gameboard. "There's really not much in Plinius's volume, but Viator said these were full of details about how different glasses are made. After I read them, I'll discuss what I've learned with Ceraulo and see if what I've read is what he does."

"Viator wouldn't give you something that was wrong."

"I know, but there are often small changes that can make something better. I saw that in the pottery workshop at the estate. Sometimes not better so much as different so people want to buy it because it's novel."

Volero took a sip. "It would appear that Father chose the right thing for your inheritance."

"I think so, too." She leaned back in her chair and swept the room with her hand. "Especially since it came with this town house. Living here is very pleasant."

"Did you bring enough people with you?"

"I did. The household is running smoothly."

She picked up her goblet, and Lepus went back to the kitchen. With her middle finger, she traced the rim. "The only thing disturbing my peace is the tribune. He was here again this morning."

"What did my young friend want?"

"From me, only conversation while his optio was going around visiting some of the shops near here. It's something to do with the counterfeiters he's hunting."

She set the goblet on the table beside the gameboard and picked up a bone rondel that was one of the tabula game pieces. "He said you and he were well matched and enjoyed playing."

"We are, and I do find him good company."

"He said he'd be coming here again. I've been quite rude to him, but he keeps showing up."

"Hmph. You being rude is hard to imagine."

"Well, maybe not rude like Priscilla or Sufina, but I did let him know that I didn't want to spend my time talking with him."

"And you only made him want to talk with you more." He rubbed his jaw. "He wants to get to know you. It's time to be nice enough to let him feel he knows you as well as he wants. Nice enough, but not too nice."

"How on earth will I know what's nice enough but not too nice?"

"You'll know as you do it. I've watched you get Artoria to change what she's doing and think it was her idea. You'd have done well on the council if you were a man." He took a sip. "You interest Glabrio because you aren't impressed by him like most young women. But he said he learned some useful things from you. What did you tell him?"

"Nothing of importance, but he says I told him Roman arrogance would offend people, so he's been trying not to show it."

Uncle's guffaw ended as a chuckle. "You told him he was arrogant and offensive. No wonder he's intrigued by you. I'd be willing to bet no one ever told him that before."

"That wasn't exactly what I said, but he heard it that way."

"Any man would." Uncle shook his head as his grin faded.

"This morning he showed too much interest in whether I was betrothed or not. I told him it was not his concern."

"When he asked me, I used Father's excuse that your father had arranged something years ago. He's planning to marry a Roman woman from a powerful political family, one that his father chooses. He told me so himself, so whatever he asks, it's only curiosity."

"His curiosity is dangerous. He teases me about committing some crime against Rome that he hasn't figured out yet."

Uncle Volero leaned forward and patted her hand. "You can let him get to know you enough to lose interest without him learning of your faith. If you don't want him seeking you out, that's all you have to do."

"You make it sound easy." She wrapped the lamb necklace in her hand. "And with God's guidance, perhaps it will be."

Uncle snorted. "You can't count on your god's guidance. He'd have to be real to give any." He swirled the wine in his goblet. "But rest assured, you can count on mine."

Chapter 26

Sooner Than Expected

Carthago council chamber, afternoon of Day 20

Glabrio stood at the back of the council chamber, leaning against the wall, arms crossed. The council usually adjourned for the day by lunchtime, but today they'd only taken a two-hour break and returned.

An argument over raising the fees for docking in the inner harbor had pitted the men owning businesses that serviced the ships there against the ones who serviced ships on the seafront quays where his ship from Rome had landed. Higher fees would mean more captains choosing the quays over the inner harbor and fewer customers at the harbor-side shops.

It was a far cry from the politics of empire that Father and his senatorial friends debated, but who was he to say it wasn't just as important for the men and their workers who would be affected?

When Volero stood and raised his hand, the angry murmuring in the room quieted. "I've heard excellent arguments presented on both sides, but before we make a decision, I believe we should consider an easy solution that is fair to all."

Glabrio straightened. Volero had all eyes upon him, and he turned to face the councilmen, not Duumvir Paternus, who'd been calling on each speaker.

"How would the money raised by the added fee be spent? Would it contribute to things that the whole city would benefit from? If only the harbor area would benefit, then the fee for only the inner harbor might be justified. But if the whole city benefits, why should the fee be applied only in the harbor?"

Scowls had relaxed to frowns, and some crossed arms dropped to men's sides.

"What if both harbor and quay add a much smaller fee that is the same for both? Then it wouldn't change where captains choose to unload their cargos merely to save some money. They can continue to choose harbor or quay, as best suits their ship and what it carries. If we add a suitable small amount based on ship size and cargo instead, can we end the division I've heard here today and act for the benefit of all Carthago?"

Murmured agreement spread through the gathering as Volero took his seat. Duumvir Paternus raised both hands. "Martinus has proposed a possible solution. Does anyone else have something they want to say about this matter?"

No one stood to speak, and Paternus pointed to the left side of the chamber with his right hand. "Those who support Martinus's proposal that a smaller fee be applied for both harbor and quays go to my right."

His left hand pointed to the right side. "Those who do not support Martinus's proposal go to my left."

The councilmen rose and divided into two groups with the group to his right being several times larger than the other.

"The council has decided to add a fee to both harbor and quays. The aediles will determine the details of those fees and present them to us next week. This session is now ended."

Glabrio leaned against the wall again as several smiling men surrounded Volero. It was obvious now why a man as young as Volero was listened to with respect.

What wasn't obvious was why Volero would leave his admirers to join him. Volero raised a hand in greeting, then strolled over. "It was an angrier session than usual, but I trust you were here solely for entertainment. My colleagues and I have never needed the Urban Cohort to settle a dispute."

"With you here to propose a solution like you did, I don't expect you ever will."

Volero chuckled. "It made some happy and some unhappy. But the unhappy ones won't be plotting how to get rid of their opponents permanently. We're still more like the old Republic in how we govern the city. Many of your men might be needed to control the people at the circus and the amphitheater, but you standing at the back is more than I need to feel safe here."

Paternus joined them. "You've always spoken your mind here, even before our young friend was here to watch over us." He twisted his signet ring. "I'm planning a dinner later this week. Are you free, Volero?"

"Mostly, except for a dinner with my niece."

"Doesn't Martina dine with you whenever you're home?"

"She did, but she moved into the small town house Father left her."

Paternus chuckled. "I suspect that was to the satisfaction of all the women in your household."

"It is more peaceful since she moved out, but conversation at family dinner... You raised daughters, Paternus. You know what girls want to talk about is often not worth listening to, and some get no better when they're grown women." Volero rested a hand on Glabrio's shoulder. "So, it's a refreshing change when our city's tribune joins me for conversation and tabula in exchange for better food than his garrison cooks prepare."

Glabrio stepped away from the wall. "I'd want to join you even if the food was just as bad…or worse."

An amused snort was Paternus's response. "Volero's daughters probably want you to join their father as well. But the conversation of most young women is boring at best."

"A wise man once told me the reason we have two ears and one mouth is so we'll listen first, then speak, then listen again. I'm finding that especially true for me here in Carthago. Volero's niece is worth listening to, even if most young women aren't."

"Martina's grandfather educated her as if she were a grandson. He made her an interesting companion for a man of any age." A wry smile lit Paternus's eyes. "But for a young man like yourself, her beauty is more likely to impress."

"For some men of any age, that's true, but beauty can fade quickly. A woman with a store of knowledge both wide and deep can captivate even when she's old."

Paternus's eyes mirrored the approval his broad smile declared. "I see why you find him fitting company at dinner, Volero. Perhaps I'll have you both to dine soon."

Glabrio accompanied his nod with a broad smile. "That would be my great pleasure."

Three councilmen in serious conversation motioned for Paternus to come.

"We can dine next week." Paternus turned his smile on Glabrio. "If you're free when we do, have Volero bring you."

"I'd be honored." They were words he meant whole-heartedly. Paternus wore the purple-edged toga of a magistrate of Rome, but even when his term as duumvir ended, he'd be a man whose good opinion Glabrio wanted.

After a single nod, Paternus crossed the room to join the others.

Volero rubbed his palms together. "Martina will be having me as her first dinner guest in a few days. She took her cook from my house, so I know the food will be good. But she's my ward, so I'd accept her invitation even if it wasn't."

"I enjoyed speaking with her this morning, but we were interrupted before we finished."

Her uncle didn't need to know that it was his own optio who interrupted and that she was pleased because she was trying to get him to leave when Sartorus came.

"Would you like to finish your conversation?"

"Finish…not necessarily. But continue…definitely."

Volero motioned toward the door, and they merged with the crowds outside in the Forum. "I can arrange that. I'll let her know I'll be bringing you as my companion."

"Will she mind if you do that?"

A chuckle was Volero's first response. "I'm her guardian. As long as I don't bring my wife or daughters, she'll be fine with me bringing a guest, and the conversation will be better if you're there."

It was all Glabrio could do not to grin. "In that case, I'd love to join you."

When he and Volero parted outside the council chamber, he gave in and let the grin out. An evening with Volero's intriguing niece was coming sooner than he'd expected. He would love to see the look on her face when Volero told her he was joining them.

The grin faded. Then again, maybe he wouldn't.

Near the agora, morning of Day 21

After breakfast, Glabrio left the garrison dining room with Sartorus beside him. "You were right that a little rosemary could turn bland into delicious."

"As good as my mother made." Sartorus patted his stomach. "And much appreciated by your troops."

The two guards posted at the entrance to headquarters snapped to attention and struck their chests as he passed. Dubitatus sat at his desk, rolling a stylus between thumb and middle finger as he stared at a wax tablet.

Glabrio turned into the centurion's office. Verus should have his list of metalworkers ready soon. Time for Dubitatus to do the same.

Dubitatus stood. "Did you want something, Tribune?"

"A list of all the jewelers and shops with metalworkers in your district."

Dubitatus's head drew back. "All the jewelers and metal workshops? In the whole district?" He wrinkled his nose.

"That's what I said." The edge Glabrio put on his voice made Dubitatus's eyebrows lower.

"I meant no disrespect, Tribune, but no one ever asked for something like that before. It could be a very long list. It might take a long time to make it. But if that's what you want, then I'll look into making that list."

Look into making it? It was all Glabrio could do not to roll his eyes. Instead, he donned the emotionless tribune mask he'd learned from Titianus "Make it top priority."

Dubitatus's nod seemed half-hearted. Nepos's neglectful approach to command was probably responsible, but his least-capable centurion was about to learn he was not Nepos.

"When you finish that, make a list of all the bakeries in the district as well."

It was hard not to laugh when Dubitatus's eyes saucered and his mouth opened and closed like a fish before saying "Yes, Tribune."

Glabrio strode into his own office and settled into his chair. With elbows resting on the desktop, he rubbed his forehead. Verus would provide what he requested, but Dubitatus... His name meant "doubtful." Perhaps it fit too well.

Adding the bakeries was probably too much, but it was too late to change that without looking indecisive.

With the council not in session that day, Glabrio had nothing better to do than walk through Dubitatus's district with Sartorus, making note of the shops of interest.

He returned to the antechamber and tapped Sartorus's desk with his knuckles. "Bring a few tablets." He dropped his voice so Dubitatus couldn't here. "I want that list of metalworkers in this district sooner than I'm expecting him to make it."

"Will I be making a bakery list, too?" He cleared his throat. "If so, I'll need a lot of tablets."

"Too much to ask?"

Sartorus's shrug gave an answer without words as he reached for his helmet on the end of his desk.

"We won't need the helmets today."

His optio's smile proclaimed his approval of that choice.

Africa was too hot for surrounding your head with metal for appearances only. From everything he'd seen of Carthago so far, his helmet served no purpose beyond projecting authority. His bronze cuirass was enough for that. Today was only a scouting trip, anyway.

As Glabrio passed Dubitatus's open door, the centurion was staring off into space, his mouth curved into a frown. Their eyes met, and Dubitatus dropped his gaze to the tablet in front of him and began writing.

"Dubitatus."

The centurion turned resentful eyes upon him.

"I won't need the bakery list right now. You can wait on that until I ask for it later."

"Yes, Tribune." The frown relaxed into straight lips, and Glabrio headed for the exit.

A fist hit each station guard's chest, and they moved from parade rest to attention as Glabrio passed. When they were out of earshot, Glabrio motioned Sartorus to move closer.

"I don't know where the counterfeit coins are being made, but we'll assume for now it's in or near Carthago. The workshop will have a furnace hot enough to melt the metals. Glassworks and metal foundries will all have what's needed."

Sartorus shifted the satchel strap on his shoulder. "Do you think one of the glassworks Titianus's captain bought from made the counterfeits?"

"Maybe, but I don't want to narrow the search too quickly. If we spot anything that matches one of the customers of Martina's glassworks, mark that for special attention. When we start visiting workshops, we'll be looking for molds for making disks of copper or bronze and some way of coating the disks with gold or silver. The front and back patterns will be stamped using a die, and someone has to sculpt or engrave that die."

"That's why the jewelers?"

Glabrio had turned down the street that led to Martina's. "Yes, and they're used to working with gold and silver to make small coated statues and goblets and such. They sometimes buy and resell fine glassware as well as what they make themselves. They could have paid with their counterfeits."

Her house was just ahead.

"The coins from Martina's workshop were bronze coated with silver and gold, but Melis said sometimes tin is coated onto lead. It looks like silver when it's fresh."

As they neared her threshold, Sartorus glanced at the door, then at him. His ever-observant optio raised an eyebrow as Glabrio led them by without slowing.

He'd like to stop and see her, but it might not be wise today. What if she told him she didn't want to see him again before he could join Volero there for dinner?

Her uncle said she was a gracious woman. She was more likely to welcome him if Volero was watching, so he'd time his arrival so her uncle would already be there. And if she didn't want to talk with him, he could at least listen to what she and her uncle discussed.

The more a man knew about another person, the easier it became to find common ground.

Paternus had spoken the truth when he declared Martina a worthwhile companion for a man of any age. All Glabrio had to do was convince her he'd be worth talking with as well.

Chapter 27

Not the Best Idea

Martina's town house, late afternoon of Day 21

Martina was on her knees by the loom, tying the ends of the warp threads for her new project to the stone weights. As she knotted the last one, someone knocked on the door.

She looked up at Platana at the loom beside her. She clasped her hands, as if praying. "Please don't let that be the tribune again." Then she faked a shudder.

The shudder triggered Platana's chuckle. "He's left you alone for a day and a half now, even though he said he'd be back. Maybe he's given up?"

Lepus trotted past on the way to admit whoever it was.

"One can only hope." Martina stood and brushed off her tunic. "Uncle Volero. It's good to see you again."

"I'm on my way home from the baths, and I wanted some sensible conversation before I got there." One corner of his mouth lifted. "When it's only the family, my daughters make certain there's plenty of the other kind."

"Do sit, and Platana will get something from the kitchen. Fruit, cheese?

"Either or both." He settled into his chair by the fountain, leaned back against the cushions, and released a satisfied sigh. "It's a good thing I bought three chairs for you. You're going to need them."

Martina tipped her head. "Why would I need them?"

"Because you're going to invite me to dinner so I can bring a friend."

Platana returned with a plate of dried figs and cheese slices, then withdrew.

Uncle folded a cheese slice and popped it into his mouth. "This is tasty. It will do nicely for when we arrive."

"I'm glad you like it." She nibbled a slice as well. "It's a pleasure to have you to dinner anytime, but who will be coming with you?"

"Glabrio."

144

Martina's jaw dropped before she could stop it. "The tribune? But we agreed I should keep him at arm's length."

"We did, but as I've come to know him better, I think this is a better way to quench his interest in you." He bit off half a fig.

"But won't it make him think I want his company and conversation?" She sucked air through her teeth. "I don't think this is a wise thing to do."

"Nothing is more attractive to a man than a woman of intelligence who obviously admires him. But a woman who treats him like an uncle...that has no appeal. If you treat him exactly like you treat me or Father's old friends, he'll understand what that means."

Lepus approached with a plate of fruit pastries. Volero took it and placed it on the tabula board. "That's all we'll need." He flicked his hand toward the kitchen, and Lepus scurried away.

Uncle selected a berry-filled tart and bit off a corner. "This will be good to serve him as well."

She stared at him. "I can't believe you're telling me to invite him to dinner. How could he not think that means I want more of him? He doesn't even take the hint when I suggest it's time for him to leave."

"Most of his curiosity about you should be satisfied by seeing you like you are with family. As Artoria is so fond of saying, you're pretty, but not so gorgeous that every man's head turns, and you certainly don't know how to turn a man's head and keep his gaze locked on you like she's taught Priscilla." He took another bite. "But he's immune to that. Young women with much more to offer than a pretty face have undoubtedly used the same tricks on him before."

"Artoria will be angry when she finds out. She'll think I'm trying to lure him away from Priscilla. I already told her I don't want the kind of men Priscilla would want. She didn't believe me, and entertaining the tribune will make me look like a liar."

Uncle shrugged. "He'll come here directly without coming to my house, so she'll never know."

Martina rolled her eyes. After almost twenty years of marriage, how could Uncle not know what his wife would suspect? "Which will make it look even more like I'm luring him with a personal invitation, not including him as your guest. We can't count on him to not mention dining here."

"He won't say anything. He understands women like her. Besides, Artoria has no cause for complaint. He comes often enough to my house for tabula and conversation. She and the girls all love having him there."

"Which is why you should continue to entertain him at your house, not here at mine."

He finished the pastry. "Don't lose sight of our goal. It's not to entertain him. It's to let him see you're not the entertainment he wants."

"But it could work just the opposite. I've tried to discourage him, and it doesn't work. If I seem to encourage him, he'll think he's wearing me down and never go away."

"I think that's highly unlikely, so it's a risk I'm willing to take."

"But what if you're wrong?"

It was tempting to throw up her hands to make her point, but dramatic displays had the opposite effect on Stoic men like him and Grandfather. Quiet logic worked best, but why didn't he see what was so obvious to her?

"Martina, I understand how young men think better than you ever will. I was one myself. I was only a little younger than him when I decided Artoria would be a wonderful wife with her beauty and flirtatious charm. It took me a few years to realize what a man should want in a wife. You're nothing like what attracted me then."

But the tribune wasn't her uncle, and not all men thought alike.

"Then why was he asking about whether I was betrothed?"

"Mere curiosity. You don't have to worry about him wanting to marry you. We provincials can never satisfy the needs of a future consul of Rome."

Her eyebrows lifted. She had no intention of satisfying the needs of any man who wasn't her husband, and now that she was sui iuris, only a Christian man would qualify for that role. Certainly not an ambitious nobleman from Rome destined for political prominence.

"That's what his father was only four years ago. That's what he'll be before he's through. Your dowry is a thousand times too small to tempt him, and your political connections that could help him are nonexistent. Your main attraction is your unusual lack of interest in getting to know him."

Martina opened her mouth, then closed it without speaking. Nothing she could say would convince Uncle this was not the best idea.

And maybe he was right. Maybe it took a man to see what would make another man lose interest.

"Very well. I'll plan a dinner for three days from now. The food will be no fancier than what we usually eat, and I'll do my best to bore him to tears."

He reached over and patted her hand. "Ordinary food is fine, but don't overdo the boring part. He'll know you're acting, and that will only tempt him to return to find out why. Be the Martina he's seen so far. Just treat him like you do me or Father's old friends."

Volero moved the two plates to the vacant chair. "I don't expect Glabrio tonight." He picked up the blue game pieces. "So, before I go home to an evening of boredom with Artoria and the girls, you can play tabula with me like our tribune usually does. You play at least as well as he can." He rubbed his chin. "If you could beat him a few times and act too proud of it…that could cool his interest as well."

"It never dimmed Grandfather's desire to play with me."

"He taught you, so he took pride in your skill." He placed his first game piece as she picked up some blonde ones. "Glabrio and I haven't played *latrunculi* yet. If he's not as good at that strategy game as I am, you can beat him at that one, too."

"I can try." Martina shrugged. "But one never knows how the game will end until you play it."

As she placed her first piece, she couldn't stop the sigh.

God, please let Uncle be right that this is a good way to discourage the tribune. Please protect us all from discovery before he loses interest and goes away.

Chapter 28

Top Priority

Glabrio's quarters, late afternoon of Day 22

After another day of Glabrio walking the streets in Dubitatus's district, several tablets listing workshops of interest sat on the desk in his quarters. He'd shed the body armor and hung it on its rack. In just his tunic, he settled into his most comfortable chair to cool off and relax with something good to read.

Another day would be needed to check out the remaining streets, but today he'd found an unexpected treasure.

Fronting a town house two blocks from the Forum, he'd discovered what described itself as the best shop in the city for scrolls and codices.

It was. They had something unusual for both his father and his closest friends back in Rome. To satisfy Father's love of history, he'd bought a set of scrolls of the history of Rome written by their ancestor Gaius Acilius, starting with the founding of the city and ending in Acilius's own time two hundred years ago.

For Titus and Kaeso, he'd found something perfect for their school library—a scroll of Cincius Alimentus's account of his capture and imprisonment during the Second Punic War. It included his conversation with Hannibal about his plans to cross the Alps. Before Glabrio sent it to Rome by special courier to ensure its delivery, his aide could make a copy for his own library.

Knowing what would please Father, Titus, and Kaeso was easy. But what would appeal to Martina? Maybe poetry, but which poet? Would she already have Ovidius, Lucanus, and Statius? The shop had beautifully crafted codices of each.

Or…Kaeso's wife Sabina wrote elegant poetry, as good as anything he'd ever read. She'd made him a collection of his favorites to bring with him. Written by the poet herself on fine parchment with a leather cover she'd carved with cranes flying over a marsh, how could Martina not love it? Sabina would make him another just like it if he asked her.

His mouth curved into a wry smile. Sabina would tell Pompeia he wanted it for a woman, and they'd both let their imaginations loose trying to figure out what woman could inspire such a gift. They'd never suspect it was only for a friend…or an attempt to make her one.

A knock on the doorframe drew his eyes away from Alimentus's exciting tale. Sartorus stood before him, wax tablet in hand.

"A letter for you, Tribune. It came by military courier."

Glabrio opened the wax seal box and recognized the impression of Saturninus's signet. Only eight days since he'd sent his report…Saturninus had sent this reply as soon as his own letter arrived. He pulled the cords free from the wax and opened the tablet.

> M. Lollius Paullinus Valerius Saturninus, urban prefect, to G. Acilius Glabrio, tribune of the XIII Cohort, greetings. If you are well, then I am glad. I received your report on the state of affairs in Carthago upon your arrival, and these are your new orders based on what it contained.
>
> I am concerned that Nepos was not there to meet you. When he first informed me of his selection for a quaestorship, I told him he would have to wait for his replacement so he could explain any cases that would need to continue. He replied that he would. He obviously planned to because his father expected his ship to dock yesterday.
>
> While you wouldn't consider him especially conscientious, his reports have never failed to come on schedule, and they read like those of a tribune in charge. What he told his father was consistent with him overlapping you in Carthago so he could brief you before leaving.
>
> I fear something might have happened to him before you arrived. Your top priority is to discover where Nepos is now.
>
> He told his father that a friend had planned a farewell dinner the night before his ship sailed, but his father doesn't know who that friend was. That can be your starting point.
>
> You've proven yourself almost as skilled as the last tribune of the XI at ferreting out connections between people, so I expect you'll have no trouble identifying the friend. He might know why Nepos left early…if he did, indeed, leave.
>
> If his disappearance was sudden and surprising to the

friend and to the centurions of the Cohort, you might be looking for his remains.

While I want you to send whatever you find of him, living or dead, home to his father, make certain I don't have to command the next tribune of the XIII to look for what remains of you.

I hope all will continue to be well with you. May the gods guard your safety.

Glabrio covered his mouth with his hand and released the breath he hadn't realized he was holding.

"Is something wrong?" Concern coated Sartorus's voice.

He held out the tablet. "Read it."

As Sartorus made his way down the letter, Glabrio could tell where he was by the raising and lowering of his eyebrows. As he finished, his aide drew a deep breath and blew it out through pursed lips.

"So, Tribune Nepos didn't abandon his post early." Sartorus rubbed his lip. "It would have been better if he had."

"Saturninus is right that the place to start is Nepos's friend. I think I know who would have hosted a farewell dinner for him, but we won't know until I talk with him. Even if he didn't, he probably knows who planned one."

He stood. "I don't know where Messala lives, but I know the man who might." He strode to the rack where his body armor was stored and began putting it on. "You haven't been to Volero Martinus's home yet, but he's the one I've been joining for dinner without special invitation. I first met Messala there at a banquet. Messala and Nepos often went to the circus together. He tried to get me to go to the races like Nepos did so I'd bet with him."

He draped his sword strap across his chest. "Get your sword as well. Titianus warned me that an officer's greatest enemy might be wearing Roman armor. Until I figure out who wanted Nepos out of the way, you're the only one I trust as bodyguard."

Sartorus stepped into his room and strapped on his belt that held gladius and dagger.

As they strode past the empty centurion offices on their way to the street, Glabrio gritted his teeth. Nepos had told the leaders of Carthago he could protect himself, and they'd believed him. He'd started to believe it himself.

It was possible that he'd find Nepos alive somewhere. But logic and experience both told him they'd be looking for a corpse.

Glabrio's fist was raised for a second knock when Volero's door opened.

"Welcome, Tribune. Master Volero is in his library." The door slave stepped back behind the door as he opened it wide.

Glabrio stepped into the vestibulum with Sartorus right behind him and stopped. "Tell your master that someone needs to speak with him privately at this door. Do not say it's me."

The youth's eyes widened, but he tipped his head. "Yes, Tribune."

Glabrio stepped to the side into the part of the vestibulum that wasn't visible to someone in the peristyle garden. This was not a social visit, and the last thing he needed was Artoria or one of the sisters spotting him and insisting on a conversation.

When Volero came far enough into the vestibulum to see him, he stopped midstride. "When Canis said someone who didn't want to be named was waiting here, you were the last person I expected."

"If you'll step outside with me for a moment, I'll explain."

Volero's gaze shifted to Sartorus, standing close behind Glabrio with his hand resting on the hilt of his sword.

"Is there a problem?" Volero's voice was scarcely above a whisper.

"Not from something you've done." Relief washed over Volero's face when Glabrio smiled at him. "But I need your help."

He tipped his head toward the door, and Sartorus opened it.

"Step outside with me?" He lowered his own voice as well. "I want no one to hear but you."

"As you wish." Volero followed Glabrio outside, and Sartorus closed the door behind them.

"This is Optio Sartorus. He came with me from Rome as my personal aide. In the future, if he comes to you about something, it's as if I've come myself."

"Very well." Volero crossed his arms. "So, what don't you want to risk my household hearing?"

Glabrio kept his voice quiet. "Nepos wasn't here when I arrived, but he'd planned to be. He appears to have vanished, and I have to find him."

Volero straightened. His hand covered his mouth, and he slowly drew it down his face. "How can I help?"

"I need to talk with his friend Messala, but I don't know where to find him. I was hoping you could tell me."

"I've been to a few banquets for the younger councilmen at the family estate where he lives. I'll draw you a map." He turned to go in, then turned back. "But before I do, I have something private to ask you."

Glabrio's eyebrows rose.

Volero slapped his upper arm in response. "Martina has invited me to dine with her two days from now. I asked if I could bring you, and she agreed. It's better if certain others don't know she's entertaining us together, so you can meet me there."

Despite the reason he came to see Volero, Glabrio smiled. "I'll be there. I came across a shop today where I bought some scrolls. They have a good selection of poetry codices, both Greek and Latin. Does she have a favorite that she'd like for her library as a thank you for the help she's giving me?"

What had he said that triggered silent laughter in Volero's eyes?

"Not that I can tell you. It would be better to bring nothing but yourself." Volero sobered. "Did you want to wait inside or outside for the map?"

"Outside."

A quick nod, and Volero entered his home and closed the door.

Better to bring nothing—Volero was probably right. Coming the first time with a gift for a man would be fine, but a woman could misinterpret that simple expression of friendship.

But now was not the time to contemplate future pleasures. A tribune of Rome was missing. His first duty was to find him.

First, Glabrio needed a conversation with Messala. Then he could decide what to do next. He'd ride out to that estate first thing tomorrow morning. It was never good to wait too long when pursuing a lead.

As he released a sigh, Glabrio's shoulders drooped.

With two and a half weeks since Nepos went missing, the trail was already as cold as the body he was hunting. He had little hope that Nepos was still alive. But whether he found what he expected or nothing at all, it would break a father's heart.

Chapter 29

WHAT HAPPENED TO NEPOS?

Road to the Messala estate, early morning of Day 23

The gray stallion tossed its head and shook its mane as Glabrio waited for Sartorus to catch up on his bay gelding.

"We won't be riding as far or as fast as we did with Acceptus." Glabrio leaned forward and patted the stallion's neck.

"Good." Sartorus moved into place beside him. "I'm sure you picked me a good horse, but being a cavalryman was never one of my ambitions."

They walked the horses past the amphitheater and continued toward the aqueduct that stretched for miles ahead of them. Soon it was fields instead of buildings flanking the road.

Off to their left was a large lagoon. They were early enough that the surface was still mirror-like except where the passage of a boat had ruffled it.

Glabrio tensed his calves, and his horse moved into the mile-swallowing trot that he'd taught Sartorus to ride. He glanced at his student. As expected, he hadn't forgotten the lesson.

A handful of docks extended many tens of feet into the lagoon to reach deeper water. From a wagon parked beside one, a line of slaves carried amphorae onto a boat that had a single small sail and six pairs of oars.

Sartorus pointed at it. "That's a good way for an estate to get their goods to the Carthago harbor cheaply."

"One of those docks is probably Volero's. The villa he used before his father died is on this road. The one we're looking for isn't far past his."

The ring of hammer on metal came from the shop fronting the road just ahead.

"Volero's map shows us turning at a metal shop and heading toward the lagoon." He pointed. "That should be Messala's villa over there."

As they rode past, the double doors to the shop stood open. One man worked a bellows, and each whoosh of air was accompanied by a brightening of the coals. A second man took an orange-hot iron ring from the coals and rained hammer blows down upon it.

The villa was half a mile down the road. When they reined in by the entrance, a youth came over to hold their horses, and Glabrio strode to the front door and knocked.

Another youth opened the door.

"Tribune Acilius Glabrio to see your young master, Lucius Vipstanus Messala."

With a sweep of his arm, the youth invited them to enter, then led them to a set of chairs along the wall of the vestibulum before heading deeper into the house.

Many minutes passed, and Glabrio was about to knock on the door from the inside to draw the door slave back to his post to explain the delay. But before he could, a tousle-haired, bleary-eyed Messala appeared.

"Glabrio. I apologize for the delay. I was sleeping late after a party. To what do I owe this pleasure?"

"I'm looking for Nepos, and I would like your help."

Messala's head drew back. "Nepos is in Rome. He went back there to become a quaestor."

"That was his plan, but he left Carthago eight days before I arrived. He should have remained here until after I came so he could brief me before sailing home."

Messala's eyes narrowed. "But Nepos's commander ordered him home to Rome before he expected to go. The message to return immediately came, and he left the next day."

"Nepos was summoned by Prefect Saturninus?" Glabrio rubbed his jaw. "Where did you hear this?"

The bigger question—why had none of his centurions mentioned it?

"He sent me a letter telling me he had to be on the next ship to Rome, as ordered by the urban prefect. He apologized for having to leave before our final dinner together. I'd planned a banquet for our mutual friends to celebrate his promotion."

When his host scrunched his eyes as he rubbed his temple, Glabrio crossed his arms. A night of too much wine made even a smart man foolish and a strong one weak. He had no reason to think Messala was either of those even when sober.

Messala cleared his throat. "He said he'd make it up to me as soon as I came to Rome to visit him. We'd go to the races at the Circus Maximus and bet on the best teams in the Empire. We'd watch the games in the Flavian Amphitheater. He promised me other special entertainments he was certain I'd enjoy."

That was one promise Nepos would never keep. Through pursed lips, Glabrio blew his breath out slowly. How do you tell a man his friend is probably dead and possibly murdered?

"Prefect Saturninus did not order his immediate return. He told Nepos to delay his return until after I arrived."

Messala stared at him, then swallowed hard. "But he sent me a letter. I know his signet. The wax in the seal box bore his mark."

"I would like to see the letter and that seal."

"I don't have either handy. My father's secretary should have filed the letter in the estate archives with the other personal correspondence. The seal box has probably been filled with fresh wax and reused by now."

"Ask him to retrieve what he can as soon as possible, and let me know as soon as you have it here."

Messala turned the signet ring on his finger. "Why? I just told you all it said."

"What it said isn't true. Saturninus didn't order him home early, but Nepos disappeared eight days before I arrived. If he'd left this area right after my arrival, he would have reached Rome five days ago. That was when his father was expecting him, but four days ago his father was still waiting. He hasn't been where he was supposed to be for twenty days."

Messala's fingers tightened on his signet, but they stopped turning it. "Do you think he's dead?" His normally florid face blanched.

"I don't know whether he's alive or dead. I do know a letter can reveal much more than the words it contains. Send a messenger to my headquarters as soon as you have it available. Saturninus ordered me to make finding him my top priority."

"It's top priority for me, too. I'll have the letter fetched immediately, and I'll send someone to tell you when it's here."

"I'd also like you to think about where he might have gone, who he might have seen on the day he disappeared or a few days before, whether anyone disliked him enough to hurt him. I need something to help me find him. Maybe he is still alive somewhere. But even if he's dead, his father will want to give him a proper burial. I'd appreciate anything you can do to help."

Messala stared at him. His mouth opened, then closed. When no words came, Glabrio turned to leave, but before he could take a step, Messala touched his arm.

"I'd appreciate it if you'd keep me posted on your progress." His jaw clenched "He was a good friend. What happened to him…it's important to me."

"I will." As Glabrio walked away, the wicker chair behind him creaked, and he glanced back over his shoulder. Messala had dropped his considerable weight into it and buried his face in his hands.

He'd judged Messala to be a man who cultivated friends so he could take advantage of them. Perhaps, at least in this case, he'd been wrong.

◆

Messala kept his hands on his face until he heard the bolt slide across. Then his gaze locked on the door through which the tribune had passed.

His head felt as if it would split open. Was that from last night's wine or today's shocking news?

Twenty or so days ago, Nepos had been with him, enjoying a leisurely bath and massage and a sumptuous dinner prepared by the renowned chef his father had just purchased. They'd been to the races that day, and he'd lost to Nepos for a change. They often kept track of who owed what and settled the debt after dinner. He'd paid Nepos before they played tabula for a few hours, and he won some back before Nepos rode home. Nothing unusual in any of that.

The next day the letter came, and he'd regretted paying off his debt. In the hustle of returning to Rome, Nepos might have forgotten to collect it. Once he was in Rome, no one as rich as he was would bother with collecting a modest debt from a far-away friend.

Messala marched through the peristyle and out the door into the stable-yard.

He stopped by the young man brushing his favorite gelding. "Take him and ride to the guard station by the harbor. Tell Centurion Verus I want to talk with him as soon as possible."

The stableman dipped his chin. "Yes, Master Lucius." He set aside the brush, mounted, and rode out.

Marcella ran his fingers through his tangled hair. By the time he dressed and ate breakfast, Verus should come. His partner in their secret enterprise was Nepos's favorite centurion. If anyone knew where Nepos had gone, it might be Verus.

He strolled back to his room, where his valet waited to shave him and tend to his other needs. Within an hour, his messenger should be back. Within two hours, a conversation with Verus should tell him what he needed to know before he spoke with Glabrio again.

He'd almost finished breakfast when the stableman returned...alone.

Messala wiped his mouth, wadded up the napkin, and tossed it on the table. "Where's Verus?"

"Centurion Verus said he can't leave his duties until late afternoon. The new tribune shows up unexpectedly, and neglecting his usual duties to come immediately would seem odd. But he thanks you for the invitation, and he'll be here for dinner."

With a flick of his hand, Messala dismissed the stableman.

He didn't want to wait that long, and he didn't want to host the centurion at dinner. But Verus was probably right that anything unusual would arouse Glabrio's suspicion.

He heaved a sigh. He'd have Father's secretary find the letter, but he'd talk with Verus before he let Glabrio know he had it. Waiting an extra day wouldn't matter after a man had already been missing for twenty.

Chapter 30

THE NEXT STEP

The harbor district, Day 23

After handing their horses off to the stableman Acceptus had recommended, Glabrio crossed his arms and watched as his stallion was unsaddled and groomed.

"I need that letter Messala received. It would help me choose what to do next."

"How?" Sartorus massaged his hand.

"The tablet and the handwriting. If Nepos wrote it, it would probably be a tablet from the supply at headquarters. The shop those come from marks the back right corner. The handwriting should match the handful of reports Nepos put in the archives when he first came. I find it easier to write them myself than to dictate them to you. Since he didn't use a single man as his personal aide, I'm assuming Nepos felt the same."

"Won't Messala have it for you by tomorrow?"

"Perhaps, but I don't want to merely wait." He started toward the stable-yard gate. "We can do something before Messala produces the letter. It said he was catching the first ship to Rome the next day. We can look into that now. Verus should be able to help."

They left the stable and headed to the harbor guard station. As they entered, Optio Placidus stood and saluted.

"How can I help you, Tribune?"

"I'm looking for Verus."

"He's somewhere in the district. He didn't say what he would be inspecting today or when he'd return."

Not the answer he wanted. If Nepos deliberately left for Rome early like Messala's letter said, Verus, as centurion over the harbor, might know something about it. But if Verus didn't, who could he ask next?

Sartorus cleared his throat behind Glabrio. "The harbormaster might have useful information."

Glabrio looked over his shoulder at Sartorus before turning his gaze back on Placidus. "When Verus returns, tell him where to find us."

It was a short walk to the old military harbor. The concrete causeway connecting the circular island in the center to the wharves ended at an entryway with three arches. The harbormaster's office lay just beyond.

When they entered, the three men behind the counter merely glanced at him before refocusing on the person they were serving.

Glabrio walked to the head of one line. "Where do I find the harbormaster?"

The man being served stepped away and eyed him nervously.

The clerk pointed to a hinged section of the countertop, then to a door behind him. "Through there."

Sartorus lifted the counter flap and followed Glabrio through. A knock on the door drew a "come in."

The harbormaster sat behind a large desk with stacks of tablets and papyrus on each side. With a fringe of silver hair just above his ears, a saggy wrinkled throat, and bags beneath droopy eyes, he looked like a man who'd served for years and should be relaxing with the children of his grandchildren playing around him.

"Tribune Glabrio, isn't it? What can I do for you?" The lilt in his voice, the friendliness that lit his eyes, and a warm smile took fifteen years off his appearance.

"I have a problem I hope you can help with."

"I will if I can." The harbormaster leaned on his desk and steepled his fingers. "What do you need?"

"Can I find out whether a certain person sailed out of Carthago headed for Rome about twenty days ago? If so, can I find out which ship he sailed on?"

The harbormaster rubbed his lower lip. "There are several answers to those questions. Some yes, some no, some maybe."

Glabrio's brow furrowed. Weren't those simple questions? But sometimes the simplest question had a complicated answer.

"There are some ships that sail out of Carthago as their home port. For those, they might have a record of the people who buy passage with cabin rooms. For those who sleep on deck, it's unlikely any record of names is kept. But for ships that have different home ports, only the captain would know who sailed from Carthago with him."

"Is it possible to get a list of the ships that sailed for Portus or Ostia nineteen to twenty days ago?"

"For Puteoli as well." Sartorus's quiet comment behind Glabrio drew the harbormaster's eyes and then his nod.

"We have records of when ships arrive. For some, there might be a record of their cargo and where it came from. We have records of which ships left each day. As for where they were going…that's not something we routinely keep records on."

"This passenger would have booked a room. So, if there's a list of the ones based in Carthago that I could talk with, I'd like that. For the others, can I be notified when one of the ships that left on those days comes into port again so I can talk with the captain?"

"That can be arranged." The harbormaster pushed on the arms of his chair to rise. Then he trudged to the door. "Marmoris."

One of the three men left the counter and scurried over. "Yes, Dominus?"

"Take Tribune Glabrio to the archives and tell Custos to help him find whatever he needs."

"Thank you." Glabrio's warm smile received an even warmer one in return.

"My pleasure, Tribune." The elderly man headed back to his desk, and they followed Marmoris to another door off the main office.

Glabrio glanced at Sartorus, who felt his gaze and returned it with a slight nod and quick smile. When this posting ended, he'd definitely be recommending his ever-resourceful aide for a promotion. Titianus had been right that the optio from the warehouse district was exactly the man he needed to succeed in Carthago, and each day made it more obvious why.

Martina's town house, afternoon of Day 23

"So, that's how I'd like you to record the different kinds of expenses. Any questions so far?" Martina sat behind her desk with the papyrus sheet turned so both she and Clavus could see it.

"This seems easy enough so far." Clavus rubbed his jaw. "I can mostly see why you want it this way, but…" His voice trailed off.

Three sharp raps on the open door drew Martina's gaze from the sheet with its numbers and descriptions to her uncle in the doorway.

"Welcome, Uncle." She pulled the sheet back and slipped it into the drawer. "We'll talk about your question later."

"Yes, Mistress." Clavus tipped his head to her and then to Uncle Volero. "Master." Then he slipped from the room.

Volero settled into the plain wooden guest chair just vacated by Clavus. "Is that one working out well enough? I can find you another slave to be your house steward if he isn't."

"That won't be necessary. I have all the right people now. I couldn't be more pleased with them."

Uncle's brow furrowed. "Why is that?"

"Clavus told me that Colina, Petale, and he all suspected that Juliana was a Christian before she died. They'd figured out I was as well. They wanted to know why. So Platana and I explained it all."

She leaned back in her chair, rested her hands on her stomach, and interlaced her fingers. "For years, I've longed to live where I didn't have to hide my faith, and now I don't. They've all decided to join me as believers in Jesus. We gather each morning for worship. It's wonderful beyond words to get to pray and sing without worrying who might hear us."

Volero rolled his eyes. "You said the morning rites Grandfather performed did nothing, and now you're doing morning rites?"

"It's not the same. It's not formal words that have to be perfectly repeated or you have to start over. It's more like a conversation between two people than a performance. When I pray, I'm talking to God like I'm talking to you."

"It can't possibly be the same. I answer when we talk. I'm not something that's only alive in your mind."

"God isn't some trick of my imagination. He listens and answers my prayers. I've been praying about the tribune and how to deal with him." She leaned forward to rest her arms on the desk. "Last night, God told me Glabrio is going to figure out I'm a Christian if I spend much time with him. I know I said you could invite him, but after last night, I think it unwise for him to come here to dine."

Uncle's snort as he leaned toward her was as loud as a pig's. "My girls have no common sense, and they're stubborn about wanting to do things their way even when they should see it's foolish. They're just like their mother, but I expect more from you. I already explained why it's a good idea to invite him, and you agreed. I understand Glabrio better than you possibly could, and this is the right way to discourage him."

He relaxed again against the unpadded chair. "Besides, I've already invited him. It's too late for you to back out now."

"I know what God told me. Isn't there some way to keep him from coming?"

Volero's eyeroll was the answer she didn't want. "No. There's no good reason to even try. The gods, even if they were real, would have no interest in you or me. They don't tell us what to do about our own problems. Your god is no different."

She opened her mouth, but before she could speak, Uncle held up his hand.

"I don't want to hear more about this today. I know you're going to believe what you want, and you've convinced your slaves to at least pretend to do the same. But be certain to bolt your doors, including the one into the glass shop, to make sure no one comes in while you're worshipping. Your glassblowers have no reason to protect you, and you should assume they won't."

"I'll be careful." She returned her clasped hands to the desktop and sighed. There was no changing Uncle's mind once he'd decided on something like this. "And I guess it will be safe enough to host him one time. But please don't expect me to make a habit of it."

He leaned over and patted her hand. "You shouldn't have to. I expect him to be satisfied that he knows all he wants after this dinner. In the future, he can come to my house for the conversation and tabula we both enjoy."

He rose. "The duumvirs are joining me for dinner tonight, and Artoria will be wanting me home early so she can ask me what the girls can do to impress them." One corner of his mouth lifted. "My best advice would be to let them be seen but not heard if she wants to lure someone into marrying them. Glabrio will marry the woman his father chooses, but if he were free to select his wife, he'd never become my son-in-law. He'd pick a woman like you... except for your religion, of course."

Martina stood and walked around the desk to join him as he strolled toward the front door. "I'm delighted that he's not free to choose. I'd hate to be chosen. But since I must host him at this one dinner, I'll work on convincing him he wouldn't want me even if the choice was his own."

Chapter 31

THE PROBLEM WITH PARTNERS

The Messala estate, evening of Day 23

Verus rode into the stableyard and dismounted. It was his first time at the Messala villa. Young Messala's father was one of the wealthiest men on the council. A mere centurion was too far beneath his notice to be welcomed there.

He usually met the only son of Councilman Messala at the estate's metal shop by the main road. He always left with some item to make it look like he went there to buy something, that their meeting was a coincidence when Messala stopped in to check on the shop his father was using to develop his son's business skill.

That shop was the main reason Verus had cultivated the acquaintance. That and Nepos's comments that Messala resented his father's total control of everything, that he'd take great risks to make money that his father didn't know about, that he would consider hastening his father's death to become a very rich man if he wouldn't get tortured and executed for it. Ambition, greed, and ruthlessness were what he needed in a partner, and the moment he asked Messala if he was man enough to act to get what he wanted, he had an eager partner in crime.

He exchanged his uniform for a plain white tunic for this visit. Messala's summons had been urgent, and perhaps it wasn't wise for the estate slaves to know a centurion had called on their master. Slaves gossiped, and he didn't want them talking about him.

Two young men approached. One took the reins. The other scanned Verus hair to sandals. "Your business here?"

Verus raised one eyebrow. "Do you always greet guests of your master like this?" His mouth turned down. "Lucius Messala is expecting me for dinner."

The slave's face blanched, haughtiness replaced by deference. "I beg pardon. I wasn't told the master expected anyone. He's still with the councilmen at the baths."

"It's the councilman's son who's expecting me."

The man bowed his head, but only out of habit, not respect. "Follow me. I'll escort you to the young master."

Verus passed through an archway into a garden, three steps behind the slave as he led Verus past a pool with gurgling fountains and into the library where Messala had a scroll open on the desk. He rolled it and set it aside when Verus entered.

Messala flicked his hand. "Leave us."

After a quick bow, the man slipped out of the room.

Messala pointed at the door and signaled Verus to close it. He slid the bolt across for good measure. Then he settled into the chair across the desk from Messala.

"So, what's so urgent that you sent for me this morning? Why are we meeting here and not the shop?"

"I thought Nepos was called back to Rome early. He sent me a letter saying goodbye. But Glabrio came first thing this morning. He told me Nepos disappeared twenty days ago. That he wasn't supposed to leave early, that he never reached Rome." Messala rubbed his mouth. "But the tablet I got was sealed with Nepos's signet."

Messala picked up a stylus and rolled it between his fingers and thumb. "Nepos always said you were the best of his men. He relied on you. Did he tell you why he left early and where he went?"

"He didn't have to." Verus leaned back in the cushioned chair and crossed his arms. How does one man tell another he's responsible for someone's death? His mouth twitched. Bad news was best conveyed straight with no apologies. "He left early because he knew about the counterfeit coins. As to where he sailed...I gave him the coin to cross the River Styx."

Messala's jaw dropped. "You killed him?"

"I did, but you made me do it."

His partner's head drew back. "What are you talking about? He was my friend."

"You paid your gambling debt with counterfeit coins. Nepos showed them to me. He said you'd both been too drunk at the time to recognize the coins were counterfeits. After he sobered up, he realized what they were."

Verus rested his hand on his dagger. "Nepos thought it likely that the tribune of the XI Cohort would be transferred to replace him. He hadn't met Glabrio, but Prefect Saturninus claimed he was the second-best investigator he'd ever seen for solving cases that looked unsolvable. The man could ferret out the truth no matter how well it had been hidden. Nepos thought it would take Glabrio no time at all to track down the counterfeiters. We couldn't risk him telling Glabrio he got counterfeits from you."

Verus watched a parade of emotions march across Messala's face. Had Glabrio seen that, he wouldn't miss the flickers of guilt and fear. The tribune who paid attention to every detail would know how to interpret both.

Friendship kept Nepos from suspecting Messala, but nothing would hold Glabrio back. Some men stop thinking when they drink too much, and Messala had proven he was one of them. But even a drunk should know better than to pay a debt to a tribune with counterfeit coins. Glabrio dined at councilmen's homes often. If the too-diligent tribune reclined near Messala and Messala got drunk again, who knew what his partner might say?

Safety came from secrecy. Since his partner couldn't be trusted with secrets, he was on his own to solve this problem.

Messala set his elbows on the desktop and rested his head in his hands. His eyes closed for a long moment before he fixed his gaze on Verus again.

"Who sent the letter if not Nepos?"

"I wrote it and used Nepos's signet after taking it from his finger. The ring has since been melted down. It's either coating some coins or part of some rich woman's necklace."

Messala stared at him with his mouth half open.

"Then I laid a trail for Glabrio or whoever to follow. I was about to arrest a man who looked a lot like Nepos. I gave him a choice: pretend to be Nepos and board a ship for Italia or be sent to the mines." He stretched out his legs. "Glabrio came to my district after he left you this morning. I caught up with him in the harbormaster's archives. He was trying to figure out which ship Nepos might have left Carthago on." He only let himself smile, even though that deserved a grin. "Looks like my letter fooled Saturninus's second-best."

Messala leaned back in his chair, and his shoulders drooped. "What happened to Nepos?"

Verus scrunched his nose and shook his head. "You don't want to know. But you can be certain he won't be coming back to Carthago to cause either of us a problem."

"Well…what's done is done." After another deep sigh, Messala straightened his shoulders. "Everything I told Glabrio…I thought it was true. He never questioned my honesty, but he did say what was in the letter was a lie. He wants to see it himself. I told him Father's secretary would have to get it from the estate archives. I'd let him know when I had it. I sent the message to you right after he left."

"Has he already seen it?" Verus's whole body tensed.

"I'm not stupid. I wanted to talk with you first. I'll send a messenger to him first thing tomorrow."

"If he compares the handwriting with something Nepos wrote, he'll know it's a forgery." Verus rubbed his jaw. "If he compares it to one of the reports I've given him, he might realize I wrote it."

Messala gasped. "We can't have that happen."

Verus raised his hands to stop his partner panicking. "But if you make a copy and give him that…" He shrugged. "He won't know your handwriting, and if you change how you write the letters a little, he'll never suspect it's yours. Then destroy what I wrote."

"I can do that." Messala blew out a sigh, then inhaled sharply. "But someone will have to investigate the disappearance. Nepos was the son of an important senator of Rome."

Watching fear run hot and cold in Messala…his lack of control would disgust any soldier. If Verus had known his partner was more emotional child than grown man, he wouldn't have chosen him for this enterprise.

"Someone will, but Glabrio can't be the one to do it. At best, it would be exile to a tiny island for you. But you might get what I'd get…the mines or a cross."

Messala blanched. His hand shot up to cover his mouth. Retching sounds were followed by several deep swallows to force what he last ate back to his stomach.

Verus placed his hand on Messala's arm. "But it won't come to that. Just leave Glabrio to me. He won't remain a problem for either of us."

Messala nodded. He drew a deep breath and blew it out slowly. "I'm glad you know how to deal with this." He managed a weak smile. "You're a good partner."

"As you are." Verus faked an encouraging one. "You invited me to dinner, so we'd better eat."

As they strolled into the dining room, Verus glanced at the man-child beside him. He'd already made a lot of money. Maybe it was time to get out of the counterfeiting business. The two metalsmiths, the engraver…all three were slaves. If they revealed what they'd done, they'd be on a cross. Was that enough to ensure their silence?

About one person, he had no doubt. Messala was weak and a fool. He couldn't lie convincingly, and he'd crack under pressure.

Glabrio had to be dealt with first, and he might need Messala to get the tribune where he could take care of that problem. But before the next tribune came to find out what happened to two missing officers, Messala needed to join them.

Chapter 32

More Than He Expected

The Messala estate, morning of Day 24

As they approached the villa stableyard the next morning, Glabrio leaned forward to pat his stallion's neck before turning to Sartorus beside him. "I want you to watch Messala closely. He seemed surprised and truly concerned when I told him Nepos was missing yesterday, but first impressions don't always match the truth."

Sartorus nodded as they rode through the arched gateway. Two men scurried over to take their horses, and a youth came forward from the portico.

"Master Lucius is waiting for you in the library, Tribune. Follow me."

When they entered the room with one wall lined with mostly empty cubicles, Messala returned the scroll he'd been reading to a half-empty one.

He waved his hand toward the wall. "Our main library is in the town house. These are just a few I especially enjoy."

Glabrio resisted the urge to see Sartorus's response to that comment. Why would Messala make such an excuse to a man he barely knew who had no reason to care? But it gave an opening to their conversation that should help Messala relax.

"You're fortunate to have ready access when you're in town. I could bring only a few from Rome, but I've already found an excellent shop where I'm getting more."

Messala waved his hand toward the single guest chair by the desk. Glabrio sat, and Sartorus moved to the wall where he could watch Messala without him noticing.

Nepos's friend reached into a desk drawer and pulled out a tablet. "Here's what Nepos sent me." He handed it over, and Glabrio looked at the back. The mark he saw on all the cohort tablets was there. But they had a shop in the agora that sold tablets to many people, not just the Cohort. So, the writer might have been Nepos, but it could also be anyone who went to that shop.

He opened the tablet and read the words. The content was what Messala had said.

What Messala had said and nothing more. That anyone would say so little in a farewell letter to a good friend was odd.

He held it up, and Sartorus came to him. His optio took the tablet, slipped it into his satchel, and returned to the wall.

"I'll be taking it with me."

"Of course, but I would like it back when you're through with it." Messala's swallow was more than Glabrio expected. "As a remembrance of my friend."

Glabrio lowered his eyebrows. "But it's probably a forgery by whoever caused his disappearance."

Messala's mouth twitched. "But maybe it isn't. Maybe he really did return to Rome or is on his way there now, and I'll hear from him again. You don't know that he won't."

"No, I don't, but it's highly unlikely. Missing for twenty days is usually missing forever."

Messala's jaw clenched. "But maybe this time it isn't."

"Perhaps." He cleared his throat. "I have a few questions that I hope you can answer. They might help me find where he's gone."

Messala leaned back in his chair. "Ask me anything."

"With whom did Nepos spend his spare time?"

"There are several of us who went to the races and the baths together. Dined at each other's houses, too. You met some of them at Volero's dinner."

"I'd like a list of all their names." Glabrio signaled Sartorus, who took a blank tablet from the satchel and offered it to Messala.

Messala waved it away, then handed Sartorus a stylus and wrote in the air with his hand. Sartorus placed that stylus on the desktop and withdrew his own from the satchel.

"There were so many there. I must have been introduced to at least thirty people." Glabrio offered a rueful smile. "I don't remember all their names."

One corner of Messala's mouth lifted before he rattled off a list of a dozen or so names.

"Who were the people he would trust without question?"

"As far as I know, the same men."

"Were there any who have a reason to resent him, to dislike him enough to want to get rid of him?"

Messala's head drew back. "No. Absolutely not. Nepos was a fine man and a good friend. Everyone liked him."

Was and liked. Messala's use of past tense revealed what he really thought was Nepos's fate.

"No tribune doing his job will be liked by everyone. Was he too close to figuring out who committed a crime so someone killed him?"

Messala twisted his signet ring. "He didn't tell me about his work. We were friends, not colleagues. Aren't you Cohort tribunes supposed to keep what you're doing private? Why do you think he wouldn't?"

The defensive tone raised Glabrio's eyebrow.

"Some do. Some don't. What a man is supposed to do and what he does can be very different."

Messala's lowered eyebrows matched his deepening frown. "You're suggesting my friend didn't do what he ought to. If he hadn't, why would he have an enemy who'd want to get rid of him?"

Glabrio raised his hands in a pacifying gesture. "I'm not criticizing him. I never met him, and you knew him well. I'm hoping you can tell me who that enemy might be."

"I don't know, but I can think about it. Maybe something will come to me."

Glabrio leaned forward "If there's anything you can share that might give me some insight into where Nepos might be, I'd be grateful. His father is a good friend of my commander. Prefect Saturninus wants this solved as quickly as possible. His friend deserves to know what happened to his son."

Messala rubbed his palms on his tunic. "Right now, I haven't any idea. But I'll let you know the moment I think of anything."

"Thank you. I'll check with you later about that. After I find out what happened to him, I can return his letter to you." He nodded at Sartorus, who closed the tablet he was taking notes on and slipped it into the satchel with the letter.

"That will be all for the moment." Glabrio stood. "We passed a metal shop where your road turns off. Is that part of this estate?"

That question was met by Messala's stare. "Yes."

"What do they make there?"

After blinking twice, Messala shrugged. "Whatever is needed on the estate." He picked up a stylus and rolled it between thumb and middle finger. "But also things to sell. Bronze lamps, vases, pitchers, pots. Our shop is in the agora."

Glabrio smiled as he nodded, and Messala relaxed in his chair. "I've probably seen it there. I've been walking that district to find the glass shops and metal shops. Do your shopworkers shape metal in town?"

"Except for a goldsmith, no. He does fine custom work. For bronze and silver items, they sell what's made out here." Messala tapped the desktop with the stylus.

"Does your goldsmith do filigree work?"

"Probably." Messala set the stylus down. "He trained in Rome. We haven't owned him long."

"Could he engrave something for me?"

"Can't they all?"

"Many can. If I wanted something bronze coated with gold or silver as a gift for someone, can he do that?"

The fast blinks returned. "I would assume so. I really don't know. Why?"

"My father's birthday is coming. I want to send him something special."

Messala's smile was broader than that answer warranted, and it didn't match the cautious eyes.

"The lighting in my quarters is...less than bright. Could your shop out here make me some lamps with a stand to light my gameboard? Something unusual that either a man or woman might like."

"Probably. If you need something custom, you can tell them I sent you. They should be able to make whatever you describe to them." Messala flashed a smile as he leaned back in his chair. "Tell them I want them to put special effort into whatever you order. I take care of my friends."

"Thank you. I'll stop there now on my way back."

Messala raised his hand in farewell, and Glabrio strode from the library with Sartorus close behind.

Nothing was said by either until they had ridden beyond earshot from the stableyard.

Glabrio set their pace at a walk. "Your thoughts?"

"Back in Rome, would you keep letters from good friends in your family archives?"

"No. They're in a trunk in my room."

"Neither would I. But even if you did, would it take you almost a day to get one back?"

"No." Glabrio rubbed under his chin, a habit he'd developed when wearing his helmet. He now left the helmet in his quarters, but that habit remained. "So, you're thinking what we have in your satchel wasn't what Messala got after Nepos vanished."

"It might be the same words, but I think there was something about the tablet he says he got that he didn't want you to see." He stroked his throat, even though his helmet was still on his desk. "Maybe there was more in the letter than he wanted you to know. Or maybe he made a copy to give to you because he was afraid the handwriting would tell you something."

He shrugged. "Or maybe the letter never existed before he wrote it yesterday after talking with you." Sartorus sucked on his teeth. "He wanted me to write down the names instead of him."

"So, if this doesn't match Nepos's handwriting on the reports in the archives, I'll want something Messala has written for comparison."

Sartorus nodded. "Will he be willing to give that to you?"

"Not if he wrote the Nepos letter, but Volero Martinus can probably get me something without Messala suspecting it's for me. I'm dining with him tonight. I'll ask then."

They rode the rest of the way to the shop in silence.

Tonight, Glabrio was dining with Volero…at Martina's town house. Volero had said to bring only himself, but if Fortuna smiled, this would be the first of many enjoyable evenings.

If she didn't want to talk, they could play a board game. Her uncle thought they'd be well matched. He'd mentioned tabula, but did she play the more challenging strategy game, latrunculi? He missed ending the day playing it with the Praetorian tribune Martialis.

Titus and his wife played latrunculi often, and his friend praised her surprising tactics that often beat him. He played it like war; she was more subtle. Would Martina play the same?

If they played after dinner, the gameboard by the fountain would need extra lighting. She had no lampstand that he'd seen.

He could get one and use it a few times at his quarters. Something elegant made of bronze, like branches that arched over the table and held several lamps shaped like birds.

He would offer a lampstand he already had to light her board better for games with him or Volero. She might not take it if she thought he was buying something especially for her. But she wouldn't have to know, and he'd have the pleasure of watching her enjoy his gift every time they used it.

They reached the workshop and dismounted. After tying their horses in the shade of a gnarled olive tree, they entered the shop.

The pulsing whoosh of one man working a bellows accompanied the ring of the hammer strikes. Then the second man took a thin, glowing plate of iron from the flame and bent it around a stone cylinder to make half of the cuff for a set of shackles. He set that on a brick bench beside its mate.

Glabrio cleared his throat.

The bellows man turned, then walked over. "Welcome, Tribune. I'm Ahenus, shop foreman. Can I help you?"

The second metalsmith stayed by the forge, but he picked up the hammer and rested its head in his empty hand.

Ahenus's smile came and went too quickly, but making people nervous was something Glabrio did often. He saw it with many servants and slaves before he spoke to them. It was even worse when he was wearing his helmet.

A cuirass declared his authority. His helmet added intimidation. He'd seen

Titus remove his a few times when asking a nervous witness questions. Now he understood why.

"I've just come from visiting my friend, Lucius Messala. He said you could make a bronze lampstand for lighting a game table, something elegant that would please either man or woman."

Ahenus's smile reappeared, and this time it was genuine. "Our bronze lamps are very popular, and I have many designs in the storeroom. After you choose the lamps you like, I can show you what we have for lampstands. Several styles sell well at our shop in Carthago."

"I'm looking for something out of the ordinary. Something no one else would have. Maybe with tree branches to hold lamps shaped like birds or blossoms."

"We can make that as well." Ahenus pointed at the man by the forge. "Ferreus is renowned for his skill in making custom bronze, and any friend of Master Lucius deserves the very best."

Ferreus's head bobbed up and down as he grinned. "Whatever Master Lucius wants for a friend, that's what we'll do." He turned back to the forge and set the hammer down on the brick bench beside the cooling cuff.

Ahenus swept his open hand toward the storeroom. "This way, Tribune."

Glabrio followed the foreman through the doorway. Shelf after shelf of lamps stood before him. He rubbed his lower lip. Which among the dozens of styles would raise Martina's eyebrows and make her smile?

◆

Sartorus rubbed his jaw. There was plenty of light in the tribune quarters with lamp holders on the walls and a three-branch lamp holder on Glabrio's desk.

A lampstand of tree branches with bird lamps. Something a woman would like. One corner of Sartorus's mouth lifted. If he were a betting man, he'd bet that lampstand was destined for the peristyle of Publilia Martina. At least, that was what Glabrio intended.

But would she accept it? If a woman was that cool toward him, he'd choose another to receive his attentions. A soldier was supposed to remain unmarried for his twenty years of service. He had thirteen more to reach that. But he'd likely remain single even when marriage became a possibility.

He was Christian, and a Christian man should only marry a Christian woman. But the chances of him meeting a Christian when he was an enforcer of Roman law were almost nonexistent. Any Christian in her right mind would hide what she was from him. But maybe God had plans that he'd never imagined. When he finally left the Cohort, perhaps God would surprise him.

He drifted over to the rack of iron items. Iron tips for wooden plows, chains with a range of link sizes, blades for hoes.

The one called Ferreus shifted the still-hot shackles on the brick bench and went outside. When he returned, he pushed a wheelbarrow of wood. He began stacking the logs next to the forge.

Sartorus moved on from the hoes and chains to a set of shelves filled with pots and pitchers made of bronze. He ran his finger over a stamped pattern of dancing nymphs on a wine pitcher.

When he turned, a patch of red under the bench across the room caught his eye. Where the workbench pressed against the wall of a cabinet, something red had become caught between the two.

He crossed the room and went down on one knee for a closer look.

Horsehair dyed the same red as the crests the tribunes and centurions wore.

He reached under the bench and pulled the red fibers free.

Then everything went black.

◆

Ferreus stared first at the body of the optio, then at the log in his hand. He would have sworn he'd burned every bit of the crest when he pulled it out of the helmet. How had part of it caught between bench and cabinet, only to betray what they'd done?

That centurion who came to talk with Master Lucius under the olive tree was the one who got the young master involved in counterfeiting and forced them to become counterfeiters, too. He'd brought the first tribune into the workshop before he killed him. Then he'd ordered them to dispose of the body, to make certain anyone who found it would never know it had been a Roman tribune.

He told them to burn the leather and cloth and melt down the bronze so there'd be no trace of the dead officer.

They'd been afraid not to do exactly what he said. No one would believe the centurion killed his commander if he said they did.

The new tribune's voice drifted out from the storeroom. He'd almost finished choosing the lamps. He'd be coming out of that room at any moment. He had a sword. He'd use it the moment he saw his man lying on the floor.

Ferreus was a dead man, unless...

He stared at the log he'd used on the soldier. What was good for a soldier was good for his commander. Neither wore a helmet. With the log behind his back, he entered the storeroom.

The tribune was leaning over the table holding the bronze birds and flowers he'd chosen. He only glanced at Ferreus when he entered.

When the tribune's eyes focused on the lamps again, Ferreus gripped the log more firmly. One deep breath, and he struck.

Chapter 33

From Bad to Worse

Ahenus stepped back, bumping a shelf with his shoulder. He barely caught the lion-headed lamp as it toppled over the edge. "What did you do that for? He's a friend of Master Lucius!"

Ferreus lowered his arm but kept a grip on the log. "The other one found some of the crest that didn't get burned. I hit him, too."

Ahenus raised his hands, palm up, as his mouth opened, then closed. Then he gripped his head in both hands "But what are we going to do with them? The hoes and sickles that need sharpening are coming in today. How are we going to get rid of these two before anyone sees them?" He rolled his eyes. "It's hours until nightfall. It was hard enough after dark with only the one the centurion killed."

"Are they dead?"

The gravelly voice behind them spun them around. The Garamantian stood by the optio's body and nudged it with his foot.

"I don't know." Ahenus forced his breathing to slow. At least they knew this slave trader. They sold him a standing order of shackles, collars, and chains each time he brought slaves up from the south. He had no love for Rome or her soldiers.

The Garamantian crouched and pressed his fingertips into the optio's neck just below the ear. "You only knocked him out, but that's a bigger problem than if you killed him." A cruel smile lifted one corner of his mouth. "But I can solve it for you. What about that one?"

Ahenus knelt by the tribune and felt where the Garamantian had. His pulse was steady and strong. "This one's alive, too."

The Garamantian's one-sided smile turned into a full one. "If you give me the shackles and a couple of runner's collars, I can take them off your hands. They're just two more for me to sell for the mines or galleys."

"If you'll get rid of them, they're yours." Ahenus's glance at Ferreus found his friend nodding. "What do we need to do?"

"Strip them to their loincloths. You'll burn what will burn and melt down their armor." He tipped his head toward the forge. "You're lucky you have what you need for that."

He stepped to the door and whistled. He pointed at the two men driving his wagon-mounted cages and summoned them with a curl of his fingers.

"Help these two strip them and shackle them."

With two working on each of the motionless men, it was done in no time. Cuffs on their wrists connected by chains to the chain between the cuffs on their ankles.

Ahenus looked up from where he knelt by the tribune. "Now what?"

"Put on the runner's collars." The Garamantian leaned against the work-bench and crossed his arms. "Do you have bags that would cover their heads?"

Ahenus rubbed his lip. "In the storeroom."

"You don't want them talking to anyone before the ship leaves the dock. Tear four strips from that white tunic. Two wads to fill their mouths, two strips to hold those wads in place."

Ahenus motioned Ferreus toward the storeroom. "Get what he said."

From the shelf of bronze slave collars, Ahenus selected two open rings. Onto each, he threaded a bronze tag with "Hold me! I have run away" in-scribed on the top half. He slipped the ring around the tribune's neck and bent it to align the small holes on each end. After pushing the brass pin through the holes, he bent it over with pliers, crushing it against the ring to lock the collar in place. Then he moved to the soldier and did the same.

Ferreus held out two strips of cloth and a drawstring sack. Ahenus wadded one strip and placed it in the soldier's mouth. He wrapped the second strip tightly across it and tied it behind the man's head. Then he slipped the sack over the man's head, tightened the drawstring enough that it couldn't be pulled over his chin, and knotted it. They moved to the tribune and bagged his head, too.

"That should do it." The Garamantian came from the bench and kicked the shackled tribune's side. "Still out." He grinned at Ahenus. "I sell what's left of the men I bring up from the south to a trader on the lagoon. He takes them up the coast and sells them cheap as rowers and for the mines and quarries."

Ahenus's gaze settled on the tribune. Why did Master Lucius have to send them here? Why did that piece of crest have to fall where the soldier would see it? All the tribune wanted was a special gift for some woman.

The first tribune didn't deserve what the centurion did to him. These two men didn't deserve what he and Ferreus had done. A deep sigh drained his lungs. But what's a man to do when the only choice is between his own death and making someone else a slave?

The Garamantian scooped the tribune's purse off the floor. He emptied it into his own before tossing it on the pile of tunics and leather skirts that would soon burn. "You can have the optio's coins. He won't be needing them."

"What's next for them?"

"The trader at the lagoon. He's sending a ship north today."

"But what if they tell someone about this?"

"It won't matter. I'll make the papers for them, just like the others I bring him. I had you collar them because no one believes anything a runner says. In the mines or galleys, they'll learn not to say anything at all."

"Toss them in the second wagon." He pointed at Ferreus. "Help them."

The Garamantian tapped Ahenus's arm. "Get the shackles and chains I ordered. Time for me to head to the lagoon."

Ferreus took the shoulders of the tribune, and the bigger slaver took the feet. They no sooner went out the door than they returned for the soldier.

Ahenus picked up the box that held what the Garamantian usually ordered. He cleared his throat. "My master will expect payment for these."

A guttural laugh was the first answer. "Consider the bronze armor and the optio's coins your payment. Or...I could just leave those two here."

"No." Ahenus swallowed. "The bronze and purse should cover it." He hoisted the box onto his shoulder and led the Garamantian out the door.

As Ahenus lowered the box onto the cage floor next to the unconscious men, the tribune's stallion neighed at the slaver's horse.

His gaze locked onto the horses tied to the olive tree. "What should I do with their horses?"

"I'll take the gelding." The Garamantian pointed at the tree, and his driver went to get it. "It's a good horse, but not what someone would recognize. I know someone who'll buy it. That gray stallion...that one has expensive bloodlines. Too dangerous for me to try to sell. But the saddle looks plain enough that no one will recognize it. I'll take it, too." He called out to the second driver. "Get the saddle from the gray."

"But what do we do with the gray horse?"

A cruel smile curved the slaver's lips. "Is there someone close with mares in their pasture?"

"The Martinus estate. It's the next one toward town."

"Turn it loose near them. It looks like it can jump." A chuckle rumbled in his chest. "If any are ready to breed, it will get in. Let your neighbor figure out what to do with it." He shrugged. "Me, I'd leave it with my mares to improve my herd until someone came looking for it."

The driver tossed the saddle in with the soldiers, locked the cage door, and climbed onto the wagon seat.

The Garamantian mounted his stallion and reined it over by Ahenus. "I'll be back in six months. I'll want the same order of shackles." He grinned down at Ahenus. "But I'll expect a big discount for the favor I just did you."

"Ferreus and I thank you for it." Ahenus faked a smile.

"You should." With a cynical laugh, the Garamantian reined away and led the two wagons down the road toward the docks on the lagoon.

Ferreus moved beside him. "I'm glad that's over."

"Those two were never here." Ahenus gripped his friend's upper arm. "If anyone asks, we saw them ride by, but they didn't stop."

"But Master Lucius sent them to us." Ferreus's brow wrinkled. "He won't believe that."

"So…they stopped, and the tribune picked out bird lamps. He asked you to make a lampstand like a tree with branches to hold them. You can start making that, like he's coming back for it. His cuirass should give you enough bronze to start it."

He gripped Ferreus's other arm. "The centurion must never know what we've done. We can't tell Master Lucius, either. He'll tell the centurion, and that man would kill us to keep this and the murder from coming to light."

"Agreed." Ferreus tightened his lips and nodded. "At least there's no blood to clean up this time."

Ahenus tossed the first skirt of leather strips on the glowing coals and pumped the bellows. It burst into flame.

"Get that armor into some sacks and put them in the storeroom. We'll start melting it all down after the ones bringing the hoes and sickles leave."

While Ferreus bagged the tribune's bronze breastplate, Ahenus tossed the second skirt into the flames.

As one hand pumped the bellows to hasten its destruction, he squeezed the back of his neck with the other. How long before anyone discovered the new tribune was missing? Would that centurion suspect them? If he did, what would he do?

Ahenus drew several deep breaths, blowing each one out slowly. By the time he finished, his heart rate was normal, and what they should do was clear.

Master Lucius sent the tribune to them for a fancy lampstand. If they made part of it, it would look like he'd placed his order. They could say he was heading back toward town the last time they saw him. That was even true. The ships that loaded in the lagoon went toward Carthago on their way to the sea.

They wouldn't have to pretend for long. The goldsmith was coming in two days to gild the latest set of fake coins. Maybe it was time to claim some as their own and start a new life somewhere else…as free men.

At the lagoon

Sartorus awoke to the jostling of a cart and a splitting headache. He tried to call out, but the cloth in his mouth blocked any sound.

The cart stopped, and he strained to hear anything that would tell him where he was before any movement revealed he was awake.

A guttural voice with an accent he didn't recognize came from his left.

"I lost two men and a horse on this trip, so I have a horse and a couple of saddles to sell as well."

"I can take those off your hands." A nasal voice with the accent of Carthago replied. "And I'll take the first wagonload you brought for the usual price." A pause. "The two with their heads bagged in the second cage. What's wrong with them?"

"Nothing. I bag runner's heads so they don't see where they're taken. If they don't know how they got where they are now, they don't know how to get where they'd want to run to. It's hope that makes men run. Take that away, and they're no more than livestock."

Guttural voice chuckled. "The sooner they realize that, the easier it is for them. These two yelled and cursed and begged so much I gagged them as well. I treat my slaves well, but I don't put up with that nonsense."

"For runners, I usually pay half as much, but those two look fitter than the others. So..." Nasal voice paused. "Maybe three-fourths."

"I accept."

Sartorus's stomach clenched. Slaves. He tried to raise his hand to remove whatever covered his head, but the rattle of a chain was followed by a jerk on his ankles. A twist of his hand brought his fingers in contact with the links of a chain.

His heart started racing. Shackled. Caged like an animal.

God, where am I? How do I get out of here? Please save me from this.

He forced his breathing to slow. He'd just found that piece of a crest when someone knocked him out. Did those red horsehairs mean Nepos had died in that workshop? Had they killed Glabrio there, too?

But since whoever hit him had chosen not to kill him, maybe Glabrio was still alive.

Past his feet as he lay flat on his back, a key rattled in a lock. Creaking hinges announced the door was opening. Hands gripped both his ankles and dragged him out the door to stand him on his feet.

He wavered, then got his balance. A jerk on the chain to his hands made him almost fall before it started him walking. But toward what?

"Bring that one, too."

God, please let that one be Glabrio. Please save us both.

Each step made the chain between his ankles clank. The shackles made him stumble as he caught a link on something as he stepped up on what was probably a dock.

Two hands clamped onto his shoulders to steady him as he walked across the gangplank and onto the deck of a ship.

"Lie down."

Sartorus dropped to his knees and lay on the wood planks.

God, give me wisdom and strength for what's coming.

As he made gagging sounds, he thrashed around as if he couldn't breathe. Then he lay still.

Someone loosened the bag's cord, reached in, and pulled the cloth out of his mouth. As he faked the gasping of a man just starting to breathe again, they retied the cord to leave his head bagged.

With a thud, something or someone was dropped on the deck next to him.

"Better do that other one, too." Nasal man's voice came from some distance away. "I can't sell dead men."

God, please let that other one be Glabrio.

If it wasn't, that meant they'd killed Titianus's friend. He'd failed to keep him safe like he promised. His own chance of escaping a life of slavery if he was alone…well, if he were a betting man, he'd bet he had none.

Except God could do anything. He'd delivered all the Jews from slavery in Egypt and gave them their own land…until Rome took it away. But that was only because God allowed it. God could provide a way to freedom for him and Glabrio, but what that could possibly be…only God knew.

Somewhere at sea

As Glabrio drifted up from the darkness that enveloped him, the slow rocking of whatever he lay upon and the splash of water against the bow of a boat declared him at sea. Something covered his head, and it was thick enough to make the air inside too stale. When he tried to raise a hand to remove it, cool metal pressed into his wrist as whatever it was chained to stopped him. His head ached many times worse than he'd ever felt after a night of too much wine and too little sleep. But at least he didn't feel nauseated, like he had coming from Rome.

"Mulio."

The whisper beside him—was that Sartorus? Why would his optio call him that? "What?"

"The ones who did this, they mostly deal in men for the galleys and mines. If they think you'll bring more as something else, they'll try to sell you for that. But if they learn who you are, they'll kill you."

"I have no intention of being sold. The quaestor at the market should see to that."

"They'll have forged papers, and we're collared as runners. He won't believe you. Our best chance is to wait and convince whoever buys us that your father will pay what they spent and more to free us."

"So, what do you suggest?"

"If the trader asks your name, say Mulio or Agaso or Auriga."

"Why?"

"You can handle horses and mules. Slaves get named for what they do. One of the estates might buy you for that."

"Sartorus—that's a tailor. Can you make clothes?"

"My grandfather did before and after he was freed. I learned as a child and worked in the family tailor shop for years."

"I thought you worked in a fullery."

"Father started the fullery when I was fifteen. I worked there, too. I was eighteen when I left to join the Urban Cohort. It was a better choice until..."

Sartorus's whisper turned to silence.

"Until you volunteered to come here to cover my back. Urine vats would be better than this."

"I have no regrets. I'd still volunteer."

In his mind's eye, Glabrio saw the slight smile and shrug he got so often from Sartorus. As long as they were together, his situation wasn't hopeless. Between them, they'd figure something out.

"Well, whoever buys us would be a fool not to free us. I'll offer twice what we cost them, more if I have to. We just need to stay together until then."

"That's out of our control." Sartorus nudged him. "But I do expect you to find me and free me if we don't."

Meaty fingers wrapped around the neck ring and raised Glabrio's head before slamming it back into the deck. "No talking."

The dull ache in his head turned to throbbing pain. He drew a deep breath and blew it out slowly. After several breaths, the pain faded, but only a little.

Sartorus grunted, probably after a kick in the side. But even though the bag still covered Glabrio's head, the darkness didn't seem quite as oppressive, and the stale air inside the sack wasn't quite as stifling.

He and Sartorus would find a way to get free...somehow.

Titianus would tell him to ask what his friend called the one true god for help. But his grandfather had believed in that same god. He would have asked his god to save him when Domitian sent the Praetorians to execute him for his faith. No help came.

It was better not to ask at all than to beg for deliverance and discover no one was listening to your pleas.

Chapter 34

Could It Be Worse?

Utica, late afternoon of Day 24

Hour after hour, rhythmic creaks came from the oarlocks as a bank of rowers moved the ship forward. With each stroke, they moved farther from Carthago and closer to…Glabrio tried not to think about that.

Someone knelt next to him, loosened the cord around his neck, and pulled the bag off his head. He scrunched his eyes shut and turned his head to avoid the bright sunshine. Then he looked down to see what kept his own hands from reaching the bag. Both wrists wore iron manacles that were chained to a ring in the chain connecting the fetters on his ankles.

The man unbagged Sartorus as well, and when his aide offered his usual hint of a smile, Glabrio returned it.

Ahead, the wharves of a city awaited them. But which city? The sun was high in the sky, so it gave no help in deciding. If they went north, maybe Utica? If east, there wasn't a city that a ship could reach in the five hours the sun said had passed.

On the deck past the rowers, twenty or so other men stood, clustered together like sheep in a pen. Ranging in age from scrawny youths through gray-heads with stooped shoulders, most wore rough tunics that were far from new, and all had leg shackles.

The ship was small enough that its own rowers maneuvered it into place with the stern against the wharf. A ramp was lowered to rest on the deck. As his breaths came faster, Glabrio fought the fear that circled around him like a jackal waiting for a man to die.

The slaver kicked Sartorus in the thigh. "Stand up and get over with the others." When they got to their feet, he poked Glabrio's chest with two fingers. "Don't think you're still men. When we get to the slave market, keep your mouths shut until spoken to and your eyes down like the slaves you now are."

Glabrio opened his mouth, but Sartorus's elbow in his side closed it before he spoke the words that would cost him. He lowered his eyes to the deck and nodded instead. Then he followed Sartorus to join the others.

On the ship next to them, dock slaves carried sacks of grain up to the wharf where a cart waited. The first mate watching the unloading raised his arm. "Gisco!"

The man who'd kicked Sartorus raised his arm in response. "It's good to see you, Hanno."

Hanno moved to the closest rail. "Do you have any good rowers?"

"I do. Come over and see."

The first mate summoned another sailor to watch the unloading and boarded the slaver's ship. "What do you have today? I'm down to ten. One moved up to handling sails, and another died. So, I could use two more. Strong, healthy ones."

As the two men approached the cluster of slaves, Glabrio's mouth went dry. Of the whole group, he and Sartorus looked strongest and healthiest.

"Tell me about those two." Hanno pointed at them.

"I bought them in Carthago. As you can see, they're young and strong. Ready to work hard for many years."

Hanno fingered Glabrio's runner's collar and flipped the bronze tag. "What's the story behind this? It doesn't list his owner." He grabbed one of Glabrio's manacle chains and shook it. "And why these?"

"I bought them from a man I deal with often. He brings what he sells up from the south in wagons. So, he uses shackles. I asked what was wrong with these, and he said nothing except they both ran away. They complained some when he first got them, but they haven't since I've had them."

"He got them in the south. So, they're not rowers."

"Not yet, but they seem smart enough to train. They're fit enough for it."

Hanno pursed his lips. "Since they've never been rowers and we'll have to train them, that lowers what they should cost. No one will pay much for a runner, but since the last slaves you sold us worked out so well, I think my captain would pay three hundred denarii apiece. For runners, Captain Barca will think that's fair."

Gisco took a step back where he could survey Glabrio from head to foot. "Captain Barca is a good man, and since he's been such a regular customer, today I'll let you have them for much less than they're worth. Four hundred is what strong young men like these should bring."

Hanno scrunched his nose. "Too much for runners. But…three hundred fifty would be fair to us both."

"I'm feeling generous today, so I'll give you a great deal and settle for that." Gisco held out his hand, and the two clasped forearms. He pointed at two men ending a conversation on the wharf. "Your captain looks free now. Let's finish the trade."

The slaver took a stack of papyrus sheets out of the chest under the small canopy at the rear of the boat. He extracted two, and he and the first mate climbed the gangplank.

Glabrio couldn't hear what they said, but slaver and captain exchanged a friendly greeting. A few more words, and the two walked toward the forum, where the quaestor's booth should be.

His stomach knotted. They were going to register the sale, and he would never get within two hundred feet of the quaestor's booth. His shoulders drooped.

Sartorus nudged him and whispered, "Could be worse. At least that's a coastal ship, not one for the open sea. We'll be back on land often, and this is only a few hours from Carthago. And we've been sold to the same man." Sartorus's slight smile and shrug—Glabrio should have expected it, but it still seemed out of place from a man who'd soon be chained to a rower's bench every day for hours of back-breaking labor.

But he managed a smile as he nodded back.

In no time, the two men returned, each to his own ship. The slaver sorted a ring of keys as he approached. After freeing Glabrio's wrists from the manacles, Gisco knelt on one knee at Glabrio's feet.

When the first leg cuff opened, Glabrio's mouth twitched as he suppressed a smile. Once his legs were free, he could make a run for the quaestor's booth to declare who he was and demand his release.

But the first mate walked up behind the slaver, a set of leg shackles draped over his shoulder. He crouched and clamped the first cuff around Glabrio's free ankle. As soon as the slaver freed his second ankle, Hanno finished chaining him.

First him, then Sartorus. As Hanno tugged on the chains by each cuff to make certain they held, hope died. There'd be no chance for a run for freedom today.

"Get over there and get to work." As Sartorus started toward the gangplank, the first mate tapped Glabrio's chest with two fingers. "I expect my crew to work hard without complaining until I tell them to stop. See to it that you do. You don't want what will happen if you don't."

For the first few steps, Glabrio's stride was too long. He'd reach the end of the chain, and the jerk on his back leg almost made him lose his balance. But by the time he reached the top of the gangplank, he'd shortened his stride to the length of the chain.

As he stepped onto the new ship's deck, Sartorus walked past him with a sack balanced on one shoulder. A quick dip of his optio's head and a fleeting smile…he could almost hear Sartorus's say, "It could be worse."

He'd made a dozen trips between hold and cart before he risked speaking to the man tallying what they'd unloaded.

"I'm Tribune Glabrio of the Urban Cohort, and—" He choked on the next word as someone grabbed his fugitive collar from behind and jerked it into his throat. The first mate spun Glabrio to face him before the back of his hand smashed into Glabrio's mouth. "Stop talking and keep moving. The quarries always need fresh slaves. You'll go there if you cause problems."

Glabrio licked off the blood where the blow split his lip and nodded. In silence, he joined the line of men toiling like ants to empty the hold of the ship.

He was carrying the last of the sacks up the ramp when he was met by a man carrying an amphora down. At the top of the ramp, a wagon filled with amphorae was parked beside the cart of sacks.

Sartorus was just ahead of him. After he handed off his sack, he stepped over to the wagon. An amphora was placed on his shoulder. As they passed, Sartorus's wry smile and slight shrug tried to encourage without words…and failed.

Glabrio's deep breath turned into a deeper sigh. For almost an hour, he'd hauled sacks from hold to cart, and most of the hold was empty when he started. How long would it take to load that wagonload of amphorae?

The creaking of wagon wheels turned his head. A second wagon, just as full as the first one, came down the wharf and stopped.

His shoulders drooped. He was already as tired as he'd ever been. How much longer would he be trudging up and down the ramp? How many more trips with too many pounds pressing down on shoulders that were already sore?

But when he passed off his sack, he did as Sartorus had done. The first of what would be dozens of oil-filled cylindrical vessels was placed on his left shoulder. He gripped both handles to steady it and started back down the ramp.

With each step, his leg chains rattled. With each step, the sore spot on his ankle where the cuff chaffed his skin hurt more. The blister he couldn't see had long since popped.

He was half way down the ramp when he heard a third wagon approach, then stop.

He hung his head, but he kept trudging.

As Sartorus passed, Glabrio heard him whisper. "We can do this until we're found, Tribune. We're still together, so it could be worse."

Glabrio blew out a slow breath and raised his chin. Sartorus was right. They could have been sold to the quarries or mines. It could be much worse.

It was dark when they finished. Hanno and two sailors put leg shackles on ten other men. Then they were marched to a warehouse with bars on the windows. Glabrio followed the other exhausted men through the heavy door and down a hallway with too few lamps spaced too far apart. On each side, bars had replaced walls, and the men behind them barely glanced at the crew he'd been working with as they passed.

Several doors stood open, and when they reached them, the men in shackles turned into the second one. He and Sartorus followed the last two in.

Glabrio shuddered when the door clanged shut behind him and the key turned in the lock. The overseer from the wharf shook the door to be certain it held, then left without a word.

The others watched him, some openly, some occasionally sneaking a look. But no one spoke to him or his companion in this horror.

A man came from deeper in the building with dinner…if he could call it that. A tray carrying big bowls of porridge was placed on the floor just outside the cell, and each man reached through the bars to take one without a word.

As ten men shoveled porridge from bowl to mouth, the only sound was the scraping of metal spoons on clay bowls to get the last morsel. No one in their cell talked to them. The other men didn't talk among themselves, either. But with no one around to strike him if he spoke, it was the first chance for a real conversation since the workshop. He wasn't going to waste it.

After most of a day on the deck and the time spent carrying cargo off and onto Barca's ship wearing only a loincloth, Sartorus had to be hurting. Glabrio often exercised outdoors at the baths, so he was tanned enough to take the sun unprotected. But Sartorus always wore a tunic. Now the shoulder he didn't carry the sacks on and both chest and back were an angry red.

He picked up a bowl and handed it to Sartorus. Then he got his own. "When they come back for the tray, I'll ask for something to put on that burn."

"Don't. They won't give you anything, and you'll get punished for daring to ask."

Glabrio took a step away from the bars. He'd already learned to keep it short enough to match the chain length. He stirred his porridge and braced for the first bite. "How did we get here like this?"

"Messala's metalsmiths, but they had help. I was getting some red horsehair that was hung up under one of the benches, and the next thing I knew we were at a dock being sold by someone whose voice I hadn't heard before. I couldn't see anything, but I didn't hear the sounds of a harbor. I think we were at the lagoon."

Even as hungry as he was, it took will power for Glabrio to eat a second spoonful. Maybe the harder lumps were only grain that hadn't been crushed enough; he didn't look to find out. But what he feared it might be would have added some flavor. It was as tasteless as the garrison slop before Sartorus got the rosemary added. "So, that shop was probably where Nepos disappeared. But is he dead or a slave somewhere like us?"

"No way of knowing right now. But if he's dead, I don't think it was those two who did it. I think the bigger one panicked when he saw me find the horsehair. He was stacking logs by the forge when I saw the red. He hit me when I knelt to get it." Sartorus felt his head and cringed. "Probably with a log. If he'd used the hammer, I'd be dead now. It would only take a few blows with a log to kill me, but he only hit once."

Sartorus took a bite of porridge. A fleeting frown, and then he shrugged and took another big mouthful. "Titianus expected me to bodyguard you. Looks like I failed you both."

"No, you didn't." It was the first time Glabrio had seen regret that deep on another man's face, but what was happening now wasn't Sartorus's fault.

"I decided to stop there. It's all on me. If I'd heard you fall, I could have prevented this. But I heard nothing over the foreman rattling on about lamps. I only glanced at the smith when he came into the storeroom. That's the last thing I remember." Glabrio touched the lump on the back of his head. His wince was followed by the deepest sigh. "I was supposed to be dining with Volero and Martina tonight."

"The food would have been better there. This porridge is as bad as the garrison used to serve. But at least it's still warm, and there's plenty of it." Sartorus's slight smile and shrug as he ate another spoonful raised Glabrio's eyebrow.

How could his optio see anything good amidst the overwhelming bad?

With one knuckle, Glabrio stroked under his chin. Would he ever again wear the helmet that had trained him to do that? "Messala knows where we went, but will he tell anyone?"

Sartorus blew out a slow breath. "If he's not responsible, maybe. But someone would have to ask."

"Hmph." Glabrio squeezed the back of his neck. Sartorus was right, but surely one of his centurions would ask. Maybe not Dubitatus, but Verus and Longinus both knew Nepos was Messala's friend. When they realized he and Sartorus were missing, too, would they think to ask Messala about him? Would Messala tell them?

As each of their cellmates finished eating, they took their bowl back to the tray. Then they curled up on one of the dirty straw mattresses spread around on the floor. None had pillows or blankets.

Three mattresses were piled against the back wall. Sartorus grabbed one and dragged it to a place by the bars where there was room for two. Glabrio pulled his over next to it.

When Sartorus lay on his side and stretched out his arm to use as a pillow, he released a soft groan. "It's softer than the ship's deck, anyway." He grimaced as he lifted his head and lowered it back on his sunburned upper arm. "After what's happened today, I'm ready for some sleep. Good night, Mulio." A wry smile accompanied that name. "Sleep well."

Glabrio lay down on his back. "Good night."

Each time he closed his eyes, they opened unbidden. Finally, he gave up and stared at the ceiling, where moonlight shadows of the bars in the high, tiny windows crept across the planks. Sleep well? Impossible. Every rustle from others in the cell was accompanied by clinks from their shackle chains.

Locked up at night, chained during the day—how were they going to get to someone who might listen and set them free?

Glabrio startled when the slow, heavy breathing started beside him. Even the prospect of life as a slave hadn't kept Sartorus awake for long. Nothing fully quenched his optimism, even when everything was going wrong.

To most, their situation would seem hopeless, but thinking that could make a man give up. Maybe he'd be wiser to notice how things could be worse, like Sartorus did, than to let himself drown in despair.

Chapter 35

NOT WHERE HE SHOULD BE

Martina's town house, evening of Day 24

With a flourish, Martina placed her final game piece on the tabula board and gave Uncle Volero the smile of a winner.

"If Glabrio asks you for a game tonight, I hope you'll be less ruthless than you are with me." Uncle swept his pieces from the board.

"Perhaps it will hasten his loss of interest if I beat him too easily."

"Or fire his competitive spirit."

"It appears that question is moot. It doesn't look like he's coming." Martina picked up her winning game piece. "I can't say I'm sorry."

Volero began stacking his pieces for the next game. "I am. How a man behaves when he wins and loses is a measure of his character. I'd like to see how he reacts to you beating him."

She picked up a rondel and tumbled it between her fingers. "I know I agreed to host him tonight. I was ready to be friendly enough that he wouldn't think getting me to accept him was a challenge anymore. But…"

How was Uncle going to react to her next words?

"I need to go to my Cigisa estate for a while." She picked up a second rondel. "Glabrio not coming tonight…it might be God protecting me. He knows whether letting a tribune watch me too closely for too long would be deadly."

She added a third game piece to the first two and placed the stack beside the board. "God already told me Glabrio will learn of my faith if he spends too much time with me. This morning, when I prayed about what I should do, God told me to go to Cigisa now. I think I'm supposed to stay there until the tribune finds someone else to amuse him."

Volero's eyeroll accompanied a snort. "I don't think your god is telling you anything. But…" He resumed stacking his game pieces. "There is truth to the old saying, 'out of sight, out of mind.' A visit to your estate now might be wise. But what will I tell him?"

"I have a business reason you can use. One of my renters is moving to a larger shop. I've been considering using the space myself."

Volero leaned back in the chair and crossed his arms. "For what?"

"A shop selling the estate's red slip ware. Not just the regular pottery, but a place to display our special applique products. There's room for a kiln for making custom pieces, and Carthago has plenty of people with enough money to buy them."

She wiggled her fingers. "As a child, I was good at creating appliques. I would enjoy doing some of it again. A trip to Cigisa to consult with my pottery-works foreman is in order."

"That's a reason for you going that he'll find believable."

"I thought so, too." She relaxed in her chair. Uncle might scoff at going because God said to, but he respected a good business proposal. "Clavus will take good care of the town house for me, and he knows to go to your steward for advice if there's anything he doesn't know how to do with my renters. If it's a question about the glass shop, he'll ask you for guidance."

Approval lit Uncle's eyes. "If that's what you want, I can arrange for you to leave in three days. By sea and river is the safest way for you to travel there. Tomorrow morning, I'll send a courier to your Cigisa steward so he'll send someone to meet you in Utica. By tomorrow evening, the courier will report back when they'll be waiting for you. I'll provide a bodyguard to go on the ship to protect you."

He returned to stacking his game pieces. "When you decide to return, be sure you let me know so I can send someone to meet you in Utica to escort you back here. It's never safe for a woman to travel alone."

"I'd leave tomorrow to avoid Glabrio, if that were possible, but three days should be soon enough." She reached across the board to touch his hand. "Thank you for taking charge of this, Uncle. I haven't left Carthago since I came to Grandfather when my parents died."

"That's what guardians are for."

"It's what friends do, too."

Uncle's nod and smile declared his agreement. "My young Roman friend will be disappointed, but he'll get over it. I enjoy his company, so he'll be a frequent guest for dinner. I can let you know when he's no longer intrigued by your unusual charms."

They were sharing a laugh at that thought when Lepus came from the kitchen. "Dinner is ready, Mistress." He dipped his head toward Uncle. "And Master."

Martina rose. "It will be only the two of us. Share the rest among yourselves."

Lepus's grin over that prospect drew Uncle's chuckle. "Colina is as good a cook as Father ever had. Glabrio has no idea what he's missing by dining somewhere else tonight. But when I see him next, I'll let him know."

Utica, Day 25

Shortly before dawn, the rattle of bowls on a tray as it was set down jerked Glabrio awake. He'd lain on the thin, lumpy mattress for hours, watching the bars' shadows creep across the ceiling. Try as he might to stop it, despair circled like a vulture, moving closer and closer as it tightened its spiral in the sky. Finally, exhaustion won the battle with desperation, and he slept.

Sartorus lay on his back beside him, mouth open, softly snoring. The snore turned to a snort when the first mate kicked him hard in the side where he touched the bars. No wonder that spot had been left for their mattresses.

"Get up. Captain Barca has no use for lazy slaves." Before Sartorus could roll over, Hanno delivered another kick. "Today you two learn to row. It's half a day to Carthago. By the time we reach the harbor, you should have mastered your oars...or died trying." A cruel chuckle drifted back to them as Hanno moved on to the cage of his unshackled men.

The others were already lined up by the porridge tray, taking their bowls and spoons. Glabrio joined the end of the queue. By the time he reached the bars, Sartorus was behind him.

Glabrio stared at his bowl. Same color, same lack of aroma.

"Looks like they feed us more on rowing days. Or maybe breakfast is always bigger than dinner." Sartorus took a bite. "Prepared by the same master chef to his exacting standards of flavor." The second spoonful disappeared between his lips. "But it is hotter, and that helps."

The others in their cell were already returning their bowls to the tray.

"I think they know something we don't. We'd better eat it quickly, or we won't get to finish." Sartorus ate the next spoonfuls quicker that Glabrio had ever seen.

Good food was meant to be savored as you ate it slowly in the company of friends. This was as far from good food as he'd ever eaten, and the faster he wolfed it down, the less he'd have to taste it. But as long as Sartorus remained beside him, at least he dined with a friend.

He'd barely finished when the unshackled part of Barca's crew marched past their cell with Hanno at the rear. He stopped to unlock their cell, and the shackled men filed out to follow the others down the hallway. With Hanno right behind them, Glabrio stepped into the light of a new day.

The sun hung low in the east, painting the street and the buildings along it with its golden glow. As sunlight replaced darkness, his deep despair in the night seemed unjustified now.

Half a day and he'd reach Carthago's harbor where Verus's men patrolled. As soon as one saw him, he'd get them to fetch Placidus or Verus. He'd be free before dinner, and the metalsmiths would be in chains waiting for their execution. But before they died, he'd make them reveal what happened to Nepos and who else was involved.

His jaw clenched. Then he'd hunt down the man who sold him to die in the galleys or mines and return the favor.

Chapter 36

FOOLING THE ENEMY

Urban Cohort headquarters, Carthago, morning of Day 25

Daily report in hand, Verus trotted up the steps at the cohort headquarters. Normally Placidus would deliver it, but today he wanted to hand it to Glabrio himself.

It was always better to know exactly what your enemy was doing. Glabrio was on the hunt for Nepos's murderer, and the only way to make certain he failed was to volunteer to join the hunt himself and then lead the hunters to the wrong prey.

His mouth twitched as he erased a smirk. Fortuna had smiled when he forced someone to sail to Italia pretending to be Nepos. If he could find out which ship and to which port, Glabrio would let Prefect Saturninus know the search should be in Italia, and the investigation in Carthago would end.

If that didn't work out, then Glabrio had to die before he learned too much. But what was the best way to do it?

Verus hadn't figure that out yet, and he'd probably have to get rid of the optio first. Since word came of Nepos failing to reach Rome, Glabrio hadn't gone anywhere without Sartorus, and both went armed.

Dubitatus sat at his desk, writing his own report, and Verus raised a hand in greeting as he passed.

Sartorus wasn't in the antechamber to Glabrio's office, but his helmet sat on the side table. On the desk was a stack of three tablets. The one on top had a gouge in the frame that looked like the one he'd used for yesterday's report.

The inner door stood open, and Glabrio wasn't at his desk. A quick look inside the gouged tablet confirmed it was Verus's own report.

He returned to Dubitatus's office and leaned on the doorframe. "Where's Glabrio?"

"Last time I saw him was yesterday morning. He left right after he got a message that someone had a letter he wanted to see. He wasn't back when I went to dinner with a friend. I haven't seen him yet today."

"Did he say where he was going?"

Dubitatus snorted. "He does whatever he wants without telling me anything." He drummed on the tablet with his stylus. "Nepos was never around because he didn't spend much time doing what a tribune should. Glabrio's usually gone because he does everything he should and more." He closed the report in front of him. "I'm not his commander. He doesn't tell me where he's going."

"He and Nepos have very different approaches to serving Rome. I prefer Glabrio's. I wonder when he'll be back." Verus rubbed his jaw. "Did he sleep here last night?"

Dubitatus shrugged. "Sartorus takes care of everything for him, so I haven't been in the tribune quarters since he came. The two of them have the only keys."

"He said something about wanting to see the governor. I told him Noricus was holding court sessions in Leptis Magna this week. Maybe he and his optio went there."

Dubitatus leaned back in his chair. "Maybe. He's all business. Nothing like Nepos. That one treated us like he was an absentee owner with us being the stewards doing all the work."

Verus chuckled as he held up the report tablet for Dubitatus to see. "I guess I'll just leave this for when he gets back." A few steps and he'd added it to the pile on Sartorus's desk.

As he passed Dubitatus's office, he tapped on the doorframe to draw Dubitatus's gaze from what he was writing. "I'll see you tomorrow."

He got a smile and a wave in response.

As he strode down the steps, the guards on duty saluted. He walked toward the harbor for as long as they might see him. Then he veered onto a side street that would take him to the stable where he kept his horse.

He didn't use the stable Acceptus used or even one his fellow centurion would recommend. Any man who was so proud of his faithful service to Rome was the last one he wanted noticing when he rode somewhere or how long he was gone.

The Messala estate, morning of Day 25

The last time Verus came to see Messala, he'd come in a plain tunic so the slaves wouldn't gossip about his visit. Today he came in armor. Before he talked with Glabrio about how he could help, he needed to know what his bumbling partner had revealed to the man hunting them both.

He handed his horse off to a stable slave. At the entrance to the peristyle garden, he commanded the door slave to escort him to Messala.

When he entered the library, Messala's eyes saucered. "Centurion. What can I do for you?"

Verus pointed at the door, and his escort left. Then he closed and bolted it. "I went to headquarters this morning to tell Glabrio I'm ready to do anything I can to help him find Nepos. He'd already left, so I'll tell him later. But the centurion whose office is next to Glabrio's said he hadn't seen him since he got a message about your letter yesterday morning."

Without being invited, Verus sat in the guest chair across the desk from Messala. He undid the chin strap and placed his helmet on the desk. "What happened when Glabrio saw the letter?"

"He looked at it inside and out before he said it was a forgery. Then he gave it to his aide to take back to his office."

"It's a good thing you copied it so he wouldn't recognize my handwriting. He sees mine every day in my reports. Were you careful to change some of your letters in case he compares it to something you've written?"

"Of course, so he should be fooled." Messala's smile seemed too satisfied. "I told him I wanted it back when he was through with it. As a remembrance of my friend. He agreed."

Verus's eyebrows dipped. "But if it's a forgery and Nepos didn't write it, why would you want it back?"

Messala rubbed his lower lip. "He asked that, too. So, I told him it might not be a forgery, and I wanted it just in case Nepos had really gone to Rome early like it said."

It took some effort not to roll his eyes. No one would want a forgery back for sentimental reasons. "What did he say to that?"

"Missing for twenty days is probably dead." Messala's frown matched the accusation in his eyes.

"He's right about that. Anything else?"

"Yes. He asked about the metal shop, but we don't have to worry about that."

Verus inhaled sharply.

Messala raised both hands, as if to calm him. "That was my first thought, but he was only asking because he wanted to get something made as a gift for his father."

Verus shifted in his chair. Had Glabrio told the truth or was that a lie to trap Messala? "That sounds harmless enough." He stretched out his legs. "If anyone asks about me being here, you can tell them I was looking for my commander. Did he say anything about what he was planning to do next?"

"No, but if he comes back here, I'll let you know."

"Don't do that in a way that would make him suspect we're working together."

"I'm not stupid." Messala's lips tightened, then relaxed. "He knows Nepos and I were good friends. Why wouldn't I know his favorite centurion fairly well? He'd expect his own friends to have spoken with that optio who trails him everywhere like a puppy."

"What looks like a puppy to you is really a dog of war." Verus picked up a silver and ivory stylus and rolled it between his fingers. "Since Nepos disappeared, that optio is his bodyguard, not just his aide. Wherever Glabrio goes now, they both wear swords. His men in Rome trained like legionaries, and he's started the whole Cohort training like that here. Glabrio spars with Sartorus, and either one could quickly kill most of my men in a swordfight."

"Well, I already convinced him when he first came out here that I'll do anything to help him find Nepos. He'll keep believing that." Messala rubbed the back of his neck. "You're not the only one who can lie convincingly."

"True, but never to each other. Lies have no place between partners." Verus faked a smile.

"I agree." Messala mirrored Verus's smile with one just as genuine.

"I shouldn't be away from the harbor too long." Verus replaced the stylus. "I expect Glabrio will show up soon. We'll figure out what to do about him then." He stood and put his helmet back on. "You'll hear from me when I have a plan."

Messala rose as well. "We'll both be more careful until that's decided."

Verus strode to the door and unbolted it. He raised his hand in farewell before opening it. No one was in the peristyle garden to see him leave.

Good thing, since his disgust probably showed. Messala was like an unbroken horse, too unpredictable to be safe and too nervous to be trusted to think through how his words might be heard before he spoke.

He snapped his fingers when he entered the stableyard, and the stableman scurried over with his horse. He nudged it into a trot and headed back toward the road.

Ahead was the metal shop where he and Messala usually met. He'd told his partner to never say his name where the metalsmiths who made their counterfeit coins could hear it. He hadn't during their meetings, but what had he said to them when Verus wasn't there?

Glabrio had planned to order a gift from them. Perhaps he said something to the smiths about where he was going next.

Verus tied his horse in the shade of the olive tree. The clang of hammer striking metal got louder with each step toward the open doors.

When he entered the shop and cleared his throat, the foreman fumbled the bronze dolphin lamp he was polishing and barely caught it before it hit the benchtop. The smith set the glowing rod on a brick bench and clutched the hammer to his chest.

The foreman took two steps toward him. "Centurion. Can we help you?" He smiled, but it was fear, not friendliness that lurked in his eyes.

"The tribune who stopped here yesterday morning…what did he want?"

"He said he was Master Lucius's friend. He picked out those birds and flowers"—he pointed at a box of lamps under a workbench—"and described the lampstand he wanted for them." He pointed at a shelf holding a branch-like bronze sculpture. "Ferreus has the first sample ready for him to approve before he makes the rest." A tentative smile curved the foreman's mouth. "He said it's for lighting a game table, but with the kind of lamps he picked, we think it's for a special woman."

Verus rested his hand on the handle of his sword, and the foreman swallowed hard. Since he'd made them dispose of Nepos, it was the response he expected…and wanted. Fear made men eager to do what you told them. They were right to fear him.

Messala said the gift was for Glabrio's father. The foreman said a woman, but it was hard to picture any tribune who was the son of a consul finding a local woman worth that much effort.

"Did he say anything about the other tribune?"

The foreman blanched when Verus lifted his gladius a half inch out of its scabbard before pushing it down again. "No. The tribune only talked about what he wanted us to make, and the soldier didn't talk at all."

"When he comes back for his lampstand, don't tell him I asked about him."

The foreman shook his head, then nodded as if unsure which response promised he would obey that command. "We won't say anything to anyone, centurion."

"I know." Verus's smile was a cruel as he could make it. He focused it first on the foreman, then on the smith, and both seemed as afraid of him as he wanted.

"Get back to work." He wasn't their owner, but they obeyed immediately.

With hammer blows ringing behind him, he strode to his horse and mounted.

It was good that they feared him. After seeing what happened to Nepos, both knew he'd kill without provocation. Obedience without hesitation was what he expected from them now. He might need them soon for getting rid of another body or two. But after doing it once, they should find it easy to do everything he told them.

Chapter 37

RETURN TO CARTHAGO—ALMOST

The harbor in Carthago, afternoon of Day 25

As Glabrio worked the oar hour after hour, his feet chained to the bench and his hands growing blisters that burst, oozed, and burned, dread of doing this forever hung at the back of his mind. But if he and the other rowers joined the slaves hauling amphorae off the boat in Carthago, that wouldn't happen. Once ashore, all he needed was one of his soldiers to recognize him. And even if they didn't, he could demand they fetch Placidus or Verus. Either could identify him as tribune and declare him a free man.

"Oars out of the water." Hanno slapped both Glabrio and Sartorus on the back of their heads. "You don't know what you're doing for docking. Watch closely so you will next time."

Glabrio pulled in his oar, and hung his head. Hanno hit where the log had, and the pain that had mostly faded flared once more.

In what seemed almost a dance, the oarsmen turned the ship around and backed it into its berth against the quay. The gangplank was lowered from wharf to ship. The cover over the hold was tipped up onto its edge and dragged out of the way.

A line of dock slaves came down the ramp and stood by the hold. As the first amphora was placed on the shoulder of the first man, Glabrio's heart sank. If he couldn't get onto the quay, how would anyone know he was there?

Then the men without shackles stood and joined the dock slaves. Hanno walked past Glabrio to the first shackled man and released him, leaving the shackles under the bench. He worked his way back, releasing each man in turn.

When Hanno finally reached him, Glabrio tried for the emotionless face Titianus had worn while on duty. Any hope on his face could trigger suspicion.

He forced his breathing to slow when Hanno squatted by his bench, but he couldn't keep his heart rate from rising.

Hanno unlocked one cuff of the shackle and took it off Glabrio's ankle.

Glabrio kept his eyes turned away so the first mate wouldn't see the hope igniting there. He'd be able to run once both feet were freed, but he'd act the obedient slave while he carried his first amphora up. As soon as he set it down, he would sprint for the guard station at the harbor entrance.

He'd worn many wreaths for winning footraces as a youth. His unexpected dash would give him a lead on any pursuers that he could keep for that short a distance, even as tired as he was.

Then Hanno passed the cuff through the iron ring under the bench to free the chain and clamped it around his ankle again before he could stand. "Don't even think about running." Another slap on the back of his aching head punctuated that command.

He wouldn't. The length of chain between the cuffs was too short for more than a shuffling walk. The iron cuffs had already rubbed one ankle raw while they were loading in Utica; the second would join it before they finished here.

No rowers spoke as they each picked up an amphora and trudged across the gangplank and up the pier to a waiting cart. Resignation bordering on despair dulled their eyes as it had when they sat at the oars.

Glabrio joined them, and Sartorus shuffled up behind him, still chained.

As Hanno walked past them toward the gangplank, he threw an old tunic into Sartorus's face. "Keep that on until you finish loading the crates and casks." He strode past before either could thank him for his kindness in putting something between rough wood and Sartorus's sunburn.

Glabrio had almost reached the cart when the dock overseer nudged Hanno. "What's with those two?" His pointing finger shifted between Glabrio and Sartorus.

"They're runners that came from near Carthago They're too new to trust unchained."

Glabrio handed off his first amphora and started back down the plank. How long would it take to earn enough trust so he could betray it? Days? Weeks?

But maybe his plan to run to the station wouldn't have worked anyway. A guard stood between the amphora cart and the passageway to the station, arms crossed and glaring at each slave as they handed over their burden. Even if Glabrio's legs had been free, could he have made it past that guard?

Still, escape might be possible. If one of his soldiers was patrolling near their pier or if he could convince someone to fetch an optio from the guard station, he could prove he was Tribune Glabrio and must be released immediately.

But speaking to the first bystander earned Glabrio a jerk on his slave collar, a hard slap on the back of the head, and a chuckle from the man he'd hoped would help. The second attempt earned a backhand to his face and the threat of a whipping if he didn't keep his mouth shut. He didn't try a third time.

No one watching a line of slaves sweating under their loads was likely to listen to one wearing a runner's collar. All he could do was hope one of his men came close enough to hear when he called out. Any of them should recognize him—or would they? But even if they didn't, surely they'd get Verus or Placidus if he told them to.

But even though there should have been soldiers checking every ship at every berth, the few Glabrio saw never came close enough to his ship to hear even his loudest shout. If...no, *when* he returned, someone would pay for that dereliction of duty.

Sartorus had remarked on how few men patrolled the quay. If only he'd listened and told Verus to increase the number. But what hadn't been done then couldn't be fixed now.

Verus himself should have walked the quay at least once a day. Had their ship docked after he'd finished, or did he not do it like he should?

Like a mute beast of burden, Glabrio plodded back and forth, the leg chain rattling, until the last amphora of olive oil was unloaded and the last sack, crate, and cask of whatever was making the return voyage to Utica was stowed.

He'd no sooner carried his last load down into the hold than he was chained once more to his bench.

One of the men who handled the sails walked between the two rows of benches, handing a bread roll and a chunk of cheese to each rower. There would be no getting off the ship to go to a cellblock like in Utica. One more chance to run to the station erased.

Glabrio stared at the meager ration. It had taken four to five hours to make the trip from Utica. Another hour for unloading, two more to load. He couldn't stop the sigh.

Five more hours of rowing lay ahead of them before they returned to their cells in Utica. Surely the captain didn't expect them to row back without a rest.

He looked at Sartorus, chained to the bench across from him. His optio popped the final bite of cheese between his teeth and bounced his bushy eyebrows once. Then the slightest smile curved his mouth, and the barest dip of his head said more than a hundred encouraging words would have.

Glabrio's roll was half eaten when the rowboats began pulling the *actuaria* away from the quay. He wolfed down the remaining cheese and had just popped the last bite of bread into his mouth when the command to extend the oars came. He copied what the man in front of him did as the whistle blast ordered the first stroke and then kept the rhythm.

He'd heard about the biweekly twenty-mile marches made in five hours in full gear that his tribune friends in the legions oversaw from horseback. He'd give anything to trade places with one of those foot soldiers right now.

He glanced at Sartorus, who reached out on the forward stroke and pulled back on the return as if he'd been doing this for years. But even as Sartorus kept the rhythm, he glanced at Glabrio and offered a fleeting smile.

As Glabrio bent to the task himself, hope revived. No matter what came next, at least he wasn't alone.

Two hundred feet offshore, many other ships bobbed at anchor. A series of whistles gave the command to stop and store oars. The splash as their anchor dropped into the water brought Glabrio's smile. They would have some time to rest before going back to Utica.

The captain wasn't onboard. He'd walked away with another man just before the ship left its berth. Hanno was waiting here for him to return, no doubt. They were close enough for a rowboat to bring him out.

Or would they row in to get him? Glabrio was in no hurry to grip those oars again. Then one by one, Hanno released the shackled rowers. They stood and stretched before strolling to a place where they could sit and relax.

When Hanno had almost reached him, Glabrio slumped on his bench. If he looked too tired to do anything but rest like the others, his escape was at hand. He often swam a greater distance at the baths than the distance to the shore. Once he reached the quay, he could get to the guard station. Verus could send a rowboat out to rescue Sartorus, and this nightmare would be over.

Hanno crouched by his bench, unlocked the cuff…and replaced it as soon as it passed through the ring. He tugged on the chain to make sure it was secure. When Glabrio tried to rise, Hanno pressed on his shoulder to keep him seated. Then he freed Sartorus from his bench but left him shackled as well.

"You two follow me."

He led them to the sidewall where a length of light chain lay. He threaded it through the large link halfway along the chain between the cuffs, leaving them like two beads on a string before locking the free end to a bronze ring set in the gunwale.

Glabrio stared at his feet. A deep breath was followed by a deeper sigh. Even if Hanno hadn't chained him, the shackles weighed enough he'd drown in the sea. His last hope of escape was gone…for now. But at least Sartorus was still beside him, and the chain was long enough to give them freedom to stand or sit before lying down to sleep. His muscles were tired past aching, and his head still throbbed. But he'd made it through his first day on the oars. He could keep doing it until a pathway to freedom opened. Each time they came to Carthago was another chance.

One of the sailors brought each of them a big bowel of porridge. Glabrio sniffed it. No more aroma than the slop in the cellblock. But, the bowl was big, and the serving was still warm.

Sartorus raised his bowl as if in a toast. The smile and shrug Glabrio expected appeared before the first spoonful disappeared into his companion's mouth.

With an answering shrug and smile, Glabrio began his own silent dinner with a friend.

Midday of Day 26

The sun was near its zenith, and the ship rose and fell on the gentle waves where it lay at anchor. Sartorus sat on the deck, still chained to the sidewall beside Glabrio, but the rest of the rowers lounged on deck where they wanted. Hanno stood at the rail, arms crossed as he stared at the distant quay.

The sailor who manned the rudder strolled over to stand beside him. "Captain's taking his time this morning. Maybe a wild night with his friend."

"His brother this trip." A frown accompanied the shake of Hanno's head. "When he's this late, it's because they went to the races." He blew out a long breath. "I expect he'll come after they eat lunch." He rubbed his jaw. "That's what he usually does. Sometimes it's later, but he'll come in time for us to get back to Utica and unload before sundown."

The helmsman returned to the rudder, and Hanno strolled past the clusters of unchained oarsmen to take a chair under the canopy in the stern. One of the men who worked the sails raised his hand and rattled a set of dice. "Hanno! Join us?"

The first mate shook his head, stretched out his legs, crossed his arms, and closed his eyes.

With the first roll of dice came conversation and laughter among the sailors.

Sartorus nudged Glabrio. "Free time for us, too."

Glabrio pointed at their shackles.

"Well, almost free." Sartorus lifted his tunic's shoulders a little and let them drop back onto his sunburn. "This helps a lot."

Glabrio looked down at the tunic he'd been given before they slept. He tipped his head toward the canopy. "He surprised me when he gave you that for unloading."

"Me too." Sartorus massaged the back of his right hand, keeping his thumb away from the blisters on his palm. "New slaves often get treated worse so they'll appreciate it when the overseer starts treating them like the others. The same is true for new soldiers."

Glabrio stared at him, brow furrowed.

One corner of Sartorus's mouth lifted. "Not so much in the Urban Cohort because we don't need to be prepared for what the legionaries do."

"Is that why you joined the Cohort instead of the legion your mother's cousin served in? The easier training?"

"No. I've never avoided hard work. A man sleeps well after a day of it." Sartorus fingered his lip. It felt odd that Glabrio remembered that bit of conversation during their trip from Rome. Why did he sense it was time to tell his commander a little more of his story? Was that God's nudge or the pull of a growing friendship he hadn't expected his commander to want? "I didn't want a life spent killing to expand the Empire. Stopping the people who break the law and hurt others...that was something worth giving my life to."

"It is. Showing no favoritism as we do it—that's important, too." Glabrio's mouth twitched. "Our mutual commander didn't like that sometimes." The twitch turned into a wry smile. "That's partly why he transferred me to this posting." He glanced at Sartorus before looking away. "Saturninus has been a close friend of my father for many years. This was good for my political career, but it made me stop an investigation in Rome, too."

The smile vanished. "He never expected he'd end up with the sons of two of his friends in deep trouble because we came here. Nepos's father is his friend, too."

"We'll get you out of this. I'm not sure how, but I'm sure we will."

"Perhaps." Glabrio's sigh was deep and slow. Then his wry smile returned. "As you're so fond of saying, it could be worse. You've mostly got me thinking that, too." He bumped Sartorus with his shoulder. "I hope we're both right."

Chapter 38

ONLY GOODBYE FOR NOW

Martina's town house, Carthago, evening of Day 26

When Myrtis held out the plate of pastries stuffed with crushed dates and drizzled with honey, Martina took it and selected the smallest one. The first bite filled her mouth with a delightful taste and the perfect texture.

"Excellent. These are as tasty as the ones your mother makes."

A beaming smile lit the girl's eyes. "I'm glad you like them, Mistress."

"I do. You can go tell Colina what I just said."

The girl dipped her head and headed for the kitchen, still grinning.

Martina held out the plate to Uncle Volero. "This is her first time making these, and knowing you'd be eating them, too, had her scared half to death that she'd do something wrong."

Uncle took a large one and sank his teeth into it. "I've missed Colina's pastries. Maybe when her daughter is fully trained, I'll want to buy the girl back." He took a second bite. "But you'd probably tell me you'd never sell anyone in your household since you got them believing like you do."

"You're right." Her tongue caught the honey that tried to drip off. "A Christian familia is real family, not just household servants and slaves."

"And you'd never send any of them back under my wife's control." He finished off his first selection. "I don't blame you, but maybe I can borrow Colina sometimes when I want to impress a special guest."

He licked some honey off his finger. "Speaking of special guests, last night I had Paternus and a senior senator from Rome dine with me. Glabrio was supposed to join us, but he never came."

He reached for another pastry. "But dining with an old politician, even a Roman one, wouldn't entertain him as much as you could. He's asked more than once when you'll be joining us again."

He bit off the corner and licked the honey off his lips. "Or maybe he was afraid you'd be there. He'd have to explain why he didn't show at your dinner the night before."

"I wouldn't have asked him. That would make him think I missed his company, which I didn't."

"Well, I did. It was a small gathering with a lot of talk about imperial politics that don't involve Carthago. I would have found it more amusing to watch my daughters try to entertain a man who finds them childish and boring. Artoria's attempts at flattery can sorely test any polite young man's ability to keep his eyes from rolling."

Uncle's demonstration drew her smile.

"He has come close to showing what he was thinking when the three of them started saying unkind things about why you chose to live here instead of with me."

Martina selected another small pastry. "You must know it's not because of anything you've done. When Grandfather and Juliana were there, it was a peaceful haven where anyone who came felt welcome. With Priscilla and Sufina bickering all the time and Artoria finding fault with everyone and everything...I could ignore what was directed at me." She fingered Juliana's bracelet. "But the way they treated the whole familia...well, I wasn't going to be able to remain silent much longer."

"I've reined in the girls. They control themselves when I'm there. Since I pointed out no one wanted his son to marry a shrew or a harpy, their mother corrects the worst of their tempers. As for her too-critical nature..." His shrug said it all.

"Glabrio missing your dinner last night—that surprises me." Martina bit her lip. "I wouldn't have thought him the type of man who'd say he would be at a dinner and then not show up without sending an explanation. It seems even odder that he'd do it twice in a row."

"Nor would I." Volero reached for another pastry. "Something probably needed his urgent attention. His men patrol all the main roads, so he might not even be in the city. Tribune Nepos let the centurions police however they wanted. It was as if there was no commander here. Glabrio has stirred things up, asking about details, requiring written reports, insisting everything be done like he had his men do in Rome."

"I've seen him in action. More times than I'd like, actually. He's looking for some counterfeiters. A few of their coins were used at my glass shop, and the shop gave some as change to someone Glabrio knows. He kept what he found so they wouldn't be used again. Then he offered to replace them with real coins from his own purse."

Volero chuckled. "He probably saw how this place is furnished and thought you couldn't afford the loss. Except for the chairs I bought you, it looks like you're barely making it. Did you take what he offered?"

"Of course not. I don't want him to think I owe him anything." Her lips tightened until she saw the laugher in Uncle's eyes. "But you already knew I wouldn't. I told him he should talk with my foreman, not me, if he had any other questions. But he came back the next day to train Ceraulo and the others on what to look for to spot fakes. Actually, it was his optio who trained them. He spent that time training me."

"That should be useful when you start the red ware shop."

"Yes, but he only did it to make me talk to him. He came just to chat with me two days later when he had his aide visiting some shops near here in a plain tunic, not his uniform. Glabrio waited here out of sight while his optio did that."

Volero's head drew back. "Out of uniform?"

"Yes. He said a man out of uniform could learn things that one in uniform could not."

"Hmmm." Uncle's wry smile appeared. "I agree. A soldier watching you can make anyone nervous, even when you've done nothing wrong. Especially if you're not a Roman citizen, which many tradesmen aren't."

Uncle licked the last of the honey off his fingers. After drying them, he folded his napkin and placed it on the table. "What did he think of the new chairs?"

"I didn't let him try them. Like you suggested, I kept him in the old one so he wouldn't get too comfortable."

"I didn't expect you to use that trick on him." Uncle chuckled. "What did he say when you did?"

"Only that they were better than what he had at his quarters. Maybe that's true, or maybe he didn't want me to feel bad about having to use something so shabby with guests. But he was trying to get me to invite him to use the new ones while we played a board game."

"Well, the right company can make a mediocre meal taste better than a banquet or a tree stump seem better than the most comfortable chair. But I'd rather sit on a stump than in that chair. How did you keep him there?"

"I sat in the other old one and talked with him until his optio came. So, in a way he got what he wanted, but only under my conditions."

Uncle's laughter echoed in the small dining room. "No wonder he wants to spend more time with you. I'd be willing to wager no woman ever did that to him before."

"So, you can see why I think it wise to put some miles between us so he can't drop in to visit."

"What I can see is why he's so curious about you." He leaned over to pat her hand. "But he'll have found another interest by the time you return."

"I certainly hope so." Martina swung her legs off the hostess coach and stood. "I don't know who can play latrunculi at the estate. Maybe no one." She raised her eyebrows before batting her eyes. "I'll never learn the enticing ways Pricilla has mastered, but will you indulge me in a game tonight to tide me over until I can come back?"

The second round of fluttering eyelids was met with Uncle's heartiest laugh.

"Of course. That's what guardians are for."

She rested her hand on his arm as they strolled toward the game table. "You know, you've turned into a fine guardian, but you're even better as my uncle and friend. I'll miss your visits."

"Every guardian should have a ward who's as easy to care for as you." He patted her hand. "I'll miss you, too."

Harbor of Carthago, early morning of Day 27

Martina stood on the quay, watching two dock slaves carry her one large trunk down the gangplank to store in the hold. The box of scrolls and codices was too valuable to let out of her sight, so Uncle Volero's bodyguard Taurus would carry it. After Uncle gave final instructions, Taurus would lead her and Platana onto the ship for the five-hour trip up the coast to Utica.

It would be her first time at sea, and anticipation of the sights and sounds bubbled up within her. When she first came to Grandfather when her parents died, she'd missed the estate and the people there terribly. It would be good to see some of them again, but now she'd be missing the Christian brother and sisters she'd be leaving at her town house.

But she wouldn't be gone for long—only long enough to arrange what she'd need to open the pottery shop and for Glabrio to lose interest in her. Which would take longer, she had no idea.

"There's enough here for expenses and return passage." Uncle handed a purse to Taurus. "Some men from the estate should be meeting you. They'll take Martina upriver to Cigisa. Make certain the one escorting her has enough men to protect her. If he doesn't, I want you to stay with her for the river trip before you return. Any questions?"

"No, Master." Taurus tied the purse to the belt that held two daggers and joined Platana.

The thud of the cover being placed over the hold declared it time to go.

"As for you, Martina, I expect you to be careful. Listen to Taurus if he says something is amiss." Words of warning were sometimes word of true affection, like now.

"I will. I was told I'm supposed to be going to Cigisa right away, so I'm certain we'll get there safely."

Uncle rolled his eyes at her hidden meaning. He never believed God told her anything…at least not yet.

"If Taurus doesn't go upriver with you so he can confirm your safe arrival when he comes back here, I'll expect you to send word as soon as you get there."

"I'll do that. I'll let you know when I think it's time to return, too, so you can send Taurus back for me."

"I hope that won't be too long." He placed her hand on his arm. "The other passengers are on board. Time to join them."

As they strolled toward the gangplank, his mouth turned down. "I'll miss our lunchtime conversations. I'll miss the peacefulness of your home when I stop to check on you and play a game or two before I go to mine."

"You're welcome to use my house as your own whenever you wish. Colina will gladly feed you some of what they're eating." She hugged his arm. "I'll miss you, too, but this is only goodbye for now. Hopefully, by the time I figure out what I want to bring from the estate for starting my pottery shop, it will be safe to return."

Volero's frown turned into a subdued smile. "As soon as it is, I'll let you know."

They'd reached the edge of the quay. It was time to part.

She followed Taurus and Platana down the gangplank. Taurus continued on with the box to place it beneath a chair under the rear canopy. Then he sat, stretched out his legs, crossed his arms, and watched her.

The rowers extended their oars, and Martina went to the rail.

As the ship moved away from the quay, Uncle raised a hand in farewell, then stood, arms crossed, his eyes fixed on her.

Martina glanced at Platana when she joined her. "I feel bad about leaving him. Being home too much with only Artoria and her daughters—I wouldn't wish that on anyone."

Uncle raised his hand once more before turning to walk away.

"When he first moved in, I never expected him to be so much like Grand-father. He's become much more than my guardian. More than my uncle. He's become a good friend."

"He sees you that way, too." Platana patted Martina's hand where it rested on the rail. "But it shouldn't be long before you can come back."

When Uncle vanished into the throng moving around the quay, Martina left the rail. "I hope so. Uncle will tell me when he thinks it's safe. But it's God who told me it was time to leave. I'll return when He tells me it's the wise thing to do."

Chapter 39

BETTER THAN EXPECTED

Harbor of Utica, late morning of Day 27

Sartorus leaned his head back against the mattress and closed his eyes. When no one came to take them to the ship after breakfast, Glabrio stood his mattress on its side and leaned it against the bars so they could sit and wait in what passed for comfort in a slave's world.

When they went down to Carthago two days ago, the wind had been behind them until the shore curved south. When the sail was furled, the rowers took over. But yesterday coming back to Utica, the wind was strong against them. For a while, the sailors worked the sail to go against the wind. But they'd left Carthago late, and the captain decided they weren't making fast enough progress. So, they'd rowed the rest of the way. It must have been four times as far as the day before.

Halfway back, he couldn't keep the pace, no matter how hard he tried. Glabrio was struggling as well. When Hanno strode toward them, he'd closed his eyes and prayed for strength to bear what must be coming.

God had answered his prayer, but not how he expected. Hanno only slapped each of them on the back of their heads before ordering them to stow their oars until he told them to row again.

Sartorus spent most of that quarter-hour rest thanking God for the mercy shown by the first mate. Three more times Hanno made them stop rowing and rest before Utica came into view.

The sun had long since set and the sky fire was fading fast when the experienced rowers turned the ship and backed it up to its berth.

He'd expected to start unloading as soon as the gangplank was lowered. But the shackled rowers were herded onto the quay, and the others took the ship out to anchor for the night.

One more thing to thank God for as they trudged back to their cell for a bowl of porridge and a well-earned sleep.

Now it was late morning, and they still waited in the cell.

Sartorus leaned forward, taking the pressure off his sunburned back. Where his back and chest had been flaming red yesterday, today there were many small blisters. The skin between the blisters felt hot to the touch, and the slightest touch hurt.

God, how long will this pain last? One day? Two days? A week?

Hanno told him to wear the tunic while rowing yesterday, even though it made him too hot. But at least the burn didn't get worse while he wore it.

"I'm going to ask for something for that burn." Concern coated Glabrio's voice. "Hanno wants you to row hard. Surely, he'll see treating it will help you do that sooner."

"Let me ask him. It's better if he doesn't see us watching out for each other." He lowered his voice to a whisper. "None of the other rowers do. When a man loses hope, he stops caring about others."

Glabrio scrunched his face and whispered back. "And when he loses hope, he won't try to get free."

"Good thing Captain noticed before we were at sea. I've never seen it break like that before." The voice coming down the passage between cells drew both their gazes. The sailor who handed out food and one other walked past toward the cellblock kitchen. "They've taken the ship to get the rigging repaired. When it gets back, they'll move the cargo. This lot stays here until then, so Hanno wants them fed."

Sartorus couldn't stop the grin, and it raised Glabrio's eyebrows before he got it cooled to a subdued smile. But his companion in this mess didn't know Whom else he'd been talking to.

Thank You, God, for whatever broke. Thank You for the extra time off that bench and out of the sun. Please deliver us from this bondage. He drew up his knees and wrapped his arms around them, clutching his own wrists to keep them there. Then he bowed his head. *Please heal these burns quickly, and give me strength to bear the pain until You do. Please make both our heads stop hurting, too. Next time we get out of this cell, please bring someone who'll help us.*

Eyes closed, he slowed his breathing and kept praying. When a hand rested on his arm, he opened them.

"Are you all right?" Worry filled Glabrio's eyes.

"Yes. It hurts some, but it could be worse."

Glabrio slapped Sartorus's arm once before withdrawing his hand. He drew a deep breath and released a sigh. His mouth settled into a frown, then one corner of his mouth lifted. "Looks like a day of rest for us. That's better than I expected. But even if the day gets bad, as long as we're still together, it could be much worse."

Harbor of Utica, early afternoon of day 27

The white bird with black wingtips swooped down, grazed the surface of the sea, and rose with a fish in its beak. One flip of the bird's head and the fish became dinner.

Martina leaned on the rail, closed her eyes, and let the sea breeze caress her face. "Grandfather said he like being at sea. Now I understand why."

Platana ran her hand along the well-oiled wood of the railing. "Your uncle was right about this being the best way to go to Cigisa."

"I'm almost sorry we've reached Utica. But I'll be glad when we get upriver and reach the estate. Of the people I knew as a child, I wonder who will still be there. I wonder who's come down river to fetch me."

Two rowboats came out from the shore to pull the ship in to dock, back end first. A flurry of activity followed on deck, and Martina led Platana back to the canopy where Taurus waited with her library in a box.

Finally, a ramp was lowered from deck to dock. Martina drew in a deep breath, squared her shoulders, and headed for the ramp.

She was almost down the gangplank when Platana nudged her from behind. "That man looks just like the tribune's aide. Except for the slave collar, of course."

Martina turned to look at the slave working on the ship beside them. He was one of a line of men carrying crates and casks out of the hold, up the ramp, and along the pier to the wagons waiting to receive them. "He looks a lot like him, but it can't be him. Sartorus is back in Carthago with the tribune."

The tall man ahead of the one Platana pointed out reached the cargo overseer and swung the cask off his shoulder. As two men took it from him to place it in the mule-drawn wagon, he turned.

Her breath caught. There could be no mistake. Tribune Acilius Glabrio was walking toward her, iron shackles forcing him to shuffle and a collar that marked him as a runaway around his neck.

What on earth could have possibly brought him here? Who could have taken both him and his aide and turned them into slaves?

She fingered the lamb cameo before wrapping her hand around it.

The tribune was in deep trouble, and she should rescue him. She could buy him and free him. Her steward probably had enough money in the strong-box at the pottery shop to pay for him. If the other man was his aide, she should buy both of them.

If he weren't the tribune who could arrest her for her faith, there would be no question about what she would do. But if she freed him, what would she have to do next? Would he need to stay with her for a while to hide from whoever did this to him? Could she and Platana keep their secret from him if she took him to the estate where he could watch her day and night? Would a careless word from one of the house slaves reveal something he shouldn't know?

God, I'm afraid of him, of what he might do. But I know You tell us to help those in need, and he certainly needs my help right now.

She steepled her fingers against her nose. *When You told me three days ago to go to Cigisa right away, was this why?*

Peace poured over her, and she had her answer.

If that's what You want, Lord, then I'll do it. She drew a deep breath and blew it out slowly. *So…please protect us as I help him.*

She continued down the gangplank to the pier where Atriensis, the chief steward of the estate, waited.

"Welcome back, Mistress." Atriensis's smile was as kind as she remembered. "Let me offer the condolences of the whole familia on the death of your grandfather. I regret the reason, but it's good to see you again."

"It's good to see you as well, dear Atriensis." She rested her hand on his arm. "It's been so long. I probably look very different, but you look just the same."

He patted her hand, and the warmth of his smile and eyes wrapped around her as they had when she was a child "The years have given me my share of wrinkles, but it's a pleasure to see the master's little girl grown into a fine woman like her mother. Many at the estate will be pleased to see you again."

"I'm looking forward to seeing them, too." For good or ill, what would her next words put in motion? "But before we head upriver, I want to buy something."

"What, Mistress?"

She waved her hand toward the tribune. "That man over there."

"Which one?" Atriensis peered toward the lines of men trudging to and from the wagon.

"That handsome runaway."

He sucked air between his teeth. "We don't chain our men while they work or lock them up at night. A slave who runs once will run again without that. Why would you want to buy trouble?"

"I don't think he will be. With what I plan for him, he'll be content to stay."

Atriensis's eyebrows lowered. "Would your father have approved?"

"You don't need to worry. Father and Grandfather would both approve." She touched Atriensis's hand. He'd been like an uncle when she was a child, and eight years hadn't changed that. "Trust me. So, how do we find the one who owns him?"

"The captain of that ship does. I've dealt with Barca for years. He takes most of our olive oil to Carthago for the imperial buyers."

"Can we talk with him now?"

"If you wish. Let me make the request. Stay here with our men until I call you over."

Atriensis approached the man by the gangplank and exchanged words she couldn't hear. Then he went aboard and spoke with a brawny bearded man who stood, arms crossed, watching the slaves trudging into and out of the hold. More words too quiet to hear were followed by the captain and Atriensis joining her on the wharf.

"Mago Barca, this is my mistress, Publilia Martina." Atriensis bowed to each as he spoke their names.

"So, one of my rowers interests you?" Barca bounced his eyebrows and smiled suggestively.

"Perhaps." She rubbed her jaw, as she'd seen Grandfather do so often when negotiating with a friend. "But I need to check him out more closely before I make an offer."

Palm up, Barca's hand swept toward the line of slaves carrying cargo out of the ship. "Come with me."

Martina stopped herself before she bit her lip. She had no idea what the tribune would say when he saw her, but he might not want anyone to hear it. "I need to examine him by myself."

Atriensis's eyebrows shot up, but he said nothing.

Barca chuckled. "As you wish. Check out whatever you want. Take your time. Enjoy yourself."

She felt the heat to the tip of her ears. "Enjoyment is not what I'm shopping for today."

Barca's smirk and shrug said he didn't believe her. She raised her chin, turned on her heel, and strolled toward the wagon where Glabrio was waiting to hand off a cask.

She walked up behind him. As soon as he let go of the cask, she spoke softly. "I didn't expect to find you here, Tribune."

He spun and almost tripped on the chains of his shackles. "I didn't expect to be here." His woman-teasing smile lit his eyes as well.

"Act like you don't know me. Your captain thinks I'm shopping." She lowered her voice to a whisper. "What did he pay for you?"

He turned the smile off. "Three hundred fifty." He whispered as well.

She put her fingers on his jaw and turned his head, looking down her nose at him as she examined first one side, then the other of his face. She pushed back the hair to see the bruise on his temple. When she touched it, his head jerked back."

"I'm so sorry." She bit her lip. "I have to look like I'm inspecting you to see if I should buy you."

"It's all right. Make it look real." His smile was fleeting, but his eyes spoke a silent thank you.

She tapped his chin. "Show me your teeth." She gave the command loudly enough for Barca to hear.

He bared his teeth as if angry.

She made a circle with her index finger, and he turned around, the chains between his ankles clanking as he did.

When his face was turned away from the captain, he whispered. "Buy my optio, too."

She crossed her arms and moved to put her back toward the captain and Atriensis. "If I can."

With the slightest movement, Glabrio tipped his head toward his companion, who was coming up the gangplank with a cask balanced on his shoulder.

She pointed at Sartorus. "You. Come here."

Sartorus's eyes widened, then closed. His head tipped back, and an odd smile curved his mouth. Then he looked at Glabrio, whose nod was barely visible. Sartorus carried the cask to the cart, then returned to stand with his hands clasped in front of him, eyes downcast.

Martina repeated her inspection, then flicked her hand toward the string of men now carrying amphoras onto the ship. "Go back to work." With two fingers, she tapped Glabrio's chest. "You stay here."

After fingering her lower lip, she strolled over to Atriensis and the captain. "How much for both of them?"

"They're both young and strong. You'll get many years of work out of them. So...five hundred denarii each."

She looked at Atriensis and raised her eyebrow.

He scrunched his nose. "That seems high for runners. They might prove lazy or hard to handle. Does either have some special skill to justify that price?"

"Not that I know of, but lazy wasn't a problem on the voyage to and from Carthago. I put them on the back oars, and they kept the pace the first day. The second day they did even better. It took a few slaps on the back of the head for the tall one, but they put their backs into the rowing now. I haven't needed the whip even once."

◆

Martina's steward walked up to Glabrio and grabbed his jaw. Anger flared in Glabrio's eyes before he could stop it.

A frown was the steward's response. "This one..." He turned to Martina. "He'll be more trouble than you think."

"I want him anyway. I'm sure he'll be trainable with the right balance between punishment and reward." Martina crossed her arms.

Her steward pulled Glabrio's tunic over his head, leaving only the loincloth he wore while rowing to keep from overheating. That was all he wore when exercising outside at the baths in Rome, so the long hours in the sun hadn't burned him.

Before the tunic cleared his eyes, Martina had turned her gaze toward a nearby ship. Glabrio froze his face to stop the crooked smile her modesty inspired.

"Take a look at what you're buying." The captain chuckled. "You're sure to like the view. One like that is worth a good price."

She looked, but as her gaze met Glabrio's, her cheeks blazed. "I suppose that could please my female customers as much as the handsome face." Then she turned her eyes away.

Glabrio fought to stop his jaw clenching as the steward felt his biceps and thigh muscles and tapped on his chest and back. Being treated like a horse for sale—how did other men stand it? Thanks to Martina, this would be the last time.

The steward glanced over his shoulder at the captain. "Did either run more than once?"

"I didn't ask. I keep the ones I don't trust shackled most of the time, so that didn't matter." The captain pointed at Glabrio's ankle where the shackle had rubbed the skin raw. "No callouses there, so I doubt it. A brand on the forehead is cheaper than the collar, so I'd expect both if he had."

"Hmph." Her steward summoned Sartorus with a flick of his hand, and his optio left the line of men carrying amphorae to stand before him. Once more with hands clasped and eyes downcast, Sartorus acted as docile as a sheep. A repeat of the inspection followed, but Sartorus cringed when Martina's man removed the tunic to reveal the blisters and angry red skin on his shoulders, chest, and back.

Martina sucked air between her teeth. "We'll need some ointment for that before we head upriver."

The steward shrugged. "If he keeps his tunic on, it should heal fast enough without it."

"But we'll get it anyway. I won't let my people suffer needlessly." The smile she gave her steward took the sting from the rebuke. "Besides, he'll be able to work better if we do."

"This one..." Her steward flicked the bronze tag that hung from the neck ring. "If not for this collar, he'd seem like a good purchase." He turned away and rejoined Martina and the captain. "One's defiant; the other might be faking submission. But if you're certain you want them..."

"I do. We can always sell them if they don't work out."

Her steward slowly rubbed his jaw. "Five hundred is too high, but 450 would be fair."

The captain blew out a slow breath. "Too low. But since I've been carrying your cargoes for many years, I'll go down to 480."

"For 475, I'll take them both right now. The quaestor is over there today, and we can register the sale."

The captain held out his hand, and the two clasped forearms. "The bill of sale should say two rowers. The burned one is Sartorus. He calls the handsome one Mulio. I hadn't renamed them yet."

"They can keep loading while I get the bill of sale prepared and the money ready." The steward returned to Martina's side. "You can wait at the pottery shop while I do the paperwork with the quaestor. Then we'll head upriver. You'll be home before nightfall."

"While you're registering the sale, I want to get something for Sartorus's burns."

"The shop steward can take you." The man who'd come to meet her ship scanned her bodyguard. "But take him with you."

Her trunk had been unloaded, and two of the men who came with her steward picked it up. A third picked up the large box at her maid's feet.

"This way." With Martina beside him, her steward headed toward the forum.

Sartorus donned his tunic and walked down the gangplank to the ship. He disappeared into the hold and returned with another cask on his shoulder.

Martina looked back and gave Glabrio the smile he'd wanted from her since the first night he met her.

With a crooked smile at his new owner and a shrug, Glabrio went back to work. Before the rest of the men finished loading the ship, he'd be free and on a riverboat heading to Cigisa.

If he'd had to guess what would happen today, being rescued by the woman who tried so hard to avoid him was the last thing he'd have suggested. Sartorus had seen how she treated him. They'd have a good laugh later over this twist of fate.

It was good to be free again, no matter how it happened, but for Publilia Martina to pay to free him…that was much better than anything he expected.

Chapter 40

WHATEVER IS NEEDED

Martina walked at Atriensis's side as they left the quay and headed toward the Forum. She'd committed him to spending a lot of money for what seemed like a whim, but he'd soon understand why she had to.

"I know it seems odd that I'd insist on buying those two men, but I know them from Carthago."

"You're domina of all that was your father's. It's your right to buy whatever you want." His indulgent smile mirrored what Uncle Volero sometimes gave her. "I suppose I can find some use for them at the estate. Were they slaves of your grandfather or one of his friends?"

"Neither. I met the tall one at a dinner at Uncle Volero's house right after the days of mourning ended. He's the tribune in command of the Urban Cohort in Carthago."

Atriensis head drew back. "What was a tribune of Rome doing rowing Barca's ship?"

"I don't know, but I couldn't leave him and his optio like that. Not when I could free them."

"You didn't have to buy them. We could have taken the matter to the quaestor and asked what needed to be done to free a citizen who's been illegally made a slave."

"But wouldn't that have taken a few days, maybe longer?"

"Probably."

"And during that time, Tribune Glabrio and his optio would have to keep working like animals. Something horrible could happen to them. They might even die before we could get them freed. I couldn't do that to them."

"I suppose not." Atriensis paused to let a cart pass in front of them. "After we pay for them, then what? That's a lot of money."

"I hadn't thought past freeing them." She offered a sheepish smile. "From all I've seen, Glabrio is an honorable man, and his family is very wealthy. I'll simply ask him to repay me."

They crossed the street and entered her pottery shop. The man at the counter glanced at them, then stared. "Atriensis. I didn't expect you for another ten days. Is there a problem?"

"No. On the contrary, something good has happened. Our domina has returned from Carthago to stay at the estate for a while."

Atriensis held out his arm and flexed his fingers so Martina would come stand beside him. "Publilia Martina, this is your shop steward, Figulus. Our red ware comes downriver from the estate, and Figulus oversees the bulk sales and arranges for custom items the elite of the city order."

"I'm delighted to meet you, Figulus. I'm going to need you to teach me how to run a pottery shop like you do before I return to Carthago. I plan to open another shop there."

Figulus's eyebrows rose, then settled back into place as a smile grew. "It will be my pleasure to teach you all I know, Domina."

"Excellent. I'm going to the estate for a few days, so you'll have some time to figure out what you'll be teaching me when I return."

Atriensis cleared his throat. "We came for a more pressing reason today. Do you have enough money on hand to pay 1050 denarii for something?"

"Often, but not today."

"Wasn't the price only 950?" Martina fingered her silver bracelet. What if there wasn't enough money?

"The imperial tax on slave sales is one tenth of the sales price."

Martina nibbled her lip. When Atriensis agreed so readily to 475 denarii apiece, she'd assumed he had the money at his fingertips in Utica. Would Captain Barca let her take possession if she couldn't pay in full today? If he wouldn't and there was only enough for one, only one choice was possible. Would Glabrio be angry when she took his sunburned optio because his need was greater?

God, please don't let me have to choose.

Her steward blew his breath out between pursed lips. "How much can you give me right now? I can bring enough from the estate to replace the money in two days."

"I think about 975. Maybe 980."

"Taurus." Martina turned to her bodyguard, who stood a few feet back, arms crossed. "How much did Uncle Volero give you?"

"Fifty denarii."

"Give it to Atriensis. You'll come upriver with us to get it back with enough extra to get you home to Uncle."

As Taurus untied the purse Uncle had given him from his belt, Martina turned to Platana. "How much did we bring?"

Platana pulled a small purse from inside her tunic and dumped its contents on the countertop. With her fingertip, she moved each coin from left to right, counting out the total as she went. "You have thirty-five denarii."

Martina smiled at Atriensis triumphantly. "We have ten denarii to spare, and we didn't even need what's in your purse."

"You'll need some of mine for the ointment for that burn." He dumped his purse on the counter. From the twenty-five denarii, he took ten and added it to Platana's piles. "Take twenty. That should be more than enough."

He put a hundred denarii for the sales tax into his own purse and tossed Taurus's empty purse back to her bodyguard. "Put the 950 in a box. I'm going to register the sale now. When I get back, I'll go get the two men Martina simply had to buy."

He didn't roll his eyes, but the wry smile said he wanted to. "I want to leave for the estate as soon as I get them, so take her to a shop where she can get a burn ointment while I'm gone."

He patted Martina's hand. "I'll be back as quickly as I can, so don't shop too long."

"I won't. I don't have enough money to do that." She separated twenty denarii from the pile on the counter and gave them to Platana. "I'm not one to waste money on frivolous things, anyway."

"If we're going to get to the estate before dark, we can't waste time." Atriensis opened the door and held it for the others to exit the shop before he headed for the quaestor in the Forum.

Figulus led Martina, Platana, and Taurus to a shop selling perfumes and ointments.

"If you think you can find your way back, I'll leave you now."

Taurus crossed his arms. "Of course."

Martina's nod sent Figulus back up the street.

"If you want, you can wait outside. I've never known a man who preferred being inside a women's shop over waiting outside. When you escort Artoria and her girls when they go shopping, I hope you get some choice between in or out."

"Hmph." The first smile she'd ever seen on Uncle Volero's bodyguard warmed his eyes as well. "I'll be just outside. Call if you need me."

When they entered, Platana led the way to the counter. "I'd like an ointment that will soothe burned skin."

"We have several for that purpose." The shop girl turned to the shelf behind her and selected a jar with a cork top. She placed it on the counter and unplugged the cork. "This is one of our most popular."

The scent of roses wafted toward Martina.

"The scent is lovely." Platana sniffed the ointment and returned it to the counter. "But it won't do for us. It's for a man who's been burned by the sun. Chest, back, shoulders—everything a tunic usually covers. He doesn't need to smell good, but we will need plenty of an ointment that will help the pain while not being too expensive."

"Stay here, please. I'll get my mistress."

Platana's nod sent the girl through the curtain to the back room.

The next person through the curtain was old enough to be the girl's grandmother.

"So, you need ointment to treat a man?"

Martina and Platana nodded in unison.

"Is he just red or blistered?"

"He's very red all over, but there are blisters, too." Martina fingered her bracelet. "I've never seen anyone worse. He looks like it must hurt terribly."

The old woman disappeared through the curtain and returned with a much larger jar. "This will help. Aloe vera gel."

She offered the opened container to Platana, who sniffed it and held it for Martina to smell.

Platana handed the jar back to the old woman. "How do I use it?"

"Spread it on his burn, but very gently so the blisters don't break."

"Then I'll tend him myself the first time to show them how." One corner of Platana's mouth lifted as she glanced at Martina. "Men and gentle are not words I use together. How often?"

"Five or six times a day for a week. It will cool and soothe until the red goes away. He'll hurt less as soon as you start. He'll heal faster, too."

Martina leaned on the counter. "Then that's what we want. How much to buy enough for seven days for chest, back, and shoulders?"

"Two of these jars, nine denarii each."

Platana took the eighteen coins from her purse and paid. Then they joined Taurus for the walk back to the pottery shop.

"Do you suppose Atriensis has finished?" Platana glanced at the heavy ointment jar in her hands. "The sooner we get this on the optio's burn, the sooner he'll heal."

"He might already be at the shop." Martina sniffed the jar she was carrying. "Sartorus should be glad we didn't get the one that smelled like roses." The wry smile she gave Platana got a nod in return. "He can't apply this to his own back, and I can't see the tribune caring for him properly without you teaching him before they leave."

"About them leaving…" Platana fingered her lip. "How are they going to get back to Carthago?"

"Oh." Martina blew out a slow breath. "I hadn't thought about that. They'll have nothing but what they're wearing. Atriensis and I only have seventeen denarii between us. That's not enough to buy passage for two…or even one."

Martina scrunched her eyes as she rubbed her forehead. "We can't leave them here with nothing. Atriensis could give them enough to go home with Taurus if we take them upriver."

"And I could take care of that burn the first few times. The tribune can watch and learn."

"I expect they'll both appreciate your help with that."

Platana shrugged. "Whether they do or not, it's what our Lord would want me to do."

"Yes, and no matter what Atriensis thinks, spending a thousand denarii to set the tribune and his aide free was right in God's eyes."

They'd reached the pottery shop. As Taurus held the door open for them, Martina glanced over her shoulder toward the harbor.

Right in God's eyes? Undoubtedly. But was it wise to bring such a dangerous man home with her, even for a single night?

God, as Platana and I do whatever is needed for these two men, please protect us.

The harbor of Utica

Each time Sartorus hoisted another amphora onto his shoulder, it set off a burst of pain when the weight of it settled on his sunburned skin. But it was still easy to give thanks for each piece of cargo he carried.

Yesterday, he'd thanked God for the extra rest while the captain went to the races. But that also made them arrive too late to switch the cargo before nightfall. This morning, some part of the rigging broke unexpectedly, and he'd thanked God for more rest and the time out of the sun. But the real blessing was how the extra time it took for repairs had delayed their arrival at the quay until someone was there who would help them.

But the joy bubbling up inside him wasn't only because he'd be free before sundown.

Only God would use the woman who fascinated Glabrio but couldn't stand him. He'd brought her to the berth next to their ship at exactly the right time to see them. Sartorus had asked for someone who'd help the next time they were out of the cell, and God had delivered.

And even though Publilia Martina wanted nothing to do with Glabrio, she'd taken pity on them. Her concern over the coins Glabrio had to take, the shabby chairs in the vestibulum, the scarcity of furniture in her house—all said she didn't have money to spare. Still, she'd spent almost a thousand denarii to free them.

The man arranging the cargo in the hold took his amphora, and Sartorus headed up the ramp for the next one.

Glabrio would repay her. He'd tried to replace the counterfeit coins, so she should know that already. But it might be a few weeks before he could. Still, whether she could afford to spend that much money or not, she'd bought them.

Each time he passed Glabrio going to and from the wagon, they exchanged smiles and the occasional wink.

When he reached the wagon, only ten amphorae remained. He picked up the last one he'd ever carry as a slave and brought it to the hold.

Glabrio handed off his last amphora and came to Sartorus's side. "I never want to carry one of those again."

Sartorus bounced his eyebrows. "You shouldn't have to."

Hanno walked up behind them and slapped the back of their heads. "That pretty woman might want you for herself, but you're still Captain Barca's until she pays him for you. Sit on your benches."

Glabrio spun on him and straightened to his full height to tower over the first mate. "Don't do that again." Ice coated his voice. "We became hers the moment the quaestor certified the sale. We don't have to do what you say anymore." Glabrio's finger stabbed the air between them.

Hanno's jaw clenched. "You do if you want those shackles off." Hanno shook the ring of keys. "Now sit like you're told." He flicked the bronze runner's tag. "Captain has use for the shackles, but you can keep these. She might like you better in them."

Glabrio took a step toward Hanno, and Hanno stepped back. Then Sartorus's hand on Glabrio's arm stopped him.

"Her steward will be here shortly." Sartorus lifted one foot to make the chain jingle. "I'm ready to get these off, and the captain is welcome to them."

He shuffled to his bench and sat.

Glabrio snorted, but he turned and, head high, joined Sartorus at their oars.

Hanno knelt and unlocked Sartorus's shackles. As the cuffs fell away, his thanks rose to God yet again.

He watched Glabrio's face as Hanno unlocked the first cuff one last time. Deepest relief was written there, but his commander didn't yet know Who to thank for delivering them. Would the time come when he could tell the tribune who'd become his friend about the God Who'd saved them both?

Chapter 41

Going Upriver

As Martina and her party approached the pottery shop, her chief steward came from the other direction.

"Are they mine now?"

"Almost." Atriensis handed her two papyrus sheets. "The transfer of Mulio and Sartorus to you is recorded. I only need to take the money to Barca and claim them."

Taurus opened the door, and they entered. The three men who'd carried her baggage rose from tossing dice.

When Atriensis snapped his fingers, they came to him. "Take her baggage to the boat and get it ready to leave as soon as we join you."

As the men went out the door, Atriensis lifted the box from the counter and shook it. The jingle of gold and silver coins drew his frown. "Put something on top to keep it quiet."

Figulus disappeared into the back of the shop and returned with a rag.

"I don't want to look like I'm carrying this much money." Atriensis added the rag, and a shake of the box made no sound. "I'm taking Taurus with me, so you stay inside. I'll be back shortly with your purchases. Then we'll head upriver."

Martina placed her hand on his arm. "Thank you for helping me rescue them."

He patted her hand. "It was the right thing to do…assuming the tribune pays you back."

"He will." Martina picked up the box and handed it to him. "But even if he couldn't, it would still be the right thing to do."

As soon as Atriensis walked out the door, Figulus pointed at the curtain. "If you'll excuse me, Domina, my work is waiting."

"Of course." With a smile and a flick of her hand, she dismissed him.

"Nothing that happened today is what I expected." Martina settled onto a bench by the wall. "I thought God told me to come to Cigisa to get away from Glabrio. If anyone had said it would put me where I couldn't avoid him until he leaves tomorrow, I'd have laughed at that ridiculous idea. But now I'm certain God wanted us here to rescue him and his aide."

"I think God wanted you to rescue them, too." Platana sat beside her. "I think He'll protect us from any harm because you did. We just need to keep praying."

"I'm sure you're right, but if I seem to forget and start to worry too much, then remind me." Martina's deep breath was followed by a deeper sigh.

"Now that I've bought their freedom, what do I do with them?" She waved the sheets at Platana. "Since they weren't legally slaves, do I have to do anything special to free them?" She set the sheets aside and ran her fingers through her hair. She still wore it down for Grandfather's sake.

She sighed. Life had become so complicated since he died. "Uncle would know, but he's not here to ask."

Platana patted the ointment jar in her lap. "If I'm going to treat Sartorus's burn properly, they might need to come upriver for more than a day."

"I suppose so, but what will Glabrio think if I invite them?" Martina massaged the back of her neck. "I'm still not sure what will come of him being too close for too long."

She traced a spiral on the cork of her ointment jar. "Everyone at the estate will expect me to make the morning offerings to the household gods, like Mother used to." She bit her lip. "But I can't do that."

"Are you certain anyone's been doing it since you went to your grandfather? Maybe they will have forgotten what's expected of a domina."

"Maybe, but Atriensis was always so conscientious about everything. I can't imagine he wouldn't have done something."

"Maybe you can have him keep doing it."

"I could, but that would make my people talk about it. If Glabrio ever heard them, he could ask some dangerous questions."

"You could get him to keep you company so he won't hear idle gossip."

Martina rolled her eyes. "Now you're sounding like Uncle. He thinks spending time with me will make Glabrio lose interest if I try to be boring."

"That doesn't seem likely to me, but it might take a man to understand one." Platana's gaze settled on the ointment jar in her lap. "But keeping Glabrio busy won't keep Sartorus from hearing what's being said. The tribune uses him as a spy already."

Martina tapped the top of the jar. "You'll be spending a lot of time treating his burns. If he says anything, maybe you can explain away what he thinks he's seeing."

"I can try, but only God knows if that will work." Platana shrugged.

Martina steepled her fingers and rubbed the sides of her nose. Platana was right. They had little control over what the men saw or whether it would reveal their faith.

God, please show both of us how to keep our visitors from learning anything You don't want them to know.

Barca's ship

Glabrio stood at the rail, Sartorus beside him, watching the street down which Martina and her steward had gone.

How much longer? Time had passed fast enough while they carried the cargo, but since Hanno took off the shackles, it crept like a caterpillar.

Sartorus's arm shot out. "There he is."

Her man had entered the quay from another street. Under one arm was a box big enough to hold their ransom. From his free hand, two pairs of sandals hung by their ankle straps. Behind him walked the bodyguard who'd been on the ship with Martina.

He nudged Sartorus. "Time to change owners...at last."

Sartorus answered with a grin and a nod.

Barca was on the quay, talking with the captain of the boat that brought Martina. When her steward approached, he ended the conversation, and the two of them came down the gangplank. As they passed on the way to the canopy, her steward handed Sartorus the sandals.

Glabrio sat on his old bench and slipped the first sandal on. As he wrapped the straps around his calf and tied them, the faint clink of coins being counted came from the canopy behind him.

"A pleasure doing business with you, as always, Atriensis. I look forward to carrying your next load of oil to Carthago." Barca's voice was as warm as Glabrio expected from men who often made money together. "Keep the tunics. One burns too easily without it." A chuckle rumbled in his chest. "Tell that pretty mistress I hope she enjoys the tall one."

"After we harvest, you'll be hearing from me." Footsteps on the deck were followed by her steward appearing beside him.

"Let's go. Domina Martina is waiting, and the estate is a few hours upriver. I want to get there before dark."

Glabrio rose from the bench for the last time. "Lead the way."

Sartorus fell in beside him. A glance at the man who'd kept him from losing all hope found the slight smile that nothing seemed to quench. When everything was going wrong, when their situation looked most desperate, Sartorus and his "it could be worse" had helped him make it through.

It was time to write Titianus and tell him how perfect his choice had been and thank him for convincing Sartorus to come. He'd probably hear back that they'd been praying for his safety, and they were giving thanks for how their god had protected him. But whether gods protected anyone or not, it was certain a loyal friend did. That's what his optio had become.

With her steward ahead of him and her bodyguard behind, Glabrio climbed the gangplank beside his friend and stepped onto the quay, a free man once more.

After a short walk, Glabrio followed Martina's steward into a shop one block off the forum. On a bench against the front wall, Martina and her lady's maid sat, each holding a large jar.

Martina stood. "It's good to see you a free man again, Tribune." She offered a subdued smile.

"It's even better to be one." His woman-pleasing smile leaked out, and hers dimmed in response. With a twitch of his lips, he erased his own.

Her steward stuck his head through the curtain. "We're leaving, Figulus."

A man in an apron stained with red clay popped from behind the curtain. "May the gods protect you on your trip home." He dipped his head toward Martina. "And I look forward to teaching what I can when you return, Domina."

"It will be at least a few days, but not more than two weeks."

Her potter dipped his head again. "I'll be ready, Domina."

The steward tipped his head toward the door, and the bodyguard opened it. "The men have the boat ready at the river docks, so let's go."

He strode through the doorway, and the others followed.

Glabrio positioned himself beside Martina. "As I was saying, it's good to be a free man again, and no words can express the depth of my gratitude to you for buying both of us off that ship."

He cleared his throat. "But I have something else to ask of you."

"What would that be, Tribune?"

"Can we remain at your estate until Sartorus's sunburn heals? However long that takes. When we go back, we'll be in uniform again. Wearing armor with that burn…" He sucked air between his teeth.

Martina rubbed her jaw and looked away. Her long silence…what did that mean? His request was completely reasonable, so why wouldn't she agree to it immediately?

She glanced at him before turning her gaze back on the street ahead of them. "You may. Grandfather always said that it's a citizen's duty to help an officer of Rome when he needs it." She drew a deep breath. "But there are limits to what I can do. My steward is concerned that we spent over a thousand denarii, and I hope you're planning on paying me back. I'd hate to be forced to break Roman law by selling you to get it." She offered a cool smile. "Assuming I can sell you for as much as I paid. You are, after all, collared as runners."

Glabrio fingered the bronze tag hanging from the collar. "I can't at the moment, but I can assure you I'm good for the money. As soon as I get my next pay, I'll have it. But I don't know how soon that will be. I can't simply return as if nothing happened."

He massaged his wrist. "Just before we were knocked out and sold, Sartorus found part of a tribune's crest. I believe we found the metal shop where Nepos disappeared, but I don't know if he's dead or a slave somewhere, like us. I met the two slaves who do know, but Sartorus thinks they're not the ones who might have killed him. So, I don't know who got rid of him or why. The only two men I trust here are Sartorus and maybe Acceptus. He's my centurion charged with keeping the main roads safe."

One corner of his mouth lifted. "A wise man once told me that an officer's most dangerous enemies might be wearing Roman armor. It's not wise to be too quick to trust any man."

She stopped with her fists on her hips. "You can trust my uncle. The way he's welcomed you, I would think you'd know that."

Glabrio raised his hands to calm her. "I do, and I appreciate his friendship. I only meant among the men who report to me." His mouth twitched before his crooked smile appeared. She had a talent for hearing what he actually said instead of what he meant. "And I can trust you."

She fingered her bracelet, and a hard-to-interpret smile played on her lips. "Are you sure of that? I just broke Roman law by taking possession of a citizen who was sold to me as a slave when I knew he wasn't. I broke it twice since I bought two of you." Her puzzling smile turned wry. "Now I don't know if I need to officially free you or what."

He matched her wry smile. "I don't know if you need to free me to pay for that offense, so let's pretend it never happened…this time." He shrugged. "My men aren't stationed in Utica, so I'm not responsible for arresting the criminals here."

"But you'll soon be back in Carthago. When I return there…what then?"

"I owe you my life. That's a debt I can never repay. Rest assured, you will always be safe from me."

He expected a laugh, but her eyes sobered. The smile she offered him seemed uneasy.

"I hope so, but sometimes people make promises that others force them to break."

Atriensis was some distance ahead, but he stopped and looked back over his shoulder. "We're already late heading upriver. Let's keep moving. You'll have hours for talking on the boat."

As they followed him in silence, Glabrio stopped a grin before she saw it. With hours together on a small boat, the enigma that was Publilia Martina couldn't keep him from getting to know her now. He'd wanted her friendship since their first meeting. By the time they went back down the river, maybe she'd want his, too.

On the Bagrada River

With only two chairs and a stool under the small canopy of the riverboat, Sartorus took a seat next to Glabrio on the trunk that had come from Carthago.

He'd never paid attention to upstream versus downstream on the Tiber back home. But two days on a rowing bench had changed that forever.

Six men sat at the oars, and as soon as they shoved off, they began the arduous task of rowing against the current. Even in a slow-moving river like the Bagrada, they'd be dead tired after the four to five hours the steward had said the trip would take.

As soon as the boat moved past the last docks, the lady's maid came to him.

"I'm Platana, and I'll be putting ointment on your sunburn to help with the pain and speed your healing."

She was a pretty woman who looked to be in her mid-twenties, about his own age. But even if she'd been old and ugly, he didn't want her help. As a Christian, he'd stayed away from the intimate touches of women in Rome. He'd done the same here.

"Thank you for getting this for me." He held out his hand for the jar. "You won't need to put it on me. I can do it myself."

She held the jar close to her chest and rolled her eyes. "Your chest, maybe, but no one can tend their own back."

"I can help him." Glabrio reached for the jar.

Platana moved it behind her back. "The woman we got it from said it had to be applied very gently, especially on the blisters." She tightened her lips and shook her head. "I doubt any man could be as gentle as I can."

Martina rose from the chair under the canopy. "Sartorus. Come sit in here out of the sun while Platana tends you."

He opened his mouth to refuse. Servant or slave or whatever the lady's maid was, it didn't seem right for a woman to touch so much of him when it would feel like a caress.

"Do what she says." His commander's words raised Sartorus's eyebrows. "Martina's maid will probably do a much better job than you or I could. We can't return to Carthago until that burn is healed."

Sartorus's shoulders slumped. "Yes, Tribune."

Glabrio slapped Sartorus's arm where it wasn't burned. "It's Mulio or Glabrio until we're back in uniform. When we get to Martina's estate, we'll figure out the best way to proceed. But first, you need to heal."

Sartorus went to the canopy and sat sideways in Martina's chair. Martina's maid moved behind him. With some gel on her fingertips, she began with his back. He cringed when she first touched the inflamed skin, then relaxed as she applied the gel.

He turned his head enough to smile at her. "That does feel better. Thank you."

She returned the smile. "Good. Now, relax and let the gel do its work. I'll get all the red places. Then, we'll do it once or twice more before we get to the estate. Several times a day for a week or so—that's what's supposed to get you healed."

As the cooling gel dowsed the fiery pain, he closed his eyes and relaxed.

Thank You, God, for the ointment and for the woman who knows how to use it insisting she put it on me. Thank You for every small blessing these past three days and for bringing the woman who would know us and free us.

He opened his eyes, and his gaze fell on his commander, smiling as he sat on Martina's trunk.

Each time Glabrio glanced at her, his smile broadened until he turned his eyes back on the shore.

Why had she bought and freed them? What made her treat a man she didn't like and another she didn't know like people who mattered to her?

Platana had finished his back and shoulders. When she moved in front of him to work on his chest, he looked up at her face.

When she felt his gaze, she offered a kind smile. "This first time will be the worst. I'm trying not to hurt you, but some pain…" She shrugged. "I'm afraid that can't be avoided."

"It already feels some better. Thank you for doing this."

"It's my pleasure." Her eyes and smile declared the truth of those words.

She finished his chest and corked the jar. "I'll do this when we're halfway home and again after we get there."

"Thank you, Platana."

"You're very welcome."

He dropped the tunic over his head and stood to return the seat to its owner.

"Stay under the canopy, Sartorus." With a tip of her hand, Martina motioned for him to sit. "You need the shade more than I do."

He opened his mouth to protest.

"Do as she says." Glabrio's command must be obeyed without question, whether he wanted to or not.

Sartorus took the stool instead and motioned for Platana to take the chair. "I can't use the backrest, so I'll trade you."

With eyebrows raised, the handmaid looked at her mistress, who had moved outside the canopy. A downward flex of Martina's hand told her to stay there, and she sat in the shade beside him.

Sartorus had never lived among the wealthy, so he couldn't say firsthand how mistress and maid should act. But these two seemed more like friends or sisters than mistress and slave.

As he watched the rowers, he found himself moving in time with their strokes. With each back and forth, he gave thanks for their freedom once more.

Chapter 42

WALKING WITH MARTINA

Glabrio shifted to the edge of the trunk and patted the spot where Sartorus had been. "Since you've given your chair to my optio, this spot should be yours."

Martina leaned against the post that held the canvas. "I'm fine standing."

"But the one paying for the trip shouldn't have to. As I see it, I can stand and give you my seat, or you can come sit beside me." He stopped the crooked smile before it got too big. "After the past three days, I'd rather sit, but only if you'll join me."

Glabrio stood, and as he did, her bodyguard rose and came to stand behind her.

Martina glanced over her shoulder. "It's all right, Taurus. The tribune won't do anything he shouldn't."

She took a step toward him and stopped. "Very well. Since you undoubtedly need the rest, I'll join you. But"—she raised her finger and slowly shook it at him—"this doesn't mean I want a conversation. Watching the shoreline in silence was always my favorite way to travel the river when Mother took me with her to Utica." Her smile seemed sad. "It's been eight years, but I still enjoy the silence."

"Whatever you want suits me as well." Palm up, he invited her to sit on the trunk once more.

She sat on the opposite edge, keeping as much space between them as the length of it allowed.

Then, with the rhythmic soft splashes of the oars providing the accompaniment, she turned her eyes away from him and watched the passing scenery. Except for stealing an occasional glance at the special woman beside him, Glabrio watched it, too.

Evening of Day 27

As they moved farther upriver, Glabrio found himself watching the rowers at least as much as the passing scenery. It had been two hours since they left Utica, and the men still moved the oars with perfect synchrony and seemingly without tiring.

His one trip on the oars to Carthago and back had been more than he could manage without Hanno giving them special breaks.

As they passed another olive grove, a dock appeared just ahead. Without anyone telling them, the rowers headed for it. With skill rivaling that of the oarsmen backing Barca's ship into a quay, the rowers pulled into the dock. With oars pointing up at the sky, two of them climbed onto the dock and secured the boat to it with ropes.

One held a hand out to Atriensis, who gripped it as he moved from boat to dock.

"We stop here for a quarter hour or so for the men to rest. Feel free to walk around, if you wish."

Martina stood and took Atriensis's hand. With her free hand, she lifted her long tunic enough to let her step onto the dock. "The dock looks just as I remember it."

"They keep it in good shape for all of us who use it." Atriensis offered his hand to Platana.

Instead of taking it, she turned to Sartorus. "Are you ready for more ointment?"

"More than ready. The first time helped a lot." Sartorus's smile confirmed every word.

She turned back to Atriensis. "I'll stay here and tend the optio."

Glabrio stood. "But I welcome the chance to stretch my legs." He climbed onto the dock and hurried to catch up with Martina.

He matched his stride to hers. "Since our view of the shoreline isn't changing right now, is this break for the rowers also a break from silence for us?" She raised an eyebrow, but since she didn't say no, he pressed on. "May I ask you some questions?"

Martina's mouth opened as if to speak, then closed for a moment. "I suppose, but I might not answer them."

"Fair enough. How much farther to your estate?"

Martina tipped her head as she contemplated him. "We're halfway there."

"Is the estate on the river?"

"It is."

"So, is this your own boat?"

"Yes. For taking people and cargo to Utica, it's much faster than going by land."

She'd answered the last question with more than he'd asked. That was progress. Then her shoulders relaxed, like she was ready for a real conversation.

"At your uncle's first dinner, you mentioned how special your estate is. I'd planned to visit it to see why when I toured the Cigisa road with my centurion."

"I remember. As I told you, it's the people and the memories that make a place special. But only to those who've lived there. It will seem quite ordinary to you."

"I might have found it ordinary before, but not now."

She gave him a social smile. "Nothing has changed between then and now."

"But it has. You're giving us a refuge there when we need it most. Sartorus will remember your maid's kindness. I'll never forget how you found and rescued us without being asked."

"Anyone would have done the same."

"No, they wouldn't." One corner of his mouth curved. "I've seen much more of this world than you, and I can assure you that most would not have done what you have." He ran his fingers through his hair. "Some won't even help a friend if it costs them anything. At great cost, you helped two men you barely know, and one of us you don't even like."

A blush overspread her cheeks. "I don't dislike you, Tribune. My uncle says you're a good man, and I respect his opinion."

Embarrassing her hadn't been his intention, but any man would like the result. Pink cheeks made her even prettier.

"I hope over the next few days, you'll come to share his opinion as well as respect it."

"Perhaps I shall." She pointed at the boat. "Atriensis is signaling all of us to board again. It will be almost dark before we get home as it is."

"There are two more things I want to thank you for while he's not listening."

"He?"

"Sartorus. Getting that ointment and your maid's kind attention." He rubbed his jaw. "I wouldn't have made it through the past few days without him. He deserves the best of care."

A genuine smile curved her lips. "I understand. He's more than your aide. He's your friend, like Platana is to me. How many years have you been together?"

"Days, not years. He reported to one of my centurions in Rome, but I didn't start getting to know him until we sailed for Carthago twenty days ago."

Her head drew back, followed by a warmth in her gaze he hadn't seen before. "Sometimes it's not how long we know someone. It's the depth of what we share."

"A wise friend taught me it isn't rank or wealth or family connections that determine the worth of a man. It's his honor. I consider loyalty one measure of honor. He told me Sartorus was the best man to bring as my aide. He was right. Sartorus is one of the best men I know. Whatever you do for him, I consider it done for me."

"When you're ready to leave, Atriensis will give you both money for your passage home." A teasing smile appeared. "You can add that to what you'll be repaying me to make Atriensis happy. Until I told him why, he didn't think I should have spent so much on either of you."

"With pleasure." Just paying her back was not enough. He'd add on a bonus.

She started toward the boat, then paused. "I'll be watching the shoreline again, and you know what that means."

"You'll prefer silence to conversation."

A smile was her only answer before she turned away. But that was enough to satisfy. This had been more than a shallow conversation. As Sartorus healed over the next week, he'd have the chance for many more.

◆

As the rhythmic soft splashes of oars entering the water filled the silence, Martina found herself reflecting on the tribune's words, even though she didn't want to.

She sneaked a glance at him and found him watching the shoreline. She turned her own eyes on the opposite shore before he could notice.

He was the last man she would have expected to say rank, wealth, and relatives didn't define a man's worth. He certainly wouldn't have learned that from a father who'd risen to the pinnacle of importance in Rome. The first two consuls each year had that year named after them. Glabrio's father had been one of those only four years ago. Uncle had said one of Glabrio's ancestors had been among the first governors of their province, so he'd been an important man, too.

The tribune's wise friend...did the same man tell him his most dangerous enemies might be fellow soldiers? To never be too quick to trust anyone?

Yet he'd said he trusted her uncle, and he trusted her.

But could she trust him?

God, if he stays several days so Platana can take care of his friend, will he

*discover we follow You? I've been afraid of what that would mean, but will it be
dangerous if he does?*

The Cigisa estate, evening of Day 27

Martina's heart beat faster when the boat moved past the grove of olive
trees and her family villa came into view. It was as if the past eight years had
never happened. When they pulled up to the dock, a mule cart large enough
for several trunks waited for them. The villa was a quarter mile up the dirt
road.

Three of the rowers carried her trunk and box to the cart before returning
to the boat.

Atriensis took a stool from under the seat and set it on the ground. "Step
here, and I'll help you in."

Martina patted the closer mule's neck and stepped away from the cart.
"You can go ahead. It's been so long since I was here. I used to run down
this road to greet Father when he came home from a trip. I'd take his hand,
and we'd walk back to the villa together." She drew a circle in the dirt with her
sandal. "It seems fitting to come home that way, even if I'm only by myself."

Atriensis picked up the stool. "Tribune, would you care to ride?"

Glabrio moved to Martina's side. "I'll walk with Martina to make certain
she gets home safely."

"You and Sartorus can go with Atriensis to get cleaned up for dinner."
Palm up, she swung her hand toward Taurus. "I have Uncle's best bodyguard
to protect me."

"A woman can't have too many men watching out for her."

She rolled her eyes. "I'm not some helpless maiden wandering the dangerous streets of Carthago. I roamed the estate when I was a child, and I could
find my way safely home from any part of it even by moonlight."

"I would never describe you as helpless." One corner of his mouth lifted.
"But if I'm going to see all that makes this estate special, I'd like to make that
walk with you."

Martina fingered her bracelet. As tired as he must be after a day working
like a pack animal, why would he want to walk with her instead of riding?

"It's really no different from the estates near Carthago." She offered her
social smile. "Perhaps the walk is too long for your aide."

Glabrio looked at Sartorus and raised his eyebrows.

"A walk without shackles will feel good for a change." Sartorus's smile
mirrored his commander's.

"Very well." A deep sigh and another roll of her eyes would discourage most people, but there was no point in even trying them on this man.

The sky was starting to turn pink, and the air had cooled to make it perfect for a stroll. With Platana on her left and Glabrio on her right, Martina began the slow walk home.

Chapter 43

NOT BY CHANCE

Sartorus stood by the window, gazing across the olive orchard at the rising moon.

Before the cook served their late dinner of pork stew and fresh bread, Atriensis had taken them to the estate's blacksmith to get their slave collars removed. The shock on his face when Glabrio said he wanted to take them back to Carthago in case he wanted to wear one again was priceless. Then her steward left them at the villa's bath to remove several days of sweat and grime.

While spreading oil on sunburned skin hadn't felt so bad, scraping it off with the strigil had. The first dip in the hot-water tub had been more than he could bear. Glabrio stayed to finish a good soak, but he'd gone back to the room that was his until they returned to Carthago.

He tossed the clean tunic on his bed. When he was summoned to dinner, he would put it on. Until then, bare to the waist didn't hurt as much.

After sitting on the bed, he released a deep sigh. It would feel good to sleep on something soft again. It was even better to have a private place where he could pray undisturbed. Forearms on his knees and head bowed, he closed his eyes.

God, I thank You for rescuing us today. Thank You for bringing one of the few people who'd recognize Glabrio to the berth next to us. Thank You for making Martina see him. I thank You that she decided to buy us and had enough to do it. Thank You for Platana and the ointment she uses so well. Thank You again for all the small mercies since we were kidnapped.

Once more, he gave thanks for them staying together, for Barca buying them to row so they didn't end up in the quarries, for each time Hanno chose not to be as cruel as he could.

The soft clearing of a throat popped his eyes open. In the doorway, with an ointment jar in her hands, stood Platana.

"I beg pardon for disturbing you, but Mistress Martina wanted me to treat your burns again before we gather to eat."

"You didn't disturb me." He straightened. "Each time you tend to me, it hurts somewhat less. I'm grateful for all you're doing for me. I couldn't have done my back myself." One corner of his mouth lifted. "And you were right that neither Glabrio nor I could have done it as gently as you do, no matter how hard we tried."

"It's my pleasure to do it." She pulled out the chair from the small desk. "Sit here, and I'll try to finish as quickly as I can so you can eat."

"Will there be someplace I can sit? I don't think I could recline right now."

"There will. We dine sitting at the town house in Carthago. We'll do the same here."

"We? Does that mean you'll be eating with us?"

"Mistress Martina prefers it that way. Dining alone can be…lonely."

He looked back over his shoulder and gave her a smile. "I've never had the opportunity. Between a large family as a child and a garrison dining hall for the past seven years, I've always had mealtime companions."

"It's better that way." She smiled in return. "At least that's what I think."

She finished his back and started on his shoulders.

"Your mistress seems like a kind woman."

"She is, as was her grandmother before her."

"Generous, too. Glabrio and I are both grateful that she bought us as soon as she noticed him."

"I spotted you first. She would have helped you even if she hadn't seen the tribune after that. She does what she can to help others when she sees their need."

His head drew back. "I wouldn't have thought you'd recognize me out of uniform and so far from home. I'm not a man who stands out in a crowd like my commander." He offered a wry smile. "I'll be forever grateful that you remembered me after seeing so little of me."

"You stand out more than you think."

She moved in front of him and began working on his chest.

His mouth twitched. What would Glabrio say if he told him it was the maid who spotted an optio first, not the mistress spotting the tribune she tried to avoid? Maybe he'd tell him someday…but maybe not. It seemed too unbelievable, and the effect was the same, anyway—they'd been freed.

Platana had almost finished when he spoke again. "Have you missed this estate as much as your mistress?"

Her fingers moved from his chest to his stomach. "I've never been here before. Mistress's grandmother gave me to her when she turned twelve." She scooped up some ointment for the last untreated patch of skin. "Have you served the tribune long?"

"As his personal aide, only since he left Rome for Carthago. I've served in the XI Urban Cohort for seven years. I was optio under the centurion over the Tiber warehouses for half that time. It was the last tribune of the Cohort who recommended I come here as Glabrio's aide. Titianus and Glabrio are good friends. I'm glad my commander values Titianus's advice enough to choose a man he barely knew."

"The way we end up close to other people…it's often not an accident or mere chance." She opened her mouth as if to say something, but closed it to simply smile at him instead.

What was she going to say but decided not to?

"The best things in life are seldom pure chance." He had no doubt that was true. As his family's old neighbor who led him to Jesus had told him, God often worked the oddest things together for good.

"No, they aren't." Platana capped the jar and placed it on the desk. "I'll leave this here. Tomorrow after breakfast, we'll do this again." She swept her hand toward the door. "I'll take you to the dining room now, if you'd like. There's a portico overlooking a lovely garden there where you can wait for the others."

"I'd like that." Sartorus dropped the tunic over his head and fastened the belt loosely enough that the fabric wouldn't press too hard against his skin. As he followed her from the room, he thanked God once more for the seemingly chance meetings that had nothing to do with chance.

Martina leaned her elbows on the dressing table that had once been Mother's and stared at her face in Mother's mirror. It was almost her mother's face looking back at her, and that drew a deep sigh.

Atriensis had sent her trunk and box to the domina's bedchamber. It was tempting to sleep in her old room, but she was too tall for the bed she'd used as a child of eleven. And even though she almost expected her mother to come through a doorway and wrap her arm around Martina's shoulders in a quick hug, Martina was domina now and would be until she died.

"Dinner was more pleasant than I expected. With only the one course, it didn't last too long. I was afraid I'd have to talk too much with the tribune, but Atriensis was wonderful the way he kept Glabrio talking with him about being kidnapped and all they went through before we saw them." She tilted her head back to smile at Platana. "I'm sure Glabrio told him enough that my skeptical steward has no more doubts about my decision to buy the two of them."

Platana kept drawing the brush through Martina's hair to get it ready for braiding. "I saw something curious when I went to treat Sartorus before dinner."

"What?" Martina focused on Platana's face in the mirror.

"He was sitting on the bed, eyes closed. He looked like he might be praying."

Martina turned in the chair to face Platana. "Praying? Why do you think that?"

"You know how small smiles turn into bigger ones, then smaller, then bigger again when we're thanking God for something? That's what his mouth was doing. And he looked so peaceful sitting there."

"Is that all?"

"No. We talked some. Glabrio made him his aide without really knowing him. That started on the ship coming from Rome. The tribune before Glabrio is Glabrio's friend, and he recommended Sartorus."

"That doesn't seem odd. That tribune might have known Sartorus for years."

"By itself, it might not seem odd, but when I said how we end up close to other people is often not chance, I expected some comment about Fortuna smiling. Instead, he said the best things in life seldom are."

Martina nibbled her lip. "When we stopped for the rowers to rest, Glabrio said Sartorus was why he'd survived being taken. He'd known Sartorus for less than three weeks, but whatever Sartorus did, Glabrio called him one of the best men he'd ever known."

"He is a nice man. He talks with me and treats me like I'm free. After seeing him sitting on that bed and what he said about things not being due to chance, I wonder whether he was praying to the same God we do. I've never seen someone who wasn't a Christian do that."

Martina rubbed her jaw. "If he is, do you think Glabrio knows?"

"What I wonder is whether the other tribune he called Titianus knows. Is that why he recommended Sartorus, whether Glabrio knows or not?" Platana shrugged. "Being with someone who prays when problems come... there's nothing better. His friend might have wanted that for Glabrio. I know I would."

"There's no way to know what Glabrio knows right now." Martina raised one eyebrow. "But if he does know about Sartorus's faith, maybe we'll be safe enough from him even if he figures out we're Christians." She looked over her shoulder as Platana made the final sweeps of the brush through her hair. "But for now, let's assume he doesn't and be careful what he sees and hears."

"There." Platana set the brush down on the dressing table and divided the hair to make a braid for sleeping. "I'll be praying for Sartorus to reveal himself so we'll know for sure. If we each watch one of them, I think we'll find out what your tribune knows soon enough."

"He's not my tribune."

"Perhaps not." Platana began folding the strands of hair over each other. Sometimes lives intertwined like hair in a braid, whether you planned it or not. Mistress could deny it if she wanted, but it was clear enough to anyone watching whose he wanted to be.

Chapter 44

An Unexpected Offer

The Cigisa estate, morning of Day 28

In the shade of the portico overlooking a garden where herbs and vegetables intermingled with flowers, Glabrio stretched his arms out along the back of a bench.

"The porridge was good, even better than the rosemary porridge you taught the garrison cooks to make. I wonder what's in it."

Sartorus rested both hands on the seat beside him, leaning forward some to keep the cushion from touching his back. "It's not something I recognize. Maybe some local herb."

"If it's local, it might be cheap. If it's cheap enough, our cooks could alternate it with the rosemary to give some variety."

"I'll ask the chef before we leave." He patted his stomach carefully. "I wouldn't mind something different to start the morning."

"Still sore when you touch it?"

"Some, but it could be worse. What Platana's doing with the ointment really helps. It's hurting less all the time."

"When you heal enough that it's not tender to touch, we can think about going back." Glabrio rubbed his jaw. "But I want to have a plan of action before we get there."

He twisted to face Sartorus. "When we rode out to see Messala the first time, he seemed genuinely surprised that Nepos hadn't left early. He acted as if he believed Nepos was ordered back to Rome, like the letter said. His concern about a missing friend seemed real. I don't know if he's just a good actor, or if we saw the truth. But it was odd that he couldn't show me the letter for a full day."

Sartorus turned slightly toward him. "Couldn't or didn't want to for some reason."

"I suspect he didn't want to. At least not right away. I wonder if he wanted

242

to talk with someone before he did. If he did, who was it?" Glabrio ran his tongue over his upper teeth. "I think we can safely assume the letter you and I saw was not the one he originally received. Whether he changed it on his own or with someone else's help, we don't know. But when he gave it to us the next morning, he was nervous."

"What really made him nervous was when you started asking about his metal shop." Sartorus lifted the shoulders of the tunic as he turned to face Glabrio. A soft grunt escaped when he let them fall back in place. "Until you told him you wanted a present for your father, that is. Then he even encouraged you to visit it."

"But was that because he wanted my business or because he wanted the ones there to get rid of me?"

Sartorus shrugged, and that triggered a slight grimace. "If I had to guess, I'd say your business. I don't think the two men there would have done anything to us if I hadn't found that piece of Nepos's crest. When I knelt to get it, the bigger one panicked and hit me with one of the logs he was unloading. But they probably do know whether Nepos is dead and maybe who killed him."

"So..." Glabrio placed one arm across his stomach and rested his elbow on it. He bounced his fist off his lips. "So, when we get back to Carthago, we'll pay a visit to Messala's shop, but maybe not right away."

"Why delay?"

"As long as whoever is behind Nepos's disappearance thinks we won't be coming back, their guard will be down. If Nepos was killed because he discovered what they were doing, they should go back to doing it in the open, where we can find them like he did."

"But how do we do that?"

Glabrio steepled his fingers and rubbed the sides of his nose. "I don't know yet."

Sartorus's mouth curved into a smile, and that turned Glabrio's head so he could see what evoked that response.

What he saw triggered his smile, too, but for a different reason. Platana was coming with the ointment.

When she stopped in front of them, Glabrio rose. "We missed your mistress and you at breakfast. I think I'll join her while you take care of my friend. Is she through with the morning rites?"

Platana stopped her head from drawing back but not before he saw it. At breakfast, Atriensis had said something about his mistress attending to personal business, but was that only an excuse because she didn't want to talk with him?

"She's in the library. She's attending to business."

His lips twitched. At least steward and maid had the same story to tell him. "Which way is that? I could use something to read."

She cleared her throat. "Off the peristyle."

"The side we sleep on or the other?"

"The other." She paused before each answer, weighing her words.

Why was that? They were simple questions.

He tipped his head toward Sartorus. "Tell me later how he's doing. When I ask him, he only says it could be worse."

She glanced at Sartorus as her eyes warmed and her smile grew. "It could be, but I hope soon he can say it's completely better."

"As do I."

His gaze moved between optio and maid. When he returned it to Sartorus with a wry smile, was the red he saw on his optio's ears more than a fading sunburn?

Glabrio strode toward the entrance to the house. Past the kitchen and down a short hallway, he'd find the woman who made him smile, like her maid did his optio. Whether she intended to or not, Martina had taken what could be worse and made it good instead.

◆

A stack of scrolls lay on the desk, and Martina tidied them. Her favorite scrolls from Pliny's Natural History and a collection of quotes from Seneca that her father had used to teach her—they'd been left behind when Grandfather's steward came to fetch her after Mother and Father died. He'd said Grandfather had a superb library and his own way of teaching, and she wouldn't need them.

Reading parts of them again brought back memories of Father's hand on her shoulder as he pointed to what he wanted her to learn that day. Remembrances of his smiling nods when she recited a passage perfectly.

But the truth she valued now wasn't in those scrolls. It was in Grandmother's greatest treasure, never shared in Grandfather's house when anyone except her and Platana would hear, and passed on to her for safekeeping before Grandmother's final breath. She rested her hand on the much-worn leather cover of her Gospel of Marcus, then opened it to read a favorite passage.

A knock on the open door made her jump. Glabrio leaned against the doorframe with that half-smile he wore too often when he looked at her.

She closed the codex and placed it in the desk drawer. She wanted to lock it, but that could make him too eager to learn what she'd been looking at and didn't want him to see.

Instead, she rested her arms on the desktop, laced her fingers, and gave him a social smile.

"To what do I owe this visit, tribune?"

"Platana is tending Sartorus, and she said you were in the library attending to business."

She arched her eyebrow. Palm up, she waved one hand at the scrolls. "As you see."

He glanced at them before returning his gaze to her. She'd rather he didn't, but at least he wasn't looking at the desk.

"I was looking for something to read to pass the time until we can return to Carthago."

Her hand swept toward an open cabinet with many cubicles containing several dozen scrolls. "I'm sure you'll find something here. Take whatever you'd like. Like Uncle Volero, my father enjoyed reading. The estate is so far from a city library that he created our own. A good library is important to me as well."

He pointed at the box beside the cabinet. "Now I know what you considered important to bring, even when traveling light. I also brought a few of my favorites from Rome. I found a good vender just off the forum for adding to my library here." His half-smile turned into a full one. "Perhaps we can go there together sometime and add to both our libraries."

"Perhaps."

"When were you planning to return to Carthago?" He strolled to the desk and picked up a scroll. "You laughed when I suggested your cousins would miss you. I understand that completely. But I'm sure Volero is missing your conversations and board games." He partly unrolled it. "Pliny. I enjoy him as well."

He placed the scroll back on the pile and straightened it. "I'm sorry I missed dining with you and him, but I was unavoidably detained." His smile turned wry. "I spent that night shackled in a cage. I would have preferred to dine with you."

"No doubt. Consider your absence forgiven." She gave him a warm smile. Uncle was sure he'd lose interest if she was friendly enough but not too friendly. "But it won't happen again."

"Because you won't invite me or because I'll never be kidnapped again when you do?" He settled into the guest chair. "When are you returning to Carthago? It's not a casual question. I need to figure out when Sartorus and I will return."

Her mouth twitched. He hadn't given her time to tell him which before he changed the subject. Maybe he suspected her answer would be the one he didn't want.

"That depends. This trip is for business, not pleasure. I'll be opening a pottery shop where one of my renters just moved out. So, I came here to talk with my factory steward and his foremen about what kinds of pottery to have in the shop and what it takes to get it made and shipped to Carthago. He'll also be selecting the right man to oversee making special orders. We'll have at least one kiln, maybe more if he thinks that's what we need."

She wiggled her fingers at him. "You may recall at our first meeting I said these were good for more than displaying rings."

"I do. I've found it worthwhile to remember most of what you say."

She managed not to roll her eyes. "I'll be making appliques again for the Carthago shop. Figulus is also going to teach me some of what it takes to run a successful shop before I go home."

"Sartorus worked at both a tailor shop and a fullery before he joined the Cohort. Perhaps he'll have something useful to share."

"Perhaps, but I also have Ceraulo. A glass shop and a pottery shop aren't that different."

"Sartorus and I are trying to figure out how we can return to Carthago to investigate Nepos's disappearance. When I first return, I don't want anyone realizing we're not slaves in the quarries or already dead. It will be a few more days before he'll be healed enough, but that might fit with your plans."

Glabrio rubbed his jaw. "If we could travel with you like we're your slaves, no one will notice our return. Of course, you can add any expenses to what I already owe you."

"Well, Grandfather did always say we should help an officer of Rome when we can." She leaned back in her chair. "Since you're already staying with us so Platana can care for Sartorus until his burns are healed, I see no reason why you shouldn't return with us."

She drew a deep breath and paused before speaking the next words. *God, please don't let what I'm about to offer be a mistake. It seems like the right thing to do.*

"You once told me that a man out of uniform will learn many things a man in uniform cannot. I'm planning to open the pottery sales room soon, but you could live there for a short time if that would help with your secret investigations."

His head drew back, and satisfaction broadened his smile to an almost-grin.

"We can pretend to be working for you to get the shop ready. When we're not actually investigating, we can help."

"I'm not certain a tribune will be that useful in a pottery shop, but a tradesman like Sartorus might. Either way, I'll do what I can to help you find the ones who killed Nepos and would have killed you."

A tap on the open door announced Platana was back from treating the burns.

Glabrio rose. "I'll go tell Sartorus."

As he strode from the room, he paused by Platana. "When do you think he'll be healed enough to go home?"

"In some places, the red is gone now. But others…it will take more time."

"Whatever it takes, do it for him. He's worth it."

Platana dipped her head. "I'll do my best, tribune."

"Good. He deserves it."

After he left the room, Platana raised her eyebrows in a silent question.

"He'll be coming with us when we go home. Then they'll be staying in the vacant shop for a while."

Platana sucked air between her teeth. "Is that wise?"

"I hope so. It's too late to turn back now."

Oh, God, I certainly hope so. Please don't let me do something foolish that's not what You want me to do.

Chapter 45

MEANWHILE, BACK IN CARTHAGO

Carthago, morning of Day 28

Verus etched the last entry into the wax tablet and snapped it shut. He rotated his shoulders and tipped his head back, eyes closed.

His life had been much simpler before his drunken partner paid that gambling debt with counterfeit coins. It would have stayed simple if Nepos hadn't noticed anything when he sobered up. But a handful of gold-plated bronze turned him from a worthless figurehead into a real tribune determined to catch a criminal.

Glabrio was a nuisance with the way he wanted reports every day, even when nothing worth mentioning had happened. But he wouldn't have become a threat that must be removed if only Nepos had kept neglecting his duty until he went back to Rome.

Nepos had forced him to kill his commander to avoid dying himself. Glabrio wouldn't stop until he caught Nepos's killer, so he and maybe his aide must die, too. But only after Messala could no longer reveal what they'd done together would he truly be safe from the beasts or a cross.

Tablet in hand, he strolled from his office to Placidus at the front desk. "Deliver this to headquarters."

Placidus reached for the tablet, but his hand stopped halfway when a soldier trotted into the room.

"Centurion." The man's fist hit his chest. "You are urgently needed at cohort headquarters."

"What does Tribune Glabrio need me for?"

"Not the tribune. Centurion Acceptus ordered us to fetch you and Centurion Longinus from your districts."

"Acceptus? But you're one of Dubitatus's men."

"Yes, Centurion. But Centurion Acceptus is there, and he's very upset about something."

248

"Go tell them I'm on my way."

The messenger struck his chest and strode from the room.

"I've never seen anything upset Acceptus." He shrugged and got a shrug in return from his optio. "I'm going to headquarters. I don't know when I'll return."

It was a short walk from the harbor station to cohort headquarters, but he didn't hurry. Acceptus thinking something was urgent didn't mean it would be for him. But when he stepped into view of the guards by the headquarters entrance, he lengthened his stride.

He bounded up the steps and passed through the doorway to find Acceptus pacing and Dubitatus leaning against his office doorframe.

Verus stopped and crossed his arms. "What's so urgent?"

Acceptus mirrored his stance. "We have another missing tribune."

Verus's head drew back. "Why do you think that?"

"I just came back from my inspection tour last night, and I came to drop off my report. There are at least a dozen reports on Sartorus's desk, like no one has looked at them for days. Glabrio's optio wouldn't let reports pile up like that if Glabrio was here."

Dubitatus straightened. "I haven't seen him or Sartorus in the last four days. He left right after he got a message that someone had a letter he wanted to see."

Acceptus turned from Verus to face Dubitatus. "Who had the letter?"

"He didn't say, but he never does." Dubitatus shrugged. "I just overheard the messenger telling Sartorus his master had the letter Glabrio wanted. They left right away."

Acceptus tipped his head toward Dubitatus. "He didn't look into what happened to them even when they didn't return for four days."

Dubitatus squared his shoulders and raised his chin. "The last time Glabrio disappeared for a couple of days, he'd gone with you to Uthina. He didn't tell me he was going then. I just assumed he'd gone somewhere without telling me again."

Verus massaged his neck. Four days ago, Glabrio was supposed to ride back to get the new copy Messala had made. Verus had seen Messala at the baths yesterday. They hadn't spoken, but Messala had acknowledged him with a single slight nod, as he always did. Nothing in his eyes or face or bearing suggested a problem. The whole time Verus was at the baths, Messala was his usual congenial self with his friends.

"Well…I haven't seen Glabrio since I was at the harbormaster's archive helping him try to figure out which ship Nepos might have left on. That was five days ago." He rubbed his jaw. "But I don't expect to see him every day. Placidus and Ambustus usually drop off my reports. Even when he visits my district, I often miss him because I'm down on the wharves or inspecting warehouses."

"But…" Verus raised one finger and held it there. "Proconsul Noricus is holding court down in Leptis Magna. Do you think Glabrio might have decided to go see if the governor had any idea where Nepos had gone? Noricus might have called Nepos down there for some reason that Glabrio got wind of."

He accompanied a cynical smile with a soft snort. "Glabrio's an ambitious one. Maybe he wanted to impress the governor with his efforts to find Nepos. And maybe Nepos really is down there with the governor and they just never let us know. Tribunes don't report to us."

An emphatic shake of Acceptus's head accompanied his tightened lips. "I don't find that likely. Dubitatus didn't know Glabrio was leaving town with me because he wasn't in his office when I came and got him."

Dubitatus crossed his arms again. "You came before either of us are supposed to be at our desks. I was eating with my men. Glabrio usually joins us, but he didn't that morning."

Acceptus brushed Dubitatus's excuse away with a sweep of his hand, then glared at his fellow centurion. "You couldn't reach me, but why didn't you let Verus and Longinus know Glabrio and Sartorus hadn't been back in their quarters for days?"

Dubitatus shrugged. "Nepos never told us what he was doing. It was often days between when he showed up and spent the night here. Glabrio does what he wants without telling me, too."

"Hmph." Acceptus's eyes narrowed. "Nepos never told us where he was going because most of where he went had nothing to do with his official duties. He didn't care whether we did our duty, either. Glabrio is all about duty and honor and running the Cohort properly like the military unit we are. He would have told at least one of us where he was going and when he planned to return."

The sound of two guards coming to attention and the click of hobnails on the entrance steps was followed by Longinus entering the courtyard.

Acceptus spun on him. "Have you seen Glabrio in the last four days?"

Longinus paused midstride. "No. Is there a problem?"

"When did you see him last?"

Longinus blew out a slow breath. "More than a week ago. I took him on a tour of my district." One corner of his mouth lifted. "Messala tried to get him to end the tour and go to the races with him, like Nepos used to. Glabrio turned him down. He said he liked the races but duty comes before pleasure so he didn't stay the whole day even when he watched them." The half-smile turned into a full one. "That's how a tribune should think."

"Which is why I'm concerned that none of us has seen or heard from him for at least four days." Acceptus's gaze focused on Dubitatus until Dubitatus looked away. Then he turned to Verus. "We should talk with Messala if he's a friend of Glabrio's."

Verus fought the urge to rub his neck and won. Acceptus was the last man he wanted talking with someone who couldn't be trusted to stay calm under pressure. "I've talked with Messala a few times when he was with Nepos, and Nepos has mentioned several places they spent time together. I'll track him down and find out whether he knows anything."

"Good." Acceptus rubbed the underside of his jaw, like a man accustomed to wearing a helmet most of the time. "I know the stable where Glabrio keeps his stallion. I'll see if they know anything."

With Acceptus diverted from talking to Messala, the danger his partner posed was under control, at least for the moment.

Verus rested his hand on the pommel of his gladius. "And I'll see if Nepos's friend knows anything about where Glabrio might be. If he thinks Glabrio left the city, I'll check with the harbormaster to find what ship he might have taken."

"There are races today, so I need to be at the circus until late afternoon." Longinus fell in beside Verus and Acceptus as they headed for the door. "But if there's any way I can help, send me word, and I'll see what I can do."

With Longinus heading south toward the circus and Acceptus going to check on Glabrio's horse, Verus strode toward the stable where his own horse stayed.

Another half an hour and he'd know what Messala knew…as long as his partner didn't lie to him.

The Messala estate, midmorning of Day 28

Verus turned off the main road and rode past Messala's metal shop. The double doors stood open, giving a clear view of the forge. This time of day, one or both of the smiths should have been making something with blows from a hammer on red-hot metal. But no ringing of metal on metal reached his ears. No flickering flame or glowing coals lit the back wall.

Two days ago, the goldsmith from Rome had been brought from the shop in town to the estate workshop. Messala had bought him to engrave the molds and apply the gold coatings. After he gilded the latest set of fake bronze coins, they had another hoard of counterfeit aurei ready to distribute.

Maybe Messala had stopped production until he used up what they'd just made, and the smiths were working somewhere else on the estate.

251

He nudged his stallion into a trot and headed for the villa.

At the stableyard, he tossed his leg over the stallion's neck and slid off. "Take me to young Lucius Messala."

The stableman summoned a boy of about ten from the portico, and he led Verus through the peristyle and into the library, where Messala sat with a large goblet and a scroll open on the desk before him.

Verus's entrance drew a frown from Messala. "Why are you here?"

"Glabrio seems to have disappeared. I came to find out what you knew about that."

Messala pointed at the door. "Bolt it."

Verus slid the bolt home and took the guest chair by the desk.

Messala leaned back in his chair. "When did he disappear?"

"The last time anyone in the Cohort saw him seems to be when he got your message to come get the letter."

"Well, he came and got it. He said he'd be keeping it until he figures out what happened to Nepos. He wanted the names of the people who were Nepos's friends, the ones he would trust without question. I gave him a list."

"Did he have you write out the list?"

Messala's lips tightened. "I'm not stupid. His aide tried to hand me a tablet, but I gave him a stylus instead. I wasn't going to give him something to compare to the letter."

"Did he do anything other than get the letter?"

"He asked about the metal shop, but that was only because he wanted to get some statue gilded to send his father." A smirk twisted Messala's mouth. "And a fancy lampstand like a woman would want. I think there's someone here he's trying to impress."

"A woman? Not likely. He's planning to be a consul like his father. He'll marry the daughter of some important senator back in Rome."

"That may be, but we both know how men like him entertain themselves. Nepos did."

Verus nodded, but Glabrio wasn't like Nepos, no matter what Messala might think. "Did he say anything that would tell you where he was going next?"

"He said he would stop at the shop on his way back. I told him to tell them he was my friend and that I said to put special effort into what he wanted. Beyond that, he wanted me to think about who might be Nepos's enemy and want to get rid of him. He said he'd check back later for names, but he hasn't yet."

"It sounds like you handled him well." Verus donned a fake smile. Glabrio had asked his centurions for a list of all the metal shops in each of the districts.

When he stopped at the shop, was it to buy a gift or to check out what was going on there?

"Is your forge supposed to be shut down today?"

"No." Messala's satisfied smile vanished. "Why?"

"Because no one was working where I could see them when I passed it."

"Both smiths should be there." Straight lips turned into a frown. Messala unbolted the door and stepped into the peristyle. A youth knelt on the floor, scrubbing it with a wet rag.

"Go tell someone to saddle my horse immediately."

The boy scurried off, and Messala returned to the desk. He drained the goblet and wiped his lips with the back of his hand.

Verus rose. "We need to know what happened when Glabrio stopped there."

Messala's jaw clenched. His eyes blinked too fast as he slowly nodded. Then he strode from the library and led Verus to the stableyard.

They kept the horses at a trot until they reined in and tied them to the olive tree.

When they entered the shop, there was no sign of either metalsmith. Verus held his hand over the forge. Only coals from the last fire remained, and they were stone cold.

Messala entered the storeroom and pulled out a chest under the bottom shelf to reveal some loose floorboards. He lifted the boards out to expose the half-buried box that held the dies for fake bronze aurei.

"None of the dies are missing."

In the corner, he strained to move a barrel of scrap iron to reveal the compartment where they kept the fake coins until they could distribute them. A quick count of the bags turned his frown into a scowl.

"I had the goldsmith brought out here two days ago to gild the latest set of bronze coins. There were five bags in here. Now there are four."

Messala let loose a string of curses that would make a brothel slave blush.

Verus didn't share his anger. The men who saw him kill Nepos and who helped get rid of the body had vanished. They'd taken enough money to go anywhere in the Empire. Even if Messala hired slave hunters, it was unlikely he'd find them.

His mouth curved into a wry smile. Since they'd run away, they'd be afraid to tell anyone in authority what they'd done to gain their freedom. And as runaways, no one would ever believe them, even if they told the truth.

But Messala knew he'd killed Nepos, so he still posed a threat. Weak-willed and stupid, he couldn't be trusted, so he'd have to die. But only after Glabrio was dead. Messala might be the perfect bait to get Glabrio to go where he could kill them both.

Chapter 46

TWO MORE SECRETS TO KEEP

The Cigisa estate, afternoon of Day 28

When Platana entered the garden for Sartorus's next treatment, he was sitting under the portico, hands on the edge of the seat as he leaned forward slightly. The tribune lounged against the backrest, reading, but he looked up when she cleared her throat.

Glabrio rolled up the scroll. "I thought you'd be coming soon. Is Martina still in the library?"

"She might be."

The tribune stood. "I need something else to read." He tapped Sartorus's upper arm where it wasn't burned. "I'll leave my friend to your gentle care."

When Sartorus turned his gaze upon her, Platana pointed to a short stone bench in the deep shade of a grape arbor. "It will be easier over there where I can get to both sides of you."

He followed her to the arbor and pulled the tunic over his head after he stepped into the shade.

Back first, she applied some ointment and gently worked it into his skin. "Some of what was red isn't even pink now. You're healing much faster than the woman who sold us this said."

He looked over his shoulder to give her the smile that always made her feel like he saw a woman, not a slave. "Maybe no one she knows has asked the Great Healer for help."

Her ears felt warmer as she smiled back. Her heart warmed, too, as his careful words confirmed her suspicion that he'd been praying when she walked in on him. "Perhaps. I've been asking Him often, and I think we're seeing the result."

His eyes warmed to match his smile. "I have, too. The day you saw me loading the ship…I'd asked Him that morning to bring someone who would help us. I knew He had when I came up the gangplank and saw Martina inspecting Glabrio. Whatever made your mistress decide to come to Utica when she did, I've been thanking Him for that as well."

"About that…" Platana leaned over to put her lips close to his ear in case someone came within earshot unobserved. "The day the tribune didn't show up for dinner, God told her she needed to go to Cigisa right away. Her uncle started arranging it the next morning."

"The best things in life are seldom chance. But it wasn't just her He used to answer my prayers." He turned and tipped his head back until she could look into his eyes. "If you hadn't spotted me, she might never have noticed us. Since you told me that, I've been thanking God for you first…then for both of you."

She and Mistress Martina prayed for each other all the time. But no one had ever said they thanked God for her before.

She bit her lip. *God, should I ask him?*

Peace replaced nervousness, and the answer was clear.

"If you can keep the tribune from discovering we're Christians, would you like to join us for prayer and worship sometime?"

"It's safe for him to know. Many of his best friends are secretly Christian already. His grandfather was, too, but he died before Glabrio was born."

She moved around to work on his chest, and her cheeks heated when she felt his eyes on her as she touched him.

Sartorus's voice was a near whisper. "I don't think he knows I'm a Christian, and I need to tell him before I can join you."

"You'll also have to tell him no one else here knows about our faith." She whispered back. "Mistress Martina became a Christian after she moved to Carthago. She hasn't told anyone here yet. She might decide it's not wise for anyone to know."

"When I tell him, he might want to join us. His friend in Rome who recommended he bring me as his aide is one of us. He thinks Glabrio values truth enough that he'll become one of us, too."

As she applied some ointment to the last red area on his stomach, he looked past her.

"He's coming back with a new scroll. We can talk next time."

"With pleasure."

As she replaced the cork lid, she glanced at his eyes. They were fixed upon her face, and they warmed as his gaze met hers.

It would definitely be her pleasure to talk with him again. Perhaps it would be his pleasure, too.

◆

When Glabrio returned to the garden, he held the Seneca scroll Martina had been looking at. She'd said he could read anything he wanted, and she'd left it on the desk.

"Martina wasn't there, but she left behind something useful." He waved the scroll at Sartorus. "This scroll of Seneca quotations will tell me what her father thought important enough to teach her. The truths we learn when young stay with us when we're grown. I should understand her better after reading this."

"Well…" Sartorus rubbed the underside of his jaw. "What we thought was true as a child…it's not necessarily what we believe when we grow up. What a father thinks is best and true beyond question…sometimes we learn there's something much better when we're grown."

Glabrio scrunched his nose. "That's oddly philosophical of you."

"I'm not philosophical." Sartorus fingered his lower lip. "I'm experienced."

"What do you mean?"

"There's something Titianus didn't tell you about me."

"He told me you'd been a tradesman before the Cohort. Plus your time in the warehouse district would let you see things I'd missed. He said I could trust you to watch out for me. He certainly had that right." Glabrio let a half-smile appear. "What else was there to tell?"

Sartorus's face turned deadly serious, and Glabrio drew back his head. Even when they were in chains, he hadn't seen that grim set to Sartorus's mouth.

Then the slight smile he was used to seeing returned.

"I'm a Christian."

The last word felt like a blow to his chest. "Did Titus know that?"

"Not before he came to ask me to go to Carthago with you."

Glabrio's half-smile had flipped to a frown. "How did he find out?"

"He'd noticed my reluctance at camp worship, so he asked."

"You know that could be cause for dishonorable discharge, maybe worse, if the urban prefect learns of it. Why did you tell him?"

"It was the way he asked." Sartorus gripped his left hand and rubbed the palm with his thumb. "I knew it was safe for him to know."

As Glabrio rubbed his cheek, the frown relaxed. "You were right. He's one himself."

Sartorus's usual slight smile returned. "I know. He told me." He massaged his wrist. "He stopped coming to camp worship after someone almost killed him. I had no choice, but the tribunes did. I should have suspected it then."

"He credits the Christian god with saving him."

"So do I." Sartorus's smile broadened. "I'd been asking God to bring someone to rescue us, and He did. It was no accident that one of the handful of people in the province who would recognize you or me was just coming off a ship as we were unloading. God takes care of those of us who love Him."

Glabrio blanked his face. "Perhaps."

Admitting the Christian god took care of his followers was not something he was prepared to do. If their god cared, all of Grandfather's remains would be in the family mausoleum, not just the ashes of a body with no head.

"So, what made you decide to tell me this now?"

"An opportunity I don't want to miss."

"Which is?"

Sartorus's eyes narrowed as he massaged his palm again. A slight tip of his head followed, as if he'd had an argument with himself over what he should say.

"Platana asked me to join their private worship."

"Their?" Did he really want to know who was included in "they"?

"Hers and Martina's. It's only the two of them who follow Jesus. No one here knows about their faith, and they're keeping it that way for now."

"Hmph." Glabrio squeezed the back of his neck.

Her reluctance to tell him much about herself, her odd reactions when he teased her about breaking Roman law...she was afraid he'd discover she actually was.

"So, that's why she's tried so hard to avoid me."

"I don't know for certain, but it wouldn't surprise me. She had no way of knowing you wouldn't try to force her to sacrifice, then arrest her if she wouldn't. Governor Noricus hasn't been moving against Christians, but the next governor might decide to."

Glabrio gazed at the ridge of hills visible past the villa. "My family knows too well what can happen. My grandfather was consul under Domitian. Domitian got angry and exiled him. Four years later, he sent the Praetorians to execute him because he became a Christian. My father disagreed with his father's decision to reject the worship of the Roman gods, so Domitian let him live."

His gaze shifted to the Seneca scroll still in his hand. "My grandfather died before I was born. Father raised me to follow the Roman way in our worship and to be a Stoic in my approach to life. I first heard the full story of my grandfather's death when a rival at my school of rhetoric was taunting me with it. I went home and asked Father about Grandfather's beliefs. He told me that was something I shouldn't be asking. He said not to ask him again and changed the subject."

A quick glance at Sartorus found his friend nodding, sympathy in his eyes.

"I understand that pressure not to learn about following Jesus. I was fifteen when our neighbor told me the truth about the gods of Rome and the One True God. Father was furious about me making the decision your grandfather did."

Sartorus nudged him as they stood shoulder-to-shoulder, scanning the distant hills. "You got off easy. All your father did was tell you not to ask. My father was so angry about my decision that he put me in the fullery until I came to my senses."

He turned to face Glabrio. "But how can a man turn from the truth once he knows it? I couldn't betray the One who died on a cross to pay for my sins. So, rather than spend a lifetime with the urine vats, I got the recommendation from my mother's cousin and joined the Urban Cohort. I didn't join his legion because I didn't want to kill for Rome. But serving in the Cohort...that lets me protect innocent people from harm."

"I'm glad you made that choice." Glabrio slapped Sartorus's arm. "And I'm glad you chose to come here with me after Titus spoke with you."

"I am, too." Sartorus rubbed under his chin. "Would you like to join us?"

Glabrio inhaled deeply. Would he? He had no interest in following in his grandfather's footsteps in matters of belief or mode of death. But he'd seen the disappointment in Titus's eyes each time he refused to listen. That same eagerness to share lit Sartorus's face.

"I'll think about it."

"Then I'll tell you when we're going to meet."

"Do that. I might decide to."

Joining them might be all he needed to overcome her resistance. It should convince her that her religion was no barrier to friendship, as far as he was concerned. Adding one more Christian friend to the number whose deadly secret he must keep posed no problem at all.

Evening of Day 28

"So, how is Sartorus doing?" Martina closed the codex and slipped it into the desk drawer. It was time to dine now that Platana had treated his sunburn.

"Much better than the woman said he should. Where he hadn't blistered, even the pink was mostly gone before I applied the gel this evening." Platana set the ointment on the shelf. "Better still, he can join us for prayer and worship. He asked the tribune if he'd like to join us, too."

Before she could stop them, Martina's hands flew up to cover her mouth. "What did he say?"

"He said he might. Sartorus was so pleased about that when he told me."

Martina blew out a slow breath. "The tribune wants to join us."

"That's what he told Sartorus."

Martina steepled her fingers and rubbed her nose. "God did tell me to come to Cigisa right away, but I thought that was only so we'd see the pair of them and them free. Do you suppose He had another reason?"

"Like a chance for Glabrio to learn what Jesus did for all of us?"

"Maybe. Sartorus only needed to be freed from Barca's ship. Glabrio…he's still slave to all the lies I believed before Juliana told me the truth." She cradled her cheeks. "He's not going to be with us very long, so we won't have much time to share what he needs to know to make the right choice."

Her gaze turned on the desk. "I don't think he'll understand the way we pray and worship like we usually do. I know I wouldn't have before Juliana read me Marcus's gospel."

"You reading it helped Clavus and the others decide to believe in our Lord. He shouldn't be any different."

"Before we meet, I'll ask God to show me which parts to read to him first. That first time has to be exactly right, or he might not come a second time."

"I'll join you in that prayer." Platana's smile started shy and warmed. "I hope Sartorus can keep joining us whether the tribune does or not."

Martina tightened her lips to keep from grinning at her dear friend's blushes when she talked about the optio.

"I'd only expected them to be here with us until Sartorus healed, but Glabrio asked if they can travel back to Carthago with us, pretending to belong to me so no one will notice their arrival."

"That will keep us safer traveling, even with Taurus along." Platana glanced at the ointment jar. "I suppose that means we could return anytime, whether the sunburn's healed or not."

Platana tried to mask her regret, but Martina saw it.

"After Glabrio asked that, I offered to let them stay at the pottery shop. They might need a safe place to hide for a few days after they return."

Platana's head drew back. "Really? Your uncle will be stunned when he learns that."

"Well, it won't be the first time I've done something that surprised Uncle." Martina returned to the desk and took the codex out. "I want to pick out exactly the right thing to read to Glabrio first."

With eyes closed, she hugged the well-worn treasure. Was this how Juliana felt before she began telling Martina about her sin, Jesus's sacrifice to pay for it, and God's love and forgiveness?

God, please show me what he needs to hear, then give me the words I need to say to lead him toward You.

Chapter 47

No Harm Accepting an Invitation

Evening of Day 28

When Glabrio entered the triclinium with Sartorus beside him, the room was empty. Plates and goblets for five sat on the table. The chair at the head of the table should be for Martina, but he'd wait to sit until he was certain.

"Good evening, tribune."

Glabrio's smile grew as he turned to find Martina and Platana strolling toward him.

"It is now you're here."

She rolled her eyes as her smile dimmed. He should have expected that, so why had he said what would thrill a silly girl like Priscilla to this mature woman? Maybe because it was true.

"It would be whether I'm here or not." Her gaze and smile shifted to Sartorus. "How is your back feeling now?"

"It could be much worse. It's mostly not hurting." Sartorus smiled at Platana, triggering her blush. "Gentle fingers and the right ointment can work wonders."

"Platana told me you'd like to join us tomorrow. I'm so glad." Martina turned her smile back on Glabrio. "I hope you'll be joining us, too."

At least she'd taken no offense. But she never did, even when other women he'd known would have.

"After what you've done for us, how could I turn down any invitation from you?"

"Quite easily. Simply say 'no, thank you.'" She and Platana exchanged glances. "But we're glad you chose to say 'yes.'"

"Sartorus was quite persuasive." A glance at Sartorus caught his aide with tightened lips, trying to stop a smile before it turned into a grin. "So, what will we be doing?"

"We'll meet for a short time right after breakfast. Atriensis has some things to attend to first, and then he'll be escorting me to the pottery works. We have both red and white clay deposits, and the workshops are close to them. I need to talk with the foreman there about what's needed for opening the Carthago shop. The road was decent when I was here last, but that was eight years ago."

She'd deflected his question like a skilled politician. But the answer didn't really matter. He'd know soon enough.

A trip to watch people making pottery wouldn't normally excite him, but sharing a carriage with her was an exceptional opportunity. Comfortable conversation with no polite excuse for refusing to talk with him—that was worth a carriage ride, no matter how bad the road.

"I'd like to join you for that as well. If I'm going to work as a potter for you, I should learn how to be one."

Martina fingered her filigree bracelet. "I don't know how much you can learn about working with clay in a single visit. But I suppose you can watch how a real potter behaves and try to copy it whenever someone comes into the shop."

"That should help. I'll work on hiding my Roman arrogance so well I won't offend any of your customers."

Silent laughter lit her eyes. "I think you've already made great progress on that. Even people who are easily offended might find you pleasant company."

"Are you among them?"

"As I told you before, I'm not easily offended. I'm not the right person to ask if you've improved enough."

"She'll want the carriage tomorrow after breakfast." Atriensis's voice still in the peristyle drew Martina's eyes to the doorway.

She held a finger to her lips and lowered her voice to a whisper. "Don't mention us meeting tomorrow morning to my steward." She tipped her head toward Platana. "I haven't told him about us yet."

"Your secret is safe with me."

"Atriensis." The lilt in her voice brightened her steward's smile when he entered the room. "Will we be ready for a trip to the pottery works by mid-morning?"

"The carriage and team will be waiting when we're ready to leave."

Palm up, her hand swept toward Glabrio and Sartorus. "Our guests would like to join us as well."

"Five in the carriage..." Atriensis sucked air between his teeth. "It's not large enough. But I can have two mules saddled for them."

Her raised eyebrows asked Glabrio's opinion, and he faked a smile. His only reason for going was to talk with her. Sitting across from her in the carriage was what he'd counted on, but if there was no room...

"The mules will be fine."

Two young women entered the dining room carrying steaming bowls. The savory aroma of a hearty pork stew teased his nostrils, drawing a smile. After several days of lukewarm gruel, that stew should satisfy as if it were one of Father's banquets.

With a bowl in front of each chair and a plate of fresh bread in the center of the table, the five of them seated themselves. Martina sat at the head, so he chose the seat to her right across from Atriensis. One glance at Sartorus confirmed his friend's pleasure at sitting across from Platana.

As he raised the first spoonful to his lips, his gaze fixed on Martina. The first bite of stew was delicious, but that wasn't what inspired his satisfied smile.

He'd just caught Martina watching him, too.

After dinner, Sartorus sat on the edge of his bed, arms on his knees. Nothing ended a day better than praying before lying down to sleep. He still couldn't lie on his back, but on his side was comfortable enough now. He opened his eyes to find Glabrio leaning against the doorframe, watching him.

His back straightened. "Did you want something, Tribune?"

"What were you doing?" Glabrio stepped into the room.

"Talking with Someone."

The corners of Glabrio's mouth turned down. "But there's no one here but you."

"No one you can see."

"Hmph." Glabrio took the jar of ointment from the desk and uncorked it. "Talking…Titus says that's what he's doing when he's praying to his god."

Sartorus shrugged. "I'd expect that."

"Talking *with* someone isn't the same as talking *to* them. 'With' means a conversation where each says something." Glabrio sniffed the ointment before closing the jar and returning it to the desk. "Even when Martina didn't want a conversation, she still said a few words to me."

"Words don't have to be spoken to be heard."

Glabrio's eyes narrowed as the corners of his mouth turned down.

Silence hung in the room. It lingered much longer than Sartorus found comfortable. Silence was a tool Titianus used to manipulate people. He'd probably taught Glabrio to use it, too.

But silence could also mean a man was truly thinking about something. And if a man like Glabrio thought about something long enough, surely he'd see what was true.

God, give me the right words at the right time. Keep me from saying the wrong ones.

"So, what are the three of you going to be doing tomorrow, just sitting around in silence while I watch you?"

"I don't know exactly what they plan, but I know nothing satisfied me more in Rome than being with the people who first told me about Jesus."

"Your Christian neighbor got you banished to the fullery."

"That wasn't his fault. I tried to explain to my father, but he wouldn't listen." His gaze dropped to the floor, and he rubbed his palm. "He hasn't forgiven me. Maybe he never will." He raised his eyes to meet Glabrio's gaze. "I love my father, and I always obeyed him. But when he ordered me to reject what I knew to be true...that was something I couldn't do."

"But why would you take the word of some neighbor over what your father taught you?"

"He'd met Peter, one of the men who was there when Jesus was crucified and saw Him after He rose from the dead. After that, Peter spent the rest of his life telling anyone who would listen what Jesus had done...until Nero killed him for it."

◆

Glabrio stared at his friend. It had been more than thirty years since a different emperor killed his grandfather for believing a man could die on a cross and come back to life because he was a god. But every sane person knew once a man was dead, he stayed dead.

"Hmph." Glabrio rubbed the back of his neck. When Sartorus told him something, he could trust it. At least he could trust that Sartorus believed it was true, whether it was or not. But a youth of fifteen could easily be led to believe what someone he admired told him, especially if that person was a good friend.

But he'd heard more than enough about religion for tonight. Whatever the three of them did tomorrow, it would help him understand Martina better, and there was no harm in joining them when it would please a good friend if he did.

"I actually came to ask you something about the investigation." With one knuckle, he rubbed under his chin. "Who do you think can be trusted when we return?"

"I haven't met many people outside the Cohort. Who else are you wondering about?"

"Volero Martinus—he knew we were going to visit Messala because he gave us directions. I think I can trust him, but can I?"

"I haven't seen enough of him to make that judgement. He seemed genuinely concerned when you told him Nepos had vanished so you were hunting for him."

"But was that because he's involved? Has he befriended me to 'keep his enemy close'?"

Sartorus's brow furrowed. "Any sign that might be the case?"

"Well, no. He did have Messala at that first dinner, but Messala's young enough that Artoria might have wanted him there to meet her daughters. His father is very rich and on the council. Volero said the son would be a council-man someday."

He steepled his fingers and rubbed the sides of his nose. "Martina says her uncle is trustworthy. She got angry when I unintentionally implied he wasn't. But family loyalty can make us blind to the faults of the ones we care about. I think she'd try to excuse the bad and focus on the good."

◆

Sartorus switched hands and rubbed his other palm. "I think Martinus was genuinely surprised when you told him Nepos was missing and probably dead. He was eager to help you out."

He pulled a deep breath, opened his mouth, and paused. How would his commander respond to what he was about to say? "I can ask God whether we should trust him."

"Hmph." Glabrio's eyes laughed at him. "You think your god will tell you?"

"The morning we were kidnapped, He told Martina to leave for Cigisa as soon as she could. That's why they were getting off the boat next to Barca's and saw us."

Glabrio rested his arm across his stomach to support his other elbow, then tapped his lips with his fist. "Well…think about the question however you want to. We don't have to decide whether we trust him yet."

He rubbed under his chin. "But you do know the Cohort as well as I do. Which of my men can be trusted…that's a more urgent question." With pursed lips, he blew out a slow breath. "I'm inclined to trust Acceptus."

Sartorus rubbed his palm again. "I would agree."

"But the others…I don't have a reason to distrust any of them, but I also don't have any reason to trust them completely." One corner of his mouth lifted. "So, while you're talking with your god about Volero, you can ask him about the others."

Glabrio's half-smile turned into a broad, ironic one.

Sartorus fought to keep his own smile from broadening into a grin. "As you wish, Tribune."

"I'll come get you for breakfast. Tomorrow should be an interesting day." Glabrio turned toward the door, then looked back across his shoulder. "As long as we're not in uniform, it's Mulio. An odd name for a potter, I suppose, but I've grown accustomed to it."

He chuckled as he headed out the door.

Sartorus returned his arms to his knees. Time to finish his evening prayers. Tribune, Glabrio, Mulio…it didn't matter which name he used. God knew who his friend was better than Glabrio knew himself, and he'd be praying for his friend to know God before their time in Carthago was over.

Chapter 48

NOT WHAT HE EXPECTED

Morning of Day 29

Glabrio leaned back in his chair and rested his interlaced fingers atop his head. A breakfast of bread still warm from the oven, dried dates, and goat cheese more than satisfied when eaten with a friend. But where were Martina and her steward?

Seated across from him, Sartorus popped the final date between his teeth. Then his gaze focused on something past Glabrio's shoulder. "Good morning."

"Good morning." Platana's voice behind him was no surprise, given the shine in his optio's eyes. "Mistress sent me to bring you to the library. She'll be joining us shortly."

When they entered the library, a bench wide enough for two that hadn't been there before sat against one wall. With the desk and guest chairs, it was ready for their meeting of four.

Platana swung one end of the bench out so she could stand behind it and patted the seat. "We have time for your treatment before Mistress comes."

Sartorus pulled the tunic over his head and sat.

As she spread the gel on the blisters and any skin that was still red, Glabrio looked through the scolls to find what he might want to read when they returned.

Sartorus's heartfelt "thank you" came from behind him, followed by the scraping of bench legs on the floor. "There's plenty of room for two. Would you care to sit beside me?"

"I…well…" A blush overspread her cheeks.

Before Platana finished her answer, Martina entered, bolted the door, and settled into the chair behind the desk. "I apologize for the delay. Atriensis was showing me something."

As Platana placed the ointment jar on the desk, Glabrio set the Seneca scroll back in the cubicle and took the guest chair. "If we'll be here long, you ought to sit down." His hand swept toward the waiting Sartorus.

Platana glanced at Martina, and with the smallest dip of her chin, she approved Sartorus's request. With a quick glance at her admirer and a shy smile, Platana took her seat beside him.

From inside her tunic, Martina extracted a silver chain holding a key. She unlocked the desk drawer and took out a leather-bound codex. It looked like the one he'd seen her slip into the drawer when he surprised her yesterday.

Her eyes turned toward Sartorus. "Have you ever read from the gospel written by Apostle Peter's helper, Marcus?"

Sartorus cleared his throat. "The man who first told me about Jesus heard Apostle Peter teach in Rome. He never said anything about Marcus. His house church only had the writings of Lucas, both what Jesus did and what happened as the good news began to spread. They also had a copy of Apostle Paul's letter to the Romans about what Jesus had done and how we should live."

Martina stroked the worn leather cover. "This was my grandmother Juliana's. She used it to teach me about Jesus. It was her greatest earthly treasure, and now it's mine." She fixed her gaze on Sartorus. "I would love to know all that you learned someday."

Glabrio's leaned back and crossed his arms. Pompeia had been making copies of Christian writings for more than a dozen years. Was it one of her copies that Sartorus had seen?

A personalized copy of Sabina's elegant poetry would be a fitting gift for Martina, but maybe one of Pompeia's copies of Lucas's writings would be even better.

"Let's begin." Martina closed her eyes and tipped her head back. "We thank You, God, for this chance to gather together. We thank You for using Platana and me to rescue our brother, Sartorus, and his friend. Holy Spirit, please guide us as we offer our prayers and praise."

"Amen" came from both Sartorus and Platana.

Martina picked up the codex. "I asked God to tell me what to read this morning. It isn't what I expected, but it's something Platana and I both love."

She shifted in her chair to face Glabrio. "Jesus was traveling around Galilee, teaching people about God's love for us and what we should do in response. But wherever he went, people brought their sick loved ones to him for healing, and he restored them to health."

Glabrio fingered his lip. He'd heard this before from his friends in Rome.

"Sometimes he went across the Sea of Galilee to the east side to get away from the crowds following him. Most of the people there weren't Jews, so he could spend time alone with only his closest disciples. He'd just come back to the west side of the sea when what I'm going to read you happened."

Sartorus leaned toward him. "That's the Sea of Tiberias. When He wasn't traveling, He stayed on the north end of the sea with some of His followers who were fishermen."

Martina opened the codex to a place marked by a ribbon. "'And when Jesus had crossed again in the boat to the other side, a great crowd gathered about him, and he was beside the sea. Then came one of the rulers of the synagogue, Jairus by name, and seeing him, he fell at his feet and implored him earnestly, saying, "My little daughter is at the point of death. Come and lay your hands on her, so that she may be made well and live." And he went with him. And a great crowd followed him and thronged about him.'"

Her eyes turned on Glabrio again. "At this point, Marcus tells about a sick woman in the crowd who thought if she could only touch Jesus's clothes, she would be healed. Jesus felt power go out from him and stopped to ask who touched him. When she came forward, he told her that her faith had made her well and to go in peace. I can read it all now, if you'd like, or we can read that part of it later."

"Later is good. Go on."

"'While he was still speaking, there came from the ruler's house some who said, "Your daughter is dead. Why trouble the Teacher any further?"

"'But overhearing what they said, Jesus said to the ruler of the synagogue, "Do not fear, only believe."

"'And he allowed no one to follow him except Peter and James and John the brother of James.

"'They came to the house of the ruler of the synagogue, and Jesus saw a commotion, people weeping and wailing loudly.

"'And when he had entered, he said to them, "Why are you making a commotion and weeping? The child is not dead but sleeping."

"'And they laughed at him. But he put them all outside and took the child's father and mother and those who were with him and went in where the child was.

"'Taking her by the hand he said to her, "Talitha cumi," which means, "Little girl, I say to you, arise."'

"'And immediately the girl got up and began walking (for she was twelve years of age), and they were immediately overcome with amazement.

"'And he strictly charged them that no one should know this, and told them to give her something to eat.'"

Glabrio looked at Sartorus. The single bounce of his eyebrows and the growing smile spoke volumes without him saying a word. Had they both seen something like this happen, or was it only an illusion?

Bringing someone back from the dead...or nearly dead. That's what Titus said his wife's prayers to her god had done. Maybe they had. Maybe they hadn't. Blows to the head were unpredictable, where some men recovered while others didn't.

Maybe the girl really was only sleeping deeply, like their Jesus said. Why would any miracle worker tell them all not to tell anyone if he really could restore life to the dead?

Martina closed the codex and held it close to her chest. Her eyes closed, and her head tipped back, like a child basking in the springtime sunshine. "We thank You, Lord, for letting us hear Your words today as Marcus has written them down for us. Give us the faith of Jairus and the woman who touched Your clothing. Bless and keep us in Your will until we gather again. In the name of Jesus, we pray."

Platana and Sartorus spoke an "amen" before Platana rose.

Three knocks on the door made Glabrio jump. Platana left Sartorus's side and slid back the bolt. When the door swung open, Atriensis stood with arms crossed. "We can go whenever you're ready."

Martina stood. "Thank you. We'll meet you in the stableyard."

Platana picked up the ointment. "I'll get your palla."

Sartorus's gaze followed her as she left the room.

Glabrio rubbed his chin. Platana tending to Sartorus's burns had relieved the pain, but a few hours in the sun without protection could undo all that had been done

"Since we'll be in the sun as we ride, could we get a broad hat for Sartorus?"

Martina pulled the hidden key out of her tunic and lifted its chain over her head. "I'm sure that can be arranged. Some of the field workers wore them when I was a child. Atriensis will know who can get him one. Did you want one, too?"

"I'll be fine without."

She slipped the codex into the drawer and locked it before putting the chain on and tucking the key inside her tunic. "I hope you'll join us again tomorrow."

He'd never seen a more hopeful smile or greater warmth in her eyes. How could he say no?

"I'd like that."

"I'll meet you in the stableyard." She looked back over her shoulder as she passed through the doorway. It was worth it to sit through however many times she wanted to read to him to see that glowing smile.

Past wheat fields and olive groves that helped feed Rome, Glabrio and

Sartorus rode behind Martina's carriage. But it wasn't the passing bounty that filled Glabrio's thoughts. It was what Martina read from her treasured codex.

He reined in until the carriage moved far enough ahead of them. He wanted no one to hear what he was about to ask.

"That story Martina read."

Sartorus twisted in the saddle to face him directly. "What about it?"

"Had you heard it before?"

"I have."

"Did you tell her to read it?"

One corner of Sartorus's mouth lifted. "No. I wasn't expecting her to read to us, but I'm glad she did. I've never heard anything from the writings of Marcus before. The house church I went to had the writings of Lucas."

He turned his mule to face Glabrio straight on. "He was a physician who traveled with Apostle Paul for a few years. Paul was in prison in Caesarea Maritima for two years after appealing to Caesar. While they waited to go to Rome, Lucas talked to many people who'd seen Jesus. He started his writings by explaining that he wanted to write an orderly account based on the testimony of people who'd been there and seen what happened."

"A history is only as good as the information the writer has." Glabrio's jaw twitched. Titus claimed Lucas was as good a historian as any he'd read. But was his friend's opinion colored by him sharing faith in Lucas's god?

Sartorus adjusted his broad-brimmed hat and retied the cord under his chin. "Lucas wrote about how Marcus had traveled some with Paul, too. Nero killed both Peter and Paul after he blamed Christians for the Great Fire. Lucas's writings end a few years before that happened. I don't know where Marcus and Lucas were when Nero was hunting Christians in Rome."

"You make it sound like these men were writing about events that actually happened."

Sartorus startled when his mule cocked its rear leg. Then he relaxed and patted its neck. "I don't know about Marcus, but Lucas was a good historian. He wrote at the very beginning how he used eyewitnesses to get the true story."

"Bringing people back from the dead doesn't sound like history to me."

"Just because I haven't seen it doesn't mean Jesus couldn't do it. Titianus was almost dead. In the usual way of things, a man with a broken skull like his always dies."

Glabrio clenched his teeth as he nudged the mule back to a walk. Titus claimed his god stopped death from taking him, but that was what Pompeia told him. She believed it was true, but that didn't mean it was.

"Maybe the girl wasn't actually dead. Your Jesus told the mourners she wasn't."

"I don't know if Marcus reports it, but Lucas tells of another time when

Jesus stopped the funeral procession for a widow's son and brought him back to life. It scared the people following the corpse. Maybe he only said she was sleeping because he didn't want the local people to know what he was going to do."

Glabrio's eyebrows dipped until he forced them to relax. Maybe their Jesus didn't want anyone to know in case he failed to save her when he'd told her father he could.

When Christians prayed for deliverance, it didn't always come. Nero had killed the two men who'd been telling so many others their god could save them. Domitian had killed his grandfather. Glabrio had watched many Christians die in the arena. If their god had power over life and death, why did he let Rome take his followers' lives?

The carriage had pulled far ahead of them.

"Whether it happened or not, it makes for a good story. We're falling too far behind."

Glabrio flexed his calves, and the mule stayed at a walk. It took three good kicks to its sides to get it trotting. Stubborn resistance in man or mule never failed to irritate him.

Sartorus rode up beside him, but Glabrio kept his eyes fixed on the carriage ahead. Meeting his friend's gaze might invite conversation, and he'd talked all he wanted to about their god...at least for now.

Martina's Cigisa pottery works

After a visit to the clay deposits, where no one was gathering clay that day, Glabrio trailed Martina through the main workshop. A dozen workers were making plates, bowls, and cups destined for the tables of ordinary people. Some were plain, but most had a geometric pattern pressed into the clay before it went into one of several large kilns.

Nothing there fired his interest, but the smaller workshop where the fancier applique wares were made would intrigue anyone. Pieces of clay were pressed into molds to form each applique, which was attached to a plate, bowl, or goblet with a thin layer of runny clay that Martina called a slip. Then it went into a smaller kiln for firing.

But the most interesting of all was the potter sculpting custom appliques. As he carved the last mane on four fiery horses that would draw a chariot around a large vase, he transformed lifeless clay into a thing of true beauty. Glabrio half expected them to snort and neigh.

Atriensis led them from workshop to lodging to dining hall before excusing himself to go talk with the foreman in the office.

Martina had been satisfied with the lodging, where beds had rope frames, adequate straw mattresses, and large enough light blankets. Sleeping in shackles on the deck of a ship and the floor of a cell made those seem almost luxurious.

In the kitchen, he drifted away from her conversation with the cook to look into a pot of simmering porridge. When he leaned over and inhaled, it was as bland as what his garrison cooks used to prepare.

As they left the kitchen, he fell in beside her. "When I came, our garrison porridge was as flavorless as what your people are fed. I got the cooks to add a little rosemary. That gave it a good taste. You have plenty of rosemary bushes growing near your villa, so it wouldn't cost anything to change what you serve."

She paused and stared at him. "That's a wonderful idea. You know how to cook?"

"Actually, I don't. I was complaining about the horrible food, and Sartorus said that was what his mother did."

Her soft chuckle wrapped around him. "I salute your wisdom in adopting a change your aide proposed and your honesty in telling me it was his idea."

"Any suggestion Sartorus makes is worth considering, and most are worth acting on. I'm still alive because he knew what could make the slavers kill me and kept me from doing it."

"Having the right people to help...that's a blessing. I was only eleven when both my parents died and Grandfather took me in. I don't know what I would have done without Atriensis to look after everything here. But I want to learn how to run things myself in case I have to. Life is uncertain, and we never know when death might take someone from us."

A shadow of sadness passed across her face. "My parents, Grandfather, Volero—they've all performed Roman rites and thought they were doing the right thing. Grandfather was asking questions about Jesus the day before he died, but I don't know what he decided." The smile she forced didn't quite hide the quiver of her lower lip. "But at least I know I'll see Juliana again, and Platana loves Jesus as much as I do."

"Does it matter that much?" He'd seen no proof there was anything after death.

"Oh, yes. Where we spend eternity hangs on our decision about Jesus, about His sacrifice to pay for our sins. Didn't your Christian friends in Rome explain that?"

"They told me what they thought."

"And you don't believe them yet."

Any answer he gave wouldn't please her, so he said nothing.

She pointed toward the specialty workshop. "I want to watch the workers in there some more. I need to choose two of them to come with me to Carthago."

He opened the door and held it for her. "I watched one of your men shaping a goblet. It didn't look too hard, and I'd like to try it before I pretend to be one of your potters."

"Tribune Glabrio throwing clay on a potter's wheel?" She was laughing at him, but it felt surprisingly good. "This I have to see." She pointed at an idle wheel. "Tell one of my men that I'd like him to show you how to get started. I need to join Atriensis and my foreman for a while. We have to discuss a few final things about starting the Carthago shop."

"I don't expect it to look perfect the first time. Few things do." He offered a wry smile and got her warmest one in return. "But it will let me truthfully say I'm a potter if someone asks."

"However it turns out, Atriensis will have it fired and get it to you. Then you'll have something to remind you of your time in Cigisa. It should be one of a kind, and you can always say it tells a story."

As she walked away, his gaze followed her. One of a kind...that described her perfectly. He wouldn't need a roughly made goblet to remind him of his time in Cigisa. How could he ever forget it?

Chapter 49

BEGINNING TO SEE?

Morning of Day 30

Glabrio had risen at dawn to watch the high, thin clouds pass through shades of gray to pink and finally to white. A hearty breakfast of hot-from-the-oven rolls, eggs, dates, and cheese had been followed by Platana caring for Sartorus's almost-healed burns. But Martina hadn't joined them.

Platana said she was preparing, but she didn't say for what. Her smile suggested it was something the two of them would enjoy, but would he?

Today might be another visit to the pottery workshop to get the right potters and the tools they would need in Carthago, but that shouldn't take long. Tomorrow they'd start back to the city where a murderer waited. But Martina had planned another meeting while Atriensis attended to a few things near the villa.

When they entered the library, Martina was already there.

Marcus's codex lay on the desk before her. "I asked God what to read today while we wait for Atriensis. We can stop and talk about any of it, if you want to. I'll be shortening some parts in my own words and skipping others. But I'll read God's own words, too, when I think you'll understand that best. We can always go back and read everything."

God's own words. Can anything a man writes down be a god's own words? He felt a frown start and stopped it. But did she see it before he did?

Titus could guess his thoughts about their religion too easily, even when Glabrio tried to hide them. Sometimes his friend would say what Glabrio was thinking as if he could read his mind. Then he'd answer the question Glabrio hadn't spoken. Sometimes he'd simply say they could talk later when he might want to. Titus never got offended by his lack of interest.

But Martina wasn't Titus, and women were more sensitive than men. She said she wasn't easily offended, but...

Glabrio settled into the guest chair. "That sounds good."

The smile that lit her face declared that the right response. And it was true enough.

She set the codex on the desktop and clasped her hands atop it. "When it was time to begin what Jesus came from heaven to do, he started speaking to gatherings of people in Galilee. Marcus tells us the message he gave. 'The time is fulfilled, and the kingdom of God has come near. Repent and believe the good news.' He stayed in Capernaum on the Sea of Galilee when he wasn't going from town to town, teaching in the Jewish synagogues and healing people wherever he went."

Her gaze shifted from him to her hands, or more likely the codex beneath them. "One day a leper came to him. After Jesus healed him, he told him not to tell anyone. Instead, the man told everyone. Jesus often healed someone where people weren't watching and told them not to tell. But many of them did because...well...how could you not if you'd been healed of something terrible like leprosy or blindness? The sheer joy of it...I don't think I could stay quiet about it."

Couldn't stay quiet? He hadn't seen that. Titus claimed a miracle healed him, but he told almost no one. All the Christians Glabrio knew were very careful about whom they told what they thought Jesus had done. They knew what they risked if the wrong person found out. Martina had also thought it too dangerous for him to know.

But these were stories about Jews in a time before Rome declared being Christian illegal.

"Anyway, after that, Jesus had so many people coming that he couldn't enter towns openly. Instead, he taught and healed in deserted places outside the towns. But after a while, he returned to Capernaum where he stayed in Peter's house. People heard he was there, and so many came that no one else could even get near the door.

"When four men brought a paralyzed friend and couldn't get close, they got on the roof and dug through it to lower their friend down in front of him."

She opened the codex to the first of four ribbons. Preparing...placing those four ribbons must have been what kept Martina from eating with him.

"Imagine the faith of his friends in digging through someone's roof to get their friend in front of Jesus. They expected him to make their friend walk again. But he did something else first. Something much more important. We all have a problem that's more serious than anything that can be wrong with our body."

Glabrio crossed his arms. "Let me guess." It was hard not to smile in anticipation of her surprise that he'd know. "Sin."

Her eyes widened. "Exactly. Do you know what it is?"

"I've been told before, but you can tell me again."

Her eyebrows dipped. That was not the answer she was looking for. Then a hard-to-interpret smile curved her lips. "I probably need to."

She cleared her throat and closed her eyes. "Thank You, God, for giving us Your Word through these pages. Open our hearts and minds to hear what You're telling us with them. In Jesus's name we pray."

Two amens came from the bench. She turned the odd smile on him once more before putting her elbows on the desk on either side of the open codex. "So, what have you been told sin is?"

She leaned toward him and clasped her hands beneath her chin. He felt two other pairs of eyes on him, and he drew a deep breath. This meeting was supposed to be a few moments of her reading from her codex, not the start of an interrogation.

He rubbed his mouth. It was his own fault. He should have known any attempt to impress her could do the opposite.

"Doing things the Christian god doesn't like." He shrugged. "Rome arrests people for some of them."

"Rome also arrests those who do what God tells us to do." Straight lips accompanied sad eyes.

"Your secret is safe with me." He glanced at Sartorus and Platana. "All your secrets."

"I know." She leaned back in her chair. "What you said is only partly right. God doesn't like us to do some things, but it isn't simply that He doesn't like them. When we do them, we build a barrier between Him and us. And it doesn't have to be something horrible like murder or stealing to make us unfit to be in His presence. God wants us to love Him like He loves us, and He wants us to love others like we love ourselves."

She turned several pages, passing two of the ribbons and stopping short of the fourth. "This will explain it better than I can."

Her gaze shifted from the page to him. "Jesus had come to Jerusalem for the last time, and he knew in a few days he'd be crucified. He'd been teaching in the temple there, and the Jewish leaders had been challenging him. Many of them only wanted to get rid of Jesus because they saw him as a threat. But some really wanted to serve God, and one of those asked him a sincere question."

She looked past him, and he turned in the chair to see what drew her attention. Nothing seemed different. Was there something he wasn't seeing?

When she looked at him again, that odd smile was back. Then her gaze focused on the codex.

"'One of the scribes approached. When he heard them debating and saw that Jesus answered them well, he asked him, "Which command is the most important of all?"

"'Jesus answered, "The most important is Listen, O Israel! The Lord our God, the Lord is one. Love the Lord your God with all your heart, with all your soul, with all your mind, and with all your strength. The second is love your neighbor as yourself. There is no other command greater than these."

"'Then the scribe said to him, "You are right, teacher. You have correctly said that He is one, and there is no one else except Him. And to love Him with all your heart, with all your understanding, and with all your strength, and to love your neighbor as yourself, is far more important than all the burnt offerings and sacrifices."

"'When Jesus saw that he answered wisely, he said to him, "You are not far from the kingdom of God." And no one dared to question him any longer.'"

She stroked the words she'd just read. "So, what God commands us to do is to love Him with every part of our being and to love other people." Her eyes turned from the page to him. "When we think or do things that go against that love, we've sinned." One corner of her mouth lifted. "And there's not a single person alive who hasn't disobeyed both of those commands. We are all sinners."

"So…" Glabrio rubbed his jaw. "Your god demands total dedication to him. That might be reasonable, if he's a god with real power. But to be fair, he should tell us what's right and what's wrong in his eyes. And just saying to love other people—what that means isn't clear at all."

Glabrio crossed his arms. "So, what do you think disobeys the command to love other people? Even within families, how fond people are of each other varies. I love and respect my father. Most men would say they do, but if they spoke the truth, many would have to admit they don't. Many will do anything to get what they want, not caring whether they hurt relatives or friends. Life is a contest, and their goal is to win, whatever it takes. Loving strangers… what does that even mean? Love is only a kind of affection, and someone has to earn it."

"No, love like Jesus used the word is a decision, a decision that I'm willing to act upon. I don't even have to like a person to love them like God wants me to. It's wanting what's best for another person. Not simply what they want, but what's truly best for them. Those are often different. It's helping when they need it, even when I might not want to, even when it costs me something."

His head drew back. "Like buying the tribune you disliked and wanted nothing to do with when you saw me in chains."

"Yes. But I never disliked you. I was only afraid of what you might do, so I didn't want you getting too close. And I really did want to help you the moment I saw you in trouble. I'm so thankful I had enough money at the shop to be able to."

"We're glad, too." He glanced at Sartorus sitting contentedly by the woman who'd taken such good care of him. His friend cast a sideways glance at Platana, then a nod declared his agreement.

One corner of Glabrio's mouth lifted. Thankful was too mild a word to describe how he felt about what she'd done. "I'm also glad you've decided I'm not too dangerous to have around."

"So am I." Silent laughter lit her eyes. "Uncle told me you were a good man, but you're nicer than I expected. I'm so glad Barca agreed to sell you to me. If you were a poor man, I'd consider it money well spent doing what God commands. But since you're much richer than I am and you were both very expensive, I do hope you'll pay me back."

Three knocks on the door made her jump. "Atriensis is here." She locked the codex in the drawer and stood. "I'll be selecting the men who go with me to start the shop today. Then we'll inspect some other parts of the estate before I leave for Carthago tomorrow. Will you join us again?"

"Of course. I'm beginning to see what's special about this estate, but I'd like to see more."

Sartorus slid back the bolt and opened the door to let the steward in. Martina's smile as she passed Glabrio was all the invitation any man would need, and they followed Atriensis to the stableyard.

Chapter 50

TOO MUCH TO HOPE FOR

Carthago, morning of Day 30

Sitting at his desk in the harbor station, Verus drummed on a tablet with his stylus.

Glabrio and Sartorus had been missing for six days. Where were they and what were they doing? Had they gone after the missing metalsmiths? Glabrio might be the only one who'd believe them, even though they were runaways.

But Glabrio had disappeared six days ago, and he'd talked with the smiths himself five days ago. He ran his hand through his hair. But why had they decided to take only part of the counterfeits and run so soon after Glabrio visited?

The scrape of Placidus's chair legs and a muted "Centurion" was followed by Acceptus striding through the doorway. He dropped into the guest chair, took off his helmet, and set it on his knee.

Verus crossed his arms. "I take it you didn't find Glabrio yet."

Acceptus snorted. "When Messala gave you a copy of the list he gave Glabrio, I expected we'd find he'd gone to see one of Nepos's friends. Two near the top of the list have family estates off the Utica road. Yesterday I visited those and the estates of a few more that were within an easy day's ride along that road. I went as far as the Ad Gallinacium garrison. No one had seen a tribune and optio. If he'd ridden that far, he would have stopped to inspect the station, so I turned back there."

Verus rubbed his mouth before Acceptus saw the smirk that almost escaped. Their officious young tribune took too much pleasure in inspections to pass up an opportunity like that.

"I think you're right. How far out is that?"

"Almost sixteen miles. I got back after sunset yesterday." Acceptus leaned back in the chair. "Today I'll check the Cigisa road. It will be another long ride, so I've switched to my spare mount."

He ran his hand along his helmet's horsehair crest. "He's a good enough horse for thirty-mile rides, but to Cigisa and back is longer than that. It crosses more large hills as well. I'll probably spend the night at the Cigisa garrison and be back late afternoon tomorrow."

Verus worked to keep a straight face. Even if he had a horse good enough for a thirty-mile ride, he wouldn't want to take one.

"I've been checking into some from the list, too. No one had seen them at the two estates Messala mentioned that share the road to his family estate. Since the horses aren't at the stable, they must have gone out of town somewhere. But in case they didn't, today I'll talk with the ones on the list with town houses in Carthago."

He took Messala's list from the drawer and pretended to scan it. "This list might not include everyone we need to check. As important as his family is, Glabrio's a welcome guest when the councilmen entertain. I'll visit the baths this afternoon. Most of the council should be there. Maybe one of them knows where he was planning to go."

Verus slipped the list back into his desk. "But maybe we're looking too close to home. He did say something about talking with the governor about Nepos. If I was going to see the governor in Leptis Magna, I'd take a ship. But if Glabrio got seasick enough coming from Rome, maybe he weighed four days throwing up against sixteen days in the saddle, and the saddle won."

Accpetus's snort raised Verus's eyebrows. "Sartorus is a good soldier who would try to do whatever Glabrio wanted, but he couldn't make that ride. Glabrio wouldn't have made him try. They would have gone by sea, but then their horses should have been in the stable."

Verus massaged the back of his neck. Acceptus was going to be a hard man to fool when he disposed of another tribune before that tribune could dispose of him.

"I'll still ask around the harbor to see if anyone saw them board a ship. Maybe Glabrio changed where he stabled their horses and didn't tell you."

Acceptus's head drew back. "But the stableman would have known that and told me."

"Unless Glabrio didn't tell him. He never tells Dubitatus what he's doing."

Acceptus's mouth twitched. "I can understand that." He stood. "I'll be back tomorrow, but it might be late. If Fortuna smiles on us, you or I will have found him by then."

He settled the helmet on his head and strode from the room.

Verus leaned back in his chair and stared at the ceiling. If only Messala hadn't been drunk and stupid and paid that bet with counterfeits. Nepos would be back in Rome instead of wherever the smiths put his corpse. But what was done was done.

Maybe Glabrio had vanished because someone else wanted him dead and had beaten Verus to killing him. He closed his eyes, and his next breath ended in the deepest sigh. But that was too much to hope for. When Glabrio returned, he'd have to find the right way to make him disappear again.

Baths of Carthago, afternoon of Day 30

Even with his helmet left at the station, many who'd come to the baths eyed him curiously as he passed, still in body armor, through the changing room into the warmth of the tepidarium. He scanned the room, looking for one of the city leaders most likely to have had Glabrio at his dinners.

Volero Martinus sat facing him in one of the heated pools, listening as the man across from him spoke.

Nepos would have known Martinus, but he wasn't on Messala's list. But if they made a list for Glabrio, he'd be at the head of it.

Dubitatus had mocked their new tribune for taking two guards in full armor when he went in striped tunic and toga to a banquet at Martinus's domus on his second day in the city. But that was before Dubitatus knew Nepos hadn't left early for Rome. No one laughed at Glabrio's precautions now.

Of all the men in the room, Martinus was most likely to know Glabrio's plans. Verus took a step toward him, then turned in a casual manner to face the other direction.

He knew the voice of the man talking to Martinus all too well—Messala.

The men sitting on a bench within earshot rose and headed toward the changing room. With Messala facing away from it, Verus took the seat and bent over to loosen the sandal laces that wrapped around his calf. Inspecting a shoe would draw nothing but fleeting glances while he listened to a conversation he wished wasn't happening.

"I'm planning a banquet for a few of my friends, and I was going to invite Glabrio. But I haven't seen him for a few days. No one seems to have. But since he dines with you so often, perhaps you know when he plans to return."

"When was the last time anyone saw him?" Concern coated Martinus's voice.

"He came to ask me for a list of Nepos's friends six days ago. Then he stopped at my metal shop to see about getting something gilded to send his father. He also ordered a special lamp stand, but it wasn't the sort of thing a man would want to use." Messala forced a chuckle. "It could make a woman think she was special, whether she was or not."

"Six days ago, he didn't show for a special dinner where I expected him. That's not like him. You say no one has seen him in six days?"

"That's what I'm finding."

"Do his centurions know where he's gone?"

"I suppose I could ask one of them." Messala cleared his throat. "I hadn't thought of that."

"That seems like the first thing you would have done." Martinus's skeptical tone almost made Verus roll his eyes.

Time to stop the fool before he said something he shouldn't to the one man in the city who would never stop demanding the arrest and execution of whoever killed Glabrio.

Verus finished tying the strap and rose. It was time to join the conversation before it took a more dangerous turn.

He strode to the edge of the pool. "Martinus, Messala." He tipped his head to each in turn. "It's good I find you together. I'm looking for someone who might know where Tribune Glabrio has gone. He and his optio haven't been back to headquarters for several days."

Martinus raised his eyebrows. "We were just discussing how neither of us have seen him for some time. Seven days for me, six for Messala. I expected to see him six days ago, and he didn't show up."

"So, he didn't tell either of you where he was going or when he'd return?"

"No, but if there's anything I can do to help you find him, let me know."

Verus acknowledged Martinus's offer with a nod. "I will. Now, if you'll excuse me, I have many others of the council here that I want to ask as well. In view of Tribune Nepos's disappearance, finding Tribune Glabrio is of utmost importance."

Two heads nodded, and Verus headed toward Duumvir Paternus and the two councilmen talking with him.

He flexed his jaw before anyone saw the anger his clenched teeth proclaimed. At least he'd talked to Martinus in time to douse any suspicions his bungling partner had inspired.

Maybe he should get rid of Messala sooner than he'd planned, whether Glabrio was still alive or not.

Chapter 51

THE WISER CHOICE

Returning to Utica, Day 31

When the amphitheater in Utica finally appeared in the distance, Glabrio was more than ready for their river trip to end. Sartorus had joined him on the trunk instead of Martina. Even though she had spoken very little going upriver, Sartorus was no more talkative, and he didn't smell as good.

The river boat had seemed spacious before, but with the addition of two potters and two trunks of the special tools and supplies they thought essential for starting a custom pottery shop, the deck seemed full. The space beneath the deck was filled with crated pottery of the common sort to restock the Utica shop, and the boat sat much lower in the water than before. At least they were going downstream with the full load. Going back would be lighter.

He chuckled, and Sartorus looked at him with raised eyebrows.

"Downstream loaded, upstream empty. What more could a rower want?"

Sartorus's nod and grin reflected his own. They'd never look at a ship with oars again without checking the wind and current.

It was shortly after noon when they pulled in at an empty pier, and the trunks and crates were loaded onto handcarts to go to the shop. Except for the small library trunk, which Sartorus carried as Platana walked beside him.

Now that Glabrio knew Martina's greatest treasure lay within, he approved of his optio's choice.

Martina was his walking companion, and this time she made no objection.

He slowed their pace so he and the Christians would lag a little behind. Some conversations were best kept private.

"Are you going to read to us here?"

"No." Her voice was too quiet for Atriensis to hear. "There won't be any-place private enough." Smiling eyes looked up at him. "But I will when we get to my town house. All my people are fellow believers. Taurus used to guard Grandfather's second wife, Juliana, so he knows. But he's not one of us yet."

"What about Volero? Does he believe like you?"

"No, and other than Taurus, he's the only one outside my household who knows about my faith. He and Grandfather never trusted Artoria with the family secret they found embarrassing. Juliana told me about Jesus when I first came from the estate. She made Platana my maid so I'd know the pleasure of having a Christian sister with me."

"How will you keep your potters from knowing?"

"My glassblowers don't know yet, so I'll have the potters dine with them instead of with us. Cherida was a decent cook already, but Colina is teaching her how to do even better. But the time may come when I can trust them enough to share what we believe with them. I'd love to have us all together."

He rubbed his jaw. "That could be dangerous."

"I know, but God will tell me if and when it's the right time."

That was what he'd expect Pompeia to say. But he'd seen enough of the world to know what you thought was the right time often wasn't, and speaking too soon could be fatal.

When they reached the shop, the rowers and potters were carrying crates into the sales room and stacking them against the wall.

Figulus beamed at her. "I didn't expect you back so soon, but I do have everything you asked for ready. A new ledger like I use and notes on what people buy most and how much to stock. Also, some molds for the more popular appliques and some drawings to help whoever will be making your kilns."

"Wonderful. Blasteo and Minio are applique men from the estate, so you can show them what you have and see what else they think we might need."

"As you wish, Mistress." Figulus's smiling nod declared that no problem.

"I'd like you to show them what you do with the ledger, too." She turned her attention on the potters. "Can you read and write?"

Eyes widened as they glanced at each other. Then two heads shook. "No, Mistress."

"That's fine. My business steward in Carthago, Clavus, will begin teaching you as soon as we get home. One of my people can help with the record keeping until you learn. Ceraulo is in charge of my glass shop that's only two doors away, and he can help as well."

Sartorus stepped forward. "I come from a tradesman family. If you show me the ledger, I can explain anything unusual to Clavus and Ceraulo."

Atriensis cleared his throat. "While you figure all this out, I'll take Glabrio to buy passage to Carthago. Taurus will stay with you."

Martina raised her hand to acknowledge what he said, then focused once more on what Figulus was saying.

Glabrio followed Atriensis into the street. They'd reached the quay when Atriensis stopped and crossed his arms.

"You share the name of the consul of Rome four years ago. Any relation?"

"My father."

The corners of Atriensis's mouth turned down. "A powerful family led by an important man. I expect you'll become the same."

Glabrio's eyebrows lowered, and he returned frown for frown. Was a steward of a provincial estate about to challenge him over something? "I plan to."

"So, you won't be in Africa long. But even being here a short time, you've made some enemies who want you gone, if not dead. Make certain the trouble you're chasing doesn't get her hurt for helping you."

It wasn't simply a provincial steward standing before him. It was a man who loved Martina like a daughter and only wanted to protect her.

Glabrio placed his hand over his heart. "You have my word that she'll be as safe as I can keep her."

"One thing more." Atriensis's gaze bored into him. "Don't do anything to break her heart, either."

"You have my solemn word."

"Hmph." Atriensis's deep sigh lowered Glabrio's eyebrows again. "I think you mean that, but what a man intends and what finally happens…"

He pointed at a ship already backed into the quay with men unloading it. "We'll book passage on the Seawind. I ship grain to Carthago on her. Her captain's a good seaman and a good man."

In almost no time, Glabrio had been introduced to the captain as the man in charge of Martina's party, and passage for six was booked.

In silence, they returned to the pottery shop. The bell on the door tinkled as they entered, and Martina came out of the back room.

She took one of Atriensis's hands. "Figulus has done an excellent job of preparing everything we'll need. Please find some way of expressing my appreciation."

"I will." He placed his second hand around hers. "There are too many people here for me and the rowers to stay the night. You and Platana can share my usual room. I'll be heading upriver to beat the sunset."

"Are you sure you have to leave already?"

"Yes. Figulus will get your trunks to the ship. I trust Taurus and Glabrio to get you home safely. But I expect you to send me word as soon as you get home so I won't worry about you."

"With two soldiers and Uncle's best bodyguard, no one could be safer. You take good care of yourself. I have no idea how I'd ever be able to replace you." She stood on tiptoes and kissed his cheek. "You've always been as much an uncle to me as Uncle Volero is."

He kissed the top of her head. "Come visit us again soon."

"I will."

Eyes filled with love for her turned on Glabrio and instantly cooled. "Remember what we discussed."

Glabrio nodded once. Of course he'd remember the words of a man who loved her like a father.

"May Fortuna smile on your journey home." Atriensis summoned the two rowers with a curl of his fingers, and they left the shop.

Martina came to stand beside Glabrio. Her fingertips wiped the corner of her eye.

Glabrio looked down at her and fought off the urge to put an arm around her to comfort her. "He loves you like a father."

She smiled up at him through tears. "I know. I love him, too."

She wiped the tears away. "Atriensis repaid Figulus for what you cost me, so we can take some and eat at the taberna just down the street. Figulus says their stew is delicious, and his cook only made enough for his workers anyway."

"Whatever you want is fine with me."

"I'll get the others."

As she disappeared behind the curtain, he drew a deep breath and released a deeper sigh. Atriensis's words of warning would likely gnaw at him. What a man wants and what finally happens weren't always the same, and he'd be wise to remember that.

The sun was almost down when they returned to the pottery shop after dinner. Martina and Platana took the room Atriensis used when he stayed overnight. While Taurus placed his pallet in front of their door and the potters chose the workshop, Glabrio and Sartorus had taken theirs to the salesroom floor.

It was better than the bare deck and no worse than the cell.

Sartorus lay on his side, and his slow, deep breathing soon declared him asleep. But nothing kept him awake for long.

Glabrio rolled onto his back and placed his hands beneath his head. He stared at the shadows cast by the iron rods that barred the half-foot windows at roof level. He'd make it back to Carthago tomorrow, but what then?

The metalsmiths would be his first target. No doubt they'd played a role in selling him as a slave, but Sartorus thought selling them instead of killing them was enough to show they weren't murderers. If they'd sold Nepos like they had him, they could be made to tell who bought the missing tribune. It was a short step from there to where he'd been taken and getting him back if he was still alive. If someone else had killed him and left them to get rid of the evidence, they'd tell him that, too.

Either way, capturing them before anyone knew he was hunting them was the next move, and Martina had made that easy by letting him act like her slave until he was ready to reveal himself.

Martina—the thought of her triggered a smile. Behind those rolling eyes and twitching lips when she thought he didn't mean what he'd just said, there was a woman wise beyond her years and kind beyond any woman he'd ever seen, Titus's Pompeia excepted.

The more time he spent with her, the more he wanted to be with her. But he was an Acilius Glabrio, destined for position and power in the service of Rome. He needed a senatorial wife who could help him achieve that, and Father would find him one. It wasn't wise to want something else.

Father defined wisdom as Seneca did: proper understanding, the ability to discern good from evil, knowing what to choose and what to reject based on the true value of things, not common opinion. Until coming to Carthago, he'd agreed wholeheartedly.

But Titus had laughed when he heard that quote. He'd said that was only the start. Copying a senator's best oratorical stance with one hand upraised, he'd proclaimed, "The fear of the Lord is the beginning of wisdom, and the knowledge of the Holy One is understanding." Then he'd crossed his arms before saying a man would never be truly wise until he opened his heart and mind to knowing the one true god.

Grandfather would have agreed with Titus, and he was executed because of it.

Glabrio rolled from his back to his side. Father had made the wiser choice, and he would do the same.

◆

The three-flame oil lamp on the table beside the bed she and Platana were sharing cast faint shadows on the wall behind her. Martina lifted the Marcus codex out of its chest and unwrapped the cloth that protected it. She fingered the ribbons that were still where she'd placed them that morning.

"I wish there was a good place to read to him tonight. He asked me if I would, and he seemed disappointed when I said no. I hope the delay doesn't make him lose interest."

She rewrapped the codex and returned it to the chest. "I'm so glad he's going to be staying with us for a while." She locked the chest and dropped the key's chain over her head. "He's a nice man. I'm glad he didn't take offense all the times I tried to drive him away."

Platana lay by the wall, and she propped herself up on one elbow. "Sartorus says he's a truly good man. He couldn't be happier that Glabrio is curious about our faith. The tribune's closest friend in Rome is a believer, too."

"A truly good man. Yes, I can see that. If he were a believer, he'd be a wonderful husband for a Christian woman."

Platana slid closer to the wall and patted where Martina would lie. "He'd make a wonderful husband for you."

Martina blew out the lamp and stretched out on the bed. "But he told Uncle his father will arrange a political marriage for him in Rome, so I suppose that's something that could never happen."

She stopped the sigh before Platana heard it. He was a good man, so he wouldn't let himself get involved with anyone in Africa. He wouldn't lead someone on to think he might. He was only lonely so far from home, and he wanted some friends for conversations and board games until it was time to sail back to Rome.

But it was obvious why a woman might want to be his wife. She'd be tempted to want that herself if he were a Christian and could marry his heart's desire instead of his father's choice.

Chapter 52

RETURN TO CARTHAGO

Carthago, Day 32

Glabrio and their party stood on the wharf, waiting for their trunks and some crates of pottery to stock her shop. The trip down the coast had been enjoyable this time since he was no longer chained to a rowing bench.

Sartorus nudged him and tipped his head sideways. Placidus was ambling down the wharf toward them.

He turned away to hide his face. No one must know he was back until he'd arrested the metalsmiths. "Watch him."

A slight turn of Sartorus's body let him keep his eyes on the optio without obviously watching. Placidus passed within fifteen feet of them and continued down the quay.

"He didn't even glance our way." Sartorus's voice was almost a whisper.

Glabrio turned to watch the retreating optio, only to see him disappear as he entered a passageway leading to the inner harbor.

He blew out a slow breath. "It's good he didn't spot us."

"But he should have." Sartorus slapped his shoulder where the almost-healed sunburn had been itching. "He should have been scanning everything and everyone he passed. When we were loading Barca's ship, his men should have been doing the same."

"Do you think Verus knows what happens when he's not watching?"

"I don't think Verus cares. If he did, his men would be doing it whether he was watching or not. Even Dubitatus expects his men to do what they're supposed to without his attention, and they do."

"Verus did a thorough tour when we walked the harbor and quay."

"He knows what to do, but knowing and doing aren't the same for some men." Sartorus slapped his other shoulder. "They weren't for Tribune Nepos."

"Maybe that changed at the end. Maybe that's what got him killed."

"Maybe." Sartorus rubbed his palm. "It almost got you killed. But we had help Nepos wouldn't have had."

"You mean Martina."

"She's only part." Sartorus glanced at the potters, who were talking with Taurus, and lowered his voice. "From the moment I woke up in the cage, I was praying for deliverance for both of us. Barca buying us both even though we weren't rowers, the rigging breaking so we'd be loading cargo when Martina came, God telling her she needed to go to Cigisa right away so she'd be on that ship where she could see us...I see God's hand in all of it."

Glabrio stared at Sartorus and saw absolute certainty in his eyes. How could he be so certain a god no one could see had done anything?

"It could all be coincidence. Sometimes Fortuna smiles and works in our favor."

"That's a lot of coincidences strung together. Fortuna's smiles can't do anything, but God can make the most unlikely things, even bad things, work together for the good of those who love Him."

Sartorus's smile and shrug lowered Glabrio's eyebrows. Grandfather probably believed that until Domitian sent the Praetorians for his head.

"Hmph." What he wanted to say wasn't something he would risk the others hearing, so it was better left unsaid.

He glanced at Martina, chatting with Platana while they waited. She was happy believing as she did, whether it was true or not. As Grandfather had, would she choose to die for it?

But as long as no one else learned what she believed, he could keep her safe.

Martina's town house, afternoon of Day 32

As Volero approached the door to Martina's town house, he wouldn't say he was worried, but he was concerned.

When he'd gone home from the council chamber, the last thing expected to find was Taurus sitting in a chair in the vestibulum, waiting for him. When his bodyguard hadn't returned the day after Martina sailed to Utica, he'd assumed Taurus had gone on to Cigisa to make certain his niece reached the estate safely. No message had come telling him she hadn't, and past dealings with her excellent steward made Volero confident that Atriensis would have sent one if there'd been any problem.

But when he asked Taurus why she'd come back so quickly, the burly slave had opened his mouth, then closed it. When he opened it a second time, it was to say Martina had told him not to tell anyone, but she'd like to see him as soon as it was convenient.

Before his knuckles could strike the door a second time, it swung open to reveal a smiling Lepus.

"Mistress Martina hoped you'd come quickly."

As soon as Volero stepped in, the boy bolted it and sprinted past him to the rear of the house.

Her steward needed to teach his son proper behavior for a doorkeeper, but at least that smile erased any remaining worries he had about her return.

He'd reached the new chairs by the gameboard when she came from the back of the house. After settling into his own chair, he invited her to do the same with a sweep of his hand.

"I didn't expect you back so soon. Taurus wouldn't tell me anything because he said you'd said not to, but I hope it was a good trip."

She seated herself and leaned back against the cushions. "Even better than I expected. It was so good to see Atriensis and some of the others again. It was as if I'd never left. I've brought two applique potters back with me who'll be able to start custom production here. When we get the kilns set up, I'll have them make a few samples that you can take to your house. Maybe when you entertain, you can point them out to your guests. I'm sure many of the wives will want to buy some for themselves."

Her satisfied smile was just like his father's when he'd made a good business move. "Word of mouth among their friends will get me customers quickly."

"So, you accomplished at least part of your goal. But getting Glabrio to stay away...you didn't have to leave for that to happen."

Her doorkeeper came from the kitchen with a plate of cheese and raisins. Without a word, he placed it on the table and scurried away.

Volero picked up a slice. "I learned why he didn't come to your dinner. He seems to have gone somewhere, and he didn't tell anyone where he was going."

He took a bite. "Two days ago at the baths, Messala was asking me if I'd seen Glabrio lately. He was going to invite him to a party, but no one had seen him for several days. Then one of his centurions came over to ask if either of us had seen him. Apparently, the last time anyone saw him was the morning of your dinner." He picked up a raisin. "I hope he's all right, wherever he is."

"Wait here." Martina rose and went to the door leading to her future pottery shop. "I have a surprise for you."

She stuck her head through the doorway and said something too softly for him to catch. When she stepped back, a teasing smile lit her eyes. "I think you'll like it."

Volero's hand shot up to cover his mouth. Wearing the tunic of a slave, Glabrio stepped through the doorway.

"What happened to you?"

Glabrio and Martina joined him by the gameboard.

"Sartorus found a piece of Nepos's crest at Messala's metal shop, and the next thing I knew we were on a slave ship heading up the coast to Utica. We were sold as rowers there. Martina saw us unloading the ship when she arrived and bought us."

He directed a smile at Martina and got one in return. "I'll have enough to repay her when I get my first pay here."

Volero's gaze moved between them. The tribune that Martina had tried to discourage was receiving her warmest smiles now.

"Did she suggest that?" Volero tipped his head toward his niece.

The question drew Glabrio's eyes back toward Volero. "Yes, but I would have insisted on repaying her anyway." He directed the teasing smile she used to dislike at her, and it wasn't dislike Volero saw in her eyes. "She said it was the only way she'd get back what she spent on us because I probably wouldn't sell for what she paid for me."

The guffaw Volero couldn't hold back echoed in the peristyle. "With Martina's natural business sense, she'll do well with what Father made her inheritance." A glance at Martina caught her grinning.

Volero took a handful of raisins and offered the bowl to Glabrio, who also took a few. "You know, Messala's estate is very near mine. Do you own a gray stallion?"

Glabrio popped a raisin in his mouth. "I did, but I don't expect I'll get him back."

"Perhaps you will. One jumped my fence to get to my mares. My stableman checked with the neighboring estates, and none had lost one. I can have him brought to you, but he had no saddle and only a halter." Volero selected a piece of cheese. "I'll return him with one of my saddles as a thank you for the loan of such a fine stud."

"You can keep him for a while longer. He's too easy to recognize once you've seen him. What I need are a couple of plain horses no one would recognize."

"I'll have two brought in from the estate to the stable where I keep my stallion. You can use them for as long as you need them."

"Thank you. Tell them Mulio will be getting them."

Volero's head drew back. "Mulio?"

"Sartorus named me so the slave traders wouldn't know I was a kidnapped tribune. He said they'd kill me if they did."

"He was right." Volero leaned back in the chair and crossed his arms. "So, is there anything else I can do to help?"

"Can you get a message to one of my centurions without anyone knowing I sent it?"

"Of course. Who, and where will I find him?"

◆

When Glabrio reached for another slice of cheese, Martina rose. "Now that I've sprung my surprise, I'll leave you two to figure out what to do next." She leaned over to kiss her uncle's cheek before heading for the kitchen.

Glabrio's first thought—too bad it wasn't his. Then Atriensis's words came to mind. He would be returning to Rome to marry the senatorial daughter of Father's choosing. Nothing beyond friendship was possible between them. He should do nothing to make her think there could be more.

"Acceptus at the first station south of town on the road past your estate. I'd like him to come here alone or with only you."

"What should I tell him so he'll come?"

"Don't tell him I'm here. I don't want him telling anyone. I don't trust the other centurions, at least not yet."

Before Glabrio put the next raisin in his mouth, he inspected it. The fruit that looked good on the outside sometimes held a worm within.

"The man who told me to bring Sartorus to cover my back warned me against trusting anyone too quickly. He also said the most dangerous enemy an officer has might be wearing Roman armor. But I've seen enough of Acceptus's sense of duty to trust him."

"Your centurions are looking for you. At the baths a couple of days ago, Messala was asking me if I knew where you were. Then one of your centurions came over to ask if we knew where you'd gone, but I don't know his name. He was asking any of the councilmen who were there." Volero rubbed his jaw. "I'll tell Acceptus it's about the missing tribune. Except for those your centurion talked to and anyone who heard about your men looking for you, anyone hearing that would assume I meant Nepos."

"That should do it. When Acceptus sees me, I expect a response not unlike yours."

"Perhaps I'll bring him myself to see it."

Volero stood. "I'm eating with Paternus tonight, or I'd suggest we finally have our dinner with Martina. But it looks like you don't need my company to smooth your way."

Glabrio chuckled. "Sartorus did that. Maybe someday I'll tell you how."

As Volero stepped away from his chair, he sighed. "I'm expected to bring Artoria, so I'll leave you to more congenial company than I'll have. I'll send Taurus to tell you when the horses are here. He'll also bring you some money to tide you over until you get paid." One corner of his mouth rose. "But unlike my money-wise niece, you don't have to repay me."

Volero opened the town house door and raised a hand in farewell before disappearing into the street.

Glabrio blew out a long, slow breath. Volero was a man to be trusted, as Martina had said. But dangerous secrets should only be shared by the one they put in danger. Volero had concealed his niece's forbidden faith for many years, but his father had counted on him keeping the secret. He had no reason to shield Sartorus from discovery. Until Sartorus saw a reason for her uncle to know, his secret would remain within the walls of this Christian household.

Titianus and his familia, Martina and hers, and Sartorus—how many Christians would he end up hiding himself before he was through?

Martina's town house, evening of Day 32

Glabrio sat at the kitchen table, arms crossed. Tonight had been different from their meetings before. In Cigisa, Martina had only read to him from her Christian codex and then invited his questions. She'd done that again tonight.

But in the presence of so many others, it hadn't felt right to ask the questions her readings stirred up.

And he had several hard questions.

When her Jesus and his followers were going to Jerusalem for their celebration in remembrance of them escaping slavery in Egypt, the ones closest to him were afraid because the word was out that the Jewish leaders wanted to kill him. But rather than calm their fears and tell them they would be safe, he told them he'd be betrayed to the chief priests, who would condemn him to death and deliver him to the Gentiles, who were anyone who wasn't a Jew.

Only Rome had the right to execute, so there was no surprise in that.

But her Jesus went on to say that after they'd scourged and killed him, he would rise to life on the third day.

Titus had told Glabrio before that Jesus's death paid for the sins of everyone who chose to believe in him. Rising three days later proved that he had power over death and that everything he'd said was true.

But if Jesus actually knew he'd be crucified before he went to Jerusalem, why on earth did he go? No one in their right mind would volunteer to be tortured to death like that. And how could any sane man believe that his own death could pay for the sins of others?

Then the followers got into an argument about who was greatest, and Jesus told them whoever wanted to be great had to be a servant of all. That wasn't the way the world Glabrio had lived in worked. Great men exercised power and ruled. Servants and slaves only served, and no one would consider them great.

And what did it mean, when Jesus called himself the son of man and said he came to serve and give his life as a ransom for many?

Maybe Sartorus could explain it later. His friend kept nodding his head as she read it, so it must make sense to him.

Now Glabrio was watching as Martina and the members of her household took turns speaking prayers out loud to their god. Sartorus had joined them as if it were the most natural thing in the world for a man to do. But after his optio's prayers thanking their god for the rescue of both of them, he'd only listened to the prayers of the others. Or had he? Sometimes his eyes would close and an odd smile would come and go.

And each time when they opened again, he would look at Glabrio and smile.

Late evening of Day 32

Martina leaned her elbows on the dressing table and stared into the mirror. "I really thought I read what God wanted Glabrio to hear tonight. But he didn't ask a single question. He just sat there with his arms crossed. And then there were those frowns that would start until he saw me looking at him. He looked like he didn't want to be with us at all."

Platana drew the brush through her hair. "But he did seem disappointed yesterday when you said there was no safe place to read. Maybe all the extra people made him shy."

Martina turned to look at Platana directly. "Tribune Acilius Glabrio shy? In all my time attending Grandfather's dinners, I've never seen a man I'd call more confidant. At Uncle's dinner the day after he arrived, he talked with the important men like he was one of them. Of course, he expects to be one, like his father, so maybe that's normal for men like him. He's already at home among the senior councilmen."

"But I've also seen how he treats Sartorus as an equal, even though he outranks him. They're close friends." Platana set the brush aside and began braiding. "And I've seen how much he wants your good opinion. He has from the start, even before you rescued him."

"I've seen that, too." Martina turned back to the table, picked up the brush, and removed the hairs caught in it. She rolled them into a ball before setting them on the table. "I hope he stays for at least a few more days before he goes back to his headquarters. I want him to hear the whole story about what Jesus has done so he can decide to believe."

"I hope so, too." The blush on Platana's cheeks spoke more than her words. "It's nice having them both with us."

Martina smiled at her dear friend in the mirror. When Platana turned thirty in five years, she could give her Roman citizenship when she freed her. It was worth waiting for that.

She'd watched Sartorus, the way he looked at Platana when he thought she wouldn't see. Roman soldiers weren't allowed to marry, so even if she freed Platana right now, the future he obviously wanted was impossible.

Before she let Glabrio into her world, she wouldn't have understood the longing behind that look in his eyes.

But Glabrio would return to Rome and marry his father's choice. She's known that from the beginning, so why had she let herself start to care about him so much? He'd never choose to be the husband of a woman like her. But for as long as he stayed in Carthago, she could enjoy his company, like Uncle Volero did. And maybe before he left, she'd know the joy of him becoming her brother in Christ.

Chapter 53

First Step in the Hunt

Martina's town house, early morning of Day 33

Glabrio held one end of the board while Sartorus maneuvered the other. They lowered it onto the two stacks of bricks that turned it into the first of several shelves for storing pottery in the back room. The potters were building a kiln in an unused part of the glass shop that had been designed to take a high-temperature furnace. So, getting the shop ready to sell what Martina had brought from Cigisa had fallen to them.

The tinkle of the bell hanging on the door was followed by the click of hobnails on the brick floor. Acceptus had come.

Volero's voice drifted past the curtain. "The man who can tell you about the missing tribune is waiting here. He isn't ready for anyone but you to know." A pause, then, "Mulio?"

Glabrio swept aside the curtain and stepped into the sales room.

Acceptus's jaw dropped, and then his fist hit his chest. "Tribune." His mouth curved into a broad smile. "It's good to see you again. I was afraid what happened to Nepos had happened to you."

"It almost did. That's why I've asked you to come without telling anyone else. I need two men arrested before anyone knows I'm back. It's likely the ones I want would disappear before I could interrogate them if the wrong person knows. I don't know if I can trust any of the centurions besides you, and Volero is the only other man in the city I trust completely."

Acceptus raised his chin, and his smile broadened at the compliment. "I won't tell anyone until you say to."

Volero slapped Glabrio's upper arm. "Now that I've delivered the other man you trust completely, I'm expected by some of the council to discuss a matter before we meet today. But if I can help in any way, send someone for me, and I'll see what I can do."

"Thank you, but we can take care of it now."

Volero left, closing the door behind him.

Acceptus squared his shoulders. "What do you want me to do, Tribune?"

"Sartorus and I went to Messala's estate off the south road to get the letter he claimed Nepos had sent saying he'd been recalled to Rome. I also got a list of the people who were good friends of Nepos and might know where he'd gone."

"Verus asked Messala for a list like that as well. I used it to decide which estates on the Utica and Cigisa roads to ask if you'd been there. It was late last night after I got back from Cigisa that I got Martinus's message to come with him to meet someone who knew about the missing tribune." One corner of Acceptus's mouth lifted. "I figured that was Nepos, not you."

"I asked him to deliver my message that way so anyone overhearing would think that. On the way back, we stopped at Messala's metal shop by the main road. Messala said they could make something I wanted to give someone. While I was looking at lamps, Sartorus found a piece of a tribune's crest. One of the smiths knocked him out and then me. When we awoke, we were stripped, shackled, and collared as runners."

He felt his neck where the collar had been. "Whoever did that probably expected us to die in the quarries, but we were sold to a captain in Utica to be rowers. Two days later, Volero's niece recognized us as she got off a ship there and bought us. She's letting us hide out here until I'm ready to reveal I'm back."

"Do you think the same happened to Nepos?"

"I don't know, but the two smiths in Messala's shop undoubtedly do. They're the ones I want to arrest. They didn't kill us, so there's a chance Nepos is a slave somewhere. If he's dead instead, they'll know who killed him."

"I can bring a squad from my station to meet you south of the metal shop so they won't know we're coming. We can handle the interrogation at my station as well."

"Pick men who won't recognize me as their tribune."

"That would be all of them. None have been up to Carthago since you came."

Glabrio raised his index finger. "One more thing. Call me Mulio in the presence of others and call Sartorus Fides."

The corners of Acceptus's mouth turned down. "Fides I understand, but Mulio?"

His centurion's eyebrows rose when Glabrio chuckled. "Sartorus gave me a slave name that might get me bought for an estate. I decided to keep it until I reveal I've returned."

Acceptus's mouth twitched as he stopped a smile. "As you wish, Mulio. I'll go get my men and meet you south of the shop."

"Very good. We'll get the horses Volero is lending me and be there soon."

As Acceptus closed the door behind him, Glabrio returned to the back room to get Sartorus. It was time to start bringing the guilty to justice. He'd know who those guilty ones were after the metalsmiths talked. It wouldn't be long before Saturninus could tell Nepos's father what had happened to him.

He found Sartorus stacking bricks for the next shelf.

"It's time to ride. Acceptus is meeting us south of the metal shop. We'll soon know whether you're right about the smiths being dragged into something they wanted no part of. But the ones responsible will soon pay for what they've done."

They locked the shop door and left through Martina's vestibulum so Lepus would secure the door behind them. No one dangerous should know they were staying there, but he'd given his word to Atriensis to do all he could to keep Martina safe.

As they strode toward Volero's stable, Glabrio glanced at the man beside him. When this was all over, he'd be recommending Acceptus for special recognition. But how best to reward Sartorus—he had no idea. Nothing he'd thought of yet seemed enough.

The Messala estate, late morning of Day 33

Once more, Glabrio rode beside Acceptus with Sartorus behind them. But this time he wore no armor. Acceptus had brought one of his own white tunics for his commander and a spare red tunic like his soldiers wore for Sartorus, but if their own armor wasn't somewhere at the metal shop, he'd have to get new armor made for both of them.

But Acceptus had equipped them both with a soldier's belt with dagger and gladius hanging from them. That should be enough.

The metal shop lay just ahead, and Acceptus raised his hand. With three simple hand gestures, he ordered his men to circle the building to block any attempted escapes. Then the three mounted men tied their horses to the olive tree. The shop doors were closed, and with sword drawn, Acceptus pushed one open.

The shop was dark, and Sartorus pushed open the second door, letting the sunlight flood in.

Glabrio held his hand over the forge. No heat rose from the coals. But how long had it been since someone let the fires die?

"Time to ask Messala what he knows about where his smiths are and what they've been doing." He massaged the back of his neck. "But I'd like to leave some of your men here to watch in case they come back. I need to talk with them, so if they show up, hold them but don't kill them."

Acceptus rattled of four names. "Wait out of sight over there." He pointed to a grove of olives. "If the men who work here return, arrest them. They might be murderers, so expect them to resist. Keep at least one alive for interrogation."

Glabrio untied his horse and mounted. "It's time to pay Messala another visit. Watch him closely. He's not a skilled liar, but he'll try."

He turned his horse toward the villa and nudged it into a walk that Acceptus's four soldiers could match.

When they reached the villa, the soldiers remained in the stableyard while the others were escorted to Messala in his library.

"Glabrio. This is a surprise." Messala rose from his desk. "Centurion Verus was just asking everyone who knows you if they knew where you were. So, where were you?"

"Thanks to your metalsmiths, I took a short trip to Utica."

"My metalsmiths?" Messala's eyebrows rose more than genuine surprise would warrant.

"Yes. We came to speak with them, but no one is there. So, where are they?"

"They should be working in the shop, but they might have gone to repair something elsewhere on the estate."

Messala stood. "Let's go see." He walked past Glabrio and Acceptus, and Sartorus stepped out of the doorway to let him pass.

A youth was on his knees, scrubbing a mosaic by the peristyle pool. Messala shoved him with his foot. "Get my horse saddled immediately."

As the boy scurried away, Messala turned and crossed his arms. "I give my best slaves freedom to manage their work without overseeing them much. The smiths have been very good at supplying everything needed for the shop off the harbor, so they're among those mostly doing what they think best." His smile and shrug were meant to be nonchalant, but the smell of fear hung around him.

Glabrio strode past him toward the stableyard. "We'll soon see if that's true."

As they rode through the stableyard gate and headed toward the shop, Messala moved his horse next to Glabrio. "This workshop makes and mends the iron implements used on the estate, and they also make custom orders to sell in the shop off the harbor. I have some of their own creations in the villa. That's why I recommended them to you for your father and lady friend."

Adopting the emotionless face he'd learned from Titus, Glabrio turned cold eyes on Messala. "You mean gilding for my father and a lampstand for myself. I have no 'lady friend' in Carthago."

Messala raised both hands, palm out. "I apologize if I've misjudged, but the way you described it...it was a reasonable assumption. Nepos had some... special friends."

Glabrio tipped his head back ever so slightly to project the desired level of displeasure. "I am not Nepos. You'd be wise to remember that."

Messala blanched.

"Those special friends were not on the list you gave me. When we reach the shop, you'll correct that omission."

When they arrived at the abandoned shop, Messala flung his leg over his horse's neck, slipped off, and stomped into the shop. Fists on hips, he spun to face Glabrio. "They are supposed to be here working." He faked a scowl. "I wonder where they could be?"

"Since they aren't here, you can show us the shop records. Sartorus and I will inspect those while the rest of my men search for anything that shouldn't be in an estate metal shop."

Messala blinked fast several times. "Of course. The records should all be in the strongbox or the cabinet next to it. The key is hidden under the second shelf from the top at the rear." He cleared his throat. "If you don't need me further, I'll return to the villa."

"I'd like you to stay until the search is completed." Glabrio warmed his tone of voice. "There might be something for which I could use your explanation."

"Of course." As Messala's mouth curved into a social smile, a twitch at the corner declared how eager he was to get on his horse and ride away from the problem he was caught up in.

Acceptus and his four men probed every shelf and sack, every corner and crevice. Acceptus took an iron rod and tapped every floor plank. The hollow sound under a shelf in the storage room revealed a box holding the molds for coin blanks and dies for striking fake aurei. Under a barrel of metal scraps, another compartment was found. It held nothing.

"How dare they betray my trust like that!" Messala's glowering and bristling would have made an actor proud. "Counterfeiting! And now they've run away. I'll get the slave chasers onto them immediately."

"You can do that, but I'll find them before the hunters can." Glabrio stared at Messala until the amateur liar wiped some sweat from his lip. "But if they should show up here again, hold them for me. Counterfeiting is a capital crime, and they'll stand in the arena or hang on a cross for it." He paused for effect. "As will anyone involved in the crime with them."

"Of course." Messala's eyes widened, and then he started blinking too fast. "If you have no further need of me here, I'll return to the villa."

"You may go as soon as you give Sartorus that list of Nepos's special women." With his eyes kept cold, Glabrio offered a warm social smile. "Thank you for the help you've given in both this matter and Nepos's disappearance."

Sartorus took a wax tablet and stylus from the desk and handed them to Messala. With a slight tremor, Messala wrote several names and handed it back. Then, with a nod and a shaky smile, he left the shop.

As he watched Messala mount and trot toward his villa, Glabrio's sigh was long and deep. The red horsehair Sartorus had seen was gone. The men who knew how it got there were gone. The question remained as to whether Nepos was killed by them or another. He was inclined to believe by another. As Sartorus had reminded him more than once, they could have killed him and Sartorus, yet they didn't. They hit each of them only once when another blow or two would have ended their lives. They panicked when he found the crest, and what happened next came from fear, not malice.

But whether Messala was part of the killing of his supposed friend or not, he was almost certainly involved in the counterfeiting the metalsmiths had been doing. His slaves had no choice but to do what they were told, from making fake coins to disposing of unwanted bodies, alive or dead.

But the son of a respected councilman from one of the richest families in the area was untouchable without solid evidence of his crime. Glabrio had no evidence a judge would believe.

At least, not yet.

He turned to Acceptus. "You can send your men back to the station, but I'd like you to stay with Sartorus and me for a while longer. There's some watching to do, and I might need your help."

As Acceptus dismissed his men, Glabrio, with Sartorus at his side, walked to their horses. "We're going to ride past that grove to where the villa can't see us, then double back and watch from cover. I want you to change into your slave tunic again and be ready to follow anyone who comes from the villa. Messala's running scared since we found the coin dies, and he's likely to send a message to whomever is involved with him. You'll follow any messenger to see where they go. But don't try to stop them. Just report back. Leave now, and we'll join you in the grove shortly."

"I'll go get ready. He'll probably send his messenger as soon as we all leave the shop area." Sartorus unbuckled his soldier's belt and handed it to Glabrio. "I can't blend in wearing these."

"But that leaves you unarmed."

"But not unprotected." Sartorus bounced his eyebrows once.

Glabrio stopped his frown before Acceptus could see and ask about it. Sartorus might think his god would protect him, but Grandfather was proof that wasn't always so.

Sartorus mounted and trotted away. Glabrio draped the belt across his saddle and joined Acceptus as he watched his men marching back toward their station.

"What's the next step after this, Tribune?"

"We're going to lie in wait in that grove to see what Messala does next. Care to join us?"

"With pleasure. Messala is guilty of something, and I don't think it's only counterfeiting."

"I agree, but he's not smart enough to be the one in charge." Glabrio rubbed his jaw. "Don't leave Carthago for a few days. I'm not sure exactly how, but I might need a man I can trust in case I need more help than Sartorus." He slapped Acceptus's upper arm. "And I'm glad you're that man."

Acceptus's nod and smile declared his satisfaction that he was that man, too.

Glabrio and his fellow watchers had barely settled in when the stableman rode past at a canter on a gray mare. Sartorus mounted and rode out after him.

With Acceptus beside him, Glabrio settled in to wait and to watch for more messengers. None appeared, and it was more than an hour before the stableman returned with his horse at a trot.

In almost no time after that, Sartorus rejoined them.

"Well? Who did he visit?" Glabrio asked before Sartorus could even dismount.

"I only know part. He stopped at Messala's bronze shop and disappeared inside. When he hadn't come out in a quarter hour, I decide to do some shopping." One corner of his mouth lifted. "A brass lamp shaped like a bird for a woman I wanted to impress seemed a believable reason to be there." Sartorus's attempt at an innocent expression when he looked at Glabrio was enough to make Glabrio's ears heat.

"He wasn't in the sales room, so I asked a couple of prices and left. I waited another quarter hour and was about to come back to tell you I'd lost him when he came out of the shop. So, I followed him again, and he only came back here."

"Do you think he stayed there the whole time or went out a back door to somewhere else?"

"I can't prove it, but I suspect the second. From how long he was out of my sight, I think where he went is near the harbor or the agora, but I can't be sure. If he moved fast and didn't stay long, he could have reached the Forum."

Glabrio blew out a slow breath. "Well, that's still something, even if we don't know his final destination. But we've probably learned all we will here today."

Acceptus mounted. "Where will you be staying now? Headquarters?"

"Not yet. I still might want to check into a few things out of uniform. I'll be at the pottery shop for at least one more night. Maybe longer."

"I'll be at the first station, but I can move into town if you prefer."

"No. I don't want anyone to suspect you have a special role in the investigation yet. I can use Volero's people to get a message to you quickly. You can go back to your usual work until I send for you."

"Until later, Tribune." Acceptus's fist hit his chest, and he reined away to rejoin the road heading south where the trees blocked the view from the villas.

"Time for us to go home, too." Glabrio mounted and nudged his horse into a trot with Sartorus beside him.

Home. Odd that he'd used that word, but that was what Martina's town house felt like. Maybe she'd play that tabula game with him that he'd been wanting almost since he met her.

And maybe after dinner she'd read something that he would understand.

Chapter 54

WHAT'S THE NEXT MOVE?

Martina's town house, afternoon of Day 33

When the knocks on the front door finally came, Lepus scurried past the looms to let Glabrio and Sartorus in. Platana was all smiles as she turned from her loom. Martina couldn't stop her own smile, either.

The men had left for Uncle's stable in slave tunics. Sartorus returned in the same, but he had a red bundle under his arm, and the tip of a scabbard peeked out. Glabrio wore a clean white tunic of good linen with a military belt holding both sword and dagger. Sartorus stepped into his bedchamber to drop off his bundle. After a wave at Platana, he unbolted and passed through the door to the pottery shop.

Martina left her loom and met Glabrio by the game table.

"Did you catch the men who sold you?"

"They've disappeared. So, I didn't get to ask them whether Nepos was alive or dead when he left the shop. I'd hoped to learn who got rid of him and where they took him. If he's dead, I'd hoped to recover his body to return to his father for a proper Roman burial." He rubbed his cheek. "If I were to die here, it's what my own father would want most."

"Your father actually believes the Roman gods are real?" She bit her lip. Had her tone sounded too insulting? Would he take offense at her asking?

"Real? Not like you believe your god is real. But every good Roman performs the rites and ceremonies as if they were. We honor our ancestors as well by how we bury our dead."

His brow furrowed. "Your grandfather—didn't Volero bury him like a Roman expects and deserves?"

"Yes. But both he and Grandfather knew the gods were just stories. It was what other people would think if he didn't have what you call a proper burial that made him do it that way. Preserving Grandfather's reputation mattered to Uncle most."

She'd promised Uncle not to do or say anything at the funeral that would betray she and Juliana were Christians or that Grandfather was considering it. But Glabrio already knew about her, and he'd never repeat what she just said to anyone whose opinion mattered to Uncle.

"It was Grandfather's second wife, Juliana, who first told me about Jesus. The day before Grandfather died, he and I talked a lot, and he was considering whether to believe as well."

One corner of Glabrio's mouth lifted. "As you well know, what someone believes can get them killed. It did my grandfather. But I suppose when you're near death already, that no longer matters." His wry smile faded. "You said you don't know what he decided."

"I don't." It had been a month since Grandfather died, and the tears that came too easily then she could mostly stop now. But one trickled down her cheek. "He died in the night before he told me. But if he chose not to believe…"

One tear turned into two and then ten. She closed her eyes.

She jumped when his fingertips wiped the tears from one cheek. When her eyes opened, she found him standing close enough to wrap his arms around her and draw her close.

Maybe she shouldn't, but she wished he would. But he only stroked her upper arm and patted it twice before lowering his hand.

""I still don't understand why what he chose matters so much."

"What we choose to believe before we die determines where we spend eternity. Jesus promised us eternal life with him only if we believe he came to die to pay for our sins and rose from the grave afterwards.

"Eternal life?" His eyebrows lowered, and he took a step back from her.

"Yes. Life as we see it now"—she swept her hand toward all that was around them—"it only begins here on earth. After we die, we live on, either in heaven with God or in utter darkness separated from Him forever. What we decide to believe about Jesus in this life determines what happens after we die."

Glabrio crossed his arms and stared at her until the silence became uncomfortable. "Whatever happens after this life…no one can know that. Just because someone who knew your Jesus taught something and whoever Marcus was wrote it down…that doesn't make it true."

"But—"

"I don't want to discuss this anymore right now." His frown turned into a wry smile. "But you'll probably find something in your codex about it, and I wouldn't mind you reading it to me later."

"I'd like that, too."

Juliana had told her that timing was everything in getting a man to listen. When they didn't want to, changing the topic was best.

"So, since you didn't find the metalsmiths, now what?"

He drew a deep breath and blew it out through his nose. "We found something that might tell us why Nepos died. In a compartment under the floorboards, we found dies for making counterfeit coins. Messala was there when we found them, and he lied about not knowing his smiths were counterfeiting." His lips tightened. "But without proof that he's lying, his father is too important in the city for him to answer for what he's done."

"Even if he had a part in killing a tribune?" Martina picked up a bone rondel from the tabula board.

"Without a body, I can't even prove Nepos is dead." He rubbed his forehead. "I'm not sure what to do next."

Martina fingered the rondel before placing it on the board, like she would to start a game. "If it were me...I'd ask God to show me what to do."

His snort startled her. "Your god isn't going to tell a man who doesn't believe in him what to do."

"He might. You never know until you ask."

"Maybe I should have Sartorus ask him." The laughter in his eyes said he didn't mean it. But since he said it, she'd pretend he did.

"I think that's an excellent idea. I'll ask Him to tell you, too." She scooped up three more pieces. "You said before you like tabula. Uncle says you're good enough to beat him sometimes, and I sometimes beat Uncle. Maybe if we play for a while, something will come to you."

The crooked smile that made her cousins fluttery appeared. But she'd seen enough of him to know he wasn't trying to play with a girl's affections with it. It was just what his mouth did when something amused him.

"Whether it does or not, let's play." Glabrio settled into the chair and placed his first piece.

She took her seat and made her next move. Tabula was one of her favorite pastimes, and playing with him should entertain them both. But whether he realized it or not, their conversations about God were not a game, and winning their debate without God winning his heart was still losing.

The harbor district, afternoon of Day 33

As Verus walked along the wharf, he needed to kick a dog or strike a slave. Nothing less than hitting something could vent the anger seething within him.

Messala's stableman had come looking for him with horrible news and a request to come right away that he had no intention of fulfilling today. Only a fool would risk that. Only a bigger fool would have asked him to do it.

At least Messala had sent the man to his shop and had him exit through the back rather than come directly to the harbor station. Surely Glabrio would have had someone try to follow Messala's messenger. No matter how careful Messala told his man to be, that optio Glabrio took everywhere would be hard to shake.

Glabrio and Sartorus had reappeared with Acceptus and a squad of soldiers in tow, demanding to know where the metalsmiths were.

Wherever the two had gone with the counterfeit coins they stole, it had better be far from Carthago and hopefully outside the province.

The big one was not too bright, but the shop steward was. So how had they bungled the disposal of Nepos so badly that Glabrio's optio could find a piece of Nepos's crest? They were supposed to melt down the armor and burn the rest of anything that could be identified. Had they buried the body deep enough and in a place where no one would find it, or had they failed at that as well?

And why, in the name of all the gods, had they only knocked out Glabrio and his man and sold them as slaves instead of killing them, too?

Verus had told Acceptus he would check the most likely ships to see if Glabrio took one south to see the governor. A total waste of his time now the meddling tribune had returned, but Verus wasn't supposed to know that yet. So, he'd keep asking captains if a tribune had booked passage until Glabrio or Acceptus told him their tribune was alive and well and back in Carthago.

He approached the next captain who stood, arms crossed, watching his ship being unloaded.

"Do you sail south toward Leptis Magna?"

The captain turned calm eyes on him and uncrossed his arms. "No. Our home port is Puteoli, and I carry people and cargo between here and there. Why do you ask?"

"I'm looking for the ship our tribune sailed on."

"It's been a few weeks, but I carried a tribune across to Italia. He said he was going home to Rome."

It was all Verus could do not to grin. "Was that Tribune Nepos?"

"It was. He said he'd finished his time of service here and was going home to be a quaestor." The captain flicked his hand at a fly circling his head. "Good thing he kept mostly to his cabin."

Verus raised one eyebrow and faked a wry smile. "He commanded us here for three years, and I bet I can guess why."

"Three years under one like that..." The captain shook his head. "No one met him in Puteoli, and after four days on my ship, that didn't surprise me at all."

"That's not the tribune I'm looking for. Our new commander is everything Nepos wasn't. But when he returns, he might be interested in knowing which ship his predecessor took home."

He looked at the hull. "So, it's the Zephyr captained by?"

"Androcles of Puteoli. If your tribune is looking for passage on a fine ship to Italia, mention me."

"I will." With a dip of his head, Verus moved away.

At last, he had something he could tell Glabrio to make him stop looking for Nepos. He wouldn't have to kill another commander after all.

He rubbed under his chin where it wasn't blocked by the cheek guards. But whether he'd still have to get rid of his old partner…that remained to be seen.

Chapter 55

Probably No One Listening

Martina's town house, evening of Day 33

Glabrio leaned back in his chair and patted his now-full stomach. Colina's savory pork stew had been as good as anything Father's chefs made, and it was shared at a single table by Martina's whole household.

Sartorus sat next to Platana, enjoying her smiles and returning his own. With Sartorus on one side and Martina on the other, Glabrio felt as much at home as he had at Titus's table.

Martina wiped her lips and placed her napkin on the table beside her empty bowl. "I thought tonight that just the four of us would read in the peristyle. I put a lampstand by the chairs Uncle got me."

With Platana beside her, she led them to the circle of light around the game table. Sartorus carried the guest chair out of the tablinum to put it by the three good chairs. Platana moved to take it, but he picked it up before she could. "I brought this one for me. You should sit on the one like Martina's."

She blushed. "But I'm only—"

"Don't say it. You're not 'only' anything, and I want the guest chair."

Martina picked up the Marcus codex from the chair she'd used for their afternoon tabula and sat. Glabrio took Volero's chair across the board from her.

She laid the codex on the board and opened it to one of several ribbons. Each time he saw it, there were more ribbons in it, as if she left one at each place she'd read.

"After our discussion this afternoon, I think I have the perfect thing to read tonight."

"Our discussion?" His eyebrows lowered. Some of what he'd said to her he didn't want repeated in front of the others.

"About eternal life. You were right that I'd find something in the codex. Jesus said a lot about it, and I prayed about what to read you first."

310

"So, what did you pick?"

She gave him a smile that was one of his favorites. Eyes filled with what looked like affection focused on his. Then she turned them down on the manuscript and began to read.

"'As Jesus was setting out on a journey, a man ran up, knelt down before him, and asked him, "Good teacher, what must I do to inherit eternal life?"

"""Why do you call me good?" Jesus asked him. "No one is good except God alone. You know the commandments: Do not murder; do not commit adultery; do not steal; do not bear false witness; do not defraud; honor your father and mother."'"

Glabrio leaned back against the cushions and rested his arms on the arms of the chair. It was a list that any good Roman would agree with.

Martina glanced at him, then continued. "'He said to him, "Teacher, I have kept all these from my youth."

"'Looking at him, Jesus loved him and said to him, "You lack one thing: Go, sell all you have and give to the poor, and you will have treasure in heaven. Then come follow me."

"'But he was dismayed by this demand, and he went away grieving, because he had many possessions.

"'Jesus looked around and said to his disciples, "How hard it is for those who have wealth to enter the kingdom of God!"'"

Glabrio rubbed his jaw. Martina knew he came from an important family in Rome, but did she have any idea what that meant? That his family's wealth might be greater than anyone she'd ever meet in Carthago? Many times more than all of her neighbors around Cigisa combined?

If all a person had to do was believe Jesus died for their sins, why would he say wealth would keep people out of the kingdom?

"'The disciples were astonished at his words. Again, Jesus said to them, "Children, how hard it is to enter the kingdom of God! It is easier for a camel to go through the eye of a needle than for a rich person to enter the kingdom of God."'"

"'They were even more astonished, saying to one another, "Then who can be saved?"

"'Looking at them, Jesus said, "With man it is impossible, but not with God, because all things are possible with God."'"

The smile Martina directed at him was the warmest he'd ever seen. Her eyes matched it, and it felt like she only saw him, not his wealth and rank. He returned a smile just as warm, and her gaze dropped to the codex, but not before a faint blush overspread her cheeks. The only time she'd blushed before was when he teased her about disliking him. He'd embarrassed her then. This was something different.

"'Peter began to tell him, "Look, we have left everything and followed you."

"""Truly I tell you," Jesus said, "there is no one who has left house or brothers or sisters or mother or father or children or fields for my sake and for the sake of the gospel, who will not receive a hundred times more, now at this time—houses, brothers and sisters, mothers and children, and fields, with persecutions—and eternal life in the age to come.""""

From the corner of his eye, Glabrio caught the slow nodding of Sartorus's head. His friend's old neighbor had convinced him Jesus had done what the Christians claimed, and he'd lost his family because of that. Did he still consider it worth the loss of his father's affection and what would have been his as a son?

Sartorus had said it was. He acted like it was. But maybe he'd never known what it was like to have a father, like his own, who loved you and supported you in everything. A father who was your best friend.

Receiving a hundred times more than what you left behind sounded good, except that last part. With persecutions…why would Jesus have added that? Except for it being true. Rome had declared their religion illegal, and sometimes that carried a terrible cost.

Grandfather had been wealthy and powerful. Did he understand what it would cost when he became a Christian? When the Praetorians came, did he wish he'd never done it?

Martina's gaze was fixed on his eyes. She was waiting for a comment, a question, or some other response from him.

"So, what happened to him, the rich man?"

"We don't know. I hope he changed his mind, but it doesn't say." She fingered one of the ribbons. "A little earlier when Jesus was talking with his disciples, he asked them, 'What does it profit a man to gain the whole world and forfeit his soul?' I can find it if you want me to read it to you."

"Not right now."

Her eyes had brightened when he asked the question. Disappointment dimmed them when he didn't ask for more.

Glabrio lay one arm across his stomach, rested his other elbow on it, and tapped his mouth with his fist. "The wife of my friend Titus back in Rome makes copies of Christian writings to share with other Christians. I don't think she has this one. While we're still here, can Sartorus make a copy for me to give them?"

"I'll make the copy myself." Martina beamed at him. "And a copy for you as well, if you'd like."

He chuckled. "One copy is enough. I don't need one as long as you'll read to me from yours."

"As long as you want me to, I'll be delighted to read to you." She bit her lip...not something she did often. "But after you move back to your quarters, we won't see you every day. Would you like a copy to use there?"

One corner of his mouth lifted. "It's not the sort of thing that should be in a tribune's library." He shrugged, and she lowered her gaze to the codex.

He'd disappointed her again, but there was an easy fix.

"The garrison cooks do better than when I first arrived, but I have to be beyond hungry to look forward to what they prepare. You, on the other hand, have a chef as good as the ones Father has." He leaned over and slapped Sartorus's arm. "I think we'd both be willing to dine here when I don't have to dine elsewhere. If you'll have us, that is. You could read to us then."

Sartorus's glance at Platana brought pink to the maid's cheeks. "I'd be willing."

"Come every night if you wish. We'd love to have one or both of you join us whenever you can." Martina closed the codex. "Shall we pray now?"

Glabrio settled back in the chair and crossed his arms. It was a repeat of last night, with prayers and thanksgiving offered to their god in the name of Jesus.

There probably wasn't anyone listening. But it made them all happy to do it, and he didn't mind hearing what they said, just as he had at Titus's table back in Rome.

Night of Day 33

It had been a day of disappointments, but a day of blessings, too. Sartorus sat on his bed, forearms resting on his thighs, eyes closed. Ending the day talking with God—nothing was better than that. Listening to Martina reading from the word of God, praying with her and Platana, watching Glabrio's interest in what he was hearing grow—a contented sigh welled up from deep within him.

I thank You, God, for having me come here with Glabrio. Thank You for letting Titianus figure out I was one of Yours. Thank You for delivering us from slavery. Thank You for—

The softest rustle made him open his eyes. Leaning against the doorpost was Glabrio.

"I didn't want to disturb your talking with someone." One corner of Glabrio's mouth lifted, but the oil lamp didn't throw enough light to tell whether his eyes laughed, too. Then the half-smile vanished "I have some questions about what Martina read tonight."

Was Glabrio laughing at him praying, as he had before, or did he now understand what prayer really was? But as long as the questions were heartfelt, the interruption was welcome.

"I'll answer them, if I can."

"I'm sure you can because they're about you."

Sartorus's brow furrowed before he could stop it. "Ask me anything you want."

He pulled one knee up on the bed and turned to face Glabrio head-on. He pointed to the end of the bed. "Sit if you think this might take a while."

Glabrio sat on the end, mirroring Sartorus. "The rich man had followed what the Jewish god commanded all his life. But Jesus told him he still had to give away everything he had and join the ones who were following him around." He rubbed his jaw. "And that part about giving up brothers and sisters and fathers…"

He stared at the wall, where the oil lamp on the nightstand cast their shadows.

Then his gaze locked on Sartorus. "You gave up your place in your family. Do you regret it?"

Sartorus rubbed his palm with his thumb. "I do have regrets, but they're probably not what you think. I regret that my father wouldn't even listen when I tried to talk with him about what I knew was true. I regret what will happen to him when he dies if he doesn't let someone tell him what he needs to hear. I'm afraid he'll never believe Jesus paid with his own blood to free him from sin. To free everyone who trusts that he paid the ransom for us."

His fingers moved to massage his wrist. "But do I regret becoming a follower of Jesus? No. I've been given peace and strength to face whatever life throws at me."

Glabrio's eyebrows dipped. "It could be worse. I don't know how many times you said that when something else went wrong. I didn't understand how you could do that at the beginning, but now I think it has something to do with following Jesus."

Sartorus leaned forward. "From the moment I woke up in the cage, I was asking God to protect us, to show me what we could do to make it through and come out free. I couldn't always see how, but I always had a sense that God was taking care of us."

"Well, we made it through, whether your god helped us or not. Father raised me a Stoic, but whether it's happiness in the Elysian Fields or simply ceasing to be, I wasn't ready to have my life end yet."

"But your life won't end when you die. No one's life does. It's what happens after…that's where believing in Jesus makes the difference. He told his followers that he would prepare a place in heaven for them to join him after they died. He's prepared a place for me."

Sartorus rubbed his lip. He'd never had to explain this before. But he took a deep breath and pressed on. "After we die, we live on, either in heaven with God or in utter darkness separated from Him forever. What we decide to believe about Jesus in this life determines what happens after we die." One corner of his mouth lifted. "I know where I'm going."

The next words…how would his commander take them? "I hope you'll be there someday, too."

Glabrio closed his eyes, steepled his fingers, and rubbed the sides of his nose. When they reopened, curious intensity had been replaced by studied coolness. "My grandfather died for his faith in Jesus. Father kept me away from anyone who could tell me why when I was too young to make good choices. I understand the ruler who walked away, but not just for the wealth. The total commitment your Jesus asks…the man in the story wasn't able to make that choice. I'm not willing to make it, either. I'd be giving up everything that my father taught me matters."

Sartorus nodded. *God, what do You want me to say?*

No words came, so maybe silence was God's answer.

Glabrio slapped the bed and stood. "It's late. I'll let you get back to your talking to your god." His soft chuckle seemed forced. "Martina told me I should get you to ask him what we should do next. Now if she asks if I did, I can say yes."

Glabrio started toward the door, but he looked back over his shoulder. "Sleep well, my friend. Tomorrow we'll start trying to catch the counterfeiter who probably killed Nepos, too. Maybe sleeping on the problem will tell one of us what to do next. Good night."

Glabrio disappeared into the peristyle before Sartorus could answer. But he would do what his commander asked. He'd be asking God to show them the truth and to bring Nepos's murderer to justice.

He'd also be asking God to show his commander the truth about Jesus and to bring his friend to faith.

◆

In the wicker chair by her dressing table, Martina relaxed as Platana began braiding her hair for sleeping. "When Glabrio asked for a copy for his Christian friend, it was so hard not to show how delighted I was. I'd hoped he'd want a copy for himself. Then when he said a tribune shouldn't have one…" A deeper sigh than she intended escaped.

Platana kept folding each section of hair over another as she worked her way down Martina's waist-length tresses. "Maybe it's better if he keeps coming to hear you read. It gives you a chance to answer his questions." She reached for the ribbon to secure the finished braid. "He did say they'd come whenever he didn't have to dine elsewhere."

Martina looked over her shoulder and grinned at Platana. "And a chance for Sartorus to visit even when he can't."

The blush Martina expected washed over Platana's cheeks.

"He is a nice man. He loves joining us for prayer. I hope he does come even when his commander doesn't." She rested her hands on Martina's shoulders and leaned over to look directly in Martina's eyes. "I expect your tribune will come as often as he can to spend time with you."

Martina felt her ears heat. But after she'd teased Platana, it was only fair to be teased herself.

"He has no real interest in me. He's only lonely so far from his family and friends, like Uncle says. Remember, he told Uncle his father would soon be selecting a political wife in Rome." She shrugged, and the knowing smile that appeared on her dear friend's lips made her ears heat even more. "I'm not interested in him that way, either. Uncle has him over to enjoy some conversation and tabula. Surely, I can do the same since we both understand his long-term plans."

She patted Platana's hand. "I think God wants him to come so he'll listen to what Marcus wrote and maybe think about joining us as believers. That would be worth encouraging even if he weren't pleasant to have around."

Platana's lips twitched. "Quite so. Sharing our faith with him is why you should keep inviting him. A man has to hear if he's going to know what he should do."

"Quite so." In the mirror, Martina caught sight of Platana's barely concealed smile and start of an eyeroll.

She looked away. She did like Glabrio, more than she was willing to admit, even to Platana. If he were a Christian already and didn't have to go back to Rome, he'd be the perfect husband for her. But he wasn't, and maybe he never would be. Sometimes it seemed he listened only because he knew she wanted him to, not because he was hearing God calling him.

Even if he did want to join them in following their Lord, he was Tribune Acilius Glabrio, son of a recent consul of Rome. He was self-destined to follow in his father's footsteps. His father would never approve of a marriage to a Carthaginian woman whose family could do nothing to advance his political career, and men like him never went against their father's wishes.

The man of Platana's dreams was a soldier who couldn't marry for almost fifteen years and would probably follow his commander back to Rome. The man of her dreams…it was better not to think of Glabrio that way. She had no more hope of a heaven-blessed union with a Christian man than her maid, and she'd be wise to keep reminding herself of that. Still…

God, I know You can do anything. Would You please give at least one of us our heart's desire?

Chapter 56

THE TRIBUNE RETURNS

Early morning, Day 34

Glabrio ate his last hard-boiled egg and drained the clay goblet. "We'll be returning to quarters today."

"Will you be here for dinner?" Martina dabbed at her lips before setting her napkin down. Eager eyes said she was hoping for a yes, but he had to disappoint her.

"I don't know. I might not be. If I dine elsewhere, I'll be taking two soldiers with me. People expect that now. So, Sartorus can come by himself, but he should be back at headquarters before it gets too late. Whoever might want to get rid of me could target my aide as well."

He stood and dropped his wadded napkin on the table. "Time for us to go."

"Be careful." Martina stood as well. "I'll be asking God to keep you both safe."

Her words drew Sartorus's biggest smile, and Platana's nodded agreement drew his lingering gaze.

Glabrio nodded once. He'd almost said "You do that," but his tone of voice when he did would not be what she wanted to hear.

Lepus scurried ahead of them to open the door, and they headed for Volero's stable.

When they'd gone half a block, Glabrio kicked a small rock off the walkway. "I wish Titus was here to talk this over with."

"With all due respect, Titianus had no equal at what the Urban Cohort does in Rome, but he'd built a network of watchers who helped. Here in a new city where he knows no one…he might not do any better than you are."

"So you think the incomparable Titianus would have no more idea of what to do next than I have?" Glabrio grinned when Sartorus rubbed his mouth with the back of his hand.

"In a new city where you can only see what the locals want you to see, would anyone?"

"That's a diplomatic answer if I ever heard one." He slapped Sartorus's upper arm. "Perhaps not, but I'd still like his advice." He rubbed under his jaw with his thumb, then rested a hand on his chest. It still seemed strange not to wear his armor, but at least he wouldn't get too hot today. "Speaking of advice, did your god give you any after I left?"

"Not about this."

"Should I ask what it was about?"

"I'd rather you not."

Glabrio's grin faded. "Then it looks like we're on our own."

They walked a block in silence before Glabrio spoke again.

"So, what do we know, what do we think we know, and what do we only suspect?"

Sartorus's slight smile accompanied his shrug. "We know where something happened to Nepos. We know who knew what that was, but they're gone. I don't blame them. It was only a matter of time before whoever got rid of Nepos got rid of them for knowing."

"I agree. I'd be willing to bet Messala is a counterfeiter, whether we can prove it or not. But was he involved in killing Nepos? If you're right that the smiths acted out of panic instead of under his orders, Messala didn't expect us to find that piece of crest. So, maybe he didn't help with Nepos's disappearance. Any other thoughts?"

They were halfway to the stable.

Sartorus tightened his lips. "Messala already knew his smiths weren't at the shop when we went up to his villa. He acted too surprised. I think he knew the dies were hidden beneath the floorboard, and he'd thought through what he was going to do if we found them. He also wasn't surprised when we found the empty compartment. That was probably where they stored counterfeits before passing them off as the real thing. Either the smiths took what was in there, or Messala and his accomplice moved any counterfeits elsewhere when they discovered the smiths were gone."

Glabrio tapped Sartorus's shoulder again. "Titus would be impressed to see you thinking just like he does."

"I would have said I've learned to think like you, not him."

They reached the stable, and Glabrio led them through the open gate.

"What I'd most like to know is whether Nepos is dead or a slave somewhere. I can't simply leave him in bondage for the rest of his life. Men don't last long in the mines or quarries, and life is pure misery while they're there." Glabrio ran a hand through his hair. "Messala probably knows, but admitting that would make him the main suspect for murder or kidnapping."

"If only we knew who his messenger warned. I failed you that time."

"You couldn't know he'd sneak out the back. I need some way to get Messala to contact his counterfeiting partner again when we can see who it is. So, it's time for Tribune Glabrio to reappear in Carthago. Maybe someone will give themselves away by being too surprised when that happens." One corner of his mouth lifted. "Or not as surprised as they should be."

Glabrio approached the youth brushing Volero's stallion. "Do you know who took a message from Volero Martinus to Centurion Acceptus two days ago?"

"I did." The youth glanced at him, then returned to brushing.

"I need you to take a message to him again."

The youth scanned him head to sandals and back. "I do what Master Volero tells me. Right now, that's grooming his horses."

Glabrio opened his mouth, ready to tear into the youth for insubordination. But before he could—

"We'll finish grooming them while you take Mulio's message." Sartorus picked up a brush. "Master Volero won't be happy if he hears you refused."

The youth's eyes widened. "What's the message?"

"To come back here with you as quickly as possible." Glabrio lifted the brush out of the youth's hand. "Which ones still need brushing?"

After pointing at four stalls, the youth saddled a mare and rode out.

As Glabrio swept the brush down the horse's shoulder, Sartorus came to stand beside him. "One more thing I haven't done before."

"Neither have I, but I used to watch the horses get groomed when I was a child." He bumped Sartorus with his shoulder. "By the time I return to Rome, I'll be a master at doing many things I used to only watch."

Sartorus moved to the other side and copied what Glabrio was doing. "I heard Titianus tell Melis once that he should never say he couldn't do something. Always say, 'I haven't done it before, but I can try.' And Melis would usually do it on the first try."

Glabrio switched from shoulder to side and kept brushing. Of one thing he was certain. First, fourth, fourteenth—no matter how many tries it took, Sartorus would never give up until he got something right.

Two sets of trotting hoofbeats announced Acceptus's arrival. Glabrio set down the brush and sauntered over to where the centurion was tying his stallion.

Acceptus's fist struck his chest, and his mouth opened. But he paused before any words slipped out.

"Mulio." The respectful tone was the same as he used when he said tribune.

The youth had unsaddled his mare and was brushing her. Glabrio curled his fingers to get Acceptus and Sartorus to follow and moved to the far corner of the stableyard, where no one would overhear.

"Messala and his accomplice know we're back and that you were with us yesterday, but it's not likely anyone else does. So, it's time to make a public reappearance. First, Sartorus and I will enter headquarters. Then you can enter as if you were there for another reason than escorting us."

"I can drop off a blank tablet on Sartorus's desk as if it's a report."

"That should do. Who got the other centurions looking for me?"

"That was me. I sent two of Dubitatus's men to fetch them."

"Then Verus and Longinus shouldn't find it odd if you send out a message to come to headquarters as soon as possible." Glabrio pointed at the youth. "You can tell him Volero Martinus is helping you, and you're leaving your horse here with Mulio's for the rest of the day."

As Acceptus headed toward the youth, Glabrio and Sartorus went out the gate. Dubitatus should be through with breakfast and at his desk when they got there. His mouth tended to drop open like a fish when he was surprised.

But if his jaw didn't drop today, what would that mean?

When they started up the stairs at the entrance, the eyes of both guards widened. First one, then the other snapped to attention and struck their chests as Glabrio passed.

He did not get the same response from Dubitatus. When they passed the doorway to his office, no one sat at the desk.

Glabrio frowned as he looked at Sartorus. He got a slight smile and a shrug in response.

"Maybe he's out patrolling his district." Sartorus rubbed his jaw. "Or looking for you."

Glabrio made his eyeroll as dramatic as possible, and it earned his optio's chuckle. "Maybe Acceptus will have to send someone out to fetch Dubitatus as well."

Glabrio plucked the front of his tunic. "It will take only a moment to get out of these and into our regular tunics. Clothes don't define the worth of a man, but they declare his authority."

It only took a moment to change into the white tunic with purple stripes he normally wore under armor. When he finished, Sartorus stood in the doorway, wearing his spare red tunic. Together, they returned to the courtyard.

Acceptus sat at his desk, writing on a tablet. As they passed, he tipped his head toward Dubitatus's office and rose. A finger to Glabrio's lips triggered a nod and a wry smile.

Time to spring the surprise on Dubitatus.

When Glabrio stepped into his centurion's office, Dubitatus was leaning over a wax tablet, stylus in hand. He glanced up, then did a double-take as he threw himself back in his chair.

His mouth dropped open, then snapped shut. "Tribune! You're back." Then a broad grin joined delighted eyes. "We were afraid something might have happened to you, too. So, where were you?"

"We were knocked out and sold as rowers to a merchant ship operating out of Utica. Someone I know saw and freed us. But whoever is responsible will soon regret the day they were born."

Dubitatus's eyes widened as Glabrio let his jaw clench and anger burn in his eyes.

"Acceptus is going to send two of your men to fetch Verus and Longinus, and then we'll all discuss how we'll find the men who kidnapped us."

He looked over his shoulder at Acceptus, who stood in the doorway. "Go now."

Acceptus's fist hit his chest, and he headed for the station's barracks.

"You can get us both swords, daggers, and belts from the armory. Ours were stolen, and I doubt we'll get them back. When you return, I'll be reading reports in my office."

After Dubitatus strode out the door and headed toward the barracks where the armory was, Glabrio walked into his office. But he turned to watch the courtyard entrance as Sartorus stood at his side.

"Your thoughts?"

"His reaction when he first saw you…he seemed too happy, like you were a long-lost brother returning. His reaction when you told him where we'd been was more like the normal Dubitatus. So, I don't think he heard from Messala's messenger."

"I agree. I can't see why he'd be nearly ecstatic about me returning. But his response to us being kidnapped…that seemed normal enough. That's a relief. I would hate to think one of my centurions is a counterfeiter or murderer."

He pointed at the stack of tablets on Sartorus's desk in the antechamber. "Looks like my men kept preparing the reports I asked for, even when I'm gone. While we wait for the others to come, let's start on them. I want something other than my kidnapping for my own report to Saturninus."

Sartorus brought in an armload, and they began sorting them by district. One per day from the three city districts, one from Acceptus's just-finished tour of his many small stations…all his men were doing what a Cohort centurion should. With their help, identifying Messala's partner quickly might just be possible.

Chapter 57

No Other Choice

Harbor station, morning of Day 34

Verus sat at his desk, a tablet open before him as he rolled the stylus between his fingers. What to include in today's report eluded him. Messala's message from the day before kept bubbling up and shoving other matters from his mind.

What had Glabrio done at the metal shop that got him knocked out and sold as a slave? Why in the name of all the gods didn't the smiths just kill him and get rid of all their problems? No wonder they ran. Any other choice would have been utmost stupidity, and that shop steward was not a stupid man. One bag of coins was enough to let them go almost anywhere in the empire and start over as free men. The steward would probably set up a shop so no one would be wondering where their money came from.

He leaned back in his chair. But maybe that was for the best. He and Messala had split the four bags of gilded coins between them when they found the smiths gone. With the dies seized by Glabrio, his partnership with Messala was over.

There was still the goldsmith, but he wouldn't tell anyone. Verus had already ensured his silence with a detailed explanation of what could happen to the niece who'd been brought from Rome with him. The gladiator trainers were always looking for new girls to entertain their fighters, and when they were no longer good enough for that, they'd finish at a brothel on the waterfront.

A knock on the doorframe shifted his gaze from the ceiling to Placidus standing in the doorway.

"Centurion. A messenger from headquarters for you."

He stepped aside to reveal a Cohort soldier.

Verus leaned forward and rested both arms on his desktop. "What's the message?"

A fist struck the man's chest. "Centurion Acceptus sent me to tell you you're needed right away at headquarters."

He'd been expecting Glabrio to call him to headquarters ever since Messala's messenger came. Why their tribune waited a day… he didn't know and didn't really care. Why Acceptus sent the message and not Glabrio…that was odd, but not worth worrying over.

"Tell him I'm on my way."

The soldier saluted, executed a parade turn, and left.

Verus closed the tablet and scooped up his helmet from the end of his desk. He rapped Placidus's desktop with his knuckles as he passed. "I don't know when I'll return. When Acceptus thinks it's important, it usually is."

Placidus raised a hand in farewell, and Verus strode into the street past his saluting guards.

He'd taken his time before when Acceptus called them to raise the alarm about Glabrio being missing. Today his walk was brisk. A meeting with the other centurions so soon after Glabrio's return was the perfect time to announce he'd found the ship Nepos took back to Rome.

Telling Glabrio the name of the captain and ship that took his imposter to Italia should be enough to get their too-persistent tribune to stop hunting for Nepos around Carthago. Then he wouldn't have to kill Glabrio, which might mean killing Sartorus as well.

As he neared the headquarters entrance, Longinus came from the other direction.

"What's this about?" Irritation colored Longinus's voice. "There are races today, and I should be there."

Verus shrugged as they climbed the steps together and entered the courtyard.

Acceptus was leaning against the doorframe of Glabrio's office. He stepped aside and Glabrio himself appeared.

Longinus stopped and saluted, and Verus copied him.

"Welcome back, Tribune." Longinus's smile looked genuine.

It wasn't hard for Verus to summon a genuine smile of his own. By the end of this meeting, Glabrio's search for what happened to Nepos would be over. In a few years, he could retire from the Cohort, take the money he'd made counterfeiting to some other city, and start living like the rich young tribunes he'd served for too many years.

"Come in, and I'll tell you what's happened and what we'll be doing next." Glabrio seated himself behind his desk, and his four centurions lined up in front of him. Sartorus, tablet and stylus in hand, stood against the wall.

"We found a metal shop where counterfeiting was going on, but I don't know if that's the only shop involved or who all the counterfeiters are. It's on the estate of Vipstanus Messala and is overseen by his son. The metalsmiths involved knocked us out and sold us as slaves. That's why we were missing for a few days. But someone I know saw us and freed us. What I don't know is whether Tribune Nepos was taken as a slave, as we were, or was killed at that shop."

Verus cleared his throat. "I can answer that question, Tribune. I was talking to ships' captains to see if one had taken you south to Leptis Magna to see Governor Noricus. Instead, I met Androcles of Puteoli. He captains the Zephyr, and he remembered taking Tribune Nepos to Puteoli around the time he disappeared from Carthago. So, Nepos really did go back to Italia early without telling any of us his plans."

"Interesting." Glabrio leaned back in his chair and crossed his arms. "Just before we were knocked out, Sartorus found a piece of a tribune crest in Messala's metal shop. I'm convinced that his armor was melted down there and that Nepos is either dead or a slave. The one on the ship was an imposter someone hired to lay a false trail back to Rome. We'll keep looking here."

Verus drew a deep breath and blew it out slowly. "I hadn't thought about that, but I believe you're right. If we can find the ones who sold you, we should be able to find where Nepos is now."

Glabrio's smile and nod were the response Verus wanted. The arrogant young often trust the ones who make them feel smart by agreeing with them, and the next step required his tribune's trust.

Since Glabrio refused to believe Nepos left for Rome, he'd have to die.

Glabrio uncrossed his arms and leaned on his desk. "As I was saying, we've found one metal shop where counterfeiting was going on, but I don't know if that's the only one. The smiths who attacked us have vanished. I suspect young Messala knew what was happening in his shop, but I can't prove it yet. He acted surprised when we told him the smiths were gone but his manner as Acceptus's men searched the shop thoroughly makes me think otherwise."

He picked up a stylus and drummed on the desk. "Messala is my primary suspect for directing the counterfeiting operation, and he may have played a role in getting rid of Nepos. We will all be trying to gather the evidence that will tell us. That means we'll be watching Messala and the people with whom he spends his time."

He pointed the stylus at Verus. "Messala's main shop for selling what the workshop makes is in your district. Sartorus trailed a messenger Messala sent after he thought we'd left. The man went to that shop and out a back door. So, we don't know who he warned about us discovering the coin dies, which we confiscated. I want someone watching Messala's shop to see if messengers come to it again and to follow them if they do."

"I'll put my best men on it. I can train several in how to watch for suspicious behavior and how to follow without drawing attention to themselves. Maybe I should have them watching in plain tunics instead of uniforms."

"Good idea." Glabrio pointed at Longinus next. "You patrol the circus area. Messala likes to party there with friends. Maybe you can figure out who those are and if any are not the kind of men you'd expect the son of a leading councilman to spend time with."

"I have a few men who will be good at doing this without him realizing. I'll put them on this duty as well as watching myself. I have so many men stationed around the circus anyway that most people ignore them like they were part of the building."

"Acceptus." Glabrio rubbed his jaw. "I want you to look into how slaves are sold at the docks on the lagoon and figure out who bought us and then sold us as rowers in Utica. Then find out who sold us to them. That's the one most likely to know if Nepos is a slave."

"I'll take a squad from the first station. Slavers aren't always safe to deal with alone." A wry smile accompanied Acceptus's shrug.

"Dubitatus." The stylus pointed at the least able of the centurions. "Pick out your best men for asking around the agora and surrounding streets to see if anyone is having problems with being paid in counterfeit coins. Pick men who pay attention to details and will follow up with questions that could help us spot a pattern."

Dubitatus stared at Glabrio. He opened his mouth, then closed it. Verus mouth twitched as he stopped the smile. Dubitatus had no idea how to do what he was being told.

Glabrio nodded slowly, then a slight smile appeared. "Sartorus was expert in organizing these types of inquiries in Rome. He can share what he knows with your men to make their task easier."

Dubitatus's shoulders, which had tensed, settled back into their normal position. "Yes, Tribune."

Glabrio set the stylus down. "I look forward to hearing what you each find out. We'll meet here first thing tomorrow for your reports. You're dismissed."

Four fists hit chests, and the centurions filed out of the room.

Verus kept the smile off his face until they had all gone different ways to start their investigations.

Fortuna truly smiled by having him be the one watching Messala's shop. On the way back to the station to select his men, he'd stop in to remind the goldsmith what would happen to his niece if he said anything to anyone about counterfeiters.

Glabrio didn't know it yet, but he'd finally given Verus no other choice. His stubborn insistence that Nepos never left Carthago meant he would never leave it, either. As Messala had caused Nepos's death, Glabrio had just caused his own.

◆

Glabrio rested his elbow on the desk and rubbed his face. Then he raised his eyebrows at Sartorus. "Your thoughts?"

"They all seemed pleased enough to see you back. I think Verus was disappointed that he hadn't found out what really happened to Nepos, but he saw your point quickly enough."

One corner of his mouth lifted. "If you have nothing else you need me to do right now, I should go help Dubitatus before he tries to teach the men he picks something he doesn't know himself."

"Go do that. First I get my new cuirass started at the bronze shop Volero recommended. It should only take a few days. The leather parts…less than that. Then I'll go watch from the back of the council chamber to see if anyone is both surprised to see me and unhappy about it. Messala wouldn't be the first wealthy man inspired by greed to back illegal activities to make themselves richer. Especially if they have fathers who keep them on a short rein."

He stood. "Many of the council go straight to the baths, and today I'll join them. There's something about soaking and sipping wine that gets some men saying what they never should to the men who shouldn't hear it." He bounced his eyebrows at Sartorus. "Today I'll be one of the men listening."

Chapter 58

A WELCOME DISTRACTION

Martina's town house, evening of Day 34

Martina hummed her part of the duet she and Juliana used to sing on Sundays as they worshiped behind a locked door. It always made her heart soar as their voices harmonized, and they both felt God's pleasure as they sang. It hadn't seemed right to sing it alone, and Platana was no singer. But maybe Sartorus was. If he was able and willing, she'd teach him.

Colina had made her scrumptious creamy-herb dipping sauce for the first course, so Martina sliced one more purple carrot into strips and added them to the pile.

When a hairy arm slipped past her to grab a slice, Martina jumped. The crunch by her ear could mean only one thing. Glabrio had come for dinner.

She placed the knife on the cutting board before turning to face him. Before she could stop herself, her smile turned into a grin. His woman-pleasing smile curved his lips, and silent laughter lit his eyes.

"You should never sneak up on someone using a knife."

"You forget I've trained for battle. A kind woman with a kitchen knife presents no problem."

She pursed her lips, then relaxed them. She'd subdued the grin, turning it back into a welcoming smile. "Everyone was hoping Sartorus could make it for dinner, and it's nice to have you here, too."

He reached for another carrot, and the spicy scent that Juliana liked on Grandfather wafted past her. Even though he was freshly shaved, the faint shadow of a beard remained. She stepped sideways to open some space between them. It was obvious why Priscilla got fluttery when he was around. He didn't even have to do anything deliberate to have that effect, even on a sensible woman like herself.

With another crunch, he bit the tip off the carrot slice. "Are you speaking for you or for everybody?"

"For me, but I'm sure they all agree."

Sartorus entered the kitchen and picked up the knife Martina had been using. Then he joined Platana at the other counter and seized a carrot. An exchange of gazes that spoke without words and a duet of taps as their knives cut the slices followed.

Glabrio tipped his head toward Sartorus. "It's his job to make sure I stay safe. Disarming you ensured that. But since you've lost your knife, that means you're free to spend some time with me before dinner."

"There are other knives." She reached for one on the wall rack.

He intercepted her hand and held it. A gentle pull, and she turned to face him.

"Since I brought Sartorus to take your place helping Colina, let's go play a game or two." His teasing smile faded. "I could use something to get my mind off Nepos and the counterfeiters for a while. Sometimes the answer to a problem comes at you sideways when you aren't thinking about it. At least it doesn't seem like you are, but underneath the thoughts keep bubbling away. Playing with you or Volero is always a welcome distraction."

"It will be my pleasure to distract you so you can think, but first I have something for you." As they strolled toward the chairs by the gameboard, she turned aside into her office. She rejoined him with a stack of papyrus between two sheets of leather.

"I plan to add some designs to the cover, but"—she held it out to him—"it could be read even now."

"What is it?" He took it and opened it to the first page.

"A copy of the Gospel of Marcus. I made it today."

His brows lowered. "That was fast."

"It's really not that long, and I have most of it memorized already. I don't have to look at every word while I'm writing. But I did check afterward to make sure I hadn't changed anything."

"You have pretty handwriting. You could work as a scribe." He offered it back to her. "I'd like you to keep it here until I arrange a special courier to take it to Rome or I go there myself."

She'd left the cover plain so it would be safe to take with him to read. Surely his quarters must have a strongbox only he could get into where he could keep it away from prying eyes. But maybe the time wasn't right yet.

She took it. "Are you planning on leaving?"

Leaving—that word sat like spoiled fruit in the pit of her stomach. Of course, he'd be leaving someday, but did it have to be so soon?

"Not right away, but it's only four days to Rome by sea." His mouth turned down. "If Fortuna smiles, I'll be taking Nepos's cremated remains back to his father before too long. But I'll come back before you miss me."

He'd only been gone for the day, and she'd missed him. But she shouldn't let herself.

"You found his body?"

"There is a small chance that he's a slave somewhere, but I'd be willing to bet he died in that metal shop and the smiths were told to get rid of his body. They would have buried it quickly where they thought no one would find it. They didn't have any donkeys or mules at the shop, so they had to move the corpse by hand. So, it's probably in a shallow grave not too far from the shop. A place they wouldn't expect to be disturbed by someone else working the estate."

He scrunched his eyes shut and rubbed his temples. Regret filled his eyes when he opened them. "It's hard duty if they find him. My men here have never seen war. It's over a month since he vanished, and what's left won't be pleasant. Acceptus will have his men hunt for the body, and he can probably still tell if what they find is Nepos." As his shoulders drooped, a deep sigh escaped. "I owe it to his father to at least order the search."

"Do you know his father?"

"We've only met once, but my father knows him well. If something happened to me, Father would want my remains in our family mausoleum, and he'd appreciate anything someone did to bring them to him. I don't want to just send them home as cargo. A tribune of Rome who dies while serving her deserves better, and so does his family."

"You're a kind man, Gaius Glabrio."

"That's the first time you've spoken my first name." Straight lips curved into his teasing smile. "It sounds good when you do. Feel free to use it all the time."

She felt the heat sweep from her cheeks to her ears. "Perhaps I shouldn't be so informal. Certainly not where others might hear. Someone might assume things about us that aren't true."

That tiny shrug—had she hurt him by declining to call him what only family and close friends were allowed to use?

"Then use my nickname...Mulio. Sartorus gave it to me to keep me alive, so it's as good a name as any to use among good friends."

"I'll call you whatever you want here where no one but family will hear it." Good friends...it warmed her heart to hear him say it. Family...the future he planned for himself would prevent that, but he was as welcome as Uncle Volero at her gameboard and table. "But when others are present, I think Glabrio is more appropriate."

"As you wish." The smile that could hasten her heartbeat appeared. "As long as you invite me to join you, whatever you choose to call me is what I'll be."

She settled into her chair by the tabula board and placed the codex in her lap. It could stay with her until he was ready for it. If he was only going to give it away, perhaps a plain cover was the better choice.

She picked up the pair of dice and handed him one. High number would get to go first. With a flick of her wrist, she dropped the die on the gameboard and got a one. No matter what he rolled, Glabrio, as her guest, would go first.

He grinned at her instead of rolling and placed his first game piece. "Your turn."

She made her move and picked up another piece while he made his.

Her turn. But how was she to make the most of it so he'd want what God was offering him...and maybe what she had to offer, too?

Chapter 59

No Ordinary Man

Dinner was over, and Glabrio followed Martina into the peristyle for another time of reading and prayer. But tonight, he had questions he wanted answered before she read anything that raised still more questions.

He settled into Volero's chair and waited for her to join the three of them with her Marcus codex.

As before, she placed the codex on the gameboard and started their meeting with a prayer to her god.

"Lord, please be with us this evening as we read Your word and offer You our prayers. In Jesus's name we pray."

A trio of amens followed, and she opened her codex to yet another ribbon that she'd added. But before she could begin reading—

"I have some questions before you start tonight."

Her eyes brightened, and she closed the codex. "Ask whatever you like. Between the three of us, I hope we can answer them."

She beamed as if he'd given her a present, but it was doubtful she'd like what he was about to say.

"The way your Jesus talked and acted, it was as if he was what mattered most. Follow him, believe in him. He seemed to do miracles, healing people and such, but he was only a man. Maybe his god listened to him more than to most of the Jewish people, but he was still only a man."

Martina opened her mouth as if to speak, but he raised one finger and shook it at her. He wanted the whole question clear before she tried to answer.

"Saying a man's sins were forgiven…it's obvious why the religious leaders thought he had no right to say that. I can choose to forgive what someone does to me, but I have no right to tell them what they did to someone else is forgiven. Only that other person can forgive them."

He wasn't a Jew with any strong opinions about their god's sole right to forgive sins, but the next point hit him close to home.

"Telling the rich man who'd done everything his god commanded that he had to give up all that he owned and follow him to inherit eternal life, that seems far beyond what any man should ask of another."

He glanced at Sartorus and found his friend leaning toward him, fully focused on what he was saying.

"I know you Christians believe Jesus's death on the cross did something to pay for sins committed by other people. You say if people believe his death reconciles them with your god, then it does. Just believing is what makes it work. But how could his death do that? Why would you think any man was able to do anything that could pay for the sins of any person who decided to believe it did? Simply believing something doesn't make it true."

Solemn-eyed, Martina slowly nodded. What did that mean? What he'd said was just leading up to the heart of the question.

"So, if the greatest command from your god is to love him with all your heart, mind, and strength, doesn't Jesus claiming you have to follow him and believe in him require you to give your loyalty to a man instead of to your god? And to a dead man at that."

She didn't draw away from him, like he expected. Instead, she leaned forward and rested both arms on the gameboard. Then a smile like the one she used when she'd just made a clever move that trapped him curved her lips.

"If he were only a man, that would be true. But he was much more than a man. He was also the Son of God."

Glabrio's eyes narrowed. "Son of your god, like Hercules is supposed to be the son of Jupiter and a woman?"

"No. This is real, not a children's story. God has three aspects to Himself: Father, Son, and Holy Spirit. Jesus is the Son."

"So, you have three gods, not one?"

"No. Remember when the scribe asked Jesus what the most important commandments were? Jesus quoted what God Himself had told the Jews hundreds of years before when He brought them out of slavery in Egypt. 'The Lord our God, the Lord is one.' I can't explain how it works, but the three together are one God. It's not something you'll understand at all until you believe in Jesus and experience what comes next. And even then, exactly how it works is beyond what I know."

What comes next. His lips tightened, but he relaxed them as soon as he realized they had. He had no intention of becoming a Christian, so how that three-yet-still-one worked would remain a mystery to him.

"Would you like me to read you some of what lets me know Jesus is the Son of God?"

Hope filled her eyes. What she read wasn't likely to prove anything. It was only the writings of a man who'd been told what someone thought had happened. But he couldn't say no when it meant that much to her.

"Go ahead." He leaned back in his chair and crossed his arms.

Martina opened the codex at the beginning. "The first one is when God said something from heaven. A Jewish prophet named John was calling people to come and confess their sins and be baptized in the Jordan River. People were coming from all over Judea to hear him preach as well."

She lowered her gaze from him to the codex. "Here's what John was telling them. 'One who is more powerful than I am is coming after me. I am not worthy to stoop down and untie the strap of his sandals. I baptize you with water, but he will baptize you with the Holy Spirit.'

"'In those days Jesus came from Nazareth in Galilee and was baptized in the Jordan by John. As soon as he came up out of the water, he saw the heavens being torn open and the Spirit descending on him like a dove. And a voice came from heaven: "You are my beloved Son; with you I am well-pleased."'"

Glabrio fingered his lip. "Did Marcus hear that?"

"It doesn't say. But if he didn't, someone who did must have told him about it." She shrugged, but the certainty in her eyes didn't waver.

Still, second-hand reports from people who didn't actually see something were hearsay. Useful, but never conclusive in an investigation.

"What next?"

She moved her finger down the page, then turned it. "Some of his main disciples were fishermen. He lived with them in Capernaum on the Sea of Galilee when they weren't traveling."

"Which is on the north end of the Sea of Tiberias." Glabrio glanced at Sartorus and saw his raised eyebrows. "You thought I'd forget."

Silent laughter lit Sartorus's eyes. "I expect you to remember every detail, Tribune."

Martina cleared her throat, and his gaze returned to her.

"Jesus would teach in the Jewish places of worship in the different towns he visited, and this happened in Capernaum." Her fingertip settled on the codex. "'They went into Capernaum, and right away he entered the synagogue on the Sabbath and began to teach. They were astonished at his teaching because he was teaching them as one who had authority, and not like the scribes.

"'Just then a man with an unclean spirit was in their synagogue. He cried out, "What do you have to do with us, Jesus of Nazareth? Have you come to destroy us? I know who you are—the Holy One of God!"

"'Jesus rebuked him saying, "Be silent, and come out of him!"

"'And the unclean spirit threw him into convulsions, shouted with a loud voice, and came out of him. They were all amazed, and so they began to ask each other: "What is this? A new teaching with authority! He commands even the unclean spirits, and they obey him.""'

Glabrio crossed his arms and leaned forward to rest them on the table. "Unclean spirits?"

"You could also call them evil spirits or demons. They take possession of people, make them do what they wouldn't do if the spirit didn't have control of them."

"But this one called Jesus the holy one of god. That's not the same as son."

"It happened many more times than this."

She turned some more pages. "People were coming to hear him and to be healed from all over the region. He was in Galilee, but they came from Judea, Idumea, Tyre, and Sidon. Here it is. "'The large crowd came to him because they heard about everything he was doing. Then he told his disciples to have a small boat ready for him, so that the crowd wouldn't crush him. Since he had healed many, all who had diseases were pressing toward him to touch him. Whenever the unclean spirits saw him, they fell down before him and cried out, "You are the Son of God!" And he would strongly warn them not to make him known.'"

She tapped the page. "So, the evil spirits knew Jesus was the Son of God, too."

"Why didn't he want them saying it if it was true?"

"For the same reason he often told people not to tell anyone he'd healed them. He healed out of compassion, but he really came to destroy the barrier between us and God that our sins had built. He did that when he bore them on the cross. The huge crowds made it harder to spend time preparing the people, like Peter, who would take the news of what he'd done to all the world."

Sartorus leaned in. "Jesus had to keep sneaking out of Galilee into Syria where people didn't recognize him to get private time with the people he was training."

"It's one of those private times I want to read next." Martina flipped past several pages.

She smiled at Sartorus. "They did sneak out of Galilee to Caesarea Philippi just before this, and they might still have been in Syria. It's six days later, but there's a huge crowd waiting for them right after this, so they might be back in Galilee."

Syria, Galilee—it was all the same to Glabrio, but the way Marcus kept saying where things took place did make it seem more like a history than a story, even if what was happening seemed more story than fact.

"They had gone to the top of a mountain to get away from the crowds." She cleared her throat. "After six days Jesus took Peter, James, and John and led them up a high mountain by themselves to be alone. He was transfigured in front of them, and his clothes became dazzling—extremely white as no launderer on earth could whiten them. Elijah appeared to them with Moses, and they were talking with Jesus.'"

At the mention of laundry, Glabrio turned his gaze on Sartorus and got the signature smile and shrug in return.

"Moses and Elijah…who are they?"

"Moses led the people of Israel out from slavery in Egypt. Elijah was one of the greatest prophets of Israel a few hundred years ago."

"So dead people came to talk to your Jesus?" Glabrio raised an eyebrow.

Her smile was warmer than he expected. "Remember when we talked about eternal life? We don't cease to exist when our body dies. Somehow, God made it so they could talk with Jesus. They were two very special men who served God so well."

"Read on."

Her eyes refocused on where her finger rested on the page. "'Peter said to Jesus, "Rabbi, it's good for us to be here. Let us set up three shelters: one for you, one for Moses, and one for Elijah"—because he did not know what to say, since they were terrified.

"'A cloud appeared, overshadowing them, and a voice came from the cloud: "This is my beloved Son; listen to him!"

"'Suddenly, looking around, they no longer saw anyone with them except Jesus. As they were coming down the mountain, he ordered them to tell no one what they had seen until the Son of Man had risen from the dead. They kept this word to themselves, questioning what "rising from the dead" meant.'"

Glabrio placed an arm across his stomach and rested his elbow on it. Then he rubbed his mouth with the palm of his hand. "So, Jesus was discussing what he was going to do with two men who died hundreds of years earlier. Then your god spoke aloud to three of Jesus's followers telling them to listen to Jesus."

"Yes. And then he told them not to tell anyone until after he'd risen from the dead." She rested her hand on the words she'd just read. "Many of the people he healed couldn't resist telling everyone, even after Jesus said not to, but Peter, James, and John obeyed."

Glabrio glanced at Sartorus. Had he heard this story before? Sartorus sat there, nodding as if he agreed with everything she was saying.

"Ready for more?" Her brightest smile accompanied the question.

Was he? She wouldn't be happy with any answer other than yes.

"I am."

She flipped ahead to where there weren't many pages past where she stopped. "Now we get to Jesus's trial and his crucifixion." She bit her lip. "Even knowing how it ended, it's still hard to read this."

"You can stop if you want." He'd actually prefer that she did.

"No, what I'm going to share is too important for you to hear. This first part is right after he was betrayed by one of his twelve closest followers and taken to the Jewish high priest for trial. It's where Jesus himself tells the Jewish rulers that he's the Son of God, and they decide to kill him for it."

She drew a deep breath. "'Then the high priest stood up before them all and questioned Jesus, "Don't you have an answer to what these men are testifying against you?" But he kept silent and did not answer. Again the high priest questioned him, "Are you the Messiah, the Son of the Blessed One?"

"'"I am," said Jesus, "and you will see the Son of Man seated at the right hand of Power and coming with the clouds of heaven."

"'Then the high priest tore his robes and said, "Why do we still need witnesses? You have heard the blasphemy. What is your decision?" They all condemned him as deserving death.'"

A shiver ran up Glabrio's spine. But why? It was only a book written by a man who wasn't even there to see what he was describing. Or was it? What if it reported true history and not just religious stories?

Martina wiped at the corner of her eye. Was that the start of tears?

"This next part is after Jesus was scourged and nailed to a cross to die. 'When it was noon, darkness came over the whole land until three in the afternoon. And at three Jesus cried out with a loud voice, "Eloi, Eloi, lema sabachthani?" which is translated, "My God, my God, why have you abandoned me?"

"'When some of those standing there heard this, they said, "See, he's calling for Elijah." Someone ran and filled a sponge with sour wine, fixed it on a stick, offered him a drink, and said, "Let's see if Elijah comes to take him down."

"'Jesus let out a loud cry and breathed his last. Then the curtain of the temple was torn in two from top to bottom.

"'When the centurion, who was standing opposite him, saw the way he breathed his last, he said, "Truly this man was the Son of God!"'"

She swept a tear from the corner of each eye and wiped her fingers on her tunic. "Do you have any questions?"

Did he have questions? He'd blanked his face, as Titus had taught him, because she shouldn't see his thoughts. She wouldn't like any of them. But there was one question he had to ask.

"If Jesus is the son of your god and also your god, that three-but-still-one mystery, why did he cry out about your god abandoning him?"

She looked at Sartorus, who nodded and offered a slight smile. Then eyes still moist with tears turned back on him. "It's because of our sins. We build the barrier between us and God because He can't abide sin in His presence.

He can't just choose to ignore it. Sin has to be atoned for, be paid for. But an ordinary man couldn't do it. Only Jesus, who was both the Son of Man and the Son of God, could."

She tipped her head back and closed her eyes, and they stayed closed longer than he expected. Then the corners of her mouth rose, and her gaze turned on him again.

"Remember the first night you were here? We read where Jesus said, 'For even the Son of Man did not come to be served, but to serve, and to give his life as a ransom for many.' He paid a ransom by dying to free us from our slavery to sin, just like I paid a ransom to free you from slavery. During those three hours of darkness, all the sins of all of us for all time were placed on the Son of God, and God the Father had to turn away from the Son while he bore that sin. And when it was done, when every last sin was paid for, he called out and chose to die. That's what the centurion saw, and his words prove he understood who Jesus was."

Glabrio squeezed the back of his neck. Three hours of darkness. Titus was reading Phlegon's *Chronicles* just before he left Rome. Phlegon had reported an unexpected darkness at midday, but he claimed it was an eclipse. Titus had scoffed at that because the moon was always full at the Jewish Passover, and only a new moon can eclipse the sun.

"I see." Not really, but he didn't want to hear any more tonight. That was certain. He pursed his lips and blew out a long, slow breath. "You can pray now. I have enough to think about for one night."

Why did his words that were intended to end the discussion make her almost glow with happiness?

Martina leaned her elbows on the table, clasped her hands, and rested her forehead against them. "Dear Lord, we thank you for..."

It was all the things she usually prayed, with Platana and Sartorus saying amen several times.

He tried to listen, but his mind kept refocusing on one thing. If their Jesus really was the son of their god, really was a god himself, why would he choose to die on a cross to save people from being separated from him? Not just the respectable people who tried to live like their god said and might deserve help, but even those who never used to care what that god thought but now they did. Even people like himself, who were afraid to care because of where that could lead.

Chapter 60

TOO HIGH A COST

Night of Day 34

One side of the street was in deep shadow, and Glabrio followed Sartorus across the street to walk in the bright moonlight. Then his ever-watchful aide, hand on his sword, walked on the side nearer the alcoves leading to doorways, leaving him on the street side where it was easy to see if anyone approaching posed a threat.

Overall, this evening with friends had been a pleasant ending to a mostly satisfying day. He had good men working on finding the ones responsible for both counterfeit coins and the missing tribune. The metalsmiths would have made it all easy, but maybe what his men learned today would be enough to direct what should be done tomorrow.

Tabula had been diverting, dinner had been delicious, but the after-dinner discussion had been…disturbing.

Maybe not disturbing, but certainly thought-provoking. Like Titus back in Rome, they were all so certain of the truth of what they believed. But believing something was true and it actually being true were not the same. Titus had taught him that about investigating crimes.

When what was true wasn't clear, the wise man kept asking questions.

"What Martina talked about tonight…I saw you nodding. So…" He drew one finger along his eyebrow. "That part about your god speaking directly to men to tell them Jesus was his son, did those nods mean you think it really happened?"

"The Peter who was up on the mountain with Jesus when Moses and Elijah came, that was the Peter my neighbor knew. He heard God call Jesus His Son. He saw the empty tomb where Jesus had been buried. He talked with Jesus after He rose from the dead. Peter was there when Jesus told his disciples to go into all the world and tell people what He'd done. He heard Jesus say that those who believe and are baptized will be saved. He saw Jesus return to heaven where He's sitting now at the right hand of the Father. So, yes, I know it really happened."

"So…" Glabrio wasn't quite sure how to ask the next question. "This baptism Martina read about, do you know anything about that?"

"I've been baptized both ways that the John who was baptizing talked about."

"Both ways?"

"Yes. When John was baptizing, people would confess their sins, and he would baptize them in the waters of the Jordan River as a sign of their repentance. I've done that in the Tiber. The second baptism—Jesus baptized me with the Holy Spirit when I declared that I believed and would follow him as my Lord. That's why I'm never alone. When we believe in Jesus, the Spirit is with us all the time. That's not explained in what Marcus wrote, but what Lucas wrote is longer. And Peter taught about it when my neighbor heard him. It's true for anyone once they believe."

"Hmph." For a man as smart as Sartorus to talk like that…it made no sense, but the same could be said for Titus and his closest friends back in Rome.

"Just before Jesus returned to heaven, he gave his disciples orders, like an officer sending out his men. 'Go into all the world and preach the gospel to all creation. Whoever believes and is baptized will be saved, but whoever does not believe will be condemned.'"

Sartorus kicked a stone off the walkway. "And they did what He told them. That's why Peter was in Rome so my neighbor heard him. It's why Marcus came to Africa."

"But how could a handful of men have spread what they thought Jesus did to so many? Especially when it sounds…"—Glabrio tightened his lips—"totally unbelievable."

"Jesus himself explained it before he returned to heaven. It's in Lucas's writings." Sartorus closed his eyes and took a deep breath. When his eyes opened, their intensity made Glabrio look away. "'You will receive power when the Holy Spirit has come on you, and you will be my witnesses in Jerusalem, in all Judea and Samaria, and to the end of the earth.'"

"Titus has Lucas's writings." Glabrio scratched the back of his head. "And something by another of the ones who followed Jesus around…I forget the name."

"Have you read them?" Eagerness coated Sartorus's voice.

Glabrio kept looking straight ahead, not wanting to meet that focused gaze. Titus had offered them many times, but he'd always passed on the offer. "Not yet."

"If you get a chance again, I think they'll answer a lot of questions." Glabrio glanced at his friend, and the so-familiar smile and shrug appeared. "Even some you haven't thought to ask."

Questions…Glabrio was wrestling with more than enough of them already. He didn't need even more.

"That order to go tell everyone…you shouldn't be doing it. Talking to me is fine, but I don't want you killed for talking to others."

Sartorus's chuckle drew Glabrio's stare. Getting killed for following a forbidden religion was no laughing matter.

"Yes, Tribune. I won't do anything to make you need a different optio before you go back to Rome. But after I finish my years of service in the Cohort, I make no promises. Even before then, I'll do what my true commander asks of me. I owe my allegiance to Someone who outranks the Urban Prefect or any emperor of Rome."

Glabrio's jaw clenched. Titus and his family knew the risks and were careful. So were Martina and her household, but an unmarried man like Sartorus…would he always be as careful as he should be? Or would he end up like Grandfather?

They walked on in silence until they reached headquarters and parted for the night.

It was long past midnight, but sleep wouldn't come. For what must be the fiftieth time, Glabrio rolled from his back to his side and stared at the patch of moonlight moving slowly across the wall.

It was obvious why the Christian teaching appealed to people, especially that promise of forgiveness of whatever you've done and the promise of eternal life in heaven after you die. If he didn't have so much to lose by becoming a Christian, he might be tempted. But even though two of the men he admired most had made that choice, they didn't have as much to lose as he did.

Titus was paterfamilias and had to answer to no one. Sartorus…maybe he wasn't that close to his father even before his choice, and no one in power cared whether a man from a tailor shop or fullery turned away from the state religion.

But for Glabrio…Father's opinion mattered more than anyone else's, and there was no way he could step off the political path he was on without people asking why. The next step required him to perform Roman rites frequently, at least paying lip service to the gods of Rome in public displays of piety.

Titus had told him their god wouldn't share the worship of his people with any other god. It was the Christian god alone, and no others were allowed. In the arena or facing a cross or sword, so many Christians chose death over a meaningless sacrifice to the genius of Caesar and the Roman gods.

He was not going to be one of them.

Father felt betrayed by Grandfather choosing the Christian god over his own life. He'd feel doubly betrayed if Glabrio did the same.

Still, if everything Titus and Sartorus and Martina claimed was true, how could a man of honor not choose to admit the truth and follow wherever that might lead?

But the cost of that decision...it could cost him everything he and Father both valued. His own political future, his family's reputation, his father's respect, maybe even his father's love. How could a man ever be so certain that what his friends said was true that he could risk losing everything?

Chapter 61

TIME TO MAKE HIM SWEAT

Urban Cohort headquarters, morning of Day 35

When Glabrio came from his quarters, the centurions had already gathered. With a curl of his fingers, he invited them to follow him into his office.

As soon as he settled into his chair, he pointed his stylus at Acceptus. "What have you learned?"

"I found the ship on the lagoon that bought two runners with bagged heads. They had the receipts for the sales, and the sales had been registered at the quaestor's station. He got you from a slaver who brings men up from the south but not on a regular basis. His paperwork always seems in order, and he always sells men in shackles because he brings so many over a long distance. The quaestor's assistant who records sales on the lagoon has always approved the sales without questions."

"So, we still don't know who collared and sold us."

"No, Tribune, and without that slaver, we might never be able to figure that out."

The stylus moved on to point at Longinus. "What did you see?"

"Messala was at the races, seated with his usual group of friends, the ones who often watched the races together when Nepos joined them. I didn't see him talking to anyone unusual, and he wasn't acting like anything was wrong. There was betting among them, and Messala won more than he lost."

Longinus rubbed under his chin between the cheek guards. "He acted as if everything was fine. But my men who will be watching know what he looks like now and who sits with him. They'll stay alert to see what he does at future races."

"Dubitatus?"

His least capable centurion squared his shoulders and raised his chin. "My men haven't found any counterfeit complaints yet, but they haven't finished talking with everyone."

Glabrio avoided looking at Sartorus where he stood by the wall with an open tablet. Before he could trust that report, he'd have to make certain the soldiers of that district were following Sartorus's instructions, not Dubitatus's.

He pointed at his final man. "Verus."

"No messengers have come to Messala's shop. At least, no one has ridden up, gone inside for a short time, and left without buying something. It looks like only customers going in, with most coming out with something they bought."

Verus raised one finger. "But there are a lot of shops in my district like the ones in Dubitatus's. So, I decided to see if counterfeit coins were being used in my district, too. I've trained a handful of my men on how to find the business steward or owner and ask the right questions."

"Have they found any?"

"Nothing yet, but I'll notify you the moment I find something suspicious so you can come and take over the investigation."

"Very good. All of you." Glabrio scanned his men, meeting each one's eyes with a smile of appreciation. "If we keep watching, something will turn up. You're dismissed."

After they left, Glabrio leaned on his elbows and rested his head in his hands. Then he turned his gaze on Sartorus and shrugged. "I'd hoped at least one of them would have found something. It looks like we might be doing this for some time. Acceptus will need to be back riding his circuit of roads soon, but the others can do it for as long as it takes."

He rolled the stylus between his fingers before setting it down. "If we find Nepos, I'll need to take his remains back to Rome. Round trip, that could take a couple of weeks. I think I'll put Verus in charge in my absence. He goes above and beyond instructions now that he knows that's what his tribune expects. The shortage of inspections on the docks were probably because Nepos totally neglected his duty to set standards."

Sartorus set the blank tablet on the desktop. "Verus has been serving here for more than ten years, and Nepos was here for only three. Has this always been a place where a prefect would send a tribune who wasn't up to Rome's standards?"

Glabrio's laugh raised Sartorus's eyebrows. "Rome's standards? Titianus was not your typical Cohort tribune. I hope I haven't been either. Did you ever have any dealings with Tribune Victorinus?"

Sartorus shook his head.

"He was only there because two legates of frontier legions who were good friends of his father politely declined to add him to their staffs." One corner of

Glabrio's mouth lifted. "With good reason. Saturninus only left him in place when he became prefect because his father was a friend and too politically important to offend. Besides, the centurions were doing a good job without his help. Probably better than they would have if he'd interfered."

Glabrio massaged his neck. "Saturninus didn't like that I did my job too well. That's partly why he transferred me down here. I was investigating the client of one of his good friends, and he was getting complaints about it. The only way to get me to stop was to transfer me here."

Sartorus's eyes widened.

"With Hadrian touring the provinces on the southern coast this summer, it is a good opportunity to draw our emperor's attention if I'm doing a good job. My father saw that when our prefect told him he was transferring me here. But his main reason was to get me out of Rome without having to explain why."

Glabrio picked up the stylus and drummed on the desk. "Despite what happened to us, I like serving here more than I expected."

Sartorus's mouth twitched, but the grin leaked out anyway. "I do, too. I even enjoyed having the sunburn and what's come because of it."

What his optio enjoyed was Platana and all his new Christian friends. Glabrio might as well admit it. A big part of what made Carthago pleasant was a certain Christian woman who gave up trying to avoid him in order to rescue him. "What came because of it…I'm enjoying that, too."

Glabrio's own grin escaped. Then he cleared his throat and straightened his lips. Time to refocus on the problem at hand.

"From what Longinus saw at the races, I'd guess Messala thinks he got away with whatever he's done. He won't be contacting his accomplice without us doing something to panic him."

He tapped his mouth with his fist. "But I don't know what that is."

Sartorus set the tablet down on the side table and leaned against the wall. "What would make him feel like you're hunting him for a capital crime?"

"Two crimes, actually. Counterfeiting and Nepos's murder, if we can just find the body." He rubbed his cheek. "Do you think he's fool enough to put counterfeit coins in a strongbox at the estate?"

"That would be pretty stupid, so maybe." A wry smile accompanied Sartorus's slow headshake.

"I agree, which is why you and I are going out to his estate to ask him to show us the contents of their strongboxes. I don't expect to find fake coins, but it should still panic him into consulting his partner."

Sartorus's mouth straightened. "Are we going alone?"

"Not into the jackal's lair. We'll pick up some men from Acceptus's squad that's hunting for Nepos near the workshop." Glabrio's own mouth straightened. "The ones we take will think Fortuna smiled when they get off that duty."

He stood. "Let's go turn up the heat and watch Messala sweat."

The Messala estate, midmorning of Day 35

When Glabrio and Sartorus reached the metal shop, Acceptus's stallion was hobbled under the olive tree. Arms crossed, the centurion stood a short distance away, and they rode over to join him.

As Glabrio reined in beside him, Acceptus glanced at Glabrio, then turned his gaze back across the wheat field. "Welcome, Tribune." He tipped his head toward a line of his soldiers. They were spread out along the edge of a grove a hundred feet from the shop. "I have them looking for any sign the earth has been disturbed."

Glabrio. "Anything yet?"

"No." He pointed back at the grove where they had hidden after searching the metal shop. "We've checked out that grove already, around the edge and within. They would have buried him where it wouldn't be obvious the soil was disturbed. So, we're checking edges first."

"I need to borrow four of your men. From what Longinus saw at the races yesterday, Messala's too relaxed. He thinks he's in the clear. We're going to pay him a visit to make him want to consult his accomplice."

Acceptus raised an eyebrow. "How?"

"Does he know you're searching his land?"

A wry smile curved Acceptus's mouth. "I don't need to ask his permission, and no one has ridden by who might tell him."

"Good. I'll inform him, and I'll tell him to show me the content of the estate strongboxes. But I want enough men with me to keep him from thinking he can get rid of me again."

Acceptus looked at Sartorus as he pointed toward his men. "Take any four you want."

With a nod, Sartorus nudged the horse into a trot across the field.

Glabrio patted his horse's neck. It was good of Volero to lend him two mounts, but he was ready to reclaim his stallion. Or not. He'd check to see if Volero had bred him with all the mares he wanted for now. When he finally left Carthago, he'd make of gift of the horse as a thank you to a good friend who'd introduced him to the woman whose friendship he valued even more.

When Sartorus returned with four men marching behind him, Glabrio turned his horse toward the road to the villa. He set the pace to be comfortable for the soldiers.

It wasn't yet noon, and it was already hot. But a gentle breeze blew across the wheatfield, and he welcomed its cooling effect. He'd lost his cuirass at the metal shop, but he couldn't say that he missed it. It trapped the sweat that was meant to cool him, even if it would stop a sword or dagger from inflicting a killing wound. The replacement should be finished in a day or so. He'd need it when he went back to Rome. That might be soon if Acceptus's search was successful.

He glanced at Sartorus astride the horse beside him. His aide needed new armor as well. Dubitatus should know where to get that done.

At the villa, he left escort and horses in the stableyard while he and Sartorus were taken to Messala in his library...without being announced first. His suspect's first reaction would reveal more truth than any words Messala would speak.

When Glabrio stepped into the library, Messala only glanced at him. Then a jolt went through his body as he straightened. His eyes widened, and his mouth opened then shut.

Then a social smile curved his lips. "Glabrio. To what do I owe this pleasure?"

"While my men are searching the area around your metal shop for what remains of Tribune Nepos, I've come to see what's in the estate strongboxes."

"Searching for Nepos?" Messala blanched. "And you want to see our strongboxes?"

"Yes. All the strongboxes in the villa. I assume you have a private one for which you alone have a key. We can start there and move on to those your father's steward can open."

Messala stood so fast his chair fell backward. "You have no right to come into our house and make that demand."

"As Tribune of the XIII Urban Cohort, I have the right to inspect anything I think related to a crime I'm investigating. I have the dies used to make counterfeit coins in a workshop you direct for your father, and that gives me the right to inspect any strongbox you might have access to."

Messala swallowed hard, as if he was trying to keep his breakfast down. Then he raised his chin to look down his nose. "Very well, but I'll expect an apology when you find nothing like what you're looking for. My father will be writing to your commander in Rome, and you'll regret that you ever made this ridiculous accusation."

He strode past Glabrio into the peristyle. On the way to his room, he kicked a youth tending the garden. "Get Father's steward right now."

The young man scurried deeper into the house as Messala led Glabrio and Sartorus into his bedchamber. He pulled a key out from beneath his tunic, dropped on one knee, and opened the small strongbox in the corner.

Glabrio pointed at it, and Sartorus lifted each item out and placed it on the floor. At the bottom, a leather bag held coins. He handed that to Glabrio, who dumped the contents onto the bed.

Several dozen denarii spread across the striped bedcover, but not one golden aureus shone amidst the pile of silver.

Glabrio pointed at the coins. "Check each to see if they're genuine."

As Sartorus began the inspection, the steward appeared at the door. "Is there a problem, Master Lucius?"

Messala jumped at the sound of the man's voice. "No. Tribune Glabrio wants to inspect the estate strongboxes for counterfeits. The metalsmiths who ran away were counterfeiting coins, and the tribune wants to see if any made it into the house. Since we had nothing to do with what the smiths were doing, there will be no problem."

The steward's gaze bounced from Messala to Glabrio to Sartorus and settled on Messala. Then the deepest frown formed. "When did all this happen?"

"Glabrio and I discovered they were gone two days ago. His men found dies for making fake coins when they searched the shop." He glared at Glabrio. "Of course, I knew nothing about what those two were doing without my permission when no one was watching them. They overpowered the tribune and his aide and sold them as slaves some days ago, again without my knowing. And they might have killed my friend Nepos there."

Sartorus stood, and Glabrio asked the question with a raised eyebrow.

"There are three counterfeits that I can tell." He pointed to the three coins he'd set to the side. "They don't appear to be freshly made."

The steward steepled his fingers and rubbed both sides of his nose. "I see." Then he swept his hand toward the door. "If you'll follow me, I'll show you the coins in the estate strongbox in my office. If you want to see inside my master's strongboxes, you'll have to wait until he returns from the council meeting."

"Does young Messala have access to those?"

"Only the master has keys."

"Then it will be enough for now to inspect yours."

As Glabrio followed the steward from the room, he glanced back at Messala. The bluster was gone, and Messala was as pale as the men who'd lost their breakfast into the rolling sea.

Mission accomplished.

Chapter 62

NO LONGER MISSING

Martina's town house, late afternoon of Day 35

Glabrio had settled into Volero's chair for some tabula with Martina before dinner when the pounding on the front door came. Lepus scurried past, only to return with Acceptus right behind him.

The centurion scanned the gameboard as he approached, and his gaze settled on Martina. His mouth twitched as he stopped a smile. It was obvious she was winning.

He came to attention and saluted. "Tribune, we found Nepos."

Martina summoned Lepus with a curl of her fingers. He bent over so she could whisper in his ear. Then the boy disappeared into the pottery shop, where Sartorus was teaching the potters to write.

Glabrio set down the rondel he was about to play. "Where?"

"By the edge of the grove where my men were searching when you came. He was buried about four feet down. He only had a loincloth, so we couldn't use clothing to identify the body. But he was in better shape than I expected after a month, and the hair is the right shade of brown."

"Any possibility it was someone else?"

"I had the estate steward come to see where he was buried. He said there hadn't been a death on the estate recently, and they cremate instead of burying their people, anyway. I'm confident it was him. I left a guard there until I could ask you how to proceed."

Glabrio glanced at Martina. This was not a conversation to have in front of a young woman, but it wasn't shock or horror he saw, only a gentle sadness. Her eyes were focused on him, as if she was worried about how he would take it.

"Could you tell how he was killed?"

Acceptus glanced at Martina and cleared his throat. "It's been too long to say for sure. Could have been a throat cut from behind."

Glabrio closed his eyes and rubbed his forehead. It was what he both expected and feared. But what to do now?

When her fingertips touched the back of his hand, he opened his eyes.

"I can take Clavus and talk with the undertaker right now to arrange for cremation tomorrow out where you found him. I'll ask him to do what he considers necessary for Nepos's father to feel it was a proper Roman funeral. I'll also arrange a box for his remains to return to Rome so his father can place them in their family mausoleum."

Glabrio's eyebrows rose. "Is doing it that quickly even possible?"

Sadness filled her eyes. "I've dealt with him twice in the last six months. He's a good man and very good at what he does. When I explain what's happened, he'll have his men work as late as needed to be ready for tomorrow. I'll send a message to your quarters about what time he'll be out there and ready for the ceremony."

Sartorus had come from the shop and stood behind Acceptus. His face looked as grim as Glabrio felt.

Releasing a deep breath, Glabrio stood. "Take us out to see where he was buried. There's time to inspect it well enough before dark."

After a quick nod, Acceptus lead them toward the door. But before it closed behind Glabrio, he looked back at Martina, who raised a hand and offered a smile of encouragement.

There would be no tabula, no delicious dinner with satisfying conversation, no reading from Marcus's writings with her answering his questions before he went to bed tonight. And strange as it might seem, he wasn't sure which he'd miss most.

Urban Cohort headquarters, early morning of Day 36

The last traces of pink had barely faded from the eastern sky when the soldier from Dubitatus's station delivered the message to Verus.

Come immediately to headquarters. The current tribune was too quick to issue an urgent summons. Hopefully, the next one would care less about duty and efficiency, like Nepos until he got those coins.

Verus strode up the steps and past two saluting guards into the headquarters courtyard. The other three centurions were there ahead of him, and everyone was grim-faced. His stomach knotted.

Glabrio stood in his office doorway, arms crossed. "Verus."

Shoulders back and head raised, Verus struck his chest. "Tribune. I came as soon as I got the message."

With cold eyes, Glabrio nodded. "I just told the others that we've found

Nepos. He was buried at the edge of a grove across a field from the metal shop on Messala's estate. We are now hunting a counterfeiter who is also a murderer, so tell your men to be alert. Someone who killed once has no qualms about killing again to avoid being caught."

Verus's jaw twitched as he clenched it. His commander had no idea how true that was. Nor did he suspect it would soon be acted on.

Glabrio's hand closed into a fist before he hit his own thigh. "I want that murderer caught and executed before Hadrian visits the city this summer. I'm almost certain the one who killed him is Messala's partner in the counterfeiting business. So, you are to continue doing what you have been to figure out who that is. If you have any ideas of other things we might do to hasten that discovery, let me know immediately, and I'll consider adding it. Any questions?"

Four heads shook, triggering Glabrio's icy smile. "Then let's go hunt that murderer down. You're dismissed."

They saluted, and the other three headed out to do as their commander had ordered.

As Verus headed back to his station, he wanted to hit something, anything. Fortuna had frowned on him over and over and over for the past month. But the end of that was in sight.

Messala's stupidity in paying Nepos with counterfeits, the smiths' incompetence in disposing of a corpse, Glabrio's stubborn refusal to stop hunting until he found Nepos—all had conspired to force his hand.

Glabrio needed to die before Messala broke and revealed what they'd done. But where and how to make that happen without anyone discovering he was behind it…a wry smile twisted his mouth as the way forward suddenly became clear.

The Messala estate, midday of Day 36

Glabrio and Sartorus arrived at the burial site to find the undertaker had already assembled a bier and placed the wood beneath it. Atop the bier, the linen-wrapped body rested on its funeral couch.

Messala stood to one side with the estate steward beside him. Glabrio's mouth twitched. Messala would play the part of a man mourning his good friend, and perhaps there was some truth to it. He looked like he had a hangover, which was no surprise. But it was probably more guilt than grief that he was trying to drown with too much wine. If he and his accomplice hadn't been counterfeiting, Nepos would be a quaestor back in Rome instead a corpse on a bier.

Like the closest male relative should, Glabrio took his place at the head of the funeral couch. "Marcus Haterius Nepos was a loyal son of Rome who gave his life in her service. His sacrifice will not be forgotten, and I will do all I can to make certain justice comes to the ones who killed him."

He locked his gaze on Messala. Blinks that were too fast accompanied a nervous twitch of the supposed friend's mouth.

Then he took the torch from the undertaker and lit the wood under the bier. Smoke rose around the linen-wrapped remains of a young man who once had ambitions just like his own. Flames licked at the plain burial couch, then surrounded the body in dancing yellow tongues of fire. Glabrio, Sartorus, Acceptus, and a squad of eight soldiers stood at attention until the flames died and nothing was left but smoldering ash.

Glabrio poured wine on the ashes and bone fragments to cool them. Then he scooped what was left into the stone box which had been inscribed with Nepos's name.

Martina had selected one with a pre-carved garland of laurel leaves, like an athletic crown, surrounding the chiseled name. It was a good box for a soldier to return home in. He would thank her later for choosing something his own father would have thought fitting.

He placed the lid on it and stood. A soldier lifted it back into the wagon that had brought the bier, couch, and wood from town. Then he mounted to lead the procession back to headquarters, where the box would remain in his quarters until he took it back to Rome.

But first he turned his horse to face Messala. "Rest assured that I will find the one who killed him, and justice will be served."

Messala swallowed hard, but he still nodded as if he approved.

Glabrio reined away and rode to the head of the procession. Acceptus gave the command, and his men took their positions beside the wagon. In silence, they started the slow walk back to town.

Martina's town house, afternoon of Day 36

It was only midafternoon, but Glabrio was ready for the day to end. As he walked with Sartorus toward Martina's town house, he tried to turn off the frown. Tried, but didn't quite succeed. Nepos's ashes would remain at his quarters until he returned them to Rome. Each time he saw that box, it was an unwelcome reminder of what had happened and how it might not be possible to find the one responsible, no matter how hard he tried.

His fist made his usual pattern of one then three knocks, and they waited until Lepus opened the door. Sartorus turned toward the door into the pottery shop, where he was teaching the potters to write.

Martina stood just inside the peristyle, waiting for him. Time with her was exactly what he needed to push the funeral from the front of his mind.

"How are you?" Her voice was soothing balm for a weary man.

"What you arranged, it was exactly what I would want to describe to Nepos's father when I deliver the box. Your choice of box with the laurel wreath is what my own father would think fitting to place directly into our family mausoleum."

She touched his arm. "But how are you?"

"A man's death should count for something. His didn't."

"I'd rather say that a man's life should count for something, and maybe his did before he died."

He shrugged. "I'll never know whether that's true." He ran a hand through his hair. "I never met him. I don't know why it's bothering me so much."

She took his hand and led him to Volero's chair. "Because you're a good man, Gaius, and you know how much pain this will cause his father. But having you bring his son's body home will help ease that. Not knowing where his son was and what happened to him would be much worse, and you've spared him that pain."

He leaned back in the chair and closed his eyes. She'd called him by his first name, like the good friend she'd become.

"Would you like me to read to you?"

Her persistence drew his smile. She was determined to read to him until he decided to believe like she did. And maybe there was truth in what Marcus had written. Titus and Sartorus and Grandfather thought so. But facing what that would mean…he wasn't ready for that.

His eyes opened to find her leaning on the gameboard, concern in her eyes. "Not now, but I could use some distraction. Let's play."

He picked up a rondel, and after her eyes searched his face once more, she did, too.

Chapter 63

SETTLING FOR WHAT'S POSSIBLE

Martina's town house, late evening of Day 36

The dinner table had been too quiet, and although prayers with her people always warmed Martina's heart, something was missing tonight.

Two somethings, or rather two someones. Glabrio and Sartorus had gone back to the station right after their tabula game. He didn't say why.

"I'm glad I volunteered to arrange what Gaius needed for Nepos." She picked Juliana's bracelet off the dressing table and traced the curve of one of the wires.

"I missed them tonight." She looked at Platana's reflection in the mirror and saw her friend sigh. "I wish they'd stayed. He seemed so sad, almost as if it was a friend he'd lost. They'd never even met."

Platana drew the brush through her hair for the last time that night. "Maybe he was remembering the death of someone he did care about. Funerals do that to people." She separated the tresses into thirds and started the braid. "They do it to me, especially when the one who dies never knew Jesus."

The lockable box that they'd taken to Cigisa sat by the wall. It still held the codex.

"I offered to read to him when he first came, but maybe it wouldn't have helped. Nepos wasn't a Christian, and thinking about where that left him when he died…" Her sigh was deep. "It might have made things worse."

Platana folded a section of hair over the one next to it. "It's funny how he asks for the reading, then questions everything you read to him."

"Sometimes I think he asks me to read only because he knows I get pleasure out of doing it. But other times it feels like he's asking all those questions because deep in his heart, he knows it's the truth. He's trying to convince himself it isn't because he knows what he'll have to do if he ever admits it is. His grandfather was a consul of Rome, like Gaius wants to be, but after he became a Christian, the emperor killed him. I think that holds Gaius back."

353

Platana finished the braid and tied it with a ribbon. "I wish he'd join us in believing. Then he'd be the perfect husband for you." She rested her hands on Martina's shoulders and leaned over to look directly into her eyes. "I think he's very close to being in love with you. He might already be there. It gives him such pleasure when you call him Gaius, like a wife would."

"I know I shouldn't let myself, but I'm close to loving him as well." Martina closed her eyes and shook her head. "But you and I both know nothing will ever come of it. He'll go back to Rome soon and follow in his father's political footsteps until he becomes consul, too. He told Uncle that was his plan from the start. He's told me several times as well. He doesn't want me to hope for something that can't happen."

She fingered the silver bracelet that Grandfather had given Juliana when he asked her to marry him. "Grandfather married my father's mother because his father chose her. They had a comfortable marriage. But he chose Juliana himself, and they truly loved each other. What if Gaius's father chooses a woman like Artoria for him? How could a man like him ever be happy with that?" She wrapped her fingers around the bracelet. "He'll never be with me, but I still want him happy."

"But maybe God will change that." Platana opened a trunk and took out Martina's sleeping tunic. "Maybe they'll both stay longer than we expect."

"Maybe." Martina closed her eyes as Platana pulled the day tunic over her head and replaced it with the other.

God, You used us to rescue them from the plans of evil men. Please rescue Gaius from the plans he's made himself that will force him to settle for less than Your best.

She bit her lip. Maybe the next prayer was selfish, but God knew her heart, whether she prayed it or not. *Please let it be Your will that I'll be part of what You consider best.*

Urban Cohort headquarters, morning of Day 37

Sitting at the desk in his office, Glabrio leaned back in his chair and laced his fingers atop his head. The report to Saturninus telling him that he had recovered Nepos's body near where he found a piece of his crest in a metal shop had been a challenge to write.

He chose not to report being made a slave and only escaping because a woman he knew bought them. He'd look like a fool for letting that happen, and Saturninus would blame Sartorus for not protecting him.

He'd jumped ahead to the further search that uncovered the molds and dies used for making the fake aurei. The smiths involved had run away before that search, leaving him uncertain of all who were involved. But it wouldn't be long before he knew.

He scanned the end of the letter again. Saturninus might show it to Nepos's father, so it needed to be done right.

> I want to again commend Centurion Flavius Acceptus, this time for his perseverance and skill in discovering where Tribune Nepos had been buried so his body could be treated as a noble Roman deserves. I have overseen his cremation in accordance with Roman custom, and I will be escorting his remains back to Rome as soon as I catch the counterfeiter who is responsible. Until then, please assure Nepos's father that his son died honorably in the service of Rome, and his memory will undoubtedly be honored by those who knew him well.
>
> I hope all will continue to be well with you. May the gods guard your safety.

He laid down the stylus and closed the tablet with a snap. His own father would take comfort in that reason for a son's death, even as he mourned him deeply. Perhaps Nepos's father would do the same.

When Martina said she'd take care of all the details of preparing to send Nepos home, he could have hugged her for sparing him from that burden. If Acceptus hadn't been watching, he would have been sorely tempted. But it was probably good that he hadn't.

If he were free to choose his wife and if she wasn't a Christian, she was exactly the woman who would suit him. But he'd seen how the faith of a woman or man defined who they were. Titus's Pompeia would not be what she was without her thoughts about her god guiding her choices.

Father expected to choose a wife for him based on political advantage. If he even suspected his son was at risk of committing himself to a woman he'd consider unworthy of an Acilius Glabrio, Father would be on a ship to confront him and rid him of that foolish notion. Or would he? Father was so well connected. Could he take a wife without connections to a senatorial family and still be the next Acilius Glabrio to become consul? Even if he did marry the right woman by Father's standards, would that guarantee his own political success?

The smile that thought triggered faded. If he married Martina, she would have to return to Rome with him. She'd be scrutinized by the pagan women who resented her winning the matrimonial prize his father always joked that he was. Except it wasn't a joke; it was true. To make himself happy, would he be putting her at risk of exposing her faith and causing her death?

The snort escaped before he could stop it. He was assuming she wanted to marry him. Titus often joked about Pompeia trying her best to discourage him before God spared his life. Then she worked hard to convince him to believe as she did before he asked her to marry him. Martina had done exactly the same with him.

It was only after Titus decided that Pompeia followed the only true God that she considered him suitable as a husband. He hadn't done that, and he didn't intend to. So, maybe it was pointless to worry about what Father would do. Martina would have the final say on whether it was a suitable match, and her answer would be no.

And Father's approach was right for any man with high political ambition. His marriage had been the union of two prominent senatorial families, and his father-in-law had helped him both survive Domitian's execution of Grandfather and recover his property after Domitian's assassination the following year.

As for that marriage, they'd been contented enough together until she died when Glabrio was a small boy. He didn't remember her much because she wasn't interested in being a mother, only in producing heirs who would become leaders of Rome.

But now he'd seen what a marriage could be. Not a political partnership, but a covenant based on love, not duty. Titianus and Pompeia had one. Kaeso and Sabina had one. If he were to marry Martina, he'd be willing to bet that he'd have one, too.

His deep breath was followed by a deeper sigh. Father was paterfamilias. He had to approve any marriage his children made, and a Carthaginian Christian of moderate means was not what he'd want for his son. If Father said no, Roman law gave him the power to block it. So, he'd have to marry for political connection and hope they could develop the kind of marriage that was more than Father ever had. Most men had to settle for what was possible, not what they wanted most. If you've never sipped the finest wine, you can be content with a cheaper vintage.

He picked up the stylus and drummed on the desktop. The Christian teachings had a certain appeal. That promise of forgiveness—no matter what you've done. Eternal life in heaven after you die. He might consider joining them if he was an ordinary man like Sartorus. No one in power cared whether a man from a tailor shop or a fullery turned away from the state religion.

Or an equestrian paterfamilias like Titus, who was content to run his businesses and teach history and mathematics at Kaeso's school of rhetoric. He'd never cared what anyone thought of him, even the rich and powerful. Only truth and honor drove his decisions.

But an Acilius Glabrio was destined to serve Rome at the highest levels. His family had done it for generations, and Father had raised him to be the next man to shoulder that responsibility. Before coming to Carthago, he'd never doubted that he wanted it as much as Father had.

He clasped his hands atop his head and stared at the ceiling. Rome had plenty of men willing to serve her, but the relationship he had with Father was one of a kind. What would it do to his father if he threw everything away to follow the Christian god?

He closed his eyes and ran his fingers through his hair. If what his friends claimed was true… The deepest sigh drained his lungs. A man of honor had to accept the truth. But what if that led where he didn't want to go?

Sartorus's knock on the doorframe pulled him back from that dangerous reflection. A youth stood behind his aide, peering into the room.

"Verus sent a messenger to bring us to where he's discovered something. He said to come right away."

Glabrio stood and reached for the belt that still held his sword and dagger. His new cuirass and skirt of leather straps were waiting to be picked up, but the worker in bronze had needed a pattern before he could make the helmet. If Verus really had discovered something that would lead him to the ones he was hunting, he could be on a ship to Rome in less than a week. Maybe he'd just get it made there.

He joined Sartorus, and they followed the youth into the street. He led them toward the part of Verus's district west of the harbor where many businesses had their offices and shops.

When this was all over, Glabrio would be commending both Verus and Acceptus for special recognition by Saturninus. Verus volunteering to do what Dubitatus's men were trying was already paying off.

Chapter 64

NOTHING COULD BE BETTER

An alley in Verus's district west of the harbor

Verus wanted to pace, but the thugs he'd hired couldn't know how nervous what they were about to do made him. Still, it needed to be done today, before Glabrio picked up his new armor that afternoon.

He'd hired one man to club Sartorus, to knock him out but not kill him. Glabrio would fight, but with two against one and no armor to protect him, they'd kill him.

A man's guard always dropped when his enemy lay dead before him. They'd never expect the one who hired them to walk up behind and kill them both. Then he'd wake up Sartorus to serve as a witness to his stopping the ones who killed Glabrio.

He'd paid them with counterfeits, so their purses held what he needed to claim they were the ones who killed Nepos, too.

It was hard not to smile. When the prefect in Rome heard how he'd killed the men who'd murdered two of his tribunes, he'd receive a special commendation and bonuses. Maybe even rewards from the dead men's fathers. Maybe enough to make up for what he'd lost by Glabrio ending their counterfeiting before he made what he needed to buy an estate far from Carthago when he retired.

The door was open a crack, just enough to let the thug watch the alleyway. When the youth Verus had sent to headquarters turned the corner and started toward them, the thug eased the door shut and nodded.

There was a wide crack between the boards covering the window, and Verus watched for the youth to pass. He raised his hand, signaling his men to be ready. When Glabrio and Sartorus passed, he counted to three. That should let them move just far enough past the door for his men to strike before they realized what was happening.

With a flick of his fingers, he told the brawny one with the club to step out first. A second flip of his hand, and the dagger man followed.

◆

They were halfway down an alley when the youth that Verus sent for them broke into a run. The sound of a door scraping the ground behind them made Glabrio turn just in time to see a burly man hit Sartorus's head with a club. His aide crumpled and hit the ground as Glabrio's sword cleared its scabbard. Faster than a man could take a deep breath, his dagger was in his other hand.

The many hours he'd spent sparring with Sartorus had honed his reflexes. But would it be enough when it was one against two?

One man shifted left, his club ready to strike. The second man drew a circle in the air with the tip of his dagger. Dagger man waited to the right of club man, ready for the killing thrust once Glabrio was dazed or down.

But the training with Brutus's gladiators before taking this post kicked in. Surprise was a powerful ally, and he who hesitated when outnumbered usually died.

As the club was drawing back for its first blow, Glabrio leaped forward. A slash with his sword across the forearm, a thrust to the side with his dagger, and another slash to the back of the leg dropped club man to the ground.

An anguished cry exploded from his lips. He was out of action, but he wasn't dead. And if Glabrio could take down the one with the dagger, he'd still have one who could tell him who hired them.

And that would be Nepos's killer as well.

Dagger man lunged at him, and a swing of Glabrio's gladius as he twisted and leaped sideways caught the man's knife hand. The dagger clattered on the stone street, and the man grabbed his wrist, his right hand now useless.

Glabrio moved toward him, gladius poised to thrust, and the man backed up against the wall.

But instead of defeat or fear, defiance lit the dagger man's eyes. "Looks like you lost, Tribune." His mouth twisted into a sneer.

"Who hired you?" Glabrio placed the sword tip at the man's throat. "Speak now if you want to live."

Dagger man broke eye contact to look over Glabrio's shoulder. "Verus—" His sneer vanished as his eyes widened.

The flash of a polished blade to his right caught Glabrio's eye as the clatter of metal on stone sounded at his feet. A sword passed above his right shoulder to hit the throat of the thug, knocking his own blade aside. Glabrio spun away to the left.

He expected to see Sartorus, but it was Verus instead. He lowered his sword.

Verus pulled the blade tip from his attacker, and the dead man slumped to the ground. The centurion bent to pick up a dagger that lay beside the fallen man.

When he turned to face Glabrio, Verus was breathing heavily, as if he'd been running. "Good thing I came looking for you. He was about to put this second blade into your side." Verus held up the dagger.

"Too bad you had to kill him. He was about to tell me who hired him, but the other one is still alive."

He kicked the club away from the groaning man and held his sword to the man's throat as he pulled a dagger from the sheath on the thug's belt and tossed it away. Then he slipped the sword into its scabbard and crouched by the man whose answer would finally give justice to a murdered tribune and his father.

"Who—"

Before he could finish the question, a hand grabbed Glabrio's hair and jerked his head back. Verus was poised to draw dagger man's blade across his throat.

But before the blade made the cut, Sartorus's arm slipped between blade and throat, and the spurt of warm blood that hit Glabrio's chin was not his own. Sartorus wrapped himself around Verus and jerked back and sideways to pull his attacker away.

As they rolled on the ground, Glabrio waited for the moment to strike when his sword would hit murderer, not friend.

When the opening came, he drove the blade home, and the centurion he'd trusted completely, the one who'd betrayed all he'd sworn to defend, was no more.

Glabrio rolled the body off Sartorus and offered his hand to help him up.

But Sartorus didn't take it. He lay on his back, eyes closed, breathing hard. From the wound at the elbow of the arm that stopped the dagger, blood came out in spurts. A lot of blood. Too much blood.

Glabrio dropped to his knees, placed his hands on the wound, and pressed to slow the bleeding. "Don't you dare die on me."

Sartorus's eyes opened halfway, and that slight smile he so often wore appeared. "It could be worse. Death will just take me to be with Lord Jesus." He laid his hand on Glabrio's shoulder. "Don't let death take you before He's your Lord, too."

Then his eyes closed, and his hand fell away. His chest still rose and fell, but each rise took longer and was harder to see.

And the blood kept flowing, no matter how hard Glabrio pressed.

He fought to swallow the lump in his throat as he stared at the back of his hands, now coated in his friend's blood.

Titus had told him many times it was Pompeia's and Kaeso's prayers to the one true god that saved him. Would the god he'd refused to acknowledge before listen to his own prayers now and spare his friend?

God, if you're real, don't let him die because of me. Like you saved Titus, please save him, too.

What had been a pulsing flow turned into a trickle, then stopped.

Had Sartorus's god heard and answered? Did he stop the bleeding? But dead men don't bleed, either, so was that all he was seeing?

If you're all that he said, you can still save him. If you do, I'll know for certain that you're the One True God, and I'll follow you, too. No matter what it costs.

For a long moment, he held his breath. Everything around him stopped moving, as if somehow time stood still.

Then he saw the chest rise and fall and rise again. No fresh blood oozed out of the wound.

He felt Sartorus's neck by his ear. A steady pulse triggered his broadest smile.

God had answered his prayer. He'd seen with his own eyes what the only God with real power could do. No matter what came from his decision, the God of Sartorus and Titus would be his God, too.

"You." He pointed at a young man who'd joined the cluster of people watching. "Run to the ludus and bring back the gladiator physician immediately. The sooner you're back, the more I'll pay you."

The young man sprinted away in the direction of the amphitheater.

Glabrio stood and gazed down at his friend, whose chest rose and fell with the rhythm he'd seen in the Utica cell. Then Sartorus's eyelids fluttered. Glabrio dropped to one knee beside him just as Sartorus's eyes opened.

"I've sent for the physician from the ludus. How do you feel?"

One corner of Sartorus's mouth lifted. "It could be worse. I figured I was dying, and you'd have to find a new optio to watch out for you."

"You almost did, but I asked the Great Healer for help. He delivered."

"Like with Titianus?"

"Yes." If he spoke the next words, there was no turning back. He drew a deep breath. "Like with Titus, and I've come to the same conclusion he did."

Sartorus's smile grew into a grin. "Nothing could be better."

"Make way." The gladiator physician and the young man pushed through the gathering crowd. "I have a litter coming. We'll get your man fixed up in no time."

Glabrio stepped away to give the physician room. He took three denarii from his purse and gave them to the young man, whose grin was almost as broad as Sartorus's.

He turned back to watch the physician binding the wound of the man who'd now saved him several times over.

Sartorus closed his eyes, but the big smile remained, and Glabrio thanked God yet again for giving him back the best friend he'd ever had.

Chapter 65

SHARING THE NEWS

Martina's town house, afternoon of Day 37

Martina stood beside Platana, working at her loom. She glanced at her friend, who raised her eyebrows when they heard Glabrio's pattern of one knock, then three. It was still early afternoon, and when all was well with him, he came shortly before dinner.

He'd come early yesterday when his heart was hurting from dealing with Nepos's funeral. What was grieving him today?

"Lepus." Her call brought the youth from the kitchen, and he broke into a trot at the second set of knocks.

She parked her shuttle on its shelf and turned, expecting Glabrio to already have passed through the vestibulum and be almost to his chair. But he still stood in the doorway, speaking too softly to Lepus for her to hear. Lepus hadn't looked that grim since she rescued him from Artoria.

Past him were two men, each holding the poles of a litter.

A soft gasp accompanied Platana's hand flying up to cover her mouth. "Where's Sartorus?"

"I don't know." Before the last word was out, Platana had reached the chairs and was striding toward the tribune. Martina hurried to catch up.

When she reached the door, Platana stood beside the litter, holding Sartorus's right hand. He drew hers over to rest on his chest, but he didn't raise his left hand to join it. A large bandage encircled his left elbow.

"You're hurt." Platana's voice quavered. "Will you be all right?"

Sartorus drew her hand to his lips and kissed it: "I will now."

"He should be well enough in time, if your mistress will grant my request." The trace of amusement in Glabrio's voice swept Martina's worry away.

She turned her gaze from the pair to him. "What would that be?"

"One of my centurions tried to kill me, and Sartorus got hurt stopping him. Verus from the harbor district turned out to be the counterfeiter who killed Nepos."

A gasp escaped before Martina could stop it.

Glabrio's mouth twitched. "I was surprised myself. Titus told me that an officer's deadliest enemies sometimes wear Roman armor. This time, he was right." He rested a hand on the litter. "But his greatest friend might wear it, too."

He tapped Sartorus's right shoulder. "Now that I know who was responsible for Nepos's death and that man is also dead, it's time to take his remains back to Rome. I'll be going alone because Sartorus needs to recover."

Glabrio rested his hand on his sword. "I was hoping he could stay with you until I return. He stopped a blade from slitting my throat, but the cut he got doing that…" He sucked air between his teeth. "He lost a lot of blood, and he'll be laid up for a while. He'll get better care with you than at the garrison infirmary. For treating knife wounds, you can't beat a gladiator physician, but I expect you know more about what will hasten his healing."

His veiled request that they pray for their friend, was that only a short step from praying himself?

Platana's head bobbed as her gaze met Martina's before returning to Sartorus's face.

"He's always welcome here, and we'll start doing that right away. We'll give him the best of care. We even have the perfect room off the peristyle for him."

Her hand swept toward the room he'd stayed in before.

Glabrio pulled down the rod that held the top of the second door in place as Lepus lifted the bottom rod. The door swung in, making the entry wide enough for the litter. The bearers carried it to the doorway of Sartorus's room. With Glabrio at his shoulders and one of the bearers taking his legs, they moved him to the bed.

Platana stayed beside him.

After Glabrio paid the lead bearer, they shouldered the litter and left.

As soon as Lepus shut both doors and bolted them, Glabrio leaned against Sartorus's doorframe. "I'd like to get that copy of Marcus's codex from you now. I'll be taking the first ship I can get to Rome tomorrow. While I'm there, I'll meet with my Christian friends and spend time with Father."

He looked at Sartorus. "I'll be taking ginger and licorice roots, like a wise man taught me to do."

"That's good to know, Tribune." Sartorus grinned. "Remember to watch where sea meets sky as well."

"I still have to pick up my new armor before I tell Paternus what's happened and who will be in charge in my absence. So, I can't stay long." He tipped his head toward her office. "Let's go get the codex."

"Of course." Martina forced a smile. What she'd made for him would delight his friends, but as she wrote each word, she'd imagined him reading it. Knowing that would never happen left a hollow feeling.

In the tiny tablinum, she unlocked the strongbox and lifted out the codex. She was still on her knees when she handed it to him. He offered his free hand to help her stand.

"Titus and his familia will be delighted to get this. They'll be thrilled when I tell them what I'll be telling my father." The gleam in his eyes faded. "But Father's going to hate it."

"What would that be?" She released his hand, even though she'd rather not. *God, please let it be what I hope it is.*

"I discovered there's only one decision a man of honor who values truth can make, and I made it today."

"What did you decide?" Her breaths came faster. Had he made the right choice?

He tipped his head toward the room where Platana was watching over Sartorus.

"He did more than save my life today. He was dying, and I asked the Great Healer to save my friend." His teasing smile appeared, and laughter danced in his eyes. "He did, and then He saved me as well."

"What are you saying?" If it was what she thought it was…joy coursed through her.

"I decided what you and Sartorus and Titus have been telling me is true. I've decided to follow Jesus as my Lord." He rubbed his jaw. "I don't know where that will lead, but I guess I'll find out."

"Oh, Gaius!" She took his hand and drew it to her chest. "Nothing in this world could make me happier. But do be careful who you let know about it."

The heartiest laugh she'd ever heard from him echoed in the room. "Beside this household, Titus's family and, when the time is right, my father, I'm not planning to tell anyone. You taught me that lesson well."

"You can safely tell Volero. He's been hiding Christians for years."

"I might when I get back from Rome." He moved their clasped hands to his chest and wrapped his other hand around them. "This is the best day of my life." His grin faded. "But it came at a cost."

He placed his fingers on the crook of his elbow. "Where Sartorus got cut at his elbow, the gladiator physician said it's not likely to heal well. He'll probably end up with permanent weakness that would keep him from using a shield. My men all have to train as soldiers with sword and shield. He'll probably be getting an honorable discharge from the Cohort, and he still needs thirteen more years to retire."

"I can solve that problem." Martina locked the strongbox and hung the key around her neck. "If he's going to need a place to work, he can work for me. I need someone to manage the pottery shop and find us new customers." She bit her lip. "He'll be able to marry after he's discharged, won't he?"

"Yes. Why?"

How could he ask that question? Wasn't it as obvious to him as it was to her that their best friends belonged together? But there was no teasing in his eyes, so maybe it wasn't.

She lowered her voice so no one outside the room could hear. "Platana would love to marry him, and if it takes a weakened arm to get him out of the Cohort so they can marry, she'll be thanking God for that injury. I was waiting until she was thirty to free her to give her citizenship, but she won't want to wait that long. It's not that important for a woman, anyway."

Glabrio waggled a finger at her. "You're wrong about that. It's important for her children. But a man can free a woman he owns to marry her and give her citizenship right away. I'll gladly pay what it costs for Sartorus to buy and free her." The half-smile she'd grown to love appeared. "You can add the amount to what I owe you for buying me. We'll work out the details when I get paid. I only make 1500 denarii a month, so it might take me two months to clear my debt."

She narrowed her eyes. "Well, I suppose I can extend you more credit … this time. But if it goes beyond that, I'll have to charge interest."

The half-smile grew into a grin. "Volero said you'd be as good at business as your grandfather. But you already know I'll pay you. I'm only alive because he risked dying one more time to save me. The least I can do is help him marry the right woman."

Martina fingered the filigree bracelet. Juliana got the husband she wanted. Platana soon would as well. But was there any hope for her?

God, if it's possible, please…

He patted the codex. "Let's wrap this up so it's well protected until I give it to Titus."

"I can lend you a seal box if you want to use twine around the wrapping and a wax seal."

His chuckle wrapped around her and made her smile in return. "Sometimes the safest way to keep a secret is to make it look like you don't care if someone knows it. That seal box would be certain to make someone want to open it. Twine with bows around a canvas wrapping will do fine."

"Clavus should have some." She led him toward the door.

"There is one more thing."

She glanced back over her shoulder. "What?"

"Promise you'll all pray for me often until I return. That should be less than two weeks. I'll be eight days at sea and a few days in Rome."

"I've been praying for you often since the first time I read to you. Nothing could keep me from doing it now."

His broadest grin declared how much that pleased him.

"I'll talk with Sartorus while you get that ready." He bounced his eyebrows at her. "If I can get his attention away from Platana."

He followed her into the peristyle and crossed to his friend's room. As he stepped inside, her smile dimmed.

He was now the perfect man to be her husband, if only he weren't an Acilius Glabrio on the way to political greatness. That door was definitely closed.

God, thank You so much for claiming his heart. Thank You for making him my brother forever. Please make me content with whatever You plan, for I know Your plans will be better than my dreams.

Chapter 66

BACK IN ROME

The Titianus town house in Rome, evening of Day 42

It was late evening when Glabrio turned up the street toward Titus's town house. He'd arrived midday in Portus, and Titus's warehouse manager had lent him a horse and a canvas bag big enough for the stone box containing Nepos's remains and the codex. The box was lighter than a small child, so with the bag's strap across his chest, it had been easy enough to hold it on the saddle in front of him as he rode back to Rome. His travel chest would be delivered to Father's town house sometime after dark when the streets opened to wheeled vehicles. Since Father didn't know he was coming, he wanted to beat the trunk home.

But first, he needed to talk with his Christian friends before he faced the hardest conversation of his life. In seeing the friends he left behind, surprising them with his decision, nothing but pleasure lay before him. Being with Father again...the first moments would bring heartfelt delight to both. But when he told Father about the decision he'd made and the changes that must bring... would deep disappointment be followed by anger and rejection or resignation and acceptance?

When he rode through the stableyard gate, he was spotted by Theo, who waved before dashing into the house. So much for surprising Titus by suddenly appearing to lean against a doorframe.

He'd barely dismounted and lifted the bag down when he felt the hand clamp on his shoulder and turned to find a grin Saturninus would have thought impossible on Titus's face.

"Welcome back. To what do we owe this pleasure?"

Glabrio rested his hand on the bag. "I'm returning what remains of my predecessor to his father."

The light faded from Titus's eyes. "That's hard duty. Does he already know you're coming?"

"I've only told Saturninus I'd be bringing this back when I caught the one who killed him. I don't know what he's told Nepos about his son. I got here by ship faster than the report of my success could have reached him." He slipped the strap off his shoulder and lowered the bag to the ground. "I only arrived this morning, and that horse is one of yours that I borrowed from your Portus warehouse."

"You're welcome to use it for as long as you're in Rome. Will that be long?"

"A few days. I came here first, but I can't stay long. There's something I need to tell you and something I need to ask." He rubbed his jaw. "The first will surprise you, but the second won't."

"Come to the library. Pompeia's with one of her former students who's in labor. Kaeso and Sabina are dining with her father, so I hope you'll be able to come again before you leave. They'll all want to see you."

"As I want to see them. But it's better if only you and I talk tonight."

"Something serious?" The emotionless mask Titus wore in his tribune days replaced the smile.

"Maybe deadly serious."

They reached the library, and Titus waved Glabrio in ahead of him. He closed the door before sitting at the desk. "What's happened?"

"First, the good thing that will make Pompeia do that little dance she does when she's excited." He drew a deep breath. "What you've all been praying for finally happened in Carthago."

Titus leaned forward and rested crossed arms on the desktop.

"From the beginning, you told me that truth and honor matter, but truth matters most. I've decided you and everyone else here were telling me the truth after all. I didn't want to believe it because that would cost too much. But I've been convinced that Jesus of Nazareth is the Son of God, and I've decided to follow him, no matter what."

Titus leaned across the desk, his biggest grin replacing straight lips, and slapped Glabrio's arm. "I was hoping that was the first part. But since you came here straight from the port, I think I can guess the second part." He leaned back in his chair. "You haven't told your father yet, and you're not sure what he'll do when you tell him."

Glabrio sighed as he nodded. He hadn't yet started looking at everything to see how God worked it together for good, but there was no doubt Titus did. "Exactly, and when I do, it will be like Grandfather all over again. Everything we planned together...whatever involves pretending the Roman gods are real is something I can't do. This will change a lot between us, and I'm afraid of what that will mean. Father will feel betrayed by my decision, even though it isn't a rejection of him at all. It's embracing the truth."

"You can never be certain beforehand how someone will react. Quintus

Sabinus had special plans for someone, but he accepted them choosing to follow Jesus. He's kept it secret ever since. If a man like him can do that, surely an honorable man can. God can touch any heart, even one that doesn't yet believe."

Titus fingered his lip. "The only way to find out is to talk with your father privately and see where it leads. I know you'll be praying as you do, and I'll be praying for you here. You've met the Holy Spirit already?"

"Sartorus and Martina explained everything, and when I confessed my sins and declared my faith, He came."

Remembrance of that day when his confession and declaration were followed by baptism, first in the water of her pool and then by the Spirit, as Sartorus had described...even with what lay ahead, he couldn't stop the smile.

"Remember to ask Him to guide you in what to say and when to say it. Jesus told his disciples to rely on the Spirit when facing judges and kings. Your father will be easy compared to that."

"Is that in the writings of Lucas you have?"

"It is." Titus closed his eyes and looked up before focusing them on Glabrio again. "It's a promise worth remembering. 'Whenever they bring you before synagogues and rulers and authorities, don't worry about how you should defend yourselves or what you should say. For the Holy Spirit will teach you at that very hour what must be said.' He'll tell you when to speak about your faith to the ordinary people you know as well."

"Like you and Sartorus did with me."

"So, he convinced you?"

"Indirectly. Martina read to me, and they both answered my questions. But it was when he was bleeding to death from taking a knife that was meant for me that I yielded. I asked God to save him like He saved you. When He did, I had no choice but to admit the truth and follow where that leads."

"Martina?" Titus's grin reappeared. "Pompeia and Sabina will want to hear all about her later."

"I brought you something she made for me, but she'll make me another." He reached into the bag and pulled out the codex. "The writings of the apostle Marcus. She made me a copy of hers, but she approved of me giving it to you. But in exchange, I'd like to take copies of the gospels and letters you have back to her."

Titus took the codex and stroked the leather cover. "Come get them whenever you want. Pompeia will have a set ready for you. When I tell her that you've joined us and give her this...if she was a woman who squealed with delight, that's what I'd hear."

"I haven't said anything to Martina yet, but she's the woman I want to marry if I can persuade Father to let me make my own choice instead of a political marriage."

Glabrio sucked air through his teeth. "That might be hardest of all." He stood. "I'd rather stay and talk, but I'd better go so I beat my trunk to Father's house. I don't want to explain why I came here first."

"I'll be praying for you, as will the others as soon as they return. But the answer to our prayers isn't always what we want. At least not right away. Sometimes the longed-for yes is a no or a not yet. But I don't expect a no. The bond between you and your father will survive this. It might even grow stronger because of it."

Titus rose, and in companionable silence, they returned to the stableyard. Glabrio mounted, but before he turned the horse's head toward the gate, Titus rested a hand on his thigh and bowed his head. "Be with him, Lord, as he faces this challenge. Give him all he needs to say, and bless the outcome. In Jesus's name."

Glabrio joined him in the amen and nudged the horse into a walk. As he rode out the gate, he looked back. Titus stood watching with arms crossed. Then he raised a hand in what some might think a farewell, but even as a new Christian, Glabrio knew a blessing when he saw it.

Chapter 67

FACING FATHER

The Glabrio town house, late evening of Day 42

In a fine linen tunic that he'd left behind, Glabrio lounged in one of the cushioned wicker chairs in Father's library. The one Volero had at Martina's was better, but that might be more because of the woman across the game-board than the actual chair.

He'd asked for bread and a bowl of the stew served to the important household slaves since Father was dining with close friends. Saturninus would be among them.

The commotion when Father returned with his bodyguards made him set the codex aside. Rapid footsteps approached; the doorkeeper must have told Father he was home.

When Father stepped into the room, Glabrio rose. His father opened his arms, and Glabrio stepped into them for a quick embrace ending with a slap on each back.

"This is a surprise. Marcus Saturninus sad nothing at dinner about you coming back to Rome."

"He might not have known. I must have beaten the report I'd written the day before I left Carthago. It might have been on the same ship with me, but I borrowed a horse from Titianus's warehouse and rode up."

Father took a decanter of white wine from a cabinet carved with a hunting scene and poured some into two gold goblets After diluting each with twice as much water, he swirled one and handed it to Glabrio. While swirling his own, with a sweep of his other hand, he invited Glabrio to sit in the wicker chairs that faced each other.

"So, to what do I own this pleasure? Some special success or a problem?"

"A problem solved. I wrote you about Tribune Nepos disappearing."

"Did you find him?"

"Yes, and I brought him home. I found where he was killed, and one of my centurions had his men hunt until they found his grave. I oversaw his cremation and brought his remains back to his father."

Father's smile had turned into a sad frown. "His father wanted a safe posting for his only son until he could become quaestor. Carthago should have served that purpose." Father raised the goblet to his lips, but lowered it without drinking. "What happened?"

"I don't know exactly, but I found part of his crest in a metal shop involved in counterfeiting. I do know who killed him because he tried to kill me, too."

Father's eyebrows plunged. "When?"

"Twice, actually. The first I'd rather you not mention to Saturninus. It was unavoidable, but it makes me look like a fool. My optio and I stopped at that metal shop to get a custom lampstand made, and he found a piece of Nepos's crest while I was looking at lamp designs. The smiths knocked us out, and someone sold us as slaves for the mines. We ended up rowers on a coastal ship until the niece of one of the councilmen spotted us in Utica and bought us to free us."

He took a sip. "I'll be paying her back as soon as I get paid." He inhaled the wine's bouquet. "Brutus's vintage for the honorable."

Father's eyebrow rose. "It is, but how did you know?"

"I've had it before with a friend Brutus admires for his integrity."

"The incorruptible Titianus, no doubt. And the second time?"

'I had my centurions trying to find where the counterfeits were being passed so I could identify who was passing them. I took one of Titianus's warnings too lightly. He told me an officer's greatest enemy might be wearing Roman armor. The centurion over the harbor district went beyond his duty several times, and I trusted him. He sent a youth to lead me into an ambush where he tried to kill me himself after his thugs failed. I'm only alive because my optio stopped the knife that was meant for my throat with his arm."

"The man you persuaded Marcus to let you take from here?"

"Yes. Sartorus. He kept me alive while we were slaves, and he almost died from that wound. I'll be asking Saturninus for special recognition and a bonus for him."

Father swirled his wine, inhaled the aroma, and took a sip. "Whatever else you're doing, the leaders of the city are happy with it. The duumvirs wrote Marcus thanking him for sending a tribune who actually tried to learn what the needs of the city were so he could fulfill them." Father raised his goblet in a toast. "To 'the best tribune in twenty-five years,' as they described you to Marcus. He was congratulating himself on his wisdom in sending you there."

"I'm glad he did. I've found Carthago suits me very well."

"If they repeat that praise to Hadrian during his visit this summer, we'll have succeeded in using the XIII Cohort tribuneship to great advantage. In a few months, we can begin looking for a better posting."

Glabrio raised the goblet to his lips to conceal the frown that thought triggered. A better posting? When he sailed from Rome, he'd looked at Carthago as only a stepping stone to better things. Now it felt like home. Could any other posting, regardless of its political advantage, ever be better?

Another swirl and sip, then Father set the goblet down. "It's probably time to arrange the right wife for you. I have a few in mind, and we can have their fathers meet you while you're in Rome. Although any of them would be willing to unite our two families without meeting you based on my recommendation."

Glabrio swallowed hard. Father had just opened the door for the conversation he both wanted and dreaded. *God, is this the opening we're praying for? A strange calm settled over him. Give me the right words, and take this where it needs to go.*

He set his goblet beside Father's. "That might be a problem now. Something important has happened that changes what would make a suitable wife for me. Especially what would make a woman unsuitable or make her think I was."

Father leaned back in the chair. "You're talking in riddles. What do you mean?"

"What's happened in Africa, what I've seen, what I've experienced…they make marrying a woman from a political family potentially dangerous."

Father's head drew back. "Dangerous? What kind of dangerous?"

Glabrio's next words…if he said them, there was no turning back.

"Dangerous like what happened to Grandfather."

Father flicked his words away. "No matter what some of the senators say, Hadrian is no Domitian. He'll be emperor until he dies a natural death, and he'll probably adopt a good man to succeed him, like Nerva and Trajan did. I expect our family to remain in the next emperor's good graces. Neither you nor I would do anything stupid enough to change that opinion."

"I would never call it stupid, but I've done something already."

Plunging eyebrows and a deepening frown transformed Father's face. "What have you done?"

"I've thought about it long and hard. I've asked every question I could think of, and I've come to a conclusion." Glabrio drew a deep breath. "I've decided Grandfather was right. Jesus of Nazareth died on a cross to pay for my sins. I believe that he's the Son of God who came from heaven to do that and that he rose from the dead afterward. He destroyed the barrier between me and God, and I've decided to follow him as my Lord for the rest of my life."

Father's jaw dropped. When it snapped shut, hot anger burned in his eyes.

"Don't you remember what that delusion cost your grandfather? What it almost cost me? No god is real, no man can pay for what another man has done, and only an utter fool would believe what the Christians do. What on earth convinced you to believe something so stupid?"

"Praying to God is nothing like the rites we perform for the gods of Rome. He listens, and He answers. You've been to war. You've seen men bleed out and die. I watched my optio do both, and I asked God to bring him back. When He did, I knew God was real, and I told Him I'd follow Him for the rest of my life."

Father gripped the arms of his chair. "I have seen war, and dead men do not come back to life. It's impossible for you to have seen what you think you did."

"If he wasn't dead, he was so close to it that he never would have survived without God acting." Glabrio drew his hand across the crook of his elbow. "Cut right here, blood spurting everywhere. No matter what I did, I couldn't stop it. He passed out, stopped breathing. Only then did the bleeding stop. I'd been resisting what I could see was true because of what happened to Grandfather. But when I finally asked the Christian God to save my friend, He did. I left Sartorus in Carthago to get his strength back and came to Rome alone to return Nepos's ashes."

He squared his shoulders. *God, please give me the words and make him understand.*

"And to tell you what I've done. I can't deny the truth anymore after seeing with my own eyes what God can do."

"As your father, I can order you to give up this foolishness. You'll end up dead if you don't." The anger had cooled and was replaced by dismay. "I don't want you to die like Father."

"I don't plan to. But even if you forbid it, once a man knows the truth, he can't just walk away from it. Above all else, you raised me to be a man of honor. There is no honor in staying alive if you have to deny the truth."

Father scrunched his eyes and rubbed his forehead. "I tried and tried to get Father to turn from this madness, and he wouldn't." Weary eyes focused on Glabrio. "Is there anything I could say or do to get you to turn?"

"Truth is truth, and I can't turn my back on it. I'm not doing this to hurt you, Father. But I have to follow the truth, no matter the cost."

Father slumped in his chair. With elbows on his knees and eyes closed, he buried his face in his hands. Silence filled the room, broken only by the sound of Father's heavy breathing.

God, please let him see that I must follow You, that I can't deny the truth. Please don't let this be the end for us.

Jesus's own words about losing a father because of him echoed in Glabrio's mind. The ache that thought triggered spread out like ripples from a stone tossed into a pond. Was he losing forever the man who'd been both father and friend? But there was no turning back.

Then, deep inside of him, like someone whispering in the dark, a still, small voice spoke. *But you won't have to.*

After a shuddering sigh, Father straightened. In his eyes, dismay had changed to resignation.

"Well, if you're determined to do this, then we need to figure out what to do next to keep it from killing you."

"I can't go on to be quaestor. I couldn't lead the Roman rites that are required in that position. God says we're to worship only Him and no other gods. So somehow, I need to withdraw from the *cursus honorum* before I take that step. But I'm not sure how to do that without drawing too much attention and inspiring questions about why."

Father leaned back in his chair. "Would you want to stay in Carthago if I can arrange it?"

"I would. Do you think that's possible?"

Stay in the same town as his best friend and the woman he loves? Nothing could be better.

"A man never knows what's possible until he looks into it." Father rubbed his jaw. "I want to talk with Marcus before you do. He was glad to get you out of Rome where you asked inconvenient questions and refused to stop when he wanted you to. He's heard from Carthago how well they like you there. So…I want to get him thinking about leaving you there for a while. That would give us time to figure out something more permanent."

Glabrio stretched out his legs and relaxed. No one was better than Father at navigating Roman politics. "He'll probably be Urban Prefect for as long as he wants the post while Hadrian rules. If he would leave me tribune over the XIII Cohort, that would be ideal. You could remind him that having me out of Rome where I won't be disturbing his political and personal obligations is desirable, and I've already shown how well I can handle what's amiss in Carthago by finding Nepos's murderer and stopping the counterfeiters."

"I can't tell Marcus why you want to do this. He's my friend, but there are limits to what he can to do protect you, limits to what he'd be willing to do."

"You could tell him I told you nothing satisfies more than keeping a city safe from the violent and the thieves. That's actually true. His eyes roll when I say truth and justice matter, but I can make a difference there."

"What you want won't matter to him." A wry smile lifted the corner of Father's mouth. "He doesn't like you."

"I know. 'The friend of your father isn't always your friend, but he usually won't strike at you as long as he wants your father's friendship.' I've seen that in action."

Father's laugh was a sweet sound in Glabrio's ears. "Is that something Titianus told you?"

"It is."

"Marcus couldn't stand him, but he was so good at his job that removing him would have raised too many questions. He dislikes you because you turned out just like him. Titianus never had ambitions beyond being tribune. Perhaps it won't surprise Marcus that you feel the same."

Father slapped the arms of his chair. "Tomorrow before salutation, I'll pay him a visit. Now, tell me about your adventures and what's good about Carthago. It's only four days by sea, so I can come visit easily."

As they settled into a conversation between two good friends, Glabrio gave thanks that choosing God as his heavenly father hadn't ended his earthly father's love.

Chapter 68

CHARTING A NEW PATH

Saturninus's town house, early morning of Day 43

The clouds of early dawn had just passed from gray to the first blush of pink when Manius Glabrio led his two bodyguards up to the stable-yard entrance of Marcus Saturninus's town house.

The line of clients already forming by the front door would be taken care of by Saturninus's secretary since his friend started his day at cohort head-quarters in the Praetorian Fortress, spent midday at his office near the Forum attending to city matters, and ended his day with his fellow senators at Trajan's baths.

But what Manius wanted to discuss with his friend was too sensitive for any of those locations. He'd catch him before breakfast in this attempt to arrange a future that would keep his son alive.

The house slave who went to announce his presence returned with an invitation to join Saturninus for breakfast. An auspicious start to the most important conversation of his life.

When he was escorted into the private triclinium, Saturninus waved a hand at the center couch. "Join me, Manius. After seeing you last night, I'm surprised to see you so early."

The slave escorting him brought a small plate and another goblet from the side table to place in front of him. After filling it with diluted wine, he bowed and left.

Manius took a sip and nodded his approval. "Normally, I wouldn't disturb you this early, but I found my son in my library when I got home. I had no idea he was coming. I left him sleeping after his long journey. He'd escorted Tribune Nepos's remains home and is planning to deliver them to you today."

Saturninus's head drew back. "That's the first I've heard of that."

"He said he might have beaten his report here, depending on which ship brought it and how fast it came up from Portus."

Saturninus released a deep sigh. "I'm glad your son found the body. When I told Nepos his son had disappeared, he didn't want to believe that meant he was dead. No father would. But at least he can take some comfort in having his son's remains in the mausoleum of his ancestors."

"Sometimes we must sacrifice our sons to the service of Rome, and they bring honor to our families. But as a father myself...I understand how he feels. That's why I came to speak with you this morning."

Saturninus's eyes narrowed. "I don't understand."

"Last night, we had a long talk about his political ambitions and how his time in Carthago has changed them. He wants to step away from the political career we all expected for him. At first, I opposed it, but the more I think about it, the wiser it seems to me."

He sat on the edge of the couch but didn't swing his legs up. "Gaius has become even more fixated on always doing what he thinks is the most honorable thing, regardless of whom he makes angry."

From the serving plate of cheese and dried fruit, Manius selected a slice. "With the wrong emperor, I'm certain that will get him exiled and maybe even executed. Just as Domitian did to my father. It would be better if my son serves where he can't get himself into trouble with those who don't value truth and justice as much as he does. He'll continue in the cursus honorum if I tell him to, but we both know a man must be pragmatic to serve Rome well. I don't think he has that in him."

Saturninus pinched his lower lip. "You might be right. It's all black and white with him, and a career serving the empire requires a man to be comfortable with shades of gray." He reached for a dried fig. "But there might be a choice that would be good for both him and the empire. Perhaps I should leave him in Carthago as tribune of the XIII instead of you looking for a legion posting or a quaestorship. He's done an excellent job. Both duumvirs have sent letters praising his performance in looking after their city. They said they would like to keep him there for as long as possible."

As Manius selected a second cheese slice and moved it to his plate, he offered his friend his most appreciative smile. "What you propose is an excellent solution. I'm certain Gaius will be more than happy to take that assignment for as long as you remain Urban Prefect. He can serve Rome doing what he does best, and he won't get himself or anyone else into trouble while he's doing it."

He picked up a raisin and popped it into his mouth. "He'll be coming to see you later this morning to deliver Nepos's remains. I'll let you tell him what you've decided." He raised his goblet in a toast. "You've proposed a solution that serves the best interests of everyone, including Rome herself."

Saturninus pushed a bowl of hard-boiled eggs toward him. "Try the sauce. I have a new cook who's creative with spices, and I'm sure you'll like this one."

Manius swung his legs up on the couch and settled in for a good breakfast with a good friend. The friend of a man's father might not be that man's friend, but he still might take care of him as if he were.

Urban Cohort headquarters, morning of Day 43

It seemed more than five and a half weeks since Glabrio last strode across the courtyard of the Urban Cohort's headquarters. The stone box was still in the canvas bag as he carried it to the man who would deliver it to a grieving father. But what would happen after he presented it to Saturninus, only God knew.

Father had returned from Saturninus's house with a satisfied smile, but he wouldn't say what they had discussed or whether they had agreed on anything. *Let your commander tell you* was all he would say.

There hadn't been time to get a new helmet made in Carthago, so Glabrio was bare-headed when he approached the door of Saturninus's headquarters office. Still, the guards on each side saluted as if a tribune's crest was atop his head, and one opened the door for him. Perhaps they still recognized him, or the new cuirass was enough to declare his authority over them.

But would Saturninus comment on the disrespect implied by the helmet's absence? Father's steward was going to get one started that morning at the metal shop that had made the one he lost in Carthago. It would be ready before he sailed home.

The prefect sat at his desk, and most of the stack of tablets had moved from the unread to the read side. One had been pushed forward. Was that his?

He marched to the desk and saluted. "Prefect."

Saturninus set down his stylus and focused unsmiling eyes on Glabrio. He tapped the lone tablet. "I believe you have something for me."

"Yes, Prefect." He set down the bag and lifted out the stone box. "I've brought Tribune Nepos home."

Saturninus rose and walked around the desk to take the box from him. As he read the name, a sad smile flitted across his face. "A laurel wreath...Nepos's father will appreciate what you chose for his son." Then he set it on the floor and sat on the edge of his desk.

"Your report said you'd be bringing him home after you caught his killer. Can I assume you have?"

"Yes, Prefect." He drew a breath. "One of his centurions was counterfeiting aurei, and Nepos was killed in the shop where they were doing that. The metalsmiths melted down his armor, burned the rest, and buried him across a field. My optio, Sartorus, found part of his crest that they failed to burn. We also found counterfeit dies in the shop. The smiths who knew exactly what happened ran away before I could interrogate them, so we'll never know everything."

He cleared his throat. "But I thought they must have buried him within a short distance from the shop. Centurion Acceptus and his men searched until they found the grave. I oversaw his cremation, so you can tell his father all was done in a proper manner for a noble Roman."

Saturninus crossed his arms. "If you couldn't talk to the smiths, how do you know who killed him?"

"Because he tried to kill me to keep me from discovering who he was. Verus killed Nepos after he began investigating the counterfeits in Carthago. He tried to kill me after I recovered Nepos's body and was getting close to discovering his killer's identity. Optio Sartorus prevented it. He came with me from the warehouse district here in Rome."

"Hmph." Saturninus glanced at the stone box by his feet. "So, it appears you were wise to take a man you knew you could trust from here. Your greatest enemy actually was wearing Roman armor. Titianus's inflexibility in interpreting Roman law was excessive at times, but he understood the criminal mind."

"That loyalty cost Sartorus more than I expected. He was severely injured saving me. I would be promoting him to centurion over Verus's district, but his injury is severe enough his arm might not recover enough to use a shield again. He might need a medical discharge. Until that's clear, I'm putting Centurion Longinus in charge of two districts. If Sartorus doesn't recover sufficiently, I'll consult Centurions Acceptus and Longinus as I decide whom to promote centurion over the harbor district."

"It sounds like you have Carthago well in hand." Saturninus rubbed his jaw. "Which brings us to the question of what to do with you going forward."

Glabrio straightened. Whatever Father and Saturninus had discussed this morning was about to be revealed.

Saturninus chuckled. "You're not as good as Titianus at masking what you're thinking. I see I've surprised you. I had planned on you serving in Carthago for a year, which would put you there when Hadrian inspects the city in late summer. But I've changed my mind."

Glabrio's heart rate ramped up. *God, please let the change be a good one.*

"It seems a better plan to leave you there as tribune of the XIII for much longer. Your unusual skills as an investigator let you solve the murder of your predecessor. Frankly, I didn't expect that. You appear to be doing a good job in general, at least according to the letters I've received from the duumvirs. The provincials lack the broader perspective of those serving the entire empire, not just their local interests. It might be best for all concerned if I leave you serving where they are delighted to have you."

Glabrio's mouth twitched as he fought to suppress a grin. "As long as you remain urban prefect, I'd be please to serve there. I agree that the needs of the city and what I can bring to them are well matched."

He cleared his throat. "About my optio Sartorus, he kept me from being killed, but he may have lost much of the use of his shield arm as a result. If that turns out to be the case, I would like to request that he be given an honorable discharge for medical reasons with a bonus payment for the courageous sacrifice he made to save his tribune. He served exceptionally for seven years, and his injury will limit what he can do in the future."

"That seems reasonable. I'll authorize the bonus now whether he remains in service or not."

"If he requires that discharge, I'd like to continue to use him as my personal aide, at least part time, rather than train a replacement from the Carthago troops. If need be, I'll pay the cost myself. Loyalty nearly unto death is hard to find. Besides, I couldn't find anyone as good to replace him."

"It was fortunate that you took him as your aide from Rome. But now that you've killed your disloyal centurion, I expect the rest of the cohort will serve you and Rome faithfully enough."

Saturninus chuckled. "Do what you feel most appropriate with Sartorus. I'll authorize it. I have no doubt a man of your inflexible honesty will do what's right."

"Thank you, Prefect."

"He saved my good friend's son. That's worth more to me than you probably realize." As he looked at the box, a shadow of sadness crossed Saturninus's face. "I wish someone had been there to do the same for Nepos."

When his eyes refocused on Glabrio, their expression hardened. "I won't be making special arrangements for you to meet Hadrian since you won't be needing the emperor's good opinion to succeed in Carthago. Since you can't resist telling people what you think is the truth instead of what they need to hear, that's better for everyone. I told your father this posting would be an excellent opportunity to make an impression on our emperor. It could have been. But I can see you telling Hadrian something he doesn't want to hear, and I don't want to have to tell your father you got yourself killed because you can't keep what you think is the truth to yourself."

Glabrio opened his mouth, but closed it before speaking. What he would have said would only have proven Saturninus's point.

"Thank you, Prefect. I appreciate you doing what's best for all concerned."

He spoke that with full sincerity, but it still drew Saturninus's snort.

"As reward for a job well done, you can stay a few days before you return to Carthago."

"Thank you, Prefect. I look forward to continuing to serve Rome and the people of Carthago to the best of my ability."

"I'm sure you will." Saturninus flicked his hand toward the door. "I'm expected elsewhere when I finish these. You're dismissed."

As Saturninus resumed his seat at the desk, Glabrio struck his chest, executed a parade turn, and strode from the office.

The doors closed behind him, and as soon as he was far enough away the guards wouldn't see, he couldn't stop the grin.

Thank You, God, for providing everything I wanted and more.

Chapter 69

COMING HOME

Martina's town house, Carthago, evening of Day 52

Martina stood at her loom by Platana, passing the shuttle back and forth. She glanced over her shoulder. Sartorus sat in in Volero's chair, watching Platana with a contented smile.

It had been so long since Gaius left. He'd said it would be less than two weeks. But today was the fifteenth day, and still no sign of him. Surely, he must be coming soon. If anything had happened to him, wouldn't she feel it somehow?

When the one-then-three pattern of knocks echoed in the vestibulum, Platana called for Lepus, but Martina herself started for the door before he came from the kitchen. He shot past her to pull back the bolt, but she was only a few steps behind him.

The door swung open to reveal her tribune in full armor—red-crested helmet, bronze cuirass, and the smell of new leather. Behind him stood a donkey cart loaded with several locked chests.

"Welcome, Tribune Glabrio." She swept her hand toward the peristyle. "Won't you come in?"

His crooked smile warmed her to the core. "Thank you, Publilia Martina. I believe I will."

He turned to the man leading the donkey. "Bring all those in and put them there." He pointed at the worn-out chairs. When the last chest was carried in, he paid, and they left.

"I've come to speak with Sartorus first, and then I'd like to show you something."

Palm up, she pointed at Sartorus. "We've been taking good care of him, like you asked."

He lifted off his helmet and handed it to Lepus. "Put this in my room."

The boy ran his hand along the red horsehair crest as he walked away.

As they strolled into the peristyle, Gaius took her hand.

She squeezed it and got a squeeze in return. "It's good to have you home, Gaius."

"It's good to be home." He settled into the chair across the gameboard from Sartorus, and she returned to her loom.

◆

"So, how are you doing?" Glabrio crossed his arms. It was good to see his friend back to his normal color.

"It could be worse." Platana turned from her loom and smiled at him. He raised a hand in response. "I've had the most attentive nurse a man could ever have." He lowered his voice. "Makes a man want to prolong his recovery. Life in quarters…it can't compete with this."

Glabrio tapped Sartorus's good arm. "No, seriously, how are you doing."

"It's too soon to tell. Losing a lot of blood tires a man out. I'm mostly over that." He flexed his left fingers. "They all seem to be working. It's too soon to tell how the elbow will heal. The gladiator physician has come twice. He shakes his head a lot, mutters something about it's not healing like he expected, but he won't say if that's good or bad." The smile and shrug summed up his feelings. "He expects it won't heal well enough, and I'll be discharged."

"I discussed this with Saturninus, just in case. He'll be sending a bonus for your service above and beyond in almost dying to save me. Half what your retirement bonus would have been. He's leaving it up to me to decide whether you take a medical discharge."

Sartorus's head drew back. "That much?"

"He appreciates what you did. He said he was sorry no one was there to do the same for Nepos."

Glabrio leaned back in the chair. "We can postpone the discharge until you're as healed as you're going to be. Then, if you can't handle a shield, I have Saturninus's permission to hire you as my aide to keep helping me as you have been. You just won't be a soldier anymore."

Sartorus's straight lips curved into a smile. "Sounds good to me. Maybe this is God's way of clearing the path to something better." He leaned over, tapped Glabrio's hand with the back of his own, and tipped his head toward Platana. "I wouldn't mind being a married man sooner than I expected."

Glabrio tapped his hand back. "I think it would be good if you were one." He lowered his voice to a near whisper. "I hope to be one myself soon."

◆

Martina jumped when she felt Gaius's hands on her shoulders. When she turned to face him, he wore his broadest smile.

"Since I'm going to be here in Carthago for a good long while, I brought some things back from Rome. Some of them are better left here than in my quarters." He slipped his hand into hers and entwined their fingers. "Come see."

He led her to the scruffy chairs and invited her to sit with a wave of his hand.

"You let me hide out here once while Sartorus was spying for me. It was the start of something I hope has given you as much pleasure as it has me."

"It has." Would he ever know how much she enjoyed his company? How great her joy had been when he told her he'd decided he believed? How much she wished she could become his wife?

He dropped to one knee by the first trunk. From inside his tunic, he pulled out a chain holding several keys and selected one. A turn of the key, and he flipped back the lid.

"Scrolls?"

"I brought my library from Rome. I was only going to be here for a year when I first came, but I find Carthago suits me so well I've arranged to stay longer. I'll be tribune here for as long as Saturninus remains the urban prefect. Since that will probably be until either he or Hadrian dies, I've moved some of my favorite things here." He handed her a scroll. "I was hoping I could leave them with you for a while. Of course, you can read anything you want."

She unrolled the scroll. It was part of Plinius's *Natural History*.

Gaius picked up another and handed it to her. "I have his complete works here. And Tacitus and many others you'll discover as you sort through the chests."

"I love his writings. I'll be glad to look after your library."

He moved over to the next trunk and unlocked it.

The top codex was bound in leather with a rosebush in full flower engraved on it. He took it out but didn't hand it to her.

"Your copy of Marcus's writings thrilled my friends in Rome. Pompeia insisted I take a copy of each of the writings she's been copying for years. But a tribune's quarters aren't a safe place for Christian writings to be kept, especially so many of them." He handed her the codex.

She opened it to the first page and gasped. "It's the gospel written by the apostle John!" She closed it and clutched it to her chest. "Juliana always wanted to have this but was never able to find one. She said it was like sitting at Jesus's feet listening to him teach."

"Pompeia always says that, too." He stood and took her free hand. "So, I was hoping to keep them at my new wife's town house."

Her stomach twisted and flipped. "New wife? Your father arranged a marriage for you here?"

He'd always said his father would arrange a political marriage for him. But she'd expected that to be back in Rome, not here where she'd have to see them together and wish it was her.

"No, but he approved of the one I hope I've arranged for myself." He drew her to her feet before taking the codex from her and placing it on the chair. "That is, assuming you and Volero find me acceptable as your husband. I'm quite sure Volero will, but can you be happy with an arrogant Roman who sometimes offends people when he doesn't intend to? You can work on improving how I deal with people."

Joy coursed through her. All that she'd dreamed of, all that she'd prayed for in a husband…God had given it all.

She slipped her arms around him. "I'm quite sure I can."

"Then everything Pompeia sent is my engagement gift to you. I'll expect you to read them to me and explain what I don't understand." He pushed a loose strand of hair back from her forehead. "I've found you're quite good at that, no matter how hard the question." He bent over and kissed where the hair had been.

She went up on tiptoes for the kiss that promised a future of delight as husband and wife.

When their lips parted, she drew her finger down his cheek and stopped on his lips. "I suppose this means you don't have to pay me back."

His chuckle warmed her from head to toes. "I always pay my debts, but not always with money. I think we can work something out over the next forty years." His mouth straightened. "I owe you my life, for ransoming me in Utica and for not giving up until I realized Jesus had ransomed me for eternal life." Then the twinkle returned to his eyes. "Father plans to come visit soon. These old chairs are good enough for me, but we should get a few new ones for the peristyle and tablinum that are fit to sit on before he gets here."

"We should, but we'll still leave those there. Sitting in one occasionally will remind us of how much we've been blessed." She stroked his stubbly cheek again. "Will you be staying for dinner?"

"I need to check in at headquarters. I came straight here from the ship. I'll come back for dinner, but I'll sleep in quarters until we're married."

"Will that be long?" She nibbled her lip. The sooner, the better.

"Father plans to sail down for our marriage. He said it would take him a few days to arrange his affairs before he could leave." His lips brushed her forehead. "Pompeia and Sabina would love to come, but they're too close to having their babies for that to be wise. Titus and Kaeso won't leave them with the births coming so soon." He wrapped a loose tendril of hair around his finger. "When they do meet you, they'll see how God has blessed me as much as He did them."

He released her hair to draw his fingertip along her jaw. "But their business manager Melis will come. He'll want to take some of your applique red ware back to test out in the glass shop in Rome. I expect he'll become a regular customer."

"I'll invite Atriensis, and they can talk. He's always been like an uncle to me, and he'll keep our faith secret when I ask him to."

"He loves you like a daughter. He warned me against doing anything to put you in danger or break your heart. As your guardian, Volero has to join us. I'd want him anyway, but not his wife and daughters."

"Artoria will hate to see me take the matrimonial prize she wanted for Priscilla, but if she gets to host a former consul of Rome at a special dinner at her house, which everyone of importance will want to attend, she'll get over it."

"Father is a master at making people think he's pleased to be in their company. He's had plenty of practice with the socially ambitious matrons of Rome. He'll find your aunt amusing."

"Is he the one who taught you how to make anyone feel like you care what they think?"

"It must be a family trait. It comes naturally to both of us."

He released her and picked up John's codex. "I do need to go to headquarters, but that can wait a little longer. I think we should celebrate my return in the best way I know."

His eyes shone with love as he held it out to her. "Would you like to read to me for a while?"

Finis

I'D LOVE TO HEAR FROM YOU!

If you enjoyed this book, it would be a real gift to me if you would post a review at the retailer you purchased it from. A good review is like a jewel set in gold for an author. Other great places to share reviews are Goodreads and BookBub. If you've read others in the series, it would be great if you post a review of those, too.

I'd also love to hear from you at carol-ashby.com or directly at carolashbyauthor@gmail.com.

Want to hear about upcoming releases in the Light in the Empire series and free gifts only for newsletter subscribers?

For free gifts and other special offers, advance notices of upcoming releases, and info about my latest writing adventures, please sign up for my newsletter at https://carol-ashby.com/newsletter/.

LIGHT *in the* EMPIRE SERIES

Dangerous times, difficult friendships,
lives transformed by forgiveness and love.

Truth and Honor is the twelfth volume in the Light in the Empire series, which follows the interconnected lives of several Roman families during the reigns of Trajan and Hadrian. Each can be read stand-alone. The fourteen novels of the series will take you around the Empire, from Germania and Britannia to Thracia, Dacia, and Judaea and, of course, to Rome itself.

Although each can be read stand-alone, here are some groupings based on the appearance of some characters in more than one story.

Drusus family: *The Legacy, True Freedom, Second Chances, Forgiven*

Lentulus family: *Blind Ambition, Faithful*

Crassus family: *Blind Ambition, Faithful, Honor Bound*

Sabinus family: *The Legacy, Honor Bound, More Than Honor, What Matters Most*

Glabrio family: *What Matters Most, Truth and Honor*

Titianus family: *True Freedom, More Than Honor, What Matters Most, Truth and Honor*

Brutus family: *Faithful, True Freedom, Honor Bound*

The Dacians: *Hope Unchained, Hope's Reward, True Freedom*

COMING IN IN 2023 AND 2024: PLEASE HELP ME CHOOSE!

Who would you like to see in a future story?

I grew to love several of the characters in *Truth and Honor* while I was writing. That usually happens, and sometimes a future story takes shape in my head even before I finish. But more often the next hero or heroine is chosen because readers tell me who needs to come back as a story lead.

Readers who loved Galen as a teen in *Blind Ambition* wanted to see him as a grown man, so he became the hero in *Faithful*. People who asked for Brutus and Africanus to have their own story found out what happened to them in *Honor Bound*.

Since people kept asking what happened to Leander's beloved but long-lost sister in *True Freedom*, it was clear Ariana would need her own story in *Hope Unchained*. People who met Ursus in *Hope Unchained* asked what happened to him, so he returned with his childhood name of Matti in his quest to know God better in *Hope's Reward*.

In *What Matters Most*, Septimus, who was rather like a Great Dane puppy in *Honor Bound*, comes back four years older, and Tribune Titianus from *More Than Honor* and *True Freedom* faces the most dangerous assignment of his life. I'm SO glad people asked for still more of them after the earlier books.

For those of you who asked for more of Titianus's apprentice Glabrio, I hope you've enjoyed his story in this book.

But there are many more characters in the books of the series that I would like to spend more time with, and I hope there are some for you, too. Who would you most like to see in a future story? What was it about them that made you want more of them? I'd love to hear what you think. It will guide what I write next.

Some possibilities:

Aulus of *True Freedom*?

Septimus or Manius of *Honor Bound, More Than Honor,* and *What Matters Most?*

Someone else I haven't mentioned? (I can't wait to see who shows up here!)

Please tell me who you'd love to see again as a comment at carol-ashby.com or directly at carolashbyauthor@gmail.com!

I'm thinking about writing a short story or novella about someone from Sextus's or Calvia's households in *Honor Bound* or Gracchus's household in *Hope Unchained* and *Hope's Reward* to give to newsletter subscribers. Which would you rather have?

Please go to my website, carol-ashby.com, and share your thoughts in the comment box. Sign up for the newsletter, and you'll get the story when I finish it. Looking forward to hearing from you!

Historical Note

In the late Republic and early Empire, two Roman coins were made with a very high content of precious metals. The aureus was a gold coin, and the denarius was made with a silver content of up to 98% with the remaining metal being copper. The coins were about the same size, but the aureus was almost twice as heavy because gold is 1.84 times heavier than the same volume of silver. Twenty-five denarii were equal to one aureus. While the silver content of a denarius varied from 98% under Julius Caesar, 90% under Augustus, 80% under Trajan (AD 107), and down to 73 to 66% under Commodus (AD 180-192), the aureus remained essentially pure gold.

Since the cost of copper was only 1/100 that of silver, counterfeiters could make a huge profit by making a coin blank of copper instead of the denarius's standard silver-copper alloy, applying a thin layer of silver or a high-silver alloy, and stamping a pattern like that of a genuine denarius into the silver. When copper is alloyed with silver, the color of the alloy is essentially the same as pure silver up to about 30% copper. Similarly, a coin blank could be gilded and stamped with the pattern of an aureus.

During the Republic, the responsibility for minting gold, silver, and copper-based coins belonged to the Senate. There was a single main mint in Rome at the Temple of Moneta. In the 2nd century BC, the Senate gave military commanders the authority to mint coins to pay their troops, so some coins were minted away from Rome where a legion was stationed. During the Empire, minting of gold and silver coins was restricted to imperial mints under the control of the emperor, although the copper-alloy coins remained the responsibility of the Senate. The imperial mints were spread around the empire, and their locations changed over time.

Each time there was a change of emperor or some important event that he wanted to commemorate, new denarii and aurei would be minted with the portrait of the emperor on one side and a pattern on the back that served to promote the emperor's authority and spread his message. Frequent changes of the back image and of the abbreviations on the front that described the emperor's accomplishments and titles made it easy for someone to miss subtle differences between genuine imperial-issue coins and decent counterfeits.

Counterfeiting gold and silver coins was considered serious enough to make it a capital crime. The first official law against it was established during the Republic in 84 BC, but the text of that law has been lost. However, in 81 BC, the *lex Cornelia de falsis* (Cornelius's Law of falsity) declared that anyone who adulterated gold or made counterfeit silver coins broke the law. Anyone who could have prevented it and didn't earned the same punishment as the counterfeiters.

The list of forbidden activities is quite explicit: anyone who adulterated gold and silver coins, washed them (to remove part of the noble metal), melted them, shaved them, corrupted them, defaced them, and rejected the coins stamped with the face of the emperor (except counterfeit ones), faced the penalty for counterfeiting. High-status Roman citizens (senators and some equestrians) might be sent into exile. People born free were sent to the mines or were crucified. For gold coins, they might be fed to the beasts. Slaves and freedmen were subject to the "highest punishment," which was often crucifixion.

The use of tin or lead to make coins that looked like silver was also prohibited.

There were several ways to apply the precious metal surface layer to the base-metal substrate. Since the denarius was roughly the wages for a day's labor of a skilled worker, many more denarii than aurei were in circulation. That made it popular for counterfeiting. The metal used for the body of the coin was usually copper but sometimes bronze or lead.

One way of applying the surface silver layer was coating the surface with what was essentially a silver-copper solder. Another way of applying the silver was with a layer of silver foil that was attached to the surface either by soldering or by heating to form a mixed layer of silver and copper that melts at a lower temperature than either pure metal (a eutectic alloy). Other ways to apply silver include dipping the coin in molten silver, brushing molten silver onto the coin, or dusting the coin with powdered silver and heating it until the silver melts.

This type of counterfeit made from a base metal core plated with a precious metal is called a fourrée (derived from the French for "stuffed").

Gold layers could be applied as thin gold foil, as with silver. Another technique popular in ancient times is called fire gilding. The gold was dissolved in mercury to make an amalgam with a buttery consistency. The amalgam was applied to the base-metal blank, and the coated blank was heated in a furnace to drive off the mercury, leaving the gold coating behind.

Blanks of copper or bronze were usually cast in round, flat molds. After the precious metal layer was applied, the blank was placed between two dies engraved with the front and back images of the coin and then struck while hot. Dies were made of either iron or high-tin-content bronzes. The obverse (front) die with the emperor's portrait was stationary, and the upper die with the reverse pattern was hand-held. Each coin blank was placed between the dies, heated, and struck individually. There was no fixed rotation between the front and back patterns.

For lower value coins made of brass, bronze, or copper, a two-piece clay mold would be made from an original coin. Molten metal, usually a leaded copper alloy, was poured into the molds. After the metal hardened, the ceramic mold was removed and any slight projection on the edge where the metal entered the mold was smoothed away.

The counterfeiting of gold and silver coins had extreme penalties applied by Roman law. Those same laws say nothing about coins made of copper or its alloys of brass and bronze. So, it appears counterfeiting of the lesser value coins that were not made in the imperial mints was not regarded as a serious crime. Low-value coins used for everyday purchases were often minted locally by cities and provinces to meet the high demand and frequent shortages. Adding counterfeits to this mix could even help reduce the shortage. In remote provinces, having an adequate supply of coins was a common problem. In Roman Britain, many of the coins in circulation were locally produced, including many counterfeits.

There were several ways to identify a counterfeit coin. Shallow cuts to see if there was a base-metal underlayer, small areas where the silver or gold surface had broken and fallen away to expose the layer beneath, and sometimes weight were used. For an aureus, a counterfeit with a copper core weighed about half as much as a pure gold coin. For the denarius, depending on the fraction of silver in the official coins (which ranged from 98 to less than 70% before AD 200), a counterfeit coin in the hand felt about the same weight as the genuine coin. For someone not accustomed to handling genuine aurei frequently, even the lightness of a counterfeit aureus could easily go unnoticed.

For a short time at the end of the Republic, the edge of the denarius was serrated, both to show that the interior of the coin was the same as the surface and to show the edge of the coin had not been shaved. While serration was meant to be an anti-counterfeiting technique, counterfeiters simply serrated their products as well.

In *Truth and Honor*, the watchful eyes of Titianus's business manager spotted counterfeit coins given to one of their ship captains in Carthago. Tribune

Glabrio's enthusiasm over assuming command of the Urban Cohort there with a serious crime to investigate drew Titianus's warning to be careful. People who would engage in a highly profitable crime that carried the death penalty would do anything to keep from getting caught. When Glabrio arrived in Carthago, he learned how wise that warning was.

For more about life in the Roman Empire at its peak, please go to https://carolashby.com . Articles on law enforcement by the Urban Cohort and a longer article on counterfeiting are there.

The Historical People

OF TRUTH AND HONOR

Many of the characters in *Truth and Honor* are based on historical people. To the extent possible, I've stayed true to what is known of them in the historical records.

Special effort was made to get the historical details right for Emperor Hadrian, and the story is set in AD 128, the year in which Hadrian toured the provinces along the African coast of the Mediterranean. Whoever was tribune of the Urban Cohort when he passed through Carthago, the capital of Africa Proconsularis, would have met the emperor, making it an ideal time for a politically ambitious man to serve in that position.

Several of the characters in *Truth and Honor* have either served as consul or want to be consuls. Under the Republic, consul was the second-highest level of the *cursus honorum,* which was a sequence of political offices of increasing importance. The first magistrate position on the cursus was *quaestor,* the post Nepos was returning to Rome to assume. Before Augustus, consuls had both military and political responsibilities. All had military experience because they served as military tribunes before starting their political climb. The two consuls were elected by an assembly of the people to govern Rome and its provinces together for one year. One was in charge, and they alternated being in charge each month. After that, they often served as the governor (proconsul) of a province.

After Augustus established the empire, most of the former responsibilities and power of the consuls were transferred to the emperor. Consuls were nominated by the emperor and then formally elected by an assembly of the people. Several consuls were selected each year, with the first pair of consuls serving in a given year (ordinary consuls) giving their names to that year in the Roman dating system. The consuls who served later in the year were suffect consuls. The ordinary consulship was more prestigious than the suffect because the year was named after them. For the year AD 124, Manius Acilius Glabrio was one of the ordinary consuls, so people around the empire would recognize his name.

After finishing their few months as consul, the ex-consuls often became governors of the provinces that were administered by the Senate. Egypt and the provinces on the frontier where legions were stationed were imperial provinces, and their governors were chosen by the emperor. The governor of an imperial province with one legion was usually the legion commander (legate). If there was more than one legion, their legates were subordinate to the provincial governor.

POLITICAL CHARACTERS

Hadrian: Caesar Traianus Hadrianus, Emperor of Rome, AD 117 to AD 138

M. Lollius Paullinus Valerius Saturninus (59): Urban Prefect 124-134, also consul in 125; (commander of fictional Gaius Glabrio),

M'. Acilius Glabrio: consul ordinarius in 124 (Jan-April) (Father of fictional Gaius Glabrio)

M' Acilius Glabrio: consul ordinarius in 91 (January–April); exiled in 91; executed in 95 by Domitian for being Christian; (grandfather of fictional Gaius Glabrio)

M'. Acilius Glabrio or Aviola: suffect consul under Nero in 54; alive when son/grandson executed in 95.

M. Acilius Glabrio: consul suffectus in 33 BC, governor of Africa 25 BC

M'. Acilius Aviola, consul in 122, cousin to Acilius Glabrio.

L. Stertinius Noricus: governor of Africa 127/128, consul suffectus in 113

L. Publilius Celsus, consul suffectus in 102, and consul ordinarius in 115; executed for plot to assassinate Hadrian in 118.

A. = Aulus, D. = Decimus, L .= Lucius, M = Marcus, M'. = Manius, Q. = Quintus

(There were only 20 common first names in use at this time, so abbreviations were often used. Only family and close friends addressed a person using only their first name.)

HISTORICAL LITERARY FIGURES

Poets:

Marcus Annaeus Lucanus (Lucan, 39-65) poet; writer of epic poem about the Julius Caesar-Pompey Civil War, friend then conspirator against Nero; forced to commit suicide.

Quintus Horatius Flaccus (Horace, 65-8 BC): leading Roman lyric poet during the time of Augustus.

Publius Papinius Statius (46-96): composer of epic and shorter poems, including odes.

Lucius Cincius Alimentus (active before 200 BC): senator and author. Served as praetor in Sicily in 209 BC, commanding 2 legions,. Wrote account of his capture and imprisonment during the Second Punic War, including his talk with Hannibal. Wrote *Annals* before 202 BC.

Pūblius Ovidius Nāsō (Ovid, 43 BC -AD 17/18: Leading poet during Augustus's reign. Exiled by Augustus in AD 8 to a town on the Black Sea. Maybe for his erotic poem, *Ars Amatoria* that was subversive to Augutus's moral legislation, maybe for knowing about a conspiracy against him by the husband of Augustus's granddaughter Julia the Younger.

Publius Vergilius Maro (Virgil, 70-19 BC): supreme Latin poet who wrote the *Aeneid*, the 12-volume epic poem about the founding of Rome.

Historians and natural historian:

Publius Cornelius Tacitus (Tacitus, AD 56-120): Historian who wrote the Annals (*Annales*) and the Histories (*Historiae*) spanning the history of the Roman Empire from the death of Augustus (AD 14) to the death of Domitian (AD 96). Other works include *Germania, Agricola, and Dialogus*. In the Annals, he describes the persecution of Christians under Nero and provides a nonbiblical report of the crucifixion of Jesus of Nazareth.

Lucius Cincius Alimentus (active before 200 BC): Senator, military commander and historian. Served as *praetor* in Sicily in 209 BC, commanding 2 legions. Wrote an account of his capture and imprisonment during the Second Punic War, including his talk with Hannibal. Wrote his Annals before 202 BC.

Gaius Plinius Secundus (Pliny the Elder, AD 23/24 - 79): Author, naturalist, army and naval commander. Admiral of the fleet at Misenum when Vesuvius erupted, took fleet to rescue people at Pompei, stayed to study the eruption, and died from poisonous gases. Wrote the encyclopedia *Naturalis Historia* (Natural History), which comprised 37 books compiled into 10 volumes.

For more about life in the Roman Empire at its peak,
please go to carolashby.com.

Discussion Guide

1) Glabrio is the son of a family that's been politically important for centuries. What kind of pressures does that put on him? Is he happy with the future his father has planned? Why does he choose "unimportant" people for his closest friends? How does that affect the decisions he makes? How did that change over the course of the story? Have you ever experienced similar pressure? If so, how did you handle it?

2) Before the story began, Martina had changed from a broken-hearted girl into a strong Christian woman because of her step-grandmother Juliana. What were the problems that caused in her life? What were the blessings? Her pagan grandfather was finally asking about Jesus just before he died, but she didn't know his final decision. Have you or someone you know faced that same uncertainty? What was the effect on the survivor?

3) When the elderly neighbor who had met Apostle Peter lead Sartorus to faith, what did that do to his family relationships? How did he deal with that? What were the challenges he faced as a soldier who was a Christian? How did he deal with them? In his position, what do you think you would have done?

4) Volero begins the story with jealousy of a long-dead brother affecting his attitude toward his niece. How did the death of his father affect his opinion of Martina? How did that change their relationship? Do you think he'll ever consider whether her faith is more than an unbelievable superstition? Why or why not? Do you have a Volero in your own life? If so, how do you handle that?

5) Artoria is a socially ambitious woman who resents her niece, Martina. How would you describe her relationship with her husband, Volero? With her daughters? How did she respond to Martina's long-suffering nature? What do you think she would do if she learned the family secret? Have you known someone like her? How did you deal with them?

6) Centurion Verus and the councilman's son, Messala, are both attracted to what counterfeiting can give them. What did each hope to gain from their partnership? When troubles come from their illegal activity, how did each react? Have you ever had to deal with a ruthless person? What did you do?

7) Tribune Glabrio and Optio Sartorus came from very different backgrounds,

and their relative ranks would normally have kept them from being close, especially in an extremely class-conscious society like ancient Rome. What started to change that? Why did acquaintance grow into close friendship? Have you ever had a close friendship grow with someone you least expected?

8) Glabrio had listened to his closest friends in Rome (Titus, Kaeso, and Pompeia) try to share their faith, and he'd been uninterested. Why? What made him listen to what Sartorus and Martina told him? What struggles did he face as he considered what he had believed versus what his friends believed? Have you or someone you know faced the same struggles?

9) When Glabrio returned to Rome to tell his father what he'd decided to do, what reaction did he expect? How did his father react? Have you ever been in a situation where what you believed was the right choice threatened relationships with family and closest friends? How did you handle that?

10) *Truth and Honor* is a story of duty and honor, of reluctance to consider what would challenge a person's chosen path, of friendship opening the door for sharing one's faith, and of courage to accept the truth and whatever that brings. What touched you most? What made you think about what your own choices would be?

Who would you like to see in a future short story or novella?

I grew to love several of the characters in *Truth and Honor* while I was writing. That usually happens, and often the next story for a character takes shape in my head even before I finish. Sometimes it's requests from readers that reveal who should be the focus of a future story. There are many people in *Truth and Honor* and all my other novels that I would like to spend more time with, and I hope there are some for you, too. Who would you most like to see in a future story? What was it about them that made you want more of them? I'd love to hear what you think.

Please go to my website, carol-ashby.com, and share your thoughts in the comment box. Sign up for the newsletter, and you'll get the story when I finish it. Looking forward to hearing from you!

Glossary

Actuaria: a merchant galley with sails and oars, usually 30 to 50

Amphora: a tall clay jar with two handles and a narrow neck used for transport of liquids

Aureus: (pl. *aurei*) a gold Roman coin worth 25 denarii

Atrium: the open central court of a Roman house with enclosed rooms on all sides; replaced in North African town houses by a wide *vestibulum* and sometimes a reception room (*basilica*) off the vestibulum

Caldarium: A hot, steamy room at a Roman bath complex with tubs of hot water sunk into the floor

Centurion: 1st level officer over 80 men; rises through the ranks based on merit

Client: one with obligations to a patron; could be of same or lower status as patron. When slaves were freed, the former owner became their patron

Cognomen: the third name of the 3-part Roman name, the surname or family name

Colonia: a settlement of retired military veterans (Roman citizens) with special political rights

Consul: highest elected political office, nominated by emperor; presided over Senate and judged special cases, could become governors of some provinces after serving

Cursus honorum: the sequence of public offices held by Roman politicians

Denarius: (pl. *denarii*) silver Roman coin worth 1.13 drachmas; worth about one day's living wage

Domina: female head of a Roman household

Domus: town house of the upper classes and wealthy freedmen with indoor courtyards (atrium and peristyle), many rooms, and a garden

Duumvir: each of two magistrates or officials holding a joint office

Equestrian order: 2nd highest class of Roman citizens; required personal wealth greater than 100,000 denarii

Familia: the Roman family unit consisting of the paterfamilias, his married and unmarried children regardless of age, his son's children, and his slaves

Freedman: a freed slave who owes support and service as a client to his former owner

Gladius: short thrusting sword used by the Roman military and some gladiators

Gorgon: Medusa and her sisters with snakes for hair and the power to turn anyone who looked at them to stone

Lanista: the head trainer of a gladiatorial school

Latrunculi: military strategy board game involving trapping and removing captured stones

Legate: commander of a legion

Legion: unit of the Roman army consisting of about 6000 Roman citizens

Ludus: (plural l*udi*) gladiator training school; also rents bodyguards

Optio: (plural *optiones*) Roman junior officer ranked below centurion

Palla: rectangular cloth wrap worm by Roman women

Paterfamilias: (plural *patres familias*) Oldest living male of an extended Roman family, the patriarch who owns everything

Peregrine: a person who is not a Roman citizen

Peristyle: a space within a building, such as a court or internal garden, surrounded by a row of columns

Praetor: a Roman magistrate ranking below consul, serves as a judge

Praetorian Guard: military unit serving as bodyguards and intelligence agents for the emperor

Praetorian Prefect: an equestrian serving as commander of the Praetorian Guard

Quaestor: the first magistrate position on the political career path for senators

Raeda: a four-wheeled closed-in carriage

River Styx: a river in Hades across which Charon carried dead souls for a fee (Greek mythology)

Salutation: daily ritual during which prominent citizens received clients and others seeking favors

Salve: hello, standard Roman greeting

Senatorial order: highest class of Roman citizens; required personal wealth greater than 250,000 denarii

Sestertius: (plural sesterces) bronze Roman coin worth 1/4 denarius

Salve: hello, the standard Latin greeting

Strigil: an instrument with a curved blade used to scrape sweat and dirt from the skin

Sui iuris: independent of their paterfamilias, most often through his death

Taberna: tavern or shop selling prepared food

Tablinum: the main office and reception room for the Roman master of the house

Tabula: popular Greco-Roman board game, often played with betting, similar to backgammon

Tepidarium: the warm room at a Roman bath complex with radiant heat from floor and walls

Toga: a long (10 to 20 feet) garment with one curved edge worn only by Roman citizens

Tribune: high-ranking officer from equestrian or senatorial order

Triclinium: dining room with couches arranged along three sides of a low table

Urban Cohort: one of four military police units under the urban prefect; 1 tribune over 6 centurions and about 500 men

Urban Prefect: senator serving as quasi-mayor of Rome with administrative and judicial powers to maintain order in the city; commander of the Urban Cohort

Vale: goodbye, the standard Latin farewell

Vestibulum: passage between the outer door and the interior of a town house (*domus*); a wide room used for a reception area for clients in North African town houses, a narrow passageway in a domus in Rome

Scripture References

The only Christian writing Martina had available was a codex of the gospel of Mark (Marcus) that had belonged to her step-grandmother, Juliana, who led her to faith. So, all her readings and almost all of the references in *Truth and Honor* are from the Gospel of Mark. Two translations were used in the text: the ESV and CSB.

Mark played a vital role in establishing the church in North Africa and Egypt. According to Coptic historical tradition, Mark had joined Peter in his missionary work during the early 40s and returned to Libya and Egypt during the reign of Claudius to start the church there. He mostly remained in Alexandria as the head of the church until his martyrdom. Coptic chronology has him in Africa (the area of Cyrene in present-day Libya or Alexandria in Egypt) from AD 43 until his death in 68.

Eusebius reported in his *Ecclesiastical History* that early Christian traditions place Mark in Africa from as early as the first years of Claudius (41-44) to as late as the reign of Nero (54-68). He provides a specific date for Mark's arrival in Alexandria as the third year of the reign of Emperor Claudius, which was AD 43. It's believed that Mark wrote down the sermons of Peter in Rome in AD 42-43. He left for Alexandria in AD 43 and, on his way to Egypt, passed through Cyrene, where his family originated and he might have been born. He was the leader of the Alexandrian church until he was martyred there in AD 68.

Since Mark was a leader in establishing the church in Africa, a wealthy woman like Martina's step-grandmother might have been able to get a copy of the Gospel of Mark.

In *Truth and Honor*, everything Martina shared with Glabrio is limited by what she could read in the gospel of Mark, which presents shorter versions of many of the events than one finds in Matthew, Luke, and John.

Chapter 48:
Mark 5:21-24, 35-43 (ESV)
Luke 7:10-17 Paraphrased by Sartorus

Chapter 49:
Mark 1:15 (CSB)
Mark 2:1-12, 23-25, 39-45 Paraphrased by Martina

Mark 12:28-34 (CSB)

Chapter 51:
Proverbs 9:10 (CSB)

Chapter 52:
Mark 10:32-45 Paraphrased in Glabrio's thoughts

Chapt 55:
Mark 10:17-30 (CSB)
Mark 8:34-36 Paraphrased by Martina

Chapter 59:
Mark 1:9-11, 21-28 (CSB)
Mark 3:8-12 (CSB)
Mark 9:2-10 (CSB)
Mark 14:60-64 (CSB)
Mark 15:33-39 (CSB)
Mark 10:45 (CSB)

Chapter 60:
Mar 16:15-16 (CSB)
Acts 1:8 (CSB)

Acknowledgements

Most of all, I thank God for the opportunity to tell this story of how faithful Christian friends were able to answer the objections of a man reluctant to believe because of what it might cost him.

No one can write the best book possible without the help of many others. Here are a few who helped me more than I can fully express.

I'm especially thankful for Lisa Garcia, my top alpha beta and dear friend who's helped me with every book in the series. She has a gift for spotting places that need additional work to get the story right. Her prayers while I'm writing the spiritual scenes and her insights on what seems real help the spiritual scenes become better. Her skill at spotting typos is as good as a copy editor. Her prayers always bless me in writing and in life.

I want to thank Sherril Stinnett, who's been my invaluable alpha beta for *Honor Bound, Hope's Reward, More Than Honor, What Matters Most,* and *Truth and Honor.* She's wonderful at spotting when something isn't quite right so I can fix it. I can tell she's praying when I'm writing the hard sections, especially where faith decisions are being made.

Christine Dillon, the inspiring author of the Grace series, was also a beta reader for this book. With an author's eye and the spiritual insight of a missionary, her help with a manuscript is always a blessing. It's such a pleasure to have her as my author buddy.

Terry Shoebotham is my local writing buddy and prayer partner for so much of life. She's a joy to talk with about books and life in general, especially over a plate of Indian food at our favorite buffet.

I want to thank Andrew Budek-Schmeisser for being my prayer partner and good friend as I've written so many of these books. Whenever I needed prayers for something that was giving me problems, an email would get him praying right away. Despite serious health problems, he's always been willing to share his knowledge of good writing, his spiritual insight, his artistic insights on the covers, and his expertise with horses, combat, and low-tech field medicine. He's helped me with *The Legacy, Faithful, Second Chances, True Free-*

dom, Hope Unchained, Honor Bound, Hope's Reward, More Than Honor, What Matters Most, and *Truth and Honor,* and with many brainstorming sessions about characters for future volumes. None of the books would have been the same without him.

I also want to thank Katie Powner for her prayers and wise comments. She is an award-winning author herself. For wonderful contemporary reads, you can't beat Katie's novels.

Thanks also to Mesu Andrews for praying with me for inspiration and for meeting deadlines when they got way too close and especially when they needed to be reset because they flew on by. As a leading writer of Biblical fiction, she shared her author insights on important spiritual scenes, too. Ancient history nerds belong together, and I can count on her to share my excitement about archeological discoveries from Old Testament and Roman times.

I'm not sure what I'd do without Ronda Wells, a fellow writer and medical doctor. She helped me figure out exactly what to do to Sartorus before his turning-point conversation with Glabrio. She teaches and writes blogs for authors on medical problems we can give our characters, and she shares my keen interest in the scientifically strange.

Dana McNeely, Tessa Afshar, and Anne Perreault have all been wonderful when I asked for prayers for inspiration and efficiency. It's also great to have people who appreciate it when I share the odd scientific results and archeological discoveries that fascinate me.

My line editor, Wendy Chorot, has once more brought her deep spiritual insight and her editorial skill to bear to make the spiritual scenes feel like real life. These are the most challenging part of the story, and she always helps me make them better. Working with her is a delight, too.

Roseanna White has designed another gorgeous cover for the series. Each one captures the location of the story and some of the key characters. Every time I think she can't possibly top the last one, but she always does.

I also thank my family (son Paul, daughter Lydia, her husband Paul, and granddaughter Payton) for the balance and joy they bring to my life.

But my greatest thanks to go my amazing husband, Jim, who makes every day a little bit better just by being here. The best of my heroes embody his kindness, patience, and humor. Having him as my husband is a true blessing.

About the Author

Carol Ashby has been a professional writer for most of her life, but her articles and books were about lasers and compound semiconductors (the electronics that make cell phones, laser pointers, and LED displays work). She still writes about light, but her Light in the Empire series tells stories of difficult friendships and life-changing decisions in dangerous times, where forgiveness and love open hearts to discover their own faith in Christ. Her fascination with the Roman Empire was born during her first middle-school Latin class. A research career in New Mexico inspires her to get every historical detail right so she can spin stories that make her readers feel like they're living under the Caesars themselves.

Read her articles about many facets of life in the Roman Empire at carolashby.com, or join her at her blog, The Beauty of Truth, at carol-ashby.com.

LIGHT *in the* EMPIRE SERIES

*Dangerous times, difficult friendships,
lives transformed by forgiveness and love.*

The Light in the Empire Series follows the interconnected lives of several Roman families during the reigns of Trajan and Hadrian. Join them as they travel the Empire, from Germania and Britannia to Thracia, Dacia, and Judaea and, of course, to Rome itself.

Although each can be read stand-alone, here are some groupings based on the appearance of some characters in more than one story.

Drusus family: *The Legacy, True Freedom, Second Chances, Forgiven*

Lentulus family: *Blind Ambition, Faithful*

Crassus family: *Blind Ambition, Faithful, Honor Bound*

Sabinus family: *The Legacy, Honor Bound, More Than Honor, What Matters Most*

Glabrio family: *What Matters Most, Truth and Honor*

Titianus family: *True Freedom, More Than Honor, What Matters Most, Truth and Honor*

Brutus family: *Faithful, True Freedom, Honor Bound*

The Dacians: *Hope Unchained, Hope's Reward, True Freedom*

Forgiven
Are some wounds too deep to forgive?

With a ruthless father who murdered for the family inheritance, Marcus Drusus plans to do the same. In AD 122, Marcus follows his brother Lucius to Judaea and plots to frame a zealot for his older brother's death. But the plan goes awry, and Lucius is rescued by a Messianic Jewish woman. Her oldest brother is a zealot and a Roman soldier killed her twin, but Rachel still persuades her father Joseph to put his love for Jesus above his anger with Rome and hide Lucius until he heals.

Rachel cares for the enemy, and more than broken bones heal as duty turns to love. Lucius embraces Joseph's faith in Jesus, but sharing a faith doesn't heal all wounds. Even before revealed secrets slice open old scars, Joseph wants no Roman son-in-law. With Rachel's zealot brother suspecting he's a Roman officer and his own brother planning to kill him when he returns, can Lucius survive long enough to change Joseph's mind?

If you're wondering what made the Drusus brothers become what they are, you can find out in *The Legacy*, set eight years earlier, and *True Freedom*, set four years earlier.

Blind Ambition
Sometimes you have to almost die to discover how you want to live.

It's AD 114 in the Roman province of Germania Superior, and being a Christian carries a death sentence. Tribune Decimus Lentulus is on the fast track for a stellar political career back in Rome. When he's robbed, blinded, and left for dead, a young German woman who follows the Way finds him. Valeria knows it's his duty to have her and her family killed, but she chooses to obey Jesus's command to love her enemy and takes him home to care for him.

It's not his miraculous recovery that shakes Decimus to his core. It's the way they love him like family and their unconcealed love for Jesus. In spite of himself, he falls in love with the Christian woman Rome wants him to kill. Can Valeria hide her faith to follow him into the circles of Roman power? Or should he abandon his ambition to help rule the Empire and choose to follow a different way?

Discover what happened to the people of *Blind Ambition* eight years later in *Faithful*.

The Legacy
When Rome has taken everything, what's left for a man to give?

Betrayed by a ruthless son who'll do anything for power and wealth, Publius Drusus faces death with an unanswered prayer—that his treasured daughter, Claudia, and honorable son, Titus, will someday share his faith. But who will lead them to the truth once he's gone?

Claudia's oldest brother Lucius arranged their father's execution to inherit everything, and now he's forcing her to marry a cruel Roman power broker. If only she could get to Titus—a thousand miles away in Thracia. Then the man who secretly told her father about Jesus arranges for his son Philip to sneak her out of Rome and take her to the brother she can trust.

A childhood accident scarred Philip's face. A woman's rejection scarred his heart. Claudia's gratitude grows into love, but what can Philip do when the first woman who returns his love hates the God he loves even more?

Titus and Claudia hunger for revenge on their brother and the Christians they blame for their father's deadly conversion. When Titus buys Miriam, a secret Christian, to serve his sister, he starts them all down a path of conflicting loyalties and dangerous decisions. His father's final letter commands the forgiveness Titus refuses to give. What will it take to free him from the hatred poisoning his own heart?

Join the people you met in *Second Chances* eight years earlier in this tale of betrayal, hatred, love, and forgiveness, where even bad things can work together for good.

  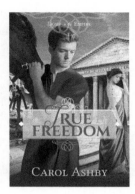

Faithful
Is the price of true friendship ever too high?

In AD 122, Adela, the fiery daughter of a Germanic chieftain, is kidnapped and taken across the Roman frontier to be sold as a slave. When horse-trader Otto wins her while gambling with her kidnappers, he entrusts her to his friend and trading partner, Galen. Then Otto is kidnapped by the same men, and Galen must track them half way across the Empire before his best friend loses a fight to the death in a Roman arena.

Adela joins Galen in the chase, hungry for vengeance. As the perilous journey deepens their friendship, will the kind, faithful man open her eyes to a life she never dreamed she'd want?

A trip to the heart of the Empire poses mortal danger to a man who follows Jesus, especially when he must seek the help of an enemy of the faith for Otto to survive. Tiberius hunted Christians when he governed Germania Superior and banished his own son when he became one.

When Tiberius learns sparing Galen offers a chance at reconciliation, he joins the trio on their journey home. Can his animosity toward the followers of Jesus survive a trip with the Christian man whose courage and faithfulness demand his respect?

Follow the continuing saga of the people you met in *Blind Ambition* from the frontier of Germany to the heart of the Empire in *Faithful*.

Second Chances
Must the shadows of the past destroy the hope of the future?

In AD 122, Cornelia Scipia, proud daughter of one of Rome's noblest families, learns her adulterous husband plans to betroth their daughter to the vicious son of his best friend. Over her dead body! Cornelia divorces him, reclaims her enormous dowry, and kidnaps her own daughter. She plans to start over with Drusilla a thousand miles away. No more husbands for her. But she didn't count on meeting Hector, the widowed Greek captain of the ship carrying her to her new life.

Devastated by the loss of his wife and daughter, Hector's heart begins to heal as he befriends Drusilla. Cornelia's sacrificial love for Drusilla and her courage and humor in the face of the unknown earn his admiration...as a friend. Is he ready for more?

Marriage to the kind, honest sea captain would give Drusilla the father she deserves...and Cornelia the faithful husband she's always longed for. But while her ex-husband hunts them to drag Drusilla back to Rome, secrets in Hector's past and the chasm between their social classes and different faiths erect complicated barriers to any future together. Will God give two lonely hearts a second chance at happiness?

Join the people you met in *The Legacy* eight years later in this tale of healing and new beginnings. Surprising things happen when God opens the door.

True Freedom
The chains we cannot see can be the hardest ones to break.

When Aulus runs up a gambling debt to his father's political enemy, he's desperate to pay it off before his father returns to Rome. His best friend Marcus suggests they fake the kidnapping of Aulus's sister Julia and use the ransom money. But when the man they hired kidnaps her for real, Aulus is catapulted into a desperate search to find her.

Torn from his childhood home by Rome's conquering armies and sold as a farm slave to labor until he dies, Dacius's faith gives him strength to bear what he must and serve without complaining. After a deadly accident makes him one of Julia's litter bearers, he overhears Marcus advising her brother to kidnap her. When Dacius almost dies thwarting the kidnapping, a Christian couple pretend Julia and Dacius are their children to keep her brother from finding them before her father returns.

But pretending to be free again makes returning to slavery more than Dacius can bear, while acting like a common woman opens Julia's eyes to dreams and destinies she never knew existed. With her brother closing in and her father almost home, can she find a way around Roman law and custom to free them both for the future they long for?

Find out what happens to Ariana's brother Diegis from *Hope Unchained* twelve years later in this tale of hope and a future never imagined until God opens the door.

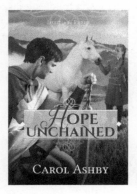 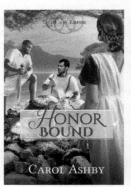 

Hope Unchained
Can the deepest loss bring the greatest gain?

Rome's conquering army took Ariana's family and freedom, but nothing can take her faith in Jesus. When she rescues a tribune's wife from certain death, her reward is freedom and a chance to free her brother and sister. But first she must catch up with the slave caravan before they vanish forever, and tracking them from Dacia to the coast seems impossible for one woman alone.

Discharged from the legion with a hand crippled by a Dacian knife, Donatus faces a future without hope. When the tribune asks him to escort Ariana on her quest, it's the only work he can find. It means four weeks with a Dacian woman and a gladiator bodyguard, but it takes money to eat. A man without options must take what he can get.

But a lot can happen in four weeks. Even battle-hardened men can be touched by love and forgiveness, and it's easier to face an enemy with a sword than to face the truth. When his moment of truth comes, what will Donatus choose, and what will that mean for both of them?

If you read *True Freedom* and wondered what happened to Leander's beloved sister Ariana, you can find out in *Hope Unchained*. If you wonder what happened to Ursus from *Hope Unchained*, he's the hero in *Hope's Reward*.

Honor Bound
Can the deepest loss bring the greatest gain?

Marcus Brutus owns estates, ships, and gladiator schools that increase his fortune daily, but his greatest treasures are his honor and his wife. When she reveals her faith in Jesus before dying after the birth of their son, he's consumed by hatred for the un-named Christian woman who led his beloved to abandon the Roman gods, making him lose her in this life and the next.

For fifteen years, Licinia's father hid her Christian faith. But now her father is dead, and a ruthless political enemy is hunting for anything to destroy her brother. When she becomes the target, her brother sends her to their estate in Germania. But is that far enough to protect her from an evil man who will stop at nothing?

When a carriage accident leaves Brutus injured and his best friend near death after rescuing Brutus's son, Licinia welcomes and cares for them. But her strange habits and his friend's unexpected recovery make Brutus suspect she's the Christian who corrupted his wife. When her brother's enemies come for her, does honor require him to protect her or turn her over as an enemy of Rome? And when Licinia's heart is drawn toward the pagan man who makes money off death, can she reconcile her growing affection with her love for Christ?

If you read *True Freedom* and wondered what happened to Africanus and Brutus, you can find out in *Honor Bound*.

Hope's Reward
Must the secrets we hide destroy our hope for a future?

For a gladiator slave, each time you step on the sand, it's kill or die. When Ursus decides to follow Jesus, he must choose to die the next time he's ordered to fight...or run away. He runs, taking again his childhood name, Matti. But he isn't just trying to escape. He's running to Thessalonica, where he hopes to find other Christians like the woman who led him to faith.

When Felicia's new husband, Falco, almost kills her in a fit of rage, her uncle won't help her end the marriage with his business partner. He will send her to her sister in Thessalonica, but only if she tells no one she plans to divorce Falco and demand her dowry back before she gets there. When Matti interrupts a robbery too late to save Felicia's money for traveling by sea, he offers to bodyguard and escort her overland to their mutual destination.

After Matti risks everything to save her from Falco's assassins, Felicia fears taking the danger to her sister's family. When his Christian friends take them in, she discovers the deepest desires of her heart. But will the secrets of Matti's past make a future together impossible?

If you wonder what happened to Ursus in *Hope Unchained*, he's the hero in *Hope's Reward*.

More Than Honor
Duty and honor had anchored his life, but only truth could set him free.

Devotion to duty and dogged determination make Tribune Titianus the most feared investigator of the Urban Cohort. Honor drives him to hunt down anyone who breaks Roman law, but it becomes personal when Lenaeus, his old tutor, is murdered in his own classroom. Why kill a respected teacher of the noble sons of Rome, a man who has nothing worth stealing and no known enemies? Had he learned something too dangerous to let him live?

Pompeia was only a girl when Titianus studied with Father before her family became Christians. She and her brother Kaeso can't move their school from the house where their father was killed. But what if the one who killed Father comes to kill again? Kaeso's friend Septimus insists they spend nights at his father's well-guarded home. But danger lurks there as well. As Titianus hunts for the murderer, will he discover their secret faith and arrest them as enemies of the Empire?

When Titianus gets too close to finding the killer, the hunter becomes the hunted. While he recovers at his cousin Septimus's house, Pompeia becomes the first woman to touch his heart. But a tribune's loyalty is sworn to Rome, no matter how he feels. When her faith is revealed, will truth and love mean more to him than honor? Does honor require more than devotion to Rome?

If you're curious about what happened with Manius's family, Kaeso's family, and Titianus a year before *What Matters Most*, you can find that story in *More Than Honor*.

What Matters Most
When faced with impossible choices, how do you decide what matters most?

For ten years, the incorruptible Tribune Titianus enforced Rome's laws. He's four days from leaving the Urban Cohort to teach at his brother-in-law Kaeso's school when Emperor Hadrian and the Praetorian Prefect draft him to secretly investigate and thwart an assassination plot...one that might involve his own commander. He can't refuse, but if Hadrian's enemies discover his Christian faith, will it mean death for everyone he loves?

Titianus's cousin Sabina returns as a widow to her father's house after six years of misery in a marriage that sealed a political alliance. She's dreading the next marriage Grandfather will arrange with someone seeking his support. When her brother's best friend Kaeso offers the encouragement and friendship she's longed for, can she escape the chains of society's expectations to gain what her heart desires?

The new tribune Glabrio wants two things as Titianus trains him: to discover for their commander who Titianus is investigating and to gain the support of Titianus's powerful relatives. Marrying Sabina would secure the backing of her grandfather, but because of the teacher, she's making choices no noblewoman should. As he gets closer to both his goals, will he realize in time what matters most?

If you're curious about what happened between Glabrio, Titianus, Kaeso, and their families almost a year before *Truth and Honor*, you can find that story in *What Matters Most*.

I'd Love to Hear from You!

If you enjoyed this book, it would be a real gift to me if you would post a review at the retailer you purchased it from. A good review is like a jewel set in gold for an author. Other great places to share reviews are Goodreads and BookBub. If you've read others in the series, it would be great if you post a review of those, too.

I'd also love to hear from you at carol-ashby.com or directly at carolashbyauthor@gmail.com.

Want to hear about upcoming releases in the Light in the Empire series and free gifts only for newsletter subscribers?

For free gifts and other special offers, advance notices of upcoming releases, and info about my latest writing adventures, I hope you'll sign up for my newsletter at carol-ashby.com.

Who would you like to see in a future story?
Help me pick what to write next!
Who would you like to see in a future story?

I grew to love several of the characters in *Truth and Honor* while I was writing. That usually happens, and sometimes a future story takes shape in my head even before I finish. But more often the next hero or heroine is chosen because readers tell me who needs to come back as a story lead.

Readers who loved Galen as a teen in *Blind Ambition* wanted to see him as a grown man, so he became the hero in *Faithful*. People who asked for Brutus and Africanus to have their own story found out what happened to them in *Honor Bound*.

Since people kept asking what happened to Leander's beloved but long-lost sister in *True Freedom*, it was clear Ariana would need her own story in *Hope Unchained*. People who met Ursus in *Hope Unchained* asked what happened to him, so he returned with his childhood name of Matti in his quest to know God better in *Hope's Reward*.

In *What Matters Most*, Septimus, who was rather like a Great Dane puppy in *Honor Bound,* comes back four years older, and Tribune Titianus from *More Than Honor* and *True Freedom* faces the most dangerous assignment of his life. The new tribune Glabrio from *What Matters Most* returns in *Truth and Honor* to face challenges he never would have expected. I'm SO glad people asked for still more of them after the earlier books.

But there are many more characters in the books of the series that I would like to spend more time with, and I hope there are some for you, too. Who would you most like to see in a future story? What was it about them that made you want more of them? I'd love to hear what you think. It will guide what I write next.

Some possibilities:

Aulus of *True Freedom?*

Septimus or Manius of *Honor Bound, More Than Honor,* and *What Matters Most?*

Someone else I haven't mentioned? (I can't wait to see who shows up here!)

Please tell me who you'd love to see again as a comment at carol-ashby.com or directly at carolashbyauthor@gmail.com!

I'm thinking about writing a short story or novella about someone from Sextus's or Calvia's households in *Honor Bound* or Gracchus of *Hope Unchained* and *Hope's Reward* to give to newsletter subscribers. Which would you rather have?

Please go to my website, carol-ashby.com, and share your thoughts in the comment box. Sign up for the newsletter, and you'll get the story when I finish it. Looking forward to hearing from you!

Lightning Source UK Ltd.
Milton Keynes UK
UKHW012036110123
415201UK00003B/64